MW01487851

CATCHING QUINN

A WAVERLY WILDCATS NOVEL

JENNIFER BONDS

This book is a work of fiction. Names, characters, places, and incidents either are the product of the author's imagination or are used fictitiously. Any resemblance to persons, living or dead, business establishments, events, or locales is entirely coincidental. The author acknowledges the trademarked status and trademark owners of various products referenced in this work of fiction. The publication and use of these trademarks is not authorized, associated with, or sponsored by the trademark owners.

Catching Quinn: A Waverly Wildcats Novel

Cover Art & Design by Cover Ever After
ISBN (Amazon): 978-1-953794-06-2
ISBN (B&N): 978-1-953794-26-0
ISBN (Ingram): 978-1-953794-30-7
First Edition 2022

www.jenniferbonds.com

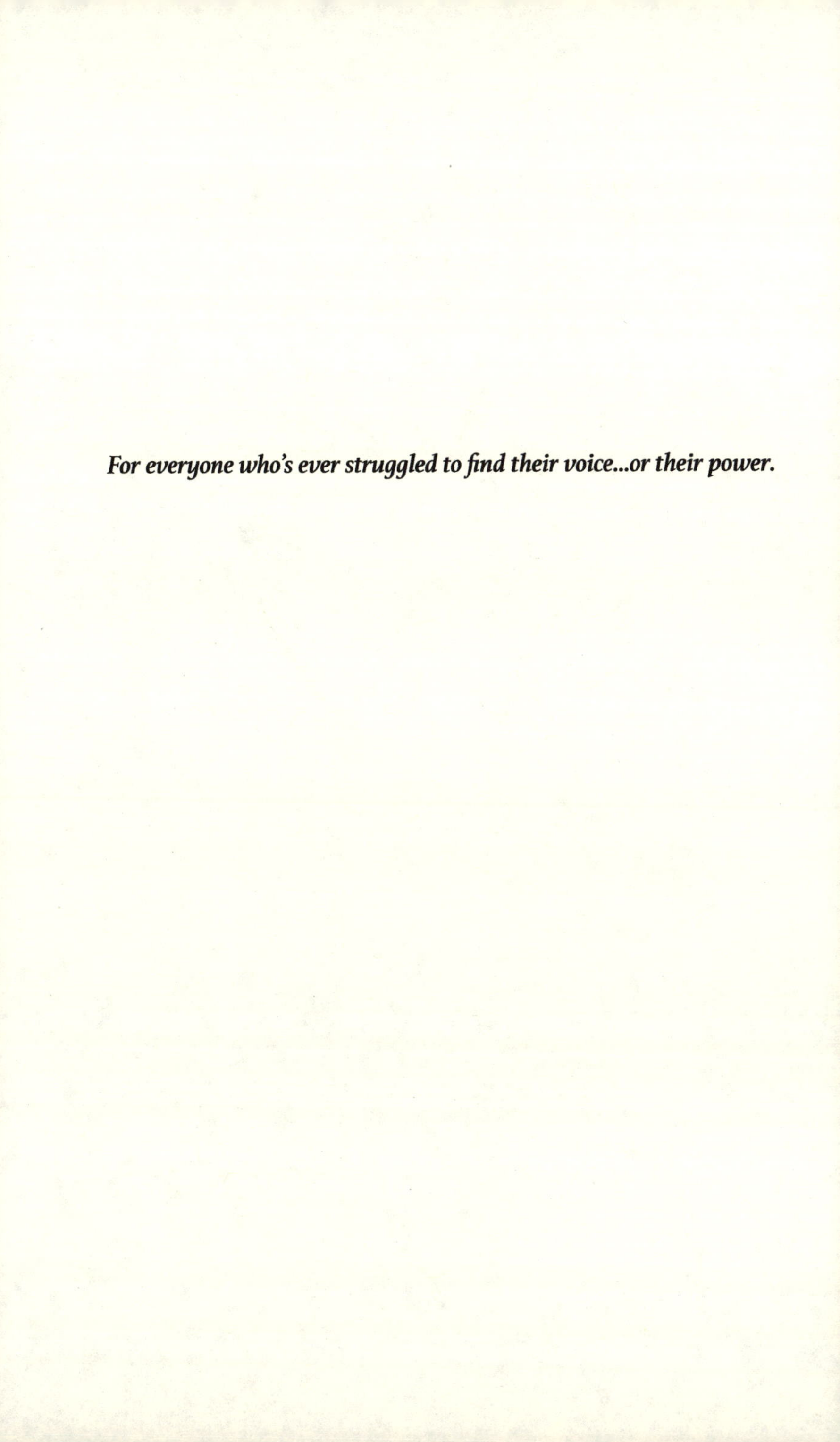

For everyone who's ever struggled to find their voice...or their power.

1

QUINN

"THIS IS LITERALLY the worst idea you've ever had." Haley arches a slender brow as she scans the room, a red plastic cup dangling from her fingertips.

"Really?" I take a sip of my beer. It's lukewarm and has too much head, but shitty beer is the least of my worries. "Worse than the time I streaked across the President's lawn?"

"Hell, yes." Haley turns to face me, dark eyes fixed on mine. "And as your best friend, I'm obligated to go on record because, girl, you are *so* going to have regrets in the morning."

Only if this plan fails.

"If there's a better place to find a hookup on campus,"—I nod toward the sea of sweaty undergrads before us—"I'm all ears."

A frown tugs at the corner of Haley's full mouth. I've got her there. Greek Row is my best option and we both know it. Sig Chi is wall to wall bodies, as if every student on campus came out to celebrate the Wildcats' first win of the season.

Hell, they probably did.

Waverly University is a football school, and the guys on the team are treated like gods. Gods who are expected to deliver a national championship.

The hardwood floor vibrates beneath our feet, but it's impossible to tell if it's from the dancing or the bass pulsing from the giant speakers in the corner of the living room.

"Come on, Hales. You're supposed to be my wing woman." I bat my lashes and jut out my bottom lip out, doing my best imitation of a pout. Haley may look totally badass, but inside she's as squishy as a Jell-O shot. "Help me, Haley-Wan. You're my only hope."

"Fine." She rolls her eyes. "But don't blame me if the sex is terrible."

I shrug, trying to play it cool despite the nervous energy coiled low in my belly. "How bad can it be?"

Haley snorts and takes a sip of her beer. "I'm not even going to dignify that with a response."

Technically, she already has, but I don't point it out, because I need her help. I'm a hot mess when it comes to the opposite sex. Not that I have much experience—or, okay, any—with sex, because every time I've tried to cash in my v-card, the universe has screwed me.

But only in the figurative sense.

Like after prom, when someone pulled the fire alarm at the hotel, and my date decided it was a sign premarital sex would send him straight to the fiery pits of hell.

Or last year, when I was hooking up with this guy from my American History class, and his cock got stuck in the zipper of his jeans. I tried to help with the zipper sitch—which, judging by his squeals, was wicked painful—but that turned out to be an even bigger mistake than hooking up with him. He bolted and never spoke to me again, like it was my fault he didn't understand the concept of manscaping.

So, yeah. I'm still a card-carrying member of Virgins-R-Us, but not for long.

Tonight I'm having sex, universe be damned.

No planning. No strings. No cosmic interference.

"What about him?" Haley gestures to a cute guy with an edgy frohawk.

I sip my beer, studying him over the top of my plastic cup. He's tall, dark, and sexy. More Haley's type than mine. I prefer my guys sweet with a side of nerdy.

And how's that working out?

"If you're not interested, maybe I'll go for it."

Bullshit. Haley and her on-again, off-again boyfriend Bryan are on a break, but there's no way she'll hook up with someone else. She might be pissed at him now, but she's convinced they're end game.

"He's all yours." I grin and call her bluff. "Not my type."

"Type doesn't matter when it comes to one-night stands." She smirks and bumps her hip against mine. "Are you sure you want to do this?"

"Definitely." I lift my chin. No way am I dying a spinster virgin. Yes, I realize that sounds dramatic, but you'd be dramatic too if the universe was conspiring to hold your virginity hostage while all your friends were getting their O on. "We just need to find the right guy."

"*Right*," she drawls, a knowing smile curving her lips. "Oh! How about the man bun? He's got a nice ass."

"Who's got a nice ass?" My brother Noah appears at Haley's side with a bottle of lager clutched in his meaty paw. Warmth floods my cheeks and he smirks at me, like he knows exactly what we've been discussing. It's not possible—not with the thumping bass—but the knowledge does little to quell my embarrassment. The last thing I need is Noah giving me shit about my virgin status. Or my disastrous love life. Or really, anything. "Don't tell me Calamity Quinn's scoping out the brothers. You know the rules." He pauses, taking a pull on his beer. "Sig Chi is off limits."

I roll my eyes—*hard*. "Trust me, we have zero interest in your brothers," I say, placing air quotes around the last word.

Noah's two years older than me and it's his last year at Waverly, but he still takes this whole *no hooking up with my friends* thing to another level. Which is ridiculous, because I have no desire to lose my virginity to a Sig Chi.

One obnoxious brother is more than enough, thank you very much.

"We just came for the free beer," Haley assures him, raising her cup.

"Good." Noah nods, and some of the tension leaves his shoulders. "Just keep Quinntessential Disaster out of trouble tonight. We don't need a visit from the plumber this early in the semester."

"That was one time!" I argue, planting a hand on my hip.

It wasn't even my fault.

Not entirely, anyway.

"Yeah," Noah says, flicking the end of my nose, "and it was one time too many. That shit's expensive, Quinntastrophe."

I glare at him, doing my best impression of a crazy ginger. Not that it takes much effort. The truth is, there are two kinds of redheads. The ones who hate the fiery temper stereotype, and those who perpetuate it.

Guess which one I am?

Haley laughs and swats Noah playfully. "Be nice."

Gross.

If I didn't know better, I'd think they were flirting. But Hales would never do that to me. Plus, it's Noah. Overprotective brother shtick aside, he's the most unevolved guy on the planet. They'd be a terrible match.

Unless it's true what they say about opposites attracting...

I shrug off the thought—no need to rot my brain with images of them getting hot and heavy—and smile sweetly at my brother. "Don't you have beer to guzzle and sorority women to woo?"

"Woo? Who the hell talks like that? Christ, it's no wonder you're single." He shakes his head and takes a pull on his lager. "No exploding faucets. And no hooking up," he adds, jabbing a finger in my direction as he disappears into the crowd.

Doubt creeps up my spine, all the ways this plan could blow up in my face taking root in my brain.

Damn Noah and his stupid wordplay.

Quinntessential disaster. Calamity Quinn. Quinntastrophe.

The childhood nicknames aren't exactly far off the mark and whisper in my ear like a backstabbing frenemy.

The kind you forget to give your address to when you move.

"Ignore him." Haley levels her gaze at me. "Stay focused on the mission."

Easy for her to say. The girl has confidence for days. She's tall and graceful, with flawless brown skin, high cheekbones, and an alluring smile that draws people in. Me? I'm a hot mess personified. It's a reality I've been fighting my entire life, which is why I'm the only one of my friends who's never had a real orgasm.

Not one that wasn't self-delivered anyway.

Haley snaps her fingers in front of my face, and I shake off the lingering doubt.

"Right, the mission." I peer over her shoulder, checking out man bun. He *does* have a nice ass. And an inviting smile. *So what the hell are you waiting for?* "Wish me luck."

I chug the rest of my beer—liquid courage for the win—and hand my empty cup to Haley.

"Go get 'em, Wildcat." She makes a roaring sound in the

back of her throat and nudges me forward, slapping my backside just before the crowd swallows me whole.

I slowly make my way across the room, doing my best to ignore the musky scent of stale beer and body spray that permeates the air. I weave between sweaty bodies, keeping my gaze locked on my target. I have to give Haley credit. The girl's got good taste, and she definitely knows my type. He's cute in a boy next door kind of way, and there are no Greek letters in sight.

Perfect one-night stand material.

But... What the hell am I supposed to say?

Nice bun, wanna fuck?

I've heard worse at these parties.

And really, who needs small talk anyway?

I square my shoulders and flash him a brilliant smile as I approach. Fake it till you make it and all that jazz. He grins back at me, and for a second, I'm feeling myself, my confidence at an all-time high. But then the heel of my boot gets caught on the most disgusting rug on the face of the planet, and I stumble forward, crashing face first into his chest.

So much for playing it cool.

"Woah." He slides his hands around my waist as someone to my left shouts *party foul*. "You okay?"

My face is on fire, and my pride is screaming at me to walk away before I make a bigger fool of myself, but I ignore it.

It's not the first time something like this has happened.

I doubt it will be the last.

"My hero." I straighten and rest a hand on his biceps, giving it a squeeze, just like they do in the movies. "I'm Quinn. And you are?"

His brows shoot up, like he can't believe I'm being this bold. That makes two of us. "Zac."

"Are you here with anyone, Zac?" I use my flirty voice, which sounds pitchy to my own ears, but it must work because now he's really looking at me, a spark of interest flaring in his eyes.

"Nah. You?"

"Nope." *Might as well own that ish.* "Want to go upstairs?"

"Seriously?" He blinks, and I can see the moment he gives himself a mental facepalm, because, yeah, not a lot of guys on campus questioning a no strings hookup. "I mean, sure, that would be cool."

He snakes an arm around my waist, fingers digging into the soft flesh of my hip, and steers me toward the stairs. I give Haley a thumbs up as we pass, and she makes an obscene gesture that has heat flooding my cheeks.

Holy shit. This is happening. I'm finally going to lose my virginity.

2

COOPER

"NEVER HAVE I EVER..." Stacy pauses, tongue gliding suggestively over her cherry-red lips as she flutters her lashes. "Hooked up with a Heisman contender."

Neither of us drinks.

She lifts a brow meaningfully—leaving no doubt she'd like to rectify the situation—as sweaty coeds press in on us from all sides. The Sig Chi party is a madhouse, and I'm feeling it, the music pulsing through my body like an electric current. I should be exhausted from today's game. It was a nail biter. But I'm wired, adrenaline coursing through my veins long after the thrill of victory should have faded.

A better man would point out that Reid's more likely to find his name on the Heisman short-list, but something tells me Stacy wouldn't care, so I keep that shit to myself.

After all, the girl is bold and unapologetic about her intentions, and I'm here for it.

"You were incredible in today's game."

She's not wrong. I had one hundred and ninety-five receiving yards *and* scored the winning touchdown. Not bad for the home opener.

What can I say? I'm awesome. The best damn wide receiver Waverly's seen in at least a decade.

Not that Stacy cares about my stats. Or the fact that it was a team effort.

Nope. She's all about the bone zone.

But hey, she wants to bag 'n' brag? I'm down.

"When you caught that last touchdown in the end zone, I swear I nearly came." She presses her tits to my chest and slides her hands in the back pockets of my jeans. The girl's like fucking Houdini. Three seconds ago, she was holding a red plastic cup. Now the only thing in her hands is my ass. Not that I'm complaining. She's a smoke show, and it's clear she's DTF. "We should go upstairs and celebrate—*privately*."

Hell yeah. "I'm always up for a one-on-one celebration."

"Perfect." Stacy grabs my hand and pulls me through the crowd, like she's afraid I'll change my mind.

Not happening. I'm horny as fuck after a game.

I leave my beer on the coffee table as we pass by and follow her upstairs. She's wearing a short as hell skirt, and judging by the glimpse I get of her right ass cheek, no underwear.

Thank you, football gods.

Lots of people throw shade at jersey chasers, but not me. I'm all about sexually empowered women getting theirs. I like to fuck, and I'm not about to judge a woman for wanting the same casual, no strings pleasure with a hard-bodied athlete.

Especially when that hard-bodied athlete is me.

At the top of the stairs, Stacy turns and extends an arm, blocking my path. She's two steps above, putting us at eye level as she leans forward and kisses me. Her lips are soft and warm, and when her tongue slides along mine, doing this swirling-sucking thing, my cock stiffens, ready to get in on the action.

Damn, it's good to be me.

I'm just getting into the kiss, imagining Stacy's lips wrapped around my shaft, when there's a thump down the hall. I glance over her shoulder—poor form, I know—and spot a couple going at it against the wall, too drunk or too horny to care that they've got an audience.

One look at that man bun and I've got my answer. Zac's planting sloppy kisses all over a redhead who—

Stacy sucks hard on my tongue—a scorching reminder to handle my own business—before she abruptly breaks off the kiss. "Lead the way, big boy." She gestures, completely undeterred by the couple dry-humping against the wall.

Welcome to Greek Row.

I climb the last two stairs and drop a hand on Stacy's lower back, guiding her toward Noah's room. I'm a member of Sig Chi—thanks to my father's legacy—but I don't live at the frat house, which makes it the ideal place for hooking up.

No sleepovers. No awkward morning after. No strings.

Noah won't mind taking one for the team. Sig Chi doesn't have a lot of rules, but rule number one is sacred.

Thou shall not cockblock.

I try the knob, and, finding it unlocked, push the door open.

Stacy slips inside, hips swaying provocatively. I follow.

The room is inky black when I enter, just a sliver of light shining through the open window, but finding Stacy isn't exactly a problem. Her mouth is on mine before I can close the door, her palms flat to my chest as she pushes me up against the wall. My hip grazes the dresser, but I barely feel it. Her tongue is in my mouth doing that swirling-sucking thing again, and the only thing on my mind is orgasms.

A woman who likes to take control in the bedroom is hot AF, and I'm a willing tribute on the path to pleasure.

I reach around and cup her ass, the tips of my fingers grazing the smooth flesh of her thighs as I pull her in close, sealing our bodies together. She must like what she feels—no surprise there—because she rotates her hips, grinding against my hard-on.

"You like that, baby?"

It's cliché as hell, but whatever. This isn't some epic romance. It's purely physical, and we both know it.

Stacy purrs in response and goes to work on my clothes. She's got my shirt half unbuttoned, and she's peppering kisses over my pecs, but it's slow going in the dark. My mind wanders—*what can I say? I have the attention span of a gnat*—back to the redhead in the hall. There was something familiar about her, but I can't put my finger on it.

Maybe we hooked up?

I've been with a lot of women, but redheads? Not so much. Then again, there was that Irish exchange student last spring.

Noah struck out with her, and when we'd busted his balls about it—

That's when it hits me. Noah's little sister—Bryn? Lynne?—is a redhead.

Shit.

Maybe it wasn't her.

Yeah-fucking-right. How many women on campus have that flaming red hair?

Stacy tugs on my belt, and I forget all about Wynn.

Before I know it, Stacy has my jeans unzipped and she's shoving them down, as desperate for release as I am. My cock strains against the thin fabric of my boxer briefs, and she brushes her thumb over the head. Once. Twice. Three times. Catching the game-winning TD was amazing, but even football can't compare to the dizzying wave of pleasure that crashes over me at her touch.

"You must be exhausted from today's game," she murmurs, sinking to her knees as a mental image of Zac and the redhead wheedles its way back into my brain. "Why don't you relax and let me take care of you?"

Fuuuck.

Any other day, I'd be all in. Problem is, I can't get Noah's little sister out of my head.

Don't be a dick.

There's a beautiful woman on her knees in front of me, and all I can think about is the redhead next door.

Fuck. Fuck. Fuck.

This is bullshit.

Not my sister, not my problem.

See rule number two, asshole.

Thou shall not fuck a brother's sister.

Which would probably break a half dozen laws outside of Greek Row.

I groan. It's the wrong move because it only encourages Stacy. She reaches for the waistband of my boxers and starts to pull them down.

I grab her wrist, regret washing over me like a Gatorade shower.

Noah's going to owe me big time.

"I'm sorry, but there's something I need to do." I take Stacy's other arm and pull her to her feet. "Just give me ten minutes. Then we can pick up where we left off."

It's pitch black, but I swear I can see the flash of anger in her eyes as she processes my words.

"Are you serious?" Her voice is dangerously low, like she can't believe this is happening.

Ditto. Of all the ways I imagined tonight ending, ditching a hot chick who wants to blow me didn't make the list.

"Yeah." I tug my pants up and button them so they don't slide back down. "I'm really sorry."

I sound like the world's biggest douchebag, but what else is there to say?

It's not you, it's me?

I doubt that would carry any more weight than my half-assed apology.

"I'm not going to sit around waiting for you like some desperate cleat chaser. If you walk out that door, we're done."

I don't bother answering. It's her choice to make, and I can hardly blame her. I'm the asshole who's bailing mid-hookup with no explanation.

Not that an explanation would make it any better.

Pretty sure she'd be pissed if she knew I was going to find another woman.

The tension in the room is so thick I'm damn near choking on it as I zip my pants and fumble with my belt. Stacy's quiet and maybe that's a good sign, but it's just as likely she's plotting my demise, so I abandon the effort of buttoning my shirt halfway through and yank the bedroom door open. The hall light slants across the room, and when I turn back to Stacy, a final apology on the tip of my tongue, she's glaring daggers at me.

"You're a real prick," she finally says, voice wavering.

"So I've been told." But at least I can be the prick who does the right thing for once.

If I'm not too late.

3

QUINN

BEST. *Idea. Ever.* I really should've thrown caution to the wind and tried this whole losing-my-virginity-to-a-stranger thing ages ago because it's finally going to happen.

I'm totally having sex tonight.

Sure, Zac's got sour beer breath, but at least he's cute. Besides, it could be worse. He could have a tiny penis. Which he very well might because technically I haven't seen it yet. Or a hairy ass.

Ugh. I really hope he doesn't have a hairy ass.

I'm down for chest hair and beards and even fuzzy arms, but a hairy ass?

Hard. Pass.

A girl's got to have some standards, amirite?

Forget his ass and get busy already.

I can almost hear Haley snorting with laughter, because, honestly, who cares if he has hair growing out of his ears? It's not like I'm going to marry the guy. Or even date him.

This is just sex.

S-E-X.

Zac at least seems to understand this because he doesn't

waste time with small talk. As soon as the door shuts, his hands are on me, roving over my body like it's his new favorite toy. They're rough and foreign, but I ignore the shiver of doubt that skates down my spine and scan the room, trying to get my bearings.

The bedroom is dark, and though the sounds of the rager downstairs are dampened, the floor still vibrates beneath my feet. There's a soft green glow coming from a terrarium in the corner, but before I can get a good look at the creature inside, Zac spins me around and walks me backward toward the unmade bed.

My knees hit the mattress, and the next thing I know, I'm flat on my back with Zac's crushing weight on top of me.

My breath escapes in a rush, and then his mouth is on mine, delivering one wet kiss after another as I gasp for air, my body sinking further into the mattress. I briefly imagine suffocating in the Sig Chi house—and the absolute shit-fit Noah will throw at the bad press—but then Zac shifts, propping himself up on one arm and thank sweet baby Jesus I can breathe again.

I gulp down a lungful of musky frat boy bedroom funk as Zac's other hand settles on my thigh, pushing up the hem of my little black dress. He trails kisses down my exposed collarbone and his fingers scrape over my bare thigh as he rotates his hips, grinding against me.

"You're so hot," he murmurs, breath warm against my skin. "You like that, baby?"

Pretty sure he doesn't want me to answer that honestly, so I make a noncommittal sound that sort of passes for a moan. I may be a virgin, but I've made out with guys before, and I know I should feel something when he's grinding on me, but I've got nothing.

Not even a tingle from down below.

Zac continues pawing and groping. I'm not exactly turned on, but it's fine. First times aren't supposed to be great anyway.

I just need to get it over with before the universe interferes.

Or before he starts drooling on your shoulder again.

I grab the hem of his shirt and pull it up over his head. His pecs are smooth and tan, not a hair in sight as I drink in the hard planes of his bare chest. Zac's got great muscle tone, and I must say it out loud because he responds.

"I worked as a lifeguard at the Jersey Shore over the summer. Gotta keep in shape for the bab—" He pauses, as if realizing that finishing the sentence could put an end to his current hookup, and hastily says, "Beach."

Whatever.

I'm not here for scintillating conversation.

"Less talking, more undressing." I reach between us and unbutton his jeans. Zac grins and wiggles out of the tight denim, clearly onboard with the suggestion. A strand of hair falls loose from his bun and tickles my cheek as he kicks off his pants.

He's wearing a pair of dark briefs, and even in the dim light, I can see he's ready to go.

One-night-stands FTW!

"Why don't we get rid of this too?" he asks, sliding my dress up over my thighs.

I nod and open my mouth to give consent when there's a knock at the door. We both freeze and listen silently, hoping whoever it is will move the eff along.

No such luck.

The doorknob rattles and I silently curse the universe.

Because *of course* someone's banging on the door.

Zac turns toward the sound, but I grab his chin and turn his face back to me, refusing to concede defeat. "You locked it, right?"

His brows knit together, and he gives a slow nod.

"Then let's just ignore it. They'll go away eventually."

Surely there are plenty of empty rooms just waiting for horny couples to hook up. It *is* a frat house.

"I guess," he says, not sounding convinced—*at all*.

FML. This cannot be happening. Not again.

I haven't even gotten my underwear off.

Desperate, I stretch up and crush my lips to Zac's, hoping the distraction will be enough to make him forget about whoever's at the door. I kiss him hard, my tongue skating along the seam of his mouth, seeking entry. He's quick to oblige and then his tongue is gliding along mine, thrusting and searching, the cock-blocker at the door forgotten.

Crisis averted.

His hand slides up my thigh, and I grab his wrist. "Condom?"

Thump. Thump. Thump.

"Open the fucking door, Zac!" a deep voice bellows from the hall.

Zac jerks upright, his gaze bouncing from me to the door, panic flaring in his eyes. "Do you have a boyfriend?"

"What? No." I prop myself up on my elbows and force a sultry smile, frustration and indignation warring for dominance. "Can we just forget about the guy in the hall already? He's probably just drunk."

Zac looks at me like I'm out of my mind, which fair, because I'm no sexpert, but I'm guessing there would be a lot of pressure to perform with some dude pounding on the door like the big bad wolf. I don't know who the asshole outside is, but he's clearly conspiring with the universe to deprive me of carnal pleasure, and I am *not* here for it.

There's another round of aggressively loud thumping, before the guy in the hall yells, "You've got to the count of three to open this door or I'm going to kick it in."

Zac leaps off the bed like his ass is on fire and bolts across the room. "Don't kick it in! I don't have the money to cover damages."

Welcome to the hot mess express—party of one.

I sigh and climb to my feet as Zac unlocks the door. The moment he turns the knob, it flies open and the cockblocker barges in, forcing Zac to take a step back as he flips the light switch.

White spots blur my vision, and I blink at the harsh glare of the overhead light.

Then I blink some more, trying to make sense of the scene before me.

Either I had more shitty keg beer than I realized or my eyes are malfunctioning because no way is Cooper DeLaurentis—Waverly's star wide receiver—glaring at us like we just stole his favorite pair of cleats.

Oh, crap. He's a Sig Chi.

Is this his room?

Awkward.

Zac recovers first and throws up his arms. "What the hell is your problem, man?"

Cooper turns to him slowly, giving me a chance to study his profile. Not that I need it. The guy is a legend on campus. There's not a woman at Waverly who doesn't have his face memorized.

Hell, there's probably not a woman on campus who doesn't have orgasmic fantasies about him, myself included.

#NoShame.

Look, I know it's what's on the inside that matters, but the guy is freaking gorgeous.

He's like a young Chris Hemsworth, with muscles for days, a chiseled jaw, and the most intense blue eyes you've ever seen. Seriously. Imagine all those drool-worthy influencer pics you've seen of the Pacific Ocean on Insta. Now imagine drowning in those placid blue waters and *boom!* you've got Cooper's eyes.

So, yeah, he's a god among mortals.

Even if, at the moment, he looks like he just rolled out of bed, his honey-blond hair tousled and his shirt half-buttoned. Which is still a step above Zac, who's in his underwear.

"*My* problem?" Cooper repeats, eyes darting to me. He looks me over from head to toe, jaw hardening as I fix the strap of my dress, pushing it back up on my shoulder where it belongs. It's the first time I've seen Cooper without his trademark smile fixed in place, but for the life of me, I can't figure out why he's so pissed. It's not like he's the one being cockblocked. "Do you have any idea who she is?"

Doubt flickers across Zac's face, then he mumbles, "Lynne?"

Oh, for fuck's sake.

"My name is *Quinn.*" I plant a hand on my hip. "With a Q."

Zach shrugs. "Music's loud downstairs."

Cooper snorts, and I shoot him a look cold enough to freeze the balls off a wildcat, which, frankly, would serve him right.

He ignores the look and turns his attention back to Zac. "Yeah, well, Quinn is Noah's little sister, so whatever you two had in mind," he says, waggling a finger back and forth between us, "isn't happening."

So much for Operation Spontaneous Hookup.

"I didn't know," Zac sputters, throwing his hands up defensively. "Nothing happened. I swear."

My temper flares, red-hot and molten. On the one hand, I can't believe I was going to have sex with a guy who can't even remember my name. On the other, who do these jerks think they are? It's my body. I can do whatever the hell I want with it.

"I have an idea," I say, infusing my words with an edge of syrupy sweetness. "How about you stop talking about me like I'm not here?"

Cooper turns to me, eyes wide in mock surprise. "You still here, Lynne?"

The jab stings, and I glare at him for all I'm worth.

"Come on, I'll walk you out," Cooper says, gesturing for me to follow.

"You're not the boss of me." I cross my arms over my chest, realizing too late I sound like Veruca Salt. "I'm a grown ass woman, and I can have sex with whoever I want."

"Not in this house you can't." He smirks and takes a step toward me, crossing his much larger arms over his chest. "We can do this the easy way or the hard way. Your choice."

I lift my chin and stare up at him resolutely. He may be the big man on campus, and I may be a quintessential disaster, but it'll be a cold day in hell before I let Cooper DeLaurentis—or any man—push me around.

He shrugs, the corner of his mouth hitching up in a crooked grin. "Don't say I didn't warn you."

"What are you—"

He bends down and hooks his arm around the back of my knees, slinging me over his shoulder. I squeal in protest as he strides out the door and into the hall, carrying me like a bag of dirty laundry.

"Put me down right now!" I thump him on the back as he lumbers down the rear staircase. "This isn't dignified."

"Neither is the clap," he shoots back, an edge of amusement in his voice. "You're welcome."

4

COOPER

TURNS OUT, carrying a chick down the stairs when she's spitting mad isn't as easy as it looks in the movies, but I manage well enough because Quinn's a tiny little thing. I've got nearly a foot on her, which should put me at an advantage, but her fury has a life of its own.

The kind fueled by sharp elbows and four-letter words.

Whatever. It's nothing I haven't heard before.

"Put me down, you cockwaffle!"

I stand corrected. That's definitely a new one.

Still, it beats the hell out of the alternative.

I shrug off the insult and carry Quinn out the back door and around to the front of the house. The party's spilled outside and red plastic cups decorate the handrail on the porch, but no one pays us any attention as I deposit her on the lawn.

Is it even a party if there aren't drunk couples arguing out front?

"Who the hell do you think you are?" she demands, planting a hand on her hip and glaring up at me. I smirk and glare right back. Quinn might be pissed now, but she'll thank me in the morning. I open my mouth to say as much, but she cuts me off, slicing her free hand through the air. "That was a rhetorical question." She huffs out a breath, nostrils flaring. "Honestly, who'd have thought Cooper DeLaurentis would be a slut-shaming hypocrite?"

"Excuse me?" Indignation flares in my gut. I step forward, closing the gap between us, and get right up in her personal space. "That's not what's happening here."

"Whatever." She rolls her eyes, completely unfazed by my advance. "If the rumors are true, you've screwed half the student body, so where do you get off cockblocking me?"

Is this girl for real?

This whole scene is killing my buzz. It's hot as hell and the humidity has my shirt clinging to my skin. The rush of today's game has worn off, and the shots of whiskey I threw back earlier are a distant memory.

The smart thing to do would be to walk away. Go find my teammates and get blitzed. Nothing good ever comes from arguing with drunk coeds.

Then again, no one's ever accused me of making good life choices.

Least of all when it comes to the opposite sex.

"Look, sweetheart, I'm all for free love, but that guy's a douche." I curl my lip, not caring if I sound like an asshole. The way she's throwing around phrases like slut-shaming and hypocrite, it's clear she's already made up her mind about me. "I did you a favor."

"A favor?" Her cheeks turn a violent shade of red and she pokes me in the chest. "Taking away a woman's agency is *not* doing her a favor. If I want to sleep with every fuckboy on campus, that's my prerogative."

Sonofabitch.

She's right.

If I'd just minded my own damn business, I'd be balls deep

inside a woman who appreciates my finer qualities instead of arguing with one who clearly thinks I'm a complete jackass.

"You're right." I throw up my hands, hoping to defuse the situation before she bursts a blood vessel. "Your body. Your choice. The thing is, I couldn't look your brother in the face if I let you hook up with Zac. The guy's a walking STD."

"Oh. My. God." She wheels around and stalks toward the house, boots sinking into the grass. "I'm going to die a virgin because of freaking bro code. How is this my life?"

Holy. Shit.

I've heard a lot of wild stuff in the locker room and on the field, but this? Not gonna lie. I'm intrigued.

I'm across the lawn and at her side in three quick strides. "Please tell me you weren't seriously going to give that douche your v-card. At a frat party."

She freezes, and I angle my body in front of her, cutting off her path.

"No judgment," I add, flashing my trademark smile. *Hasn't failed me yet.* "I lost my virginity at a house party when I was fifteen."

"Your point?"

I shrug, searching for the right words. Or at least ones that won't earn me another tongue lashing. "I'm just surprised."

"That I'm a virgin?" Her eyes narrow to slits. I've said the wrong thing. *Again.* "I realize a nineteen-year-old virgin may seem like an oddity to you, but I assure you, we aren't exactly unicorns. Not all of us can be sexual savants like—"

"I just meant..." Warmth creeps up the back of my neck, and I know without a doubt that my ears are now the color of Quinn's hair. Which is ridiculous because since when do I get flustered? I'm the king of casual sex. You want dirty talk? I'm your guy. A threesome? I'm in. Orgasms for days? No one does it better. "I mean, don't most girls want it to be special?"

My mouth snaps shut the instant the words are out.

Maybe I had more whiskey than I thought because *what the actual fuck am I saying?*

"I just want to get it over with." Quinn sighs and sweeps her hair over her shoulder, revealing a swath of creamy skin that's damn near iridescent in the moonlight. "Preferably before I die."

"Dramatic much?" I quirk a brow and give her a blatant once over. She's not old enough to buy her own beer, let alone worry about dying a virgin.

Plus, she's hot.

Not that I'm looking, because...rule number two. It's just that she's got these striking green eyes—like old Coke bottles—and that fiery red-orange hair spilling over her shoulder in soft waves.

If I didn't know she was related to Noah, I'd never believe it. Noah Mowery is your basic frat bro with collared shirts, too much product in his hair, and totally average features.

The only average thing about Quinn is her height.

"I prefer the term realist," she shoots back. "Seriously. I'm the girl who should've come with a warning label and a lifetime supply of bubble wrap."

"Bubble wrap?" What the hell does bubble wrap have to do with getting laid?

"It's just..." She lifts her chin and looks me dead in the eye. "I have terrible luck. Like, if it can go wrong, it will. Epically."

Oh-kay.

"Yeah." I hook my thumbs in my pockets and shake my head. "Still not following."

She shoots me a look that has *shocker* written all over it, because like everyone else, she thinks I'm a dumb jock.

Joke's on her. I've got a 3.8 GPA.

"Last summer, I was a server at the country club." She huffs out a breath. "One night after a wedding, this guy I worked with swiped a bottle of champagne and suggested we go for a joyride on the golf course. He was cute, so I figured, why not? Anyway, we find this nice moonlit spot on the ninth hole where we can enjoy the soothing splash of the water feature. Half-way through the bottle, we're both feeling good and we start kissing."

Sounds normal enough so far.

"Just as things are getting good," she says, her voice raising an octave, "the golf cart lurches forward and before you know it, we're up to our elbows in scummy pond water because the dumbass forgot to set the emergency brake." She pauses, and it's all I can do to keep my mouth shut. "We were both fired. To add insult to injury, I had to do community service for destruction of property. So, yeah. I'd like to lose my virginity *before* I die."

The corners of my lips quiver at the mental image she's painted, and I choke on a laugh. "That sucks, but it's not exactly a near death experience."

I'm not trying to be insensitive, but come on. That shit's funny.

She cuts her eyes at me again and tries to sidestep me, but I'm too quick. I grab her arm because no way in hell is she going back into that party.

"Okay, so you have bad luck." I swallow another laugh. "You can't just go around propositioning guys."

"Why not?" She raises a slender brow. "You do it all the time."

"Yeah, but I'm not a virgin."

She rolls her eyes—hard. "Could you maybe say it with a little less distaste?"

"There's nothing wrong with being a virgin." I throw my hands up for good measure. Could be surrender, could be self-defense. Only time will tell. "But I have a strict no virgins policy when it comes to hookups."

"And why is that?" she asks, slowly enunciating each word.

It's a trap. Do. Not. Answer.

"In my experience, they have needs I'm not equipped to handle."

So much for keeping my mouth shut.

"You don't have sex with virgins because you think they're emotionally needy?" Now she's the one curling her lip, but I have to admit, it's kind of sexy.

Not that I'm going to tell her. She's on a roll now, and despite what my teammates might think, I'm not harboring a death wish. Even if this *is* the most fun I've had all night.

"Stop putting words in my mouth."

"I'll stop putting words in your mouth," she says, smiling sweetly, "when you stop sounding like a sexist pig."

I'm a lot of things, but a sexist pig? Total bullshit.

I tamp down my annoyance and try another approach. "I'm just saying I haven't seen a lot of guys turn into emotional messes over sex."

She snorts, and if it weren't for the derisive look she throws my way, it would probably be cute. "That's because you're the reigning king of one-night stands."

Thanks for the reminder, sweetheart.

I roll my shoulders, letting the accusation slide off my back. Quinn doesn't know shit about me, and if she thinks I'm a manwhoring asshole, well, she's not wrong.

Hell, it's practically the DeLaurentis legacy.

"It seems my reputation precedes me." I force a grin and wink at her, slipping back into the carefree persona I've so carefully crafted on campus. Who cares if she thinks I'm a dick? It doesn't matter. My work here is done. "I'll see you around, Quinn."

She frowns at the brush off, her full bottom lip jutting out.

Desire flares white-hot, the urge to rake my teeth over her soft flesh striking hard and fast.

Don't even think about it, DeLaurentis.

Squashing the impulse, I jog up the front steps and stop at the door, where an underclassman is handing out cups. He jumps up from his chair like I'm the fucking pope, and I take far too much pleasure in my next words, hooking a thumb at Quinn as I deliver them. "She's cut off."

There's a splutter of outrage from behind me, but I don't look back as I slip through the front door. I've done my good deed for the night. Time to get lit.

As much fun as I had sparring with Quinn, she's Noah's little sister. Even if she wasn't, I'm not about to break the virgin rule.

Not again.

5

QUINN

WHAT THE HELL? One second I'm dead to the world, images of Henry Cavill dancing in my head, the next I'm staring at my bedroom ceiling, pulse racing. I draw in a ragged breath and blink, my eyes slowly adjusting to the darkness as the dream fades from memory.

Toss a coin to your Witcher, indeed.

The dream was a scorcher, or it would have been if it hadn't ended before I got to the good part.

FML. Now I can't even get laid in my dreams?

There's a quiet buzz, and my phone vibrates on the nightstand.

Because *of course* it does.

I debate ignoring it, but my resolve lasts exactly point two five seconds. It might be Haley. I texted her after I got the boot from Sig Chi, but she didn't answer. For all I know, she's still there drinking her face off and needs a ride home.

I roll onto my side and grab the phone, holding it up to read the messages.

Unknown: U up?

Unknown: Come on, man. Don't leave me banging

Unknown: ganging

Unknown: hanging

Unknown: ducking autocorrect

I snort laugh because at this time of night, I seriously doubt autocorrect is the cause of the sloppy texts. Besides, with the way my night's going, random texts from a drunk dude—I'd bet my right boob it's a guy—are par for the course. If I want to get back to sleep anytime soon, I need to put an end to them.

Me: Quit slurring your texts. You've got the wrong number.

I roll onto my back and watch as three little dots appear on the screen. Then disappear. I'm just about to place the phone on the nightstand when the dots reappear.

Unknown: Shit. U sure?

Is he serious?

Unknown: NM. Sorry. Lost my contacts.

Me: You can restore your contacts from the cloud.

Unknown: I could if I'd bothered to back them up.

Unknown: Damn. I really thought this was my brother's number.

I'm wide awake now and have zero self-control, so the smart-ass in me writes back.

Me: Exactly how many brothers do you have that you can't remember their numbers?

Unknown: 50ish?

I stifle a groan, my fingers flying over the screen. There are only two reasons a guy would have fifty brothers, and since a harem sitch seems unlikely, I go with the obvious.

Me: What is it with frat guys and their brothers? You know they're not your actual family, right?

I half expect him to ignore the message, but three dots appear on the screen. Curiosity unfurls low in my belly as I wait for the reply. Is he a student? The possibility that I'm texting an alumnus old enough to be my father kind of skeeves me out, but he sounds young.

Not that it matters. It's not like I'll be talking to him again after tonight.

Unknown: What do u have against Greek life?

Me: Nothing. But I've known enough douchey frat guys to last a lifetime. You're all the same.

Harsh? Maybe.

True? After tonight's misadventure? Definitely.

My phone lights up, and a *Salty AF* GIF flashes on the screen.

I laugh and send back a *Fries before guys* GIF because what do I care if some rando thinks I'm salty? After the night I've had, I've earned it.

Unknown: Let me guess, u dated a guy w letters and he broke ur heart?

Me: Hardly. I know better than to fall in love at a kegger. My roommate freshman year lost her panties and her dignity all in one night.

I follow the message with a *Hard pass* GIF.

Unknown: Smart woman. Which means u shouldn't buy into stereotypes.

*Me: Some stereotypes exist for a reason. *shrug emoji**

Unknown: Any other words of wisdom, oh wise one?

A smile tugs at the corner of my mouth as I snuggle under the comforter and type my reply.

Me: Don't underestimate the cloud.

He doesn't miss a beat. His text pops up almost instantly.

*Unknown: Was that a Star Wars reference? *smirking emoji**

Me: Was it?

Honestly, I'm impressed he picked up on it. As my brother has reminded me eleventy billion times, I'm a weirdo. Which is why I'm definitely not admitting my not-so-secret love of Star Wars.

Still, I laugh to myself as I send one last message.

Me: Remember, the cloud will be with you. Always.

I lock my phone and reach over to put it on the nightstand, but I misjudge the distance and drop it on the floor. The phone lands on the carpet with a quiet thud.

Universe 2 - Hot Mess Express 0.

Sighing, I sit up and switch on the bedside lamp. I'm just scooping the phone up from its new home under the bed when my door creaks open and Haley pokes her head in. Her hair is wild, her cheeks are flushed, and from the looks of it, her night was far better than mine.

A pang of envy hits me square in the chest, followed closely by a metric ton of guilt.

If anyone deserves a good time, it's Haley, and I shouldn't begrudge her just because my luck is trash.

"Sweet. I was hoping you'd still be up." She flashes me a mischievous grin and plops down on the foot of my bed. "Spill the tea, sis. How'd it go with man bun?"

"DOA." I sit up and lean back against the headboard. "Didn't you get my text?"

She shakes her head. "My phone died."

Haley's the only person I know who lets her phone battery die on the regular. She's a free-spirited artist who doesn't believe in being chained to technology, but honestly? Charging her phone would eliminate fifty percent of the arguments she has with Bryan.

Of course, it would also eliminate fifty percent of their makeup sex, so maybe she's onto something after all.

"Hales, you can't go out drinking by yourself with a dead phone battery." I know I'm giving off strong mom vibes, but one of us has to worry about personal safety. "What if there was an emergency? Or you needed a ride?"

Haley waves me off and tucks her feet beneath her body,

making it clear she's not leaving until she gets the deets on my disastrous evening.

I huff out a breath. "Why do I even bother?"

"Beats me." She wiggles her brows and pokes me in the leg. "Now spill."

I tell her the whole sordid story, leaving nothing out. When I'm finally done ranting about Cooper-the-cockblocker-DeLaurentis, Haley is laughing so hard tears are streaming down her face.

How's that for comforting?

"It's a good thing I love you." I smack her on the side with a pillow. "Otherwise, I'd be seriously offended right now."

"I'm sorry," she pants, swiping the tears from her cheeks. "But, come on. You know it's funny. Who does that even happen to?"

"Me!" I point to myself. "It happens to me. Every. Freaking. Time." Which is why I have no shortage of embarrassing material to write about for my column in The Collegian. I pause as reality sinks in. "I really am going to die a virgin."

"Not in this lifetime." Haley props herself up on her elbows and makes a swooning gesture. "I can't believe Cooper DeLaurentis carried you out of the house. I'd give anything to have that hottie go all caveman on me."

"He's all yours." I smile sweetly, hoping to drive the point home. "He's not my type."

Because I'm not into hard-bodied football players...said no woman ever.

"Girl, if you've got ovaries, he's your type."

Fair point. The guy is a fifteen on a ten-point scale. I didn't exactly hate the feel of his muscular body pressed against mine, but come on. He's an arrogant prick. That whole spiel about virgins? What a load of crap. I mean, who the hell does he think he is telling me who I can and can't have sex with?

If I want to get the clap, that's my prerogative.

Not that I want the clap. Or any other STI.

But it's *my* choice to make.

"Whatever." I give myself a mental shake. Cooper DeLaurentis will *not* be taking up any more of my time or headspace. "He's probably overcompensating for a small dick."

"Not from what I hear." Haley climbs to her feet. "A girl in my algebra class hooked up with him last spring. She said it was the best sex of her life." She pauses, making a lewd gesture. "Apparently, he's a man of many talents."

"Thanks for that visual." I shoot her the side-eye. "That's just what a sexually frustrated virgin needs to hear before bed."

"You're welcome." Haley blows me a kiss and flounces out of the room as I switch off the lamp.

I flop back on my pillow, trying to recall my dream about Henry Cavill. When I close my eyes, though, it's not his striking face I see imprinted on the back of my eyelids. Not his seductive smile warming my blood, or his placid blue eyes winking flirtatiously.

Nope. It's Cooper-virgins-need-not-apply-DeLaurentis.

Fan-freaking-tastic.

6

COOPER

"WHY DOES it have to be so fucking hot?" A bead of perspiration slides down my forehead as I lace up my cleats. Practice hasn't even started, and I'm already sweating. Our locker room may be state-of-the art, but with all my pads on, the air conditioner is fighting a losing battle.

"Because Science," Vaughn, our resident mountain man, deadpans from the locker to my right. "The prof didn't cover global warming in Rocks for Jocks?"

I give him the finger, ignoring Reid and Parker, who giggle like a couple of teenage girls. If they weren't my best friends, I might be offended. But after three years of playing ball and living together, we're tight.

I'd trust these guys with my life.

But not your secrets?

I shove the thought aside. Distractions have no place in the locker room or on the field. I've been in the game long enough to know it takes more than talent to win a national football championship and secure a first-round draft pick; it takes discipline.

"Worried these golden locks are going to get frizzy?" Parker asks, ruffling my hair. I swat at his hand, but he's too damn fast. "Don't be so precious. We'll all look like roadkill by the time Coach is done with us."

"Speak for yourself. I always look good."

Vaughn shoots me a disapproving look. "Could your ego be any bigger?"

I meet his stare head-on and grin. "What can I say? Everyone loves me. I'm like a calorie free taco smothered in cheese."

Vaughn snorts.

So predictable.

"You got the cheese part right," he says. "I can't believe women go for that crap."

"Don't be salty just because you're bacon and beef jerky."

Vaughn freezes, helmet in hand. "What's wrong with bacon and beef jerky?"

"Nothing." I shrug. "But when was the last time you saw a woman go down on a plate of bacon and beef jerky?"

"You're disgusting."

"If by disgusting, you mean disgustingly handsome and wise, then yeah."

Reid grins and tucks his helmet under his arm. "By mid-November, we'll all be wishing for another heatwave."

Truth. Nothing a receiver hates more than cold ass weather and stiff fingers.

I stand and grab my helmet from the top shelf of the locker. No way I'm going to be the last one on the field. Not when it's hot as balls and coach believes laps are a surefire way to improve punctuality.

"Ready?" Reid asks, holding out his fist.

"Hell, yeah." I bump his hand in solidarity. "Let's go get ourselves a national title."

I'm about to push my locker door closed when my phone lights up and the Imperial March fills the air.

Fuuuuuck.

My mood sours instantly. I have no interest in talking to my father, but if I don't answer, there'll be hell to pay.

And I won't be the one footing the bill.

"You good?" Reid asks, a note of concern in his voice.

Not even close.

"Yeah." I nod toward the exit, all cool confidence and swagger. Reid is an excellent captain and an even better friend. The last thing I want to do is drag him down, especially when I know he's got his own shit to deal with. "You guys go ahead. I'll meet you on the field."

I mutter a four-letter word as my teammates file out. Then I grab the phone, knuckles white, and hit accept.

"Dad."

"Cooper." The way he says my name—equal parts censure and long-suffering disappointment—tells me everything I need to know about the direction of this conversation. "Shouldn't you be in class?"

I don't bother answering. He's got a copy of my schedule. If he thought I was in class, he wouldn't be calling. "What's up?"

"Just checking in to see how the semester is shaping up. Hold on." There's a beat of silence. Then he rattles off a stream of commands to one of his minions before returning his attention to me. "I don't need to remind you how important this year is for your future."

No, he doesn't, but he's calling to ride my ass nonetheless, because God forbid I do anything that might tarnish his image or the upcoming Senate race.

"It's all good," I assure him, a muscle in my jaw twitching.

It's only the forty-seventh lecture I've gotten this month. I've practically got it memorized.

Not that I need it. Despite my father's total lack of confidence, I've got everything under control.

And I know better than to step one toe out of line.

I throw my head back and drag in a calming breath, exhaling the desire to put my fist through the locker door. The last thing I need is rumors of anger issues floating around campus.

Imagine how that would look in the press.

"Good." He clears his throat, and when he continues, his voice is silky smooth. *The consummate politician.* "We need a united front heading into the November election. We've all got to stay focused and keep our noses clean. Mullaney is really putting the pressure on. It's going to be a tight race, but I'm not worried."

Bullshit.

For the first time, I wonder what will happen if the great Steven DeLaurentis loses.

Nothing good, that's for damn sure.

"Take care of those grades, and we'll get you lined up with a great opportunity on The Hill next fall."

"Sure, Dad." I'm a PoliSci major, but it'll be a cold day in hell before I give up football to work in Washington with my father.

If he notices my total lack of enthusiasm, he ignores it.

Nothing new there. He's got a one-track mind. The only thing he gives a shit about is the DeLaurentis name. Like we'll be the next Kennedy dynasty or something.

Not gonna happen, old man.

"I mean it, Cooper. Your mother and I need you to stay focused this year. No parties, no women, no bad press. Understand?"

"Yes, sir." I grit my teeth, biting back the fury that's clawing its way up my throat.

I'm hardly the biggest threat to my father's re-election campaign, but pointing it out would be a mistake—one I can't afford to make. At least if I tell him what he wants to hear, we can wrap this up quickly.

"By the way, I met with Tom Anderson yesterday."

My chest tightens at the mention of my summer internship.

"Tom said you were an exemplary intern, but..." There's a long pause, giving me plenty of time to sweat his next words. It's just one of the many games he likes to play. I hate that after all these years, his manipulations still unnerve me. "He would've liked to have you stay on those last two weeks. The campaign office is always in need of extra hands."

There it is. The not-so-subtle reminder that while I returned to school early for training camp, as far as he's concerned, football is not my future.

The thing is, I enjoyed working the campaign trail. Mr. Anderson was cool. I support the party policies, and I enjoy giving back to the community. My only complaint was pounding the pavement for a man who cares more about public perception than he does his own family.

Just a few more months.

"Look, Dad, I've gotta bounce. I'm late for practice."

"Don't talk like that, Cooper. You sound like a punk." Gone is the soothing timbre he uses with the public. There's hard edge to his voice, a sure sign I've gotten under his skin. "And call your mother."

The irony of his concern has me seeing red, but I grit my teeth and swallow my anger for her sake.

"Yes, sir." I disconnect before he can reply and exhale, ignoring the way my hands shake as I drop to the bench in front of my locker. I'm late for practice, but I can't take the field like this.

Not when I'm likely to drop every pass that comes my way.

I bring up my texts and scroll through the messages, deleting two random booty calls from Saturday night. Could be girls I've hooked up with before, but since my contacts were wiped, it's hard to be sure. I spent most of yesterday hungover, so the only contacts I've reprogrammed are my parents and my roommates.

Just as well. No time for distractions.

My finger hovers over the third string of messages. I should delete them. I don't have a clue who the girl on the other end is, but...she *was* funny.

I quickly reread our exchange, a slow smile spreading over my face. Probably a closet geek like me with all those Star Wars references.

One might've been a coincidence, but two?

Not likely.

She'd probably freak if she knew she'd been talking to one of the country's top receivers.

Conceited much?

Whatever. A girl like that probably isn't into jocks. Especially ones with Greek letters and a casual outlook on sex. Plus, there's a real possibility she lives in Alaska. Or Montana. Or—

Focus, DeLaurentis.

Practice. Study hall. Call mom.

One day—*one step*—at a time. It's the only way to win a national championship and secure a first-round selection in the NFL draft.

I can't afford to settle for anything less.

7

QUINN

THE INSTANT CLASS IS DISMISSED, I'm on my feet, trudging out the door with thirty undergrads who look as excited about the homework assignment as I feel. If Professor Bates' goal was to crush spirits and Friday vibes, the man succeeded. I knew Creative Nonfiction would require some personal essays, but asking us to write a piece that exposes vulnerability the first week of class?

Stone-cold.

Asking us to share the piece for critique?

Savage.

Seriously. Who does that?

Call-me-David—who thinks he's too young and hip to go by Professor Bates—that's who. The same man who forgot to update the class syllabus, which was clearly recycled from the spring semester. Hell, if it weren't for the outdated syllabus, I'd think he designed this assignment solely to torture me.

After all, my life is one big freaking vulnerability.

It's not his fault the simple act of walking down the street is hazardous to your health.

"Is it me, or has David sharpened his teeth since last fall?"

I glance to the right and find Priya, my crit partner from Intro to Fiction, falling into step with me. "It's definitely not you. Writing something personal this early in the semester is brutal enough without suffering through a peer critique."

Especially since there's always that one pretentious asshole who shreds everyone else's work.

"It's masochistic," Priya declares, narrowing her eyes. "You better believe I'm calling him Professor Bates every chance I get. No more of this *Call-me-David* bullshit. First names are reserved for cool ass profs."

"Preach." I laugh as the stream of jostling bodies carries us out the front door of Windsor Hall and down the stone steps. "Any idea what you're going to write about?"

She shakes her head, dark ponytail bouncing. "No. You?"

I could write about my sexcapades, but there's no way in hell I'd ever put my name on them. I'd never live it down. Not even on a campus with forty-thousand students.

"No clue."

"Well, whatever you decide, don't sweat it." She hitches her bag up on her shoulder. "I've got your back during critique."

"Thanks." Gratitude wells up from the pit of my stomach and I want to hug the stuffing out of her, but that would probably be weird, so I just say, "I've got yours too."

"Cool." Priya steps off the sidewalk into the grass, letting a couple of wide-eyed freshmen with an enormous campus map pass by. "If you want a second opinion before class, you can email me your pages."

"Only if you send me yours." We did the same thing last fall, swapping feedback and tightening our pieces before sharing them with the class. Priya's a solid writer and doesn't need my help, but having her as a crit partner was a lifesaver. "You still have my email?"

She nods and we say our goodbyes, Priya heading toward the library while I head for Daily Grind.

I have time to kill before my next class, and it's too nice to be cooped up inside pouring over textbooks.

Besides, I've got all weekend to catch up on homework.

And the essay from hell.

My stomach clenches, but I can't tell if it's from the essay or hunger. The way my day is going, it's a toss-up. I overslept this morning and had to haul ass, leaving no time for breakfast.

That'll teach you to schedule an 8am class on a Friday.

I text Haley and she agrees to meet me for coffee—aka survival juice—because her next class doesn't start for an hour.

The September sun warms my face as I cross the Oak Grove, tucking my phone into my back pocket. The leaves are starting to turn and bursts of crimson and amber dot the canopy above, where squirrels race along the tree branches collecting acorns. Despite their efforts, the sidewalks are littered with fallen nuts, and I'm careful not to step on any.

Mainly because I don't want a repeat of last year.

Who the hell twists an ankle slipping on acorns?

The nurse at the student health center hadn't voiced the question aloud. She didn't need to. Her eyebrows had said it all.

But that was last year. This year I'm going to kick my bad luck—and my virginity—to the curb.

When I slip through the door of Daily Grind, the nutty aroma of fresh ground coffee welcomes me like a long-lost friend.

Haley's already in line with a dozen other caffeine deprived undergrads.

"Busy morning," I say, joining her at the back of the queue.

Most of the tables are occupied by students sipping lattes, devouring textbooks, or tapping away on tablets. I have no clue how they can work in this environment. It's not exactly noisy, but between the quiet hum of conversation, the indie rock spilling from the speakers, and the glorious whirring of the grinder, it's not exactly quiet either.

Haley makes a noncommittal sound, eyes glued to a copy of The Collegian.

A beat later, she laughs, the campus paper rattling in her hand.

"Oh, my God. Quinn... This headline." A grin splits her face as she holds up the article she was reading: *Jockblocked* by A. Ginger. "Why didn't I think of that?"

"Probably because you were too busy fantasizing about said jock." I glance around to make sure no one's listening. While I was busy documenting my failed attempt to get laid for the school paper, Haley spent most of Sunday drooling over Cooper's abs and forcing me to look at training camp pics featuring his sweat slick body. It was counterproductive, to say the least. "Keep your voice down. I don't want anyone else knowing I wrote that article."

"Why not?" She folds the paper and stuffs it in her bag as the line shuffles forward. "It's fire. A couple of people in my glass blowing class were talking about it this morning."

My heart leaps, but I press my lips flat and shrug.

It doesn't matter.

"Girl, I don't know why you're afraid to put your own name on the byline. This is pure gold." Haley levels her gaze at me, but I look away. Because apparently, I'm a coward. Who writes under a pseudonym. "You should be proud of yourself."

"Yeah, well, if you were the hot mess express, you wouldn't advertise it either." I gather my hair and twist it into a topknot, securing it with a rubber band from my wrist. I love Haley, but she just doesn't get it. Not only is she confident—in herself and her work—she's a visual artist. She lives for showcases and has the uncanny ability to let criticism roll off her back. I'd trade my soul for a skill like that. "People may laugh at my stories, but that doesn't mean I have to be the butt of their jokes."

Not anymore.

She frowns. "You really think people would laugh at you?"

"Come on, Hales. My own family doesn't even take me seriously." I force a self-deprecating laugh. "I've got half a dozen nicknames to prove it."

"Fuck Noah and his nicknames," she declares fiercely. There's no hesitation, once again proving she's loyal AF, even when it comes to family. "You give great voice. Everyone who reads your work knows it."

In the year I've been writing for The Collegian, my features have garnered thousands of comments online. The only articles that get more likes on social media are the thirst traps featuring the football team.

Still, I'm not ready to go there. Not yet.

If not now, when?

Probably never.

The line inches forward, and Haley grumbles about the long wait. The girl has zero patience—especially pre-caffeinated—and I'm not above using the distraction to change the subject.

Caffeine withdrawal FTW!

"So, what are we getting into this weekend?"

"I'm glad you asked." Haley draws the words out as she turns to face me. "I want to check out The Den tomorrow after the game. You in?"

The Wildcat's Den is a bar downtown. I've never been, but it's the place to be—if you're legal and aren't into the Greek scene.

"One tiny problem." I pinch my thumb and forefinger

together. "Neither of us is twenty-one, and I doubt even you can talk your way past the bouncer."

She nods, a mischievous glint in her eye. "That would be a problem if Bryan weren't getting us fakes. He's picking them up tonight."

"Fake IDs?" I wipe my palms on my shorts and imagine all the ways this could come back to bite me in the ass. *Spoiler alert: gingers and orange jumpsuits do not mix.* "We could get in a lot of trouble if we get caught."

"Relax. It's not a big deal." Haley loops her arm through mine, all cool confidence and low-key coercion. "Besides, we're not going to get caught."

She sounds so sure of herself that I want to believe her. The thing is, only two percent of the population has red hair, so the odds of a good fake are slim. And let's be honest, I'm not exactly what you'd call lucky.

On the other hand, The Wildcat's Den is the perfect place to find a hookup.

God knows I'm not about to try Greek Row again.

Not after Saturday night's humiliation.

"I swear, if I get arrested," I say, giving Haley the side-eye, "I'm never forgiving you."

She squeals—like there was ever any doubt I'd cave—and bumps her hip against mine. "That's the spirit!"

Spirit. Stupidity. Is there even a difference?

"I take it this means you and Bryan are back on?"

"For now." She grins and pats her dark curls. "The makeup sex was *ah-maz-ing*. You should try it sometime."

"I'll get right on that," I shoot back, scanning the chalkboard menu. "Just as soon as I lose my virginity."

There's a deep chuckle behind us, the sound raking over my skin like hot coals.

No-freaking-way.

No one's luck is that bad. Not even mine.

Warmth floods my cheeks, and I turn slowly, hoping like hell I've got it wrong. The eavesdropper wears an arrogant smirk, one my fingers itch to wipe off his face. Our eyes meet, mine no doubt horrified, his amused and the most gorgeous shade of cerulean blue.

Cooper-the-cockblocking-jockhole-DeLaurentis.

8

COOPER

QUINN TURNS ON HER HEEL, staring up at me with those big green eyes, and presses her lips flat. She's wearing a Wildcats tank top, a pair of denim cut-offs and flip-flops, which do nothing to bridge the gap in our heights. She looks positively innocent standing there with flushed cheeks and her hair piled on top of her head in a messy bun.

Yeah, well, looks can be deceiving, can't they?

After all, every time I bump into her, she's either talking about sex or attempting to get laid.

If she wasn't Noah's sister, she'd be a woman after my own heart.

"Cooper." Quinn says my name with an air of disapproval, making it clear she hasn't forgiven me for interfering Saturday night.

"Please tell me you aren't planning another random hookup." I flash her a lopsided grin. "In a coffee shop."

"That's none of your business." She adjusts her bag, gripping the strap so hard her nails dig into her palm. "You've done quite enough, don't you think?"

I open my mouth to argue—no one likes the clap—but her friend cuts me off.

"Hi, I'm Haley." She offers her hand, a knowing grin curving her lips.

Quinn obviously told her about our run-in at Sig. If I didn't know better, I'd say she approves. I like her already.

"Coop." I shake her hand, careful not to squeeze too hard, but her grip is firm and sure. "Nice to meet you. Any friend of Quinn's is a friend of mine."

Quinn huffs out a breath. "We aren't friends."

"Agree to disagree." I lean down and whisper, "As your friend, I'd like to suggest you forget about this whole random hookup business. Why not get a boyfriend and pop your cherry the normal way?"

She rolls her eyes, and the overhead lights are reflected in their emerald depths. "Told you he was a pig."

Haley gives me an appreciative once-over. "A sexy pig."

Finally, a voice of reason.

"First of all, there's nothing normal about me." Quinn lifts her chin, as if challenging me to argue before she plunges on. "Second, maybe I don't want a boyfriend," she adds, voice carrying over the steady buzz of the cafe. "I just want to get laid already."

Several heads swivel our way. Whether it's from the mention of sex or the fact that the line has moved on without us is anyone's guess.

Quinn hurries forward, dragging Haley by the arm. I follow.

For the coffee.

Keep telling yourself that, DeLaurentis.

"You know." I pitch my voice low. "If you want to get off, there are other ways."

Quinn snorts. "Thanks, Captain Obvious. I'm fully aware. I

stock my nightstand with batteries and lube, but it's not quite the same, is it?"

I do a double take. Did she just...?

Fuuuck.

My cock twitches with interest. Quinn getting herself off is a visual I don't need at nine-thirty in the morning, but it's too late. The damage is done.

How am I supposed to *not* imagine her naked and writhing in pleasure when she says shit like that?

Fuck. Fuck. Fuck.

Just the thought of all that fiery hair spread out on her pillow as she moans has me adjusting my stance, shifting my weight to mask the effect of her words. Which is so wrong, because...bro code.

Forget bro code. She's a virgin.

Totally. Off. Limits.

I rake a hand through my hair, searching for words. What is it with this girl? Doesn't she have a goddamn filter? Sure, mine slips sometimes, but it's only around the guys on the team. And only because I trust them implicitly. Growing up in a political family, I've learned to be careful about what I say and where.

Yet here Quinn is, talking about her vibrator. In a coffee shop. In broad daylight.

It's sexy as hell and—

Both women stare up at me expectantly. I've been quiet for too long.

"Depends on the guy," I finally drawl. "I can guarantee a hookup with Zac would be a distant second to your vibrator."

Quinn's mouth drops open, forming a luscious pink O.

Speechless. Probably a first.

"I tried to tell her." Haley shrugs. "But once Quinn sets her mind to something, there's no stopping her."

I'm all for slaying goals, but not if it means Quinn will hook up with any douchebag who looks her way. She deserves better than some prick who can't even remember her name.

"Are—" Quinn sputters, looking from Haley to me. "Are you two seriously ganging up on me right now?"

Haley grins. "Tough love, sis."

"Traitor."

The barista waves us up to the counter, and the girls step forward to place their order. A green tea and a croissant for Haley. A mocha latte and a pumpkin chocolate chip muffin for Quinn.

"Make that a double on the muffin." I hold up two fingers. "And a chocolate milk."

"What do you think you're doing?" Quinn demands, arching a slender brow.

"Ordering breakfast." *Obviously*.

She rolls her eyes and turns to the girl behind the counter as I fish my phone out of my front pocket. "We're not together. Ring them up separately, please."

"You can put it all on my bill." I hold my phone over the contactless reader, eyes fixed on Quinn as the payment is processed. "My treat."

"Thanks," Haley chirps as Quinn delves into her bag. She pulls out her wallet and starts counting wrinkled bills.

"Here. This should cover it." She attempts to press the cash into my hand. "We can buy our own breakfast."

"Never said you couldn't, but I thought it would be a nice gesture." I grin and push the bills back into her hand. "Unless buying you breakfast is going to get me labeled a sexist pig again?"

"Ignore her," Haley says with a wave of the hand. "It's the lack of caffeine talking. You can buy me breakfast any day."

"Same," the girl behind the counter adds, sending a flirtatious smile my way.

I know that look. It says she doesn't give a damn if I'm with Quinn or Haley or someone else altogether. Ten bucks says she slips me her digits.

And this is why Vaughn thinks you're an egomaniac.

Whatever. There's no rule that says we can't both be right.

"I've stumbled into an alternate universe." Quinn shakes her head, a puzzled expression settling over her face. "That's the only rational explanation."

The fuck?

"Because I'm such an asshole, you can't conceive of me doing something nice?" I ask as the cashier saunters off to fill our order.

Quinn blinks up at me, the picture of innocence. "You said it, not me."

A chuckle escapes before I can stop it. What can I say? I have a soft spot for sarcasm. "I think the words you're looking for are *thank you.*"

"I'll voice my appreciation, right after you apologize for being a cockblocking jackass."

"Fair enough." I cross my arms over my chest. I'm not too proud to apologize when I screw up. "I'm sorry I interrupted your hookup and prevented you from losing your virginity to a guy who couldn't remember your name and is a frequent flyer at the health clinic." I pause for effect and flash a self-satisfied grin. "Your turn."

Quinn huffs out a breath, cheeks reddening. She doesn't even look at the barista as the girl returns with our drinks.

"For the record," Haley stage whispers, grabbing her tea off the counter, "that was the shittiest apology in the history of shitty apologies."

Quinn plants a hand on her hip. "Agreed."

"Yeah? Then why don't you show me how it's done, sweetheart? I'm all ears."

"I think the words you're looking for," she says, throwing my words back at me as a calculating smile curves her lips, "are I'm sorry I was an arrogant, jockblocking jockhole. It wasn't my place to interfere, and I know better than to take away a woman's agency. I've learned from my mistakes, and I'll do better in the future."

"That was pretty good," I concede, though my apology was definitely funnier. "But aren't you forgetting something?"

She's not getting off the hook that easily. Not when she takes every available opportunity to bust my balls.

Quinn's eyes slide to the barista as she places two paper bags on the counter. "Thank you for breakfast, Cooper."

"You're welcome. Consider it a peace offering. For Saturday night."

"I suppose it's the least you can do." Quinn grabs her latte and one of the paper bags. Haley follows suit. "See you around."

Haley gives me a tiny finger wave and they hurry off, making a beeline for the front door. My stomach rumbles, and I turn back to the counter to collect my breakfast. All that remains is a bottle of chocolate milk and a napkin with the barista's number scrawled on it.

My pumpkin chocolate chip muffin is nowhere in sight.

Sonofabitch.

I stuff the napkin in my pocket and grab the chocolate milk. I don't want another random phone number. I want my muffin. The one Quinn just walked off with.

So much for making amends.

9

QUINN

THE WILDCAT'S DEN IS PACKED, the music and crowds spilling out onto the sidewalk through the roll-up doors that face College Avenue. We join the line of students celebrating Waverly's win over Buffalo, and I give my fake one last look, doing a mental comparison to my own driver's license. Red hair, green eyes, freckles. That's where the resemblance ends. The girl in the photo has a wider nose and fuller lips and...I'm totally going to get arrested.

No hookup is worth a rap sheet.

"Are you sure about this?" I turn to Haley. "I really don't think county lockup is the place for me."

"It's all good," she promises, hooking her arm through mine.

We inch toward the door, and I get my first glimpse of the bouncer. He's a big Hispanic guy with thick arms, no neck, and a shaved head. From the looks of it, he's not the sort to take any crap.

"Is it me or has that guy been eating his Wheaties?" I ask, noting the way his black t-shirt stretches over his muscular biceps, accentuating the tattoo that ends just above his right elbow.

"Don't sweat it," Bryan—Haley's on-again boyfriend and purveyor of fake IDs—says under his breath. "Just be cool."

Right. Be cool. Great advice for clubbing *and* mugshots.

When it's our turn, Bryan goes first, handing his ID to the intimidating-as-hell bouncer. The bouncer gives it a cursory glance, grunts, and hands it back.

Haley goes next. She smiles demurely and hands over her ID. He gives it the same superficial scan—barely looking up—before returning it with a bored expression.

"Hi. Nice night," I squeak, offering him my ID. He accepts, but doesn't look at it.

Nope. His gaze locks on my face and his eyes narrow, as if he's trying to place me. Or guess my age. Or—more likely—scare the crap out of me.

It's *so* working.

My stomach drops and a bead of sweat rises between my breasts. This is it. The moment of truth. Maybe I should've taken Haley's advice and put on a little eyeliner.

Right. Because eyeliner will totally age you two years.

"Birthday?" the bouncer asks, finally looking at the driver's license in his hand.

I recite the date on the ID and offer him a nervous smile.

He frowns and gives me another once-over, sending my heart rate into overdrive.

Shit. He knows it's a fake. He's going to call the cops, and they'll drag me away in cuffs and my parents will disown me and I'll never—

"You're good," he barks, interrupting my panic spiral.

He hands my ID back and relief floods my veins as Haley grabs my elbow and drags me forward, a huge grin plastered on her face.

We find a small table at the back of the bar and when the server appears, Bryan orders a round of drinks. It's a wonder she can hear him over the raucous crowd and loud music, but maybe excellent hearing is a job requirement. Right up there with not spilling beer on the paying customers.

I wouldn't last ten minutes.

"So." Haley leans forward, resting her chin on her hand. "What's the plan for tonight?"

I blink. "The plan?"

"You know. Operation Ditch Your Virginity: Part Bar."

Bryan makes a valiant attempt at hiding his laughter—*and fails miserably*.

"You told him?" I hiss, heat flooding my cheeks.

At this rate, the entire campus will know about my virgin status by the end of the semester.

"I tell him everything." Haley waves a hand dismissively. "You know this."

True, but... "That doesn't make it any less embarrassing."

"Quit stalling. I know you haven't given up on this ridiculous mission of yours."

The server returns with our drinks, and I take a big ass sip of my beer. I'm not prepared to have this conversation stone-cold sober. Not with Bryan.

"Don't sweat it, Quinn." Bryan drapes an arm across the back of Haley's chair, but the corner of his mouth is still climbing skyward in a half-smile. "Your secret is safe with me." He pauses thoughtfully. "If you're really serious, I can introduce you to some decent dudes who'd be DTF."

Haley pulls a face. "Babe, none of your single friends are decent. Trust me on this. It's why they're single." She turns to me. "And also why I haven't offered to introduce you."

"What about J?" Bryan challenges. "He's cool."

"J?" Haley echoes, voice high with disapproval. "Quinn is not losing her virginity to a guy who thinks the clit is an STI."

Bryan has the decency to look chagrined. "He was kidding. I think."

Oh. My. God. How is this my life?

"We both know J is—"

"Thanks for the offer." I cut Haley off before the discussion becomes a full-blown argument. "But losing my virginity by committee is not an option." Not one I'm willing to pursue anyway. "It has to be totally spontaneous. No planning." Bryan opens his mouth to protest, but I push forward. "Besides, it's better if it's random. That way, if it's a complete disaster, I never have to see the guy again."

"What exactly do you think is going to happen?" he asks, amusement coloring his words.

"With my luck, anything is possible." I sigh and drag a finger through the perspiration on my glass. "I couldn't even get laid at a frat party. That has to be a first."

"Y'all are overthinking this." Bryan shakes his head and takes a drink of his beer. "Trust me, if a guy gets to have sex, it's all good." He shrugs. "Guys are simple. It's women that are complicated."

Haley shoots him an arch look. "Which is why Quinn needs to find a guy who knows his way around a woman's body. Someone who's good with his hands." She grins and turns back to me. "Someone like Cooper DeLaurentis."

Like hell.

"So not happening." This time I'm the one who pulls a face, one that shows exactly how I feel about the prospect of hooking up with the cocky wide receiver. "The guy's an ass."

"He apologized *and* bought us breakfast." She shrugs. "I say forgive and fornicate."

Bryan's eyes go wide and he chokes on his beer, spraying lager all over the table when he clears his airway.

"Jesus Christ, woman! Warn me next time you say that shit."

"Sorry, babe." Haley grins and uses her napkin to mop up the mess. "Honestly, you should be used to it by now."

She's not wrong. Haley always says exactly what she's thinking, consequences be damned.

"When exactly did Cooper DeLaurentis buy you breakfast?" he asks, a jealous edge to his voice.

Here we go again.

It'll be a miracle if they make it through the night without breaking up.

Haley must have the same thought, because she tilts her head and says, "I love this song. Let's dance."

Without waiting for Bryan's reply, she jumps up and grabs his hand, pulling him to his feet. Then she turns to me with an apologetic look. "You'll be okay for a few minutes?"

"Sure." I smile and wave them off. Better alone than caught up in another one of their arguments.

Besides, maybe if I'm by myself, it'll be easier for guys to approach me.

I sip my beer as Haley and Bryan disappear into the sea of writhing bodies on the dance floor.

It's dark, and it doesn't take long to lose track of them in the crowd. Still, I watch for a while, taking in the endless tide of entwined limbs and gyrating hips before my attention drifts.

The Den is a landmark in College Park—no bar crawl is complete without a visit—so it's no surprise the walls are lined with blue and white Waverly paraphernalia or that the tabletops and hardwood floors are heavily scarred from the tens of thousands of students and alumni who've poured through the doors to eat, drink, and get shitfaced.

"Another round, hon?" the server asks, appearing at my side.

I nod and when she turns to fetch my beer, I realize she's wearing a Wildcat jersey with the number nineteen embroidered on the back.

Cooper's number.

There's no escaping the arrogant jockhole. Not in College Park, anyway.

I'm sure there are plenty of girls—and guys—wearing his number tonight, but I can't help wondering if she's hooked up with him. And if so, was it everything she'd expected?

Does it even matter?

No, no it does not.

I square my shoulders and drain my beer, ignoring the sudden warmth in my cheeks.

Cooper DeLaurentis is *not* an option, but surely there's someone in the bar who is.

Not that you'd know it. I've been sitting alone for nearly twenty minutes and so far, not a single person has spoken to me. According to every movie ever, a hot guy—or even a douchey one—should have approached by now with a terrible pickup line and a free drink offer.

So what am I doing wrong?

Only everything.

Right. What I need is a guy's opinion, but it's not like I can text Noah for hookup advice and Bryan is no help.

I drum my fingers on the sticky table, mulling it over.

The solution hits me, and I can't believe I didn't think of it sooner. It's so freaking obvious.

The drunk dialing frat bro.

Even better, he has no clue who I am, so no judgement.

I pull out my phone and start typing.

10

COOPER

Bus rides are *the fucking worst.*

I lean forward to rub the cramp in my calf, but it's close quarters and my shoulder clips Reid.

"You wanted the window seat," he reminds me, flashing a shit-eating grin. Then the asshole makes a show of stretching his legs, which are extended into the aisle. "You should know better by now."

I really should, but every once in a while, I make it a point not to be a selfish prick. Reid took some nasty hits in today's game. The last thing he needs is to be curled up like a sardine.

Besides, he's the team captain. The least I can do is give him the aisle seat.

"Yeah, yeah." I stretch and flex my right Achilles, which is tight as hell. "When we make the championship game, the university better spring for airline tickets. Preferably first class."

Reid snorts. "Don't hold your breath."

"Don't piss in my Cheerios."

"That's more your style than mine." He tips his head back and closes his eyes. Can't blame him. He'll never admit it, but he's under a lot of pressure.

Team captain. Heisman hopeful. NFL legacy.

That shit takes a toll.

I should know. I've been trapped under my father's thumb for as long as I can remember. The game is my only escape.

"Whatever. This time next year we'll be traveling in luxury." The comment is as much a reminder for me as it is Reid.

National championship. First-round draft pick. NFL contract.

Freedom.

My phone vibrates and I dig it out of my pocket. It takes some serious maneuvering because instead of joggers, which would make the four-hour bus ride from Buffalo to College Park marginally more tolerable, I'm stuck in a monkey suit. Like the fans really give a shit what we wear on the bus.

Might as well get used to it.

It'll be more of the same in the NFL. At least there I'll be compensated for my discomfort.

I glance down at my phone and find a text from an unknown number. I swipe the screen to read it, expecting a booty call. Or maybe a nude selfie.

It wouldn't be the first time.

After all, we just won our first road game, and Waverly *is* a football school.

Unknown: So, I need advice. About guys. And since you're in a fraternity...

It's the girl from last weekend. The one who loves Star Wars and hates Greek life.

Before I can respond, three dots appear, followed by another message.

Unknown: Sorry. Texting random guys for advice is weird, right? Forget I asked.

Not likely. Besides, I'm bored as hell.

Me: What's weird is texting random frat dudes 4 adv—

I backspace and erase the number four. She already thinks I'm a douche. No need to reinforce her unflattering opinion.

Me: What's weird is texting random frat dudes for advice. You know, since we're all the same.

*Unknown: What can I say? *shrug emoji* I'm desperate.*

This fucking girl. A better man might be offended, but her snark game is strong, and I'm here for it.

Me: First bit of advice, never admit to being desperate.

I stare at the screen, anticipation building low in my gut as I wait for her reply.

Unknown: That would be good advice, if I were trying to impress you.

Me: Ouch. Didn't anyone ever tell you that you'll catch more bees with honey?

Unknown: It's flies.

Me: What flies?

*Unknown: *facepalm emoji* The phrase is "You'll catch more flies with honey."*

Me: No way. That doesn't even make sense.

Unknown: The ability to speak does not make you intelligent.

Damn. She did it again. How does she work a Star Wars quote into every conversation?

I send back a *You underestimate my powers* GIF, feeling pretty smug.

That smug satisfaction? It lasts all of three seconds before she hits me with a *Much to learn you still have* GIF featuring Yoda.

I'm impressed. And annoyed I can't come up with a solid reply.

I rack my brain, but I've got nothing, so I steer the conversation back to the original message.

Me: Apparently I'm not the only one. What's this advice you need?

While I wait for her reply, I update her contact information, chuckling to myself as I type Padawan in the name field.

"Laughing at your own jokes again, princess?" Parker calls out, bumping my seatback so it jerks forward.

I give him the finger without lifting my gaze from the phone screen. If I ignore him, he'll get bored and go back to whatever movie he and Vaughn are watching on his tablet.

Padawan: I'm at a bar on College Ave and I'm trying to meet a guy, but I'm clueless. Since you're a guy, I figured you could give me some tips.

I shake my head in disbelief. Never in my life have I helped a woman pick up another man, but what the hell? It's not like we're ever going to—

I reread her message.

College Ave?

Nah. There's probably a College Ave on every campus across the country. The odds of this girl going to Waverly are probably slimmer than the odds of making it to the NFL.

I've studied those odds. They aren't great. And only half of those who get drafted have lasting careers.

Focus, DeLaurentis.

Right.

Picking up dudes. I scrub a hand over my face. Chances are, she's overthinking the situation. Women are complex creatures, but guys? Not so much. Especially when it comes to sex.

Me: What are you doing right now?

Padawan: I told you, I'm at a bar. Try to keep up.

A grin pulls at the corner of my mouth. I can practically hear the snark in her words.

Me: I mean, what exactly are you doing?

Padawan: Sitting at a table nursing a beer?

I pause at the question mark. Not quite as confident as she pretends to be, but I can work with that.

Me: First bit of advice, young Padawan. Sitting alone with your beer makes you look like a wet blanket.

Padawan: Who says I'm alone?

Me: Aren't you?

There's a long pause in the conversation. Three little dots appear on the screen and then disappear a moment later.

Way to scare her off, asshole.

My fingers fly over the screen as I type my next message. The last thing I want to do is make her feel bad when she's asking for help. Besides, it's not like I have anything else to do. Reid's zoned out, and we're still an hour from College Park.

Me: If you want to meet a guy, you need to be approachable. Most guys are scared shitless of rejection. Try hanging out at the bar. Or on the dance floor.

Padawan: Dancing? No. Freaking. Way. That's a terrible idea.

I roll my eyes.

Me: Trust me, a hot girl dancing is always a good idea.

Padawan: How do you know I'm hot? Maybe I'm a hideous troll with bad rhythm and funky breath.

Anything is possible, but if I've learned anything from the women in my life, it's this: The sexiest thing a woman can be is confident.

*Me: Girls who quote Star Wars are always hot. That's why it's what's on the inside that counts. *winking emoji**

There's a long pause. No dots. Nothing to show she's replying, but I know she read my message. It says so right on the screen.

Me: Trust me. Pop a breath mint and go shake that Star Wars loving ass.

Padawan: I don't know...

Me: Relax. It'll be fine.

Padawan: Tell that to my third-grade dance instructor. During our spring recital, my tap shoe flew off and clocked her in the face. She had a black eye for a week.

A laugh escapes before I can stop it. I mean, come on, that shit's funny.

Next to me, Reid stirs, but doesn't open his eyes.

Me: You know what? Forget everything I said about dancing and go hang out at the bar.

Padawan: That's it? That's the best advice you have for meeting a guy?

Me: Second bit of advice. You won't meet anyone if you sit around texting all night.

I brace myself, prepared for a snarky reply, but it never comes.

Padawan: What the hell. Might as well give it a try.

I hastily pull up a Yoda GIF and hit send.

Me: Do or do not. There is no try.

*Padawan: *facepalm emoji**

Padawan: I set you up perfectly.

"Yeah you did." Another laugh pushes up from my gut as I slide the phone back into my pocket.

"The fuck are you doing up there?" Parker asks, leaning over the back of my seat so his shit-eating grin is right in my face.

"Don't you worry your pretty little face about it."

He rolls his eyes, which is freaky as hell, since his head is upside down. "You wanna hit The Den tonight?"

"Is that even a question?" I smirk up at him, because it's no secret I'm always down to party.

Who knows? Maybe I'll get lucky and find a sexy Star Wars quoting hookup of my own.

11

QUINN

*J*UST HANG *out at the bar*, he said. *It'll be fine*, he said.

Thirty minutes and a shot of something red and fruity proves this was a lie. I'm wedged in between a couple of squealing woo girls who are guzzling margs like it's last call and a guy in a Wildcats tee who hasn't looked my way once. Scratch that. He asked me to pass him a napkin when one of his buddies tapped his beer bottle, creating a foam eruption to rival Mt. Vesuvius.

Who says college guys aren't mature, amirite?

I sip my beer and roll my shoulders. Maybe frat boy gave me bad advice. After all, if he's a closet nerd like me, he probably doesn't have the first clue how to pick up a stranger in a bar.

For all I know, I could be taking advice from another woefully inept virgin.

But, no. He seemed...confident.

Doesn't everyone behind the anonymity of a screen?

Whatever. Might as well order one more drink before calling it a night.

I haven't seen Haley and Bryan since they disappeared on the dance floor, and chilling at the bar is losing its appeal. You know, since I have no one to talk to and probably look like the biggest loser on campus.

Make the first move. It's the freaking twenty-first century!

I can practically hear Haley shouting the words at me, drowning out the loud bass from the overhead speakers.

God, I wish it was that easy. But after the disaster at Sig Chi, I'm not sure I've got the lady balls to make the first move again.

I signal the bartender, and he lifts his chin in acknowledgement. Judging by the number of shot glasses lined up before him, it's going to be a minute, so I turn to watch the crowd.

On the far side of the bar, there's a girl dancing on a table and I give her mental props because if I tried that crap, I'd faceplant on the hardwood floor and destroy years of orthodontic work.

Some people have all the luck.

You've got plenty of luck, Quinntastrophe. It's just all bad.

Aaaand...now Noah's in my head, too.

Great. It's just a matter of time until he and Hales get into the whole good angel-bad angel shtick and I'm left with a raging migraine.

Hard pass.

I shut out their voices—this is *my* night, dammit—and focus on the plan.

Step one: Meet a cute guy.

Step two: Invite him back to my place.

Step three: Seduce the hell out of him and kiss my virginity goodbye.

My gaze skates over the crowd, landing on a familiar face with messy black hair, tortoiseshell glasses, and the kind of shy smile that invites deep conversation. Hope surges through me and when our eyes meet, I see the instant recognition hits him. His lips flatten and his hands go immediately to his groin, like he's worried just the sight of me might cause irreparable harm to his cock.

He melts into the crowd without a backward glance.

So much for second chances.

"Try shaving your balls next time," I grumble, flashbacks of the world's biggest man-bush assaulting my brain.

"Excuse me?"

My spine stiffens, and I turn slowly to my left. The marg chugging woo girls have moved on and in their place is a guy who—judging by the big ass grin on his face—definitely heard me say balls.

Talk about first impressions.

Heat floods my cheeks. "Uh, maybe we can just pretend you didn't hear that?"

"Hear what?" His grin widens. "I'm Mike, by the way."

"Quinn."

I give him a quick once-over. He's got a friendly smile, full and inviting without being creepy. He's a few inches taller than me with shaggy brown hair, hazel eyes, and a runner's build, which is on full display under a fitted tee and equally snug jeans.

Mike leans forward, resting his arms on the bar. "Are you here by yourself?"

"My friends are around here somewhere." I make a vague gesture toward the dance floor. "You?"

"My roommates are in the back shooting pool. Figured I'd get faster service at the bar." He cuts his eyes at the bartender, who's now pouring a row of yellow shots, before he turns his attention back to me. "I don't mind waiting, though. Especially when the company is good."

I'm not sure I qualify as good company, unless he's looking for comedic relief, but he's cute, hasn't looked at my boobs once, and seems to be single, so #winning.

Go figure. Frat boy knew what he was talking about after all.

"Do you come here often?" I immediately give myself a mental facepalm because the only people who ask questions like that are sleazy guys from nineties rom-coms.

He shrugs. "I'm not big on the bar scene, but it would be sacrilege not to celebrate our first road win of the season."

"So you're toasting the football gods tonight?" I flash a teasing grin. "Good to know."

"You're not?" He leans back, pretending to be totally affronted. "If you aren't into football, I'm not sure we can be friends."

Playing along, I lift my brows and feign confusion. "A bunch of testosterone-fueled men in tight pants slugging it out over a leather ball. What's not to like?"

"Good point." He laughs. It's light and easy, as if he doesn't have a care in the world. *Must be nice.* "Can I buy you a drink, Quinn?"

Cute, single, hasn't looked at my boobs, *and* remembered my name? Hell, yes, he can buy me a drink. "Sure," I say, playing it cool for the first time in my life.

"What can I get you?" the bartender asks, appearing on the other side of the scarred bar like a freaking ninja.

I open my mouth to order another beer, but Mike cuts me off.

"A lager for me and an AMF for the lady." He shoots me that disarming smile and scoots a little closer, dropping his voice low. "Don't worry. You'll like it."

I want to point out that he has no clue what I'd like since we just met like five seconds ago, but maybe he thinks he's being chivalrous or something? Sometimes my dad orders for my mom, but they've been married for twenty-five years and she has generalized anxiety disorder, so it's not exactly the same.

Does it even matter?

No, no it does not. A one-night stand does not a soulmate make.

"Thanks." I tuck a strand of hair behind my ear. "For the drink, I mean."

"My pleasure." He leans in close and suddenly it's like we're in our own little world. It's...nice. "What's your major?"

"Undeclared." I bite my lower lip. It's the most basic getting to know you question on campus, but I hate it. It's like everyone else has their life all figured out while I'm floundering. Might as well just put a flashing light on my head that says *Hometown Hot Mess: Population Me.* "You?"

God, my conversational skills suck.

"I'm pre law." Of course he is. "With a minor in history."

"So you're an overachiever?" I tease, realizing too late that probably makes me an underachiever.

Story of my life.

"I wouldn't go that far." The bartender slides our drinks across the sticky bar. A bottle of Yuengling and an electric blue cocktail that looks like it should be served in a fishbowl. Mike hands over a twenty, and it occurs to me that maybe I should've asked more questions.

Like, what the hell is an AMF?

I stare silently at the drink as the bartender makes change. It can't be any worse than Greek Row punch, right? I lift the cup to my lips and take a tiny sip.

It's surprisingly sweet, and it goes down easy, nothing like the boozy punch I've sampled at Sig Chi. Thank God. That stuff will destroy your taste buds.

"What's the verdict?" Mike asks, turning back to me with a cheeky grin. He's so close now that our shoulders are touching. I can smell the musky scent of sweat and cologne that clings to his skin. Warmth spreads throughout my chest, but I'm not sure if it's his proximity or the alcohol hitting my system.

Either way, I don't hate it.

"Despite the offensive color, it's good." I take another sip. It goes down just as easily as the first. "Really good, actually."

"Told you so." He lifts his chin, gesturing toward the dance floor. "Want to dance?"

Um, yes, please.

So what if I'm a shit dancer? Even I can grind up against a guy without causing permanent damage.

Probably.

I take a swig of my drink, and confidence bolstered, nod.

Mike takes my hand, his skin cool against my own, and leads me onto the dance floor. There's a popular hip hop song blasting from the overhead speakers, making it damn near impossible to think, let alone talk. I take a long pull from my plastic cup as we squeeze through the crowd, letting the soft buzz of alcohol dull my senses.

I don't need to be completely sober tonight. Not when my mind is already made up.

The crush of bodies swallows us up like quicksand, and a flutter of excitement fills my chest as Mike wraps his arms around my waist. His beer bottle presses against my backside as he pulls me in close, and I loop my arms over his shoulders, careful not to spill my drink on him since that would probably be a total mood killer.

We move slowly to the beat of the music, feeling each other out, but eventually we find our rhythm. A half dozen songs later, his hips are pressed to mine in a wholly indecent manner. One that suggests I'll be ditching my virginity sooner rather than later.

Could this night get any better?

Not likely.

"Excuse me."

The familiar words echo in my alcohol-soaked brain, but I

ignore them. There's literally nowhere to go. I couldn't move an inch in either direction, even if I wanted to.

Which—spoiler alert—I don't.

Whoever it is will have to find another path to the bar.

There's a deep growl to my left—an actual freaking growl—and I jerk my head around to find a sexy blond giant smirking down at me.

Our eyes lock, and an involuntary shiver races down my spine.

Cooper-the-interfering-jockblocker-DeLaurentis.

12

COOPER

"MISS ME, SWEETHEART?" I give Quinn a slow once-over, taking in the sexy emerald tank top that complements her Coke bottle eyes and the snug, curve-hugging jeans that show off her perfect ass. "Because I sure missed you."

Her eyes narrow in suspicion, but my words have the desired effect. The handsy douchebag steps back, giving her some space.

Satisfaction surges in my chest.

And, yeah, maybe that makes me a dick, but so be it.

Quinn raises a brow. "Do I know you?"

Her tone isn't exactly friendly, but the hint of a smile tugs at the corner of her mouth.

Grindy McGrinderson looks back and forth between us, eyes going wide. Quinn can play dumb all she wants, but he knows exactly who I am. Right now, he's trying to figure out what he's gotten himself into.

What the hell. If Quinn wants to play games, I'm down.

"Don't do me like that, babe." I lean in, raising my voice to be heard over the loud music. "You've had your fun. Now let's bounce."

"I've had my—" She scrunches up her nose, a cluster of

freckles bunching across the bridge and fuck me, it's the most adorable thing I've ever seen. "What?"

I shake my head and turn to the rando.

"Sorry, man. My girl is big into role playing. She likes to do this thing where she flirts with strangers and pretends she's going to hook up with them, but she never closes the deal." Quinn makes a high-pitched squeak that would give Flipper a run for his money. I sneak a glance at her, and it's all I can do to not laugh. Her expression is priceless. I wink at her and turn back to the dude, who looks more confused than ever. "She always leaves with me." I shrug. "Says it makes the sex even hotter."

"Ignore him." Quinn shoots me a scathing look. "He's a few fries short of a Happy Meal."

"Now that you mention it." I rub my stomach. "I could go for some chicken nuggets. If we leave now, we can hit the drive-thru on the way home."

Grabby McGrabberson averts his gaze, staring over my shoulder as he mumbles, "I'm just gonna...yeah." He takes a step back and shoves his hands in his pockets. "I don't want any trouble."

He turns and pushes into the crowd.

Good riddance.

"What the hell do you think you're doing?" Quinn demands, pulling herself up to her full height. Maybe that shit works on her brother, but I spent the afternoon staring down guys three times her size. "Are you drunk?"

"No." I point to her half-empty cup. "But if you finish that drink, you will be."

Her brows furrow in confusion. "What's wrong with my drink?"

Is she for real?

"Other than the fact that it's got five kinds of liquor in it?"

"Five? Really?" She lifts the cup up and stares at it like she's seeing it for the first time. "Who'd have guessed?"

"Why do you think it's called Adiós, Motherfucker? It's meant to get you shitfaced." She giggles, probably at the name, and I scrub a hand over my face. "If you don't know what's in it, why are you drinking it?"

She cocks a hip. "Mike bought it for me."

Of course he did. "The asshole was probably trying to get you drunk and take advantage of you."

She pokes me in the chest and heat radiates from the spot where her finger landed, which is ridiculous because it wasn't even skin-to-skin contact.

Probably just leftover energy from the game.

"Maybe I was trying to get him drunk and take advantage of him." She pokes me again. "Did you ever think of that?"

"No." It's bullshit, but I'm not trying to picture Quinn seducing some random creeper at a bar. "It did, however, occur to me he might've slipped something in your drink."

She rolls those big green eyes. "I'm a virgin, not a moron. I took the drink directly from the bartender."

Thank Christ.

Relief surges through my veins. How the fuck does Noah deal with having his little sister on campus? On Greek Row?

For the first time in my life, I'm glad to be an only child. If I saw some dude playing grab-ass with my sister, I'd break his fucking hands.

Quinn's not your sister, so what do you care?

I don't.

Okay, fine. I care. But only because I'm not a trash human being.

"I can't believe you chased Mike off." Quinn's bottom lip juts out, forming a sexy little pout. "It was rude."

"Serves the fucker right." I plant my hands on my hips. If she thinks she can guilt me over Doctor Octopus, she's got another think coming. "Thirty seconds ago, he was dry humping you like a dog in heat."

"Eww." She squeals, doing that cute nose scrunching thing again. "Gross."

I flash her a wicked grin. "Tell me about it."

"Did you just—" She tilts her head and looks up at me from under her lashes. "Did you just call me gross?

"Sweetheart, there's nothing gross about you." That's half the problem. If she's really going through with this whole losing her virginity to a stranger thing, she'll have no trouble finding dudes to volunteer as tribute. "From the looks of it, I arrived just in time."

"If by just in time, you mean just in time to cockblock me again, then yes." She lifts the blue drink to her lips and takes a hearty gulp. "You can move along now." She makes a shooing motion with her other hand. "Go wreck some other virgin's night."

"Are you sure I didn't save your night?" I cross my arms over my chest, and damn if her attention doesn't lock on my biceps. Not gonna lie, I'm flattered. I figured her type was more studious. "That guy probably doesn't even know what a G-spot is, let alone how to find it."

Her gaze shifts to my face, a challenge burning in her eyes. "I suppose you think you could do better?"

Without a doubt.

I lean forward and whisper against the shell of her ear, my lips brushing against the sensitive flesh. "Sweetheart, I don't think. I know."

Her breath hitches and it's the sweetest sound I've heard all day. Forget crashing helmets and Wildcat cheers. This right here is what I need. The heat of her body warming my cheek.

"It's— It's too bad you have that virgin rule," she says, the words coming on a breathy whisper.

"Too bad." I pull back, and just like that, the moment is shattered.

Quinn swallows, throat bobbing delicately. "You're not drinking tonight?" she asks, staring pointedly at my empty hands.

"Just got here." I shrug. Normally I'd be halfway to blitzed by now. "We had an away game today."

Which, yeah, is just as stupid as it sounds. Waverly is a football school. Of course she knows we had a game today.

"I know. You played well." She smacks me lightly on the arm. "Nearly gave me heart failure in the fourth quarter when you pulled down that pass at the five-yard line."

"Did you really doubt the Dynamic Duo?" I ask, tapping into the swagger that's made me one of the most popular wide receivers in the Big Ten. "Reid and I are fire."

Even at six-two, I had to stretch like Gumby to get my hands on the ball. It was only through years of training and muscle memory that I had the presence of mind to drag my toes, making it a fair catch as the momentum of the play carried me out of bounds.

Nobody wants to hear that, though. It's not nearly as sexy in a sound bite.

"It was a great catch, but don't let your head get too big." A sexy smile curves her lips, all sass and spitfire. "Conference games will be more challenging."

Damn. She sounds just like Carter, our new placekicker, and I'm feeling it. Doesn't hurt that Quinn's actually into football and isn't over the top about it, quoting stats she doesn't understand or give a shit about.

She's the real deal.

"You two are close?" she asks. "You and Reid, I mean."

"He's my best friend." I laugh, the tension easing from my shoulders. "Scratch that. Reid's like the responsible big brother I never wanted. I'm going to miss playing with him next year."

She swirls the blue liquid in her cup, a thoughtful expression settling on her face. "I guess you'd better enjoy the next twelve games then."

"There are only ten games left in the season."

Two down, ten to go. We need ten more Ws if we want a shot at the title.

"Who says I'm talking about the regular season?" She quirks a brow. "I hear Waverly's going all the way this year."

I like the way this girl thinks. Her ass may be divine, but it's nothing compared to her big sexy brain and all the snarky sarcasm it delivers.

"You know, Emma Stone is my favorite ginger, but you're a close second."

She scowls up at me, lips pinched. "You cannot say ginger. Only redheads get to say ginger."

I want to ask what kind of sense that makes, but I bite my tongue. This is the perfect opportunity to prove I'm not a complete Neanderthal, and I'm not about to waste it.

"I'll do better," I say, remembering her apology from the coffee shop. She beams, and my stupid heart does a happy dance, emulating one of those cat memes the internet loves so much. I grab a strand of her hair, and it slides right through my fingers. It may look like fire, but it's as smooth as silk. "Let me see your fake. This hair couldn't be easy to match."

"No way." She bats my hand away. "And how do you know it's a fake?"

"You told me you were nineteen."

Surprise washes over her features. "You remember that?"

How could I possibly forget?

"Sweetheart, I remember everything." I sweep her hair back

and tuck it behind her ear. "Speaking of which, don't you think it's time to give up the Virgin Quest?"

She squares her shoulders and lifts her chin. "Not a chance."

I figured as much. Fortunately, I don't mind settling for the next best thing.

"Then I guess it's up to me to distract you." I trail a finger down her cheek. "Dance with me."

13

QUINN

"DANCE?" I repeat, pointing to Cooper's broad chest because words are not my friend right now. *AMF 1–Quinn 0.* "With you?"

I must've heard wrong. Coop's anti-virgin, and, as far as I can tell, anti-fun.

At least when it comes to me.

"Yes, Quinn." A smile plays across his lips and damn, it's sexy. "With me."

I should say no, if only because he cockblocked me—*again.* On the other hand, don't I deserve to have a little fun of my own after the stunt he pulled? It's not like I have to worry about embarrassing myself or stepping on his toes, because...*Coop.*

As long as I don't do permanent damage to the Wildcats' star receiver, it'll be fine.

Or it's the perfect recipe for a Quinntessential Disaster.

I shrug, ignoring the buzzkill in my head. "I'm game if you are."

Coop's grin widens and my belly churns with nervous energy. Or maybe that's alcohol? Hard to say which because he takes my hand, his warm, rough palm brushing against mine, and my brain short circuits.

It's a total shutdown and reboot.

When I finally get my bearings, Coop's relieved me of my drink and disposed of it God only knows where. Our eyes lock and holy shit, this is really happening. He stares down at me with the kind of intensity I thought was reserved for football. Or sex, though I don't have firsthand knowledge since, ya know, virgin.

Giiirl.

Right. So not the time. Not when Cooper DeLaurentis is staring at me like I'm a goddamn snack.

He pulls me in close, leaving a sliver of space between our bodies. The DJ drops an upbeat pop song, and he wastes no time synching up with the music, body moving with smooth precision.

The boy has moves.

Of course Coop has moves. Moves half the women on campus would give their left ovary to experience. Is this what it feels like to be lucky?

If lucky is synonymous with stiff as a corpse, then yeah.

"Relax." Coop closes a strong, possessive hand over the curve of my hip. "I won't bite."

Unless you want me to.

The words are unspoken, but they're definitely implied.

A ripple of desire spreads from my belly, heating my flesh. The prospect of Cooper DeLaurentis nibbling on my body doesn't sound half bad. Actually, it sounds pretty freaking good right now.

Nopenopenope.

No catching feelings for the campus flirt. He has a type, and I'm not it.

Still, it's not like I have any other prospects and with the warm buzz of the AMF humming through my veins—Who knew five kinds of alcohol could be so delicious?—dancing might even be fun.

I close my eyes and soak in the music's vibe. It's a steady beat even I can't screw up, so I give myself over to the moment, moving my hips slowly as I kiss my inhibitions goodbye.

Adiós, indeed.

When I open my eyes, Coop's watching me again, and damn if I don't want to know what's on his mind. In the dim light, his irises appear midnight blue, but it doesn't make them any less stunning.

A girl could get lost in eyes like those.

"You still with me?" he asks.

"Yup." *Just drowning in the deep blue sea.*

Look at me getting all poetic and stuff.

The corner of his mouth twitches, and panic briefly pierces my alcohol induced buzz. *Fuckballs.* Did I say that out loud?

Whatever. It's not like Coop and I have a future. Who cares if he thinks I'm wackadoodle?

I spin out of his grip and throw my hands up, shaking my ass because why the hell not? It's Saturday night, I'm dancing with one of the hottest guys on campus, and I feel amazing.

Sexy even.

Coop slides up behind me, easily matching my rhythm.

Feeling bold, I roll my hips, brushing my ass against his hardness. A low groan slips from his throat and satisfaction blooms deep in my chest as he tugs me up against him, fitting my body to his and keeping one possessive hand fixed on my hip. His rock-hard abs press against my back and *holy hotness, Batman.*

Those babies must be made of steel.

Fire lances through my veins, my skin hot and tight as perspiration beads along my hairline. I sweep my hair over my shoulder and sigh as the cool air kisses the back of my neck.

The relief is short-lived.

Coop leans in close, the heat of his body warming every inch of my exposed flesh. A shiver races up my spine, half longing and half pleasure.

One glance over my shoulder—one look at Coop's hooded eyes—confirms what I already know.

He's as into this as I am.

We dance like that for a while, his hand on my hip, our bodies getting sweatier and closer with each song. People press in on us from all sides, but they're easy enough to ignore with Coop at my back.

It's the most fun I've had in—*ever*.

I rake my fingers up his thigh, relishing the taut muscles, and give it a gentle squeeze. His hand settles over mine and just like that, I'm imagining those rough palms on other parts of my body. Fantasizing about all the sexy, sinful ways he could put those long fingers to good use.

Why Cooper, what big hands you have!

The better to fu—

The music changes abruptly, putting an end to my filthy thoughts. A slow song drifts across the dark bar, and Coop stiffens at my back, his hand sliding from mine.

It was fun while it lasted.

I turn, dragging a hand through my sweat damp hair. "Thanks for dan—"

Coop presses a finger to my lips, silencing me.

His cheeks are flushed and his mouth is curved in a sensual smile, one that promises sex and seduction. He slides a knee between my thighs and pulls me close, our bodies creating the kind of delicious friction that has every nerve in my body buzzing with awareness.

Nerves twist my belly, but instinct takes over. In the space of a heartbeat, our bodies are moving in harmony. Hell, it almost feels natural.

That's the AMF talking, Quinntastrophe.

Probably. The idea of Coop and me together is anything but natural. Sexy football gods and disaster-prone virgins are not a thing.

A fact you'd do well to remember.

Right. Coop isn't my friend. He's a cockblocking, beer chugging frat bro and a giant pain in my ass.

Emphasis on the *giant*.

He tangles his fingers in my hair, holding a strand up for inspection under the quick flash of a strobe light.

"Keep that up and I just might stomp on your toes." Total lie. I would never. Not just because I'm having a good time, but because I'd never jeopardize Waverly's shot at a national title. "You need those to play football, right?"

It's a throwaway question. Of course he does.

"In case you haven't noticed, I'm a big guy. I can take it." A devilish smile transforms his lips and he pulls me in closer. Which, honestly, I didn't even think was possible. "Besides, I'm not trying to sleep with you, so I have nothing to worry about, right?"

I really should've known better than to tell him about my history of disastrous hookups.

"You know what they say." I smile innocently and bat my lashes. "Never say never."

"*They* obviously haven't met me. I *always* get what I want."

I arch a brow. "Always?"

His reply is low and gravelly, barely audible over my hammering pulse. "Always."

Sweet baby Jesus. Confidence radiates from him like light from a supernova. I'm not even sure what we're talking about anymore. Coop trying to sleep with me or Coop falling victim to the hot mess express?

It could be either.

But it's so not. His pupils are blown out and his breath is coming hard and fast, as if he's imagining all the dirty things we could do to one another.

He brushes his knuckles across my cheek. His touch is feather light, almost tentative. Like he's waiting to see how I'll react.

Which is ridiculous. This is Cooper-I-can-have-any-woman-I-want-DeLaurentis. The same one who doesn't do relationships or virgins.

Is it possible he's willing to take one for the team and ditch the virgin rule? Just for one night?

Wishful thinking, sis.

Yeah, well, if you don't ask, the answer is always no.

Time to pull up my big girl panties and woman up. "Coop. I—"

My phone vibrates in my pocket.

Talk about bad timing.

You could just ignore it.

Not an option. What if it's Haley? She might be looking for me. Or she could need help. Or, more likely, she and Bryan are fighting and she's ready to go.

"Just a sec." I slide the phone out of my pocket and hold it up for inspection. The text is a little blurry on the screen, but that's probably just because it's so dark in here, right?

Haley: B and I had a fight, but it's all good. Heading out for a quick makeup sesh.

Called it. Alcohol and high drama are never a winning combo.

Haley: Do you need a ride or did you find yourself a hottie???

I bite my lip, contemplating. I may have found a hottie, but it's not like I'll be closing the deal tonight. Not if Coop has anything to say about it.

Really? Three seconds ago, you were ready to throw your panties at him.

That was the alcohol talking. Obviously.

"I can give you a lift," Coop offers.

I blink up at him. "Didn't anyone ever tell you it's rude to read other people's text messages?"

He shrugs. "You're practically pocket sized. How am I supposed to not read it when it's right there in front of me?"

He's not wrong. The guy towers over me. *Wait.* Does that mean he can see down the front of my tank top? I glance down. I'm rocking some uber pale cleavage, but I'm pretty sure the girls aren't on display. Not from my vantage point anyway.

"How about that ride?" he drawls.

My face goes up in flames at the double entendre. Every cell in my body is screaming that it's a bad idea, but you know what else is a bad idea? Riding with Haley and Bryan. If they step one foot inside the apartment, they'll never leave. I'll spend the entire night listening to makeup sex.

Hard pass.

I'm a sexually frustrated virgin, not a glutton for punishment.

I sigh. I'll probably regret this in the morning, but for now, I'm just going to roll with it. "A ride would be great, actually."

"Yeah? I thought for sure you were going to say no." Coop winks and slips an arm around my waist. "It must be my lucky night."

14

COOPER

"SHINY." Quinn slides into the passenger seat of the Audi. "And here I'd pegged you for a truck guy." A wrinkle forms between her brows and she tilts her head. "I thought for sure you'd have one of those big, noisy, gas-guzzling environmental disasters."

"What can I say?" I brace my hand on the roof of the car and lean down so we're face to face. "I like fast cars."

An impish smile curves her lips, and she wiggles her brows. "And fast women?"

I shake my head, but it's impossible not to meet her smile with one of my own when she's being so...*Quinn*. "You've got a one-track mind, you know that?"

She shrugs, the strap of her tank top falling off her shoulder. "What can I say? I'm a woman who knows what she wants."

"From where I'm standing, you look like a woman who's enjoyed one AMF too many." I hook a finger in the wayward strap and slide it back into place. Because I'm a fucking saint now. "Which is why I need to get you into bed."

Quinn giggles, and I immediately realize my mistake.

Dumbass.

"Why, yes, Cooper. I would love to take you to bed." She winks at me. "You don't even need to buy me a drink first."

I grit my teeth, searching for the words to get this conversation—hell, this night—back on track.

"I'm kidding." She rolls her eyes. "I swear, you should see your face right now. If I didn't know better, I'd think you were the blushing virgin here."

Christ. If she had any idea what kind of filthy thoughts were running through my head, she'd run the other way.

Rule number two. Rule number two. Rule number two.

Maybe if you say it enough, it'll penetrate your thick skull.

Not likely. Not when Quinn looks like temptation come to life with flushed cheeks and the kind of smile that has me thinking shit I have no business thinking.

I close her door and take my sweet ass time walking around to the driver's side. There's a gentle breeze and even the humid night air is a welcome relief after the stifling dancefloor.

Who am I kidding? It wasn't the club that had me sweating, but Quinn's firm ass pressed against my cock, rocking in that slow, seductive rhythm.

A rhythm I definitely should *not* have enjoyed.

But for fuck's sake, I'm only human. There's no denying she's got a great body. And that mouth...

I don't let myself finish the thought. It's not like this little fantasy will go anywhere, so why torture myself?

Shrugging off all thoughts of Quinn, sex, and the release I clearly need after today's game, I open the driver's door and slide in behind the wheel.

"Where to?" I dart a glance at the fiery redhead curled up in the passenger seat.

"Wildcat Ave." She flashes me a drowsy smile. "Number fifty-two."

We ride in silence, and when I pull into Quinn's driveway ten minutes later, I realize the lack of chatter is because she's sound asleep next to me. No surprise there. She's tiny. The AMF alone would have been enough to put her on her ass, and who knows what else she had to drink tonight.

"Fucking Mike," I grumble, climbing out of the car. If I ever see that kid again...

You'll what? Put your fist through his face?

Like father, like son.

The prospect is disturbing enough to dissolve my anger. I jog around to Quinn's side, open the door, and release her seatbelt.

She stirs and grumbles, "Just five more minutes."

"Not happening, sweetheart." I grin even though she can't see it. "Unless this is a ploy to get me to carry you upstairs."

Her eyelids fly open and she straightens, suddenly wide awake. "Don't even think about it."

I step back as she climbs out of the car, tottering on sky-high heels. When she heads for the front porch, I follow, easily matching her stride.

"What do you think you're doing?" She shoots me the side-eye as she fishes a single bronze key out of her front pocket.

"Walking you to the door." *Obviously*. No way I'm rolling out until she's tucked safely inside. Noah would have my ass if something happened to her, and that's the last thing I need on my conscience.

"Whatever." She rolls her eyes. "If you want to play knight in shining armor, who am I to stop you?"

"I'm nobody's white knight." I'd do well to remember it.

"Don't I know it," she mutters, stumbling on the first step. I grab her elbow on instinct, holding her upright.

"What was that you were saying?"

She straightens and pulls her arm free, shrugging one shoulder. "Watch out for the loose step."

Right. It was totally the step. "You should probably call maintenance in the morning," I say, not bothering to hide my smirk.

Quinn narrows her eyes, but doesn't respond. Instead, she hurries up the stairs and slides her key in the lock. She turns the key, and the bolt slides back with a loud *thwack*.

"Since you're here," she says, pushing the door open to reveal a dimly lit hallway. "You might as well make yourself useful."

I arch a brow. "That depends on your definition of useful."

Because no way am I having sex with her. Even if it wouldn't break rule number two—not to mention my *no virgins* policy—Quinn's not sober enough to consent.

She doesn't bother responding, just sashays down the hall, hips swinging, perfect ass beckoning me to follow.

And dammit, I do.

Quinn turns right at the end of the hall and flips a light switch, lighting up a small, neat bedroom with a full bed, overflowing book shelves, and more pink throw pillows than seems tasteful. I'm no design expert, but how many furry pink pillows can one girl need?

She perches on the end of the bed and crooks a finger, encouraging me to come closer.

Nope. Not happening.

I'm readying yet another protest when she lifts her left foot, extending it toward me to showcase her strappy black heels. "You're good with your hands, right?"

Wait. What?

Way to misread the situation, asshole.

In my defense, the girl has a one-track mind.

"You want me to..." I gesture to her foot, brows pulled low, unwilling to proceed without clarification. "Unbuckle your shoes?"

A wide smile splits her face and laughter dances in her eyes, like she knows exactly what I've been thinking. "The straps are a pain."

Talk about getting bitch slapped by humility.

But what the hell. At least if she's in bed—alone—I can leave with a clear conscience.

I cross the room and sink to my knees. Taking her left foot in my hand, I brace the heel against my thigh. Her ankle is exposed and as I shift her foot to get a better look at the buckles, my fingers brush her creamy skin. It's just as soft and smooth as it appears and desire stirs low in my gut.

Get the shoes off, and only the shoes.

Nothing else—no one else—is getting off tonight.

Or ever, thanks to the rules.

Focus, DeLaurentis.

Get the shoes off and get out.

The sooner, the better.

I make quick work of the first shoe and slip it off, letting it fall to the floor as I turn my attention to the second.

"Wow. I think that's a record." Quinn yawns, her lips forming a perfect O. Her lipstick is long gone, but the natural look suits her. "With those hands, you should definitely be the number one draft pick."

Not likely, but I appreciate the sentiment. It's a welcome distraction from the feel of her slender calf in my hand.

"Flattery will get you nowhere, Mowery."

"Yeah, yeah," she says, fighting a laugh. "You know, this mission of yours to preserve my virginity would be adorable if it weren't so infuriating."

I snort. I'm a lot of things, but adorable isn't one of them.

The second shoe drops to the floor and I rise to my feet. Quinn lets out a sigh of relief and wiggles her toes, the overhead light glinting off the shiny red polish on her toenails.

Damn. Even her toenails are sexy, which is definitely not a thought I should have about Noah's sister.

"Why don't I grab you a glass of water while you change into your pajamas?" I suggest, desperate to put some space between us.

"Make yourself at home." She waves me off. "Cups are in the cabinet above the sink."

I retrace my steps back down the hall and fill a glass with water in the tiny galley kitchen. Then, wanting to make sure Quinn has plenty of time to change, I stop in the hall bathroom, hoping to find a bottle of aspirin.

Something tells me she's going to need it.

I flip on the light and *bingo*, there's a medicine cabinet hanging above the vanity.

It's the old-fashioned kind with a mirrored door. Guilt gnaws at my conscience as I stare at my reflection, considering my options.

On the one hand, I have no business snooping in Quinn's medicine cabinet. Who knows what kind of personal girly shit is stashed in there? On the other, if I'm doing it for the right reasons—to spare her a killer headache in the morning—does that make it okay?

Fuck if I know.

I've never rifled through a woman's bathroom before, and I certainly didn't expect to be doing it tonight.

Quit being a pussy, DeLaurentis.

Just open the door and find the aspirin. How bad can it be, anyway?

"Do it for the greater good," I mutter, reaching for the latch.

I open the cabinet and swing the door wide.

"Holy hell."

It's like a pharmacy exploded in there. The shelves are jammed full and I'm half convinced this is some Hermione

Granger shit, because no way should that much stuff fit in this tiny cabinet. I scan the shelves, but I don't recognize half this stuff. There are bottles and brushes and a tube of weird green gel. And are those creepy spider-looking things eyelashes?

I suppress a shudder.

Girls are fucking weird. I could've gone my whole life without seeing this.

My gaze lands on a rectangular packet of punch-out pills and I avert my eyes.

Not my business.

Spotting the aspirin on the top shelf, I grab the bottle and slam the cabinet door.

The contents inside rattle, but that's the least of my worries.

Never. Again.

I make my way back to the bedroom armed with water and aspirin, but when I reach the half-open door, I freeze. Quinn's back is to me and she stands in the middle of the room wearing nothing but a pair of tiny black panties, miles of soft skin on display and those scarlet curls spilling over her shoulders.

Fuuuck.

My pulse quickens and my cock stirs, still not understanding that Quinn is off limits. *Way* off limits. The only action I'm going to see tonight will be the palm of my hand.

Before I can turn away, she pulls a blue nightshirt over her head. The fabric slides down her back, covering her ass.

Thank Christ for small favors.

I draw a steadying breath, willing myself to chill—it's not like I haven't seen a naked woman before—and push the door open as she climbs into bed.

Quinn makes grabby hands at the cup and I hand it over, watching as she quickly drains half the glass.

"I brought you aspirin too."

I offer her the bottle, but she shakes her head and puts the glass on the nightstand. "I never get hangovers."

"You've also never had an AMF." I quirk a brow. "There's a first time for everything."

"Don't I know it." She tucks her feet under the fuzzy pink comforter. "I mean, never in a million years did I think I'd actually have Cooper DeLaurentis in my bedroom. Not outside my dreams, anyway."

I pause, meeting her sleepy gaze. "Did you just admit to fantasizing about me?"

Quinn blinks, and her cheeks redden as she realizes what she just said. "I plead the fifth. Or alcohol induced confusion. Or...whatever." She flops back on the mountain of pillows.

"I'll keep that in mind." I pull the blanket up and tuck her in. "Night, Quinn."

I turn to leave and as I'm walking out the door, Quinn calls my name.

"Yeah?" I turn back to the bed.

"You forgot something."

"What? You want a goodnight kiss?"

She dissolves into a fit of giggles. "I'd just as soon kiss a Wookiee."

Laughing quietly, I shake my head.

I walked right into that one. Never even saw it coming.

Quinn's the last person I'd expect to make a well-timed Wookiee joke. Padawan on the other hand...

Fuck me. My stomach drops. "You made a Star Wars joke."

"Sorry. I couldn't resist."

She points to the light switch and I flip it off, my gaze lingering on her a little too long.

"Sweet dreams, Quinn."

If she answers, I don't hear it as I retreat down the hall.

The Wookiee joke was just a coincidence. It's one of the most famous quotes from the franchise. There are all kinds of memes and merch dedicated to it. Quinn reciting the line doesn't mean a damn thing. Because Quinn couldn't possibly be the anonymous woman I've been texting, could she?

15

QUINN

It's Sunday afternoon and I'm camped out on the couch working on an article for The Collegian. Despite my total lack of a hangover, it's slow going. Mainly because I'm stuck in my head, worried Coop will see the piece and realize I'm the author.

But that's stupid, right?

There are forty-thousand undergrads at Waverly.

Plus, he's busy with football. He probably doesn't have time to read the paper. Even if he did, it's all anonymous. It's not like anyone would know the article is about him.

Quit obsessing and just submit it already.

There's no doubt my readers would love another story about the cockblocking jockhole. The last one got nearly fifteen hundred comments. And, honestly, what are the odds I'd run into the same interfering jock twice?

Pretty good when you're a walking disaster.

I groan and tip my head back, letting it rest against the couch. I'm overthinking it. I know this, but I can't seem to stop. If I don't get a grip, I'm going to spiral and I really don't have time for that.

Not when I need to revise my essay for Creative Nonfiction.

According to Call-Me-David, the piece I submitted wasn't vulnerable enough. Because sending the class into fits of hysterical laughter as I described my summer working at a paint your own pottery studio where I broke half a dozen finished pieces, crowned one of the regulars with red paint, and was banned from using the kiln wasn't sufficiently deep and heartfelt.

Which just goes to show how much he knows.

Because after that reading? I was definitely feeling some kind of way.

Yeah, well, apparently stabby doesn't count.

Whatever. I'll think of something else—eventually.

I close my eyes, take a deep breath, and tap the submit button on my article.

When I open my eyes, the confirmation message flashes on the screen.

No turning back now.

"Please tell me you're not still working on that article," Haley says, flouncing into the room with a plastic tote in her hands. "Sundays are for relaxation, not homework."

I roll my eyes and close my laptop. "Maybe you could explain that to Call-Me-David because he didn't get the memo."

"Besides." She sets the tote on the coffee table and flops down on the couch next to me. "I need the tea. What happened last night?"

"Nothing." Not a total lie. I'm still a card-carrying member of Virgins-R-Us.

"Bullshit." She narrows her eyes and looks me over, as if checking to confirm my virginity is intact. Which, I'm pretty sure, isn't a thing. "You didn't have sex, but something went down." She shoots me a smug grin, victory flashing in her eyes. "Otherwise, it wouldn't have taken you so long to write that article."

Damn. She knows me too well.

"Or..." I drag the word out to buy myself some time. "It took forever because I had to make it up and I'm light on inspiration."

"I can't believe you're holding out on me." She removes the lid from the tote and tosses it on the floor at our feet. "When I lost my virginity, you were the first person I told. And who was there when you needed help picking out a vibrator? Oh, and what about the time B's piercing got stuck—"

"You promised we'd never speak of that again!" I squeal, covering my ears. Because, just no. Hearing that story once was more than enough. "Has it ever occurred to you that maybe you have a tendency to overshare?"

"Not even once." She reaches into the tote and grabs a bottle of fuchsia nail polish. It's been her signature color since freshman year. "Come on. We'll do mani-pedis while you tell me all about last night." She shoots me a stern look. "Don't you dare leave anything out."

I really should start on my revisions for Call-Me-David, but I have no clue what I'm going to write about and my toes could use a fresh coat of polish.

As if reading my mind, Haley offers me a bottle of remover and a handful of cotton balls.

We work in silence as we strip our toenails bare, but the instant I start sorting through the collection of colorful bottles, Haley makes her move.

"How did you get home last night?" she asks, expertly applying a coat of fuchsia polish to her toenails.

Leave it to Hales to get right to the heart of the matter.

"I ran into Cooper." I grab a bottle of hunter green polish, striving for nonchalance even though I'm low-key freaking out because Cooper-I-have-enough-big-dick-energy-for-the-entire-Waverly-football-team-DeLaurentis was in my bedroom. "He gave me a ride home."

Haley freezes. "Cooper DeLaurentis was in our apartment?"

"Yeah." *Be chill. It's only a big deal if you make it a big deal.*

"*Quuuiiinnn,*" Haley whines, her frustration evident. "You're killing me. I need. All. The. Details."

I bite my lip, considering. If I don't spill, she'll just keep at it until she wears me down.

Why am I holding back? Haley is my best friend. We tell each other everything. Or we did BC. *Before Cooper*. Before the annoyingly charming jockhole came swaggering into my life with his larger-than-life personality and not-so-noble mission to preserve my virginity.

"Seriously, there's not much to tell." I prop my foot up on the edge of the table and twist the top off the polish. "I ran into him at the bar. He cockblocked me—*again*. Then he gave me a ride home."

All true, but guilt noshes at my insides as I slather paint on my toenails.

I want to tell Hales every delicious detail, but there's another part of me that wants to keep them for myself. The dancing. The banter. The way his touch electrified my skin. The memory of him kneeling before me, every nerve in my body screaming for release.

It was hot AF.

Hell, just the thought of Cooper on his knees has my core tingling.

"Oh. My. God." Haley sets her polish aside and turns to study my face. "You're into him."

"What? No!" I jerk upright, leaving a trail of dark green paint on my second toe. "He's a player. And he's about as deep as a puddle. Do you really think I'm stupid enough to fall for the world's most arrogant cockblocker?"

It's overkill. I know it the moment the words are out of my mouth.

"You wouldn't be the first." She shrugs. "The only thing that's stupid is his hotness level. I swear, men like that were put on this campus just to torture us."

"Truth," I huff, reaching for a cotton ball. "It's the only explanation for the fact that out of all the bars in town, he showed up at The Wildcat's Den."

"The football team always hangs out at The Den." Haley rolls her eyes. "Everyone knows that."

Apparently not everyone.

My phone buzzes and I reach for it, knocking over the nail polish.

"Dammit!" I scramble to grab the bottle as liquid green oozes out on the table, sinking into the tiny cracks and crevices of the faux wood surface.

There goes the security deposit.

Haley hands me some more cotton balls, and I sop up the mess as she grabs my phone and reads the message on the screen.

"How was the manhunt?" A crease forms between her brows, and she holds up the phone so I can see the screen. "Unknown."

I take the phone and unlock the screen, tapping the *Create New Contact* button. Then I type in Frat Bro Yoda as Haley peeks over my shoulder.

"Who's that?"

"Just some rando who texted me a few weeks ago." I hit save and return to the message screen. "Wrong number."

She pulls a face. "You're still talking to him?"

"Sometimes." I send a GIF of a penguin falling through the ice and type #fail. Then I drop the phone on the couch so I can finish cleaning up my mess.

"Oh, a mystery guy." Haley's eyes light up. "I wonder if he's hot. Ask him for a pic."

"I am one hundred percent not asking for a pic. With my luck, I'd get a dick pic." I sigh and collect all the sticky cotton balls. "Besides, he's probably a closet nerd like me who prefers to get his geek on in private."

"Or maybe he's a super-hot nice guy." She grins. "Which, as you know, is basically a unicorn on this campus."

She's not wrong. Except...Cooper might actually be a unicorn.

Now there's a phrase I never thought I'd hear myself say.

But facts are facts. Not only is Cooper gorgeous, he was a perfect gentleman last night. Yes, he ruined my shot at hooking up, but he also made sure I got home safely and tucked me into bed. It was...thoughtful.

And definitely a side of the cocky jock I hadn't known existed.

Not that it matters. He's him and I'm me, and virgin ban or not, there's no universe where the two of us make sense.

Which is why you need to forget about Cooper and focus on the mission.

I climb to my feet. "Why would this potentially super-hot unicorn waste his time bantering with me if he could get a woman in real life?"

"Who knows?" Haley shrugs. "Why do you bother talking to some random dude?"

"Because I can't get laid, no matter how hard I try." I stick my tongue out at her. "He probably lives a thousand miles away."

"Not with that area code." A self-satisfied grin lights up her face. "My friend Avery is from eastern PA. She has the same one."

My jaw drops open, but no words come out. I snap it closed.

"You really didn't know?" she asks, suspicion clouding her eyes.

"I really didn't." I never paid attention to his number. Why would I? Even if I had, it would've been meaningless. I grew up in western PA. Those are the area codes I know by heart.

"Having second thoughts about asking for his picture?"

"Nope." I back toward the kitchen. "But, hey, if all else fails, maybe Frat Boy Yoda can be my Operation Ditch Virginity backup plan."

Actually, that's not a bad idea. God knows I can't get laid on this campus, and what could be more random and unexpected than sex with a complete stranger?

16

COOPER

"WHAT IS THAT?" I point to the bowl of leafy green shit Vaughn is shoveling down his gullet. It looks like it's already been chewed up and digested, and I swear to Christ there's popcorn in it.

Popcorn.

In a salad.

Vaughn stabs another forkful and lifts it up for inspection, like I need a close-up of the slimy greens. "It's a snap pea popcorn salad, and it's delicious."

"It's a fucking travesty is what that is." I glance around the table for support, ignoring Vaughn as he inhales the next bite, chewing with slow, exaggerated movements. "Right?"

Reid just shakes his head, a grin tugging at the corner of his mouth.

"Didn't your mama ever tell you to mind your own plate?" Parker asks, reaching over to swipe a fry off my tray. He shoots me a wicked grin and pops it in his mouth. "It's just good manners."

"Yeah, well, the next time I see your mom," I say, moving my food out of his reach, "I'll be sure to let her know your manners are shit." I know how this goes. It starts with one fry. Then another. Next thing you know, he'll be reaching for my burger—the one I shouldn't be eating since I'm supposed to be on a strict diet—but what Coach doesn't know won't hurt him.

Or me.

It's Monday afternoon and we're grabbing a late lunch in the cafeteria before heading to the field. Although we beat Pittsburgh soundly on Saturday, bringing our record to 3-0, we've got our first conference game this weekend. We're playing Iowa and it's an away game, so we're in for a grueling practice. Which is why I need fuel, and lots of it.

The kind only a greasy burger and fries can provide.

Is it healthy? No.

Am I eating it anyway? Hell, yes.

I'll burn it off during practice and Coach'll be none the wiser.

As if reading my thoughts, Reid says, "You better not be dragging ass on the field today. I'm not running extra laps because you're in a food coma."

I cock my head, letting the swagger rise to the surface. "Have I ever let you down?"

"No. No, you have not," he returns, raising his fist.

I bump it and dig into my food. Reid and I have been playing together for four years and we have great chemistry. The prospect of going our separate ways at the end of the year—of potentially facing him from the opposite side of the field next fall—is one I haven't allowed myself to contemplate.

Not when we've still got miles to go.

"Incoming," Vaughn says in that cool, casual way of his, gaze fixed over my right shoulder.

Beside me, Reid pushes his tray away, a half-eaten chicken breast still on the plate.

Fuck that noise. Between practice, weight training, mandatory study halls, and games, downtime is a luxury during the season. This is my time, and no one is getting between me and my burger.

I take a giant bite just as a dude in a faded Waverly tee steps up to the table, a messenger bag slung over his shoulder.

"Hey." Dude dips his chin in greeting and zeroes in on me immediately.

Figures.

I keep chewing, but give him a nod of acknowledgement because I'm not a total dick.

"I'm Matteo Ortiz." His voice is high and brimming with enthusiasm. The kid has zero chill. Probably a freshman. "I'm a writer for The Collegian. I sent you an email, but I guess you didn't get it."

He pauses to catch his breath, and I shoot him a look. Matteo Ortiz? He's sent me at least a half-dozen emails. All of which have gone unopened and unanswered because I only talk to the press on game days.

It's safer that way. Ensures the focus stays on the game.

"I'd like to set up an interview," he continues, completely unfazed by my silence. "To do a human-interest piece. With your father's re-election campaign ramping up, and the Wildcats poised to make a championship run, the people want your story." Right. I'm sure he's surveyed *the people* personally. He grins and pushes a mop of dark hair out of his eyes, oblivious to the tension that's settled over the table. "I've even narrowed it down to two headlines, but I can't decide between *Great Aspirations* and *Like Father, Like Son: The DeLaurentis Legacy*."

No fucking way.

My body locks up tight, muscles going rigid, and the burger spoils in my mouth, the meat suddenly dry and gritty. I swallow it down—because I can't exactly spit it out—and it lands in my gut like a stone.

Three weeks. Three weeks into the season and already my father's influence is seeping in like poison, tainting everything it touches.

But I can't say that. It doesn't fit the DeLaurentis narrative.

Handle with care.

No shit. This isn't my first run-in with the media.

Matteo might be green as grass, but he's still press. The last thing I need is a hit job because I refused the interview. Or worse, for my father to get word I trashed him publicly.

One day, the mask will come off and the world will see him for the bastard he is.

Unfortunately, today is not that day.

I take a steadying breath and exhale, forcing my muscles to relax.

"Aw, man." I stretch and lean back in my chair, locking my hands behind my head. "I wish I could, but my schedule is jammed. With football and classes, I don't have a minute to spare." Matteo opens his mouth to protest, but before he can get a word out, I continue. "If you really want a solid human-interest piece, talk to our new kicker, Carter. She's killing it. Right guys?"

I turn to my teammates and they all nod in agreement, though Reid's mouth tightens at the corners.

"I don't know...." Matteo flicks his hair out of his eyes again as he considers.

"Trust me." I flash my trademark grin and clap him on the arm, every bit the cocky receiver who only gives sideline interviews and swaggers around campus like he's got the world by the balls. "Carter's the real story. Soccer player turned football kicker? Plus, she's wicked smart. Your editor will love it. You can be all feminist and shit."

Guilt hammers my conscience for pointing this kid in Carter's direction, but she can handle it. As far as I can tell, her life isn't one big fucking lie crafted to hide her family's dirty laundry.

Matteo shrugs. "Well, if you change your mind..."

I won't. "You'll be the first to know."

When he finally leaves, Parker nearly busts a gut. "Swear to God, the DeLaurentis fan club gets bigger every day. I thought the kid was going to swoon."

I ball up my napkin and throw it at him, unable to muster a witty reply.

Nothing like a media ambush to throw a guy off his game.

Fuck. I shouldn't have put Carter's name out there. It was a dick move.

Nothing you can do about it now.

I'll make it up to her. Besides, Carter's got a steel spine. If anyone's in over their head, it's Matteo. She'll eat that kid for breakfast.

"Since when do you pass up a chance to have your face plastered all over campus?" Parker quips, reaching over to steal another fry.

Vaughn snickers and crosses his arms, leaning back in his chair. "Maybe our boy doesn't want to share the spotlight with dear old dad."

It's a struggle to keep my face neutral. Vaughn doesn't know how right he is.

You could tell them.

Not happening. Besides, who would believe me? Despite the monster lurking beneath his skin, my father's image is squeaky clean, thanks to his handlers.

"He does like to be the center of attention." Parker nods thoughtfully. "Don't they have a name for that?"

"Exhibitionist," Vaughn offers.

"Nah." Parker shakes his head. "That's not the one I'm thinking of."

Vaughn grins. "Narcissist?"

"Getting warmer."

"Egomaniac?"

"That's the one!" Parker claps his hands together, crowing in delight. "You think they make a t-shirt for that? We could get him one for his birthday."

They're only busting my balls. It's no big deal, and if anyone deserves it, I do. Problem is, the smile I normally wear like armor is just out of reach, thanks to Matteo.

Not that I blame the kid. It's not his fault I'm walking a tightrope.

Not his fault that one misstep—one mistake—could cost me everything.

"We done here?" Reid stands and collects his tray. "I promised Coach I'd review Iowa's game tape before practice."

Relief washes over me and I climb to my feet, hauling my bag up from the floor and slinging it over my shoulder. "I could stand to watch some tape."

Reid nods and turns to the others, who follow suit.

I'm ninety percent sure he only said it to take the heat off me, and I appreciate the hell out of him for it. Reid never probes, but he's not stupid. There's no way he hasn't noticed that in all the games we've played together, my family hasn't been in the stands once.

Not like his father, who makes almost every home game and would never miss Parents' Weekend.

Bitterness rises in my throat, but I choke it back down.

It's not Reid's fault my father is an asshole. Or that I'll be standing alone on the field during Senior Day.

It doesn't matter.

I just need to keep my eye on the prize. It'll all be worth it in the end.

With any luck, I'll be drafted to a west coast team, beyond

my father's reach. Once I have that NFL contract in hand, I won't hesitate to sever ties with that piece of shit. I just hope my mom has the courage to do the same.

17

QUINN

CALL-ME-DAVID IS A SADIST. That's the only explanation for the term project he assigned today.

Happy Hump Day, my ass.

A twenty-page essay on a lesson or experience that shaped our lives and made us who we are today. Twenty. Pages. It's practically a freaking memoir. What am I supposed to write about, anyway? I'm nineteen years old. *I* don't even know who I am.

You could write about your virgin quest.

Yeah, no.

Way too personal. Then again, according to Professor Bates, my last essay was lacking vulnerability, despite the re-write. The jerk gave me a C on it. A freaking *C*! Thankfully, the weekly essays are only thirty percent of our final grade. The term project, however, is fifty percent.

I can't afford to screw it up.

Which means I need to start early so I have time to swap with Priya for critique.

"Did you need something else?" The barista glances at the line behind me. There's an impatient edge to his words that suggests it's not the first time he's asked.

Get it together, Quinntastrophe.

"Sorry." I was so caught up in my mental rant, I didn't even notice him return with my order. I fumble for my card and swipe it, offering him an apologetic smile. He wordlessly hands me a receipt and I grab my order, making a beeline for the corner booth.

Daily Grind is packed, but I'm determined to brainstorm ideas for my term project. No way am I going to let it sit until the last minute. Sure, nine weeks sounds like a lot of time, but it's so not.

Not when it'll determine if I pass or fail.

I drop my bag on the bench and slide in next to it, settling the tray with my muffin and latte on the table.

My precious.

I wrap my hands around the mug, letting the warmth seep into my chilled fingers. The heatwave has finally broken and cool, crisp days have descended on College Park. Not that I'm complaining.

The heat was miserable.

I like fall. I mean, who doesn't? It's gray sweatpants season.

Plus, it brings cozy sweaters, Wildcat football, and pumpkin everything.

I take a sip of my latte, savoring the chocolate coffee goodness, before pushing it aside and pulling out a notebook and pen.

Jot down five good ideas, and then you can have the muffin as a reward.

That's what I told myself when I ordered, but now it's right there on the table, the familiar scent of pumpkin calling to me like a siren.

Just one little nibble...

I break off a Hulk-sized bite and pop it in my mouth,

chewing slowly. Because it's amazing, not because I'm procrastineating.

"Can we drop our bags while we order?" Noah's voice cuts through my carb bliss before I can even swallow. He doesn't wait for a reply. Just thunks his bag down on the bench across from me. I glance up, pissy sibling glare fully activated, and lock eyes with Cooper.

Because of course I do.

It's been a little over two weeks since he tucked me in, and in that time, he's managed to get even hotter. His hair is a little longer, and a lot shaggier, but it suits him. As does the stubble lining his chiseled jaw.

Hell, maybe it's just the glow of a 4-0 record. The Wildcats are undefeated coming off their first conference game against Iowa. It was a close game, and I may have screamed at the television once or thirty times last weekend, but Coop played well, pulling down passes the broadcasters deemed impossible.

Which totally explains his over-inflated ego.

"You know my sister, right?" Noah grins and ruffles my hair like I'm five freaking years old. "Calamity Quinn."

Heat floods my cheeks and I chew viciously, trying not to choke on the fluffy carbs before I can kill my brother. I'm sure my parents won't miss him. *Much.*

"That seat's taken." I cross my fingers under the table. Any conversation that involves Noah, Cooper, and I can't possibly end well. "Sorry."

Another lie.

It's a miracle Coop hasn't told Noah about Operation Spontaneous Hookup, and I'm not about to press my luck now.

"Really?" Noah doesn't bother to mask his doubt. Like it's so hard to believe I'm meeting someone for coffee.

Coop smirks and shakes his head, shoulders trembling with silent laughter.

Jerk.

"Who are you meeting?" Noah widens his stance and glances around the café. "Anyone I know?"

"Nope."

Coop smiles, that sexy ass grin of his extending all the way to his eyes. "Please tell me you haven't added blind dates to your playbook."

"What playbook?" Noah turns back to me, suspicion darkening his features. "You haven't played sports a day in your life."

"There's no playbook." I roll my eyes and hook a thumb toward Cooper. "You know he took some nasty hits during the Iowa game, right? His brains are probably scrambled."

Noah gives me a WTF look and glances at Coop, no doubt calculating the odds that I've offended his *brother*.

"Besides, even if I was on a blind date, it's no one's business but my own."

"Beg to differ," Noah says at the same time Coop blurts, "Bullshit."

I groan and tip my head to the sky. This cannot be happening.

Oh, it's happening.

Noah turns to Cooper, giving him the same WTF look he gave me seconds ago.

"She's your sister." Coop shrugs, like this is a perfectly normal conversation, which, *spoiler alert*: it's not. "If she's meeting random dudes, she should at least tell someone where she's going and who she's meeting." The cocky jockhole winks and adds, "Safety first."

"Yeah," I huff, piling on the sarcasm. "I'll bet you're a real safety guy."

Noah's head swivels, his gaze ping-ponging between Coop and me, before he announces, "I'm getting coffee. I need caffeine to deal with this mess."

Pretty sure the mess he's referring to is me, but I don't even care because he turns on his heel and heads for the counter.

Thank you, sweet baby Jesus.

Unfortunately, Cooper doesn't follow.

Maybe if I ignore him, he'll go away.

I reach for my muffin, but Coop gets there first, snatching the whole darn thing.

"Hey!"

He lifts it to his nose and inhales deeply. "Is this pumpkin?"

Coop doesn't wait for a reply, just takes a ginormous bite and grins down at me as he chews, a big ass smile on his face.

"You're the worst." I sigh. "Surely there's someone else you can go annoy?"

He shrugs, and I swear to God, there's a twinkle in his eye. "Turnabout is fair play, sweetheart."

"In case you've forgotten." I cross my arms. "I never agreed to play this messed up game."

My life is enough of a trainwreck without him interfering at every turn.

"Damn." Coop heaves a beleaguered sigh, but I don't miss the hint of a smile tugging at his lips. "I thought we were friends."

"Friends share." I arch a brow and stare pointedly at the muffin. *My* muffin.

"Exactly." He tears what's left of it in half and offers me the larger piece. "Which is why I figured you wouldn't mind if I sampled the goods. You know, since last time you *accidentally* took mine."

It was no accident and we both know it, but I just smile up at him with wide-eyed innocence and take the proffered muffin.

"So." He shifts his weight and adjusts the bag slung over his shoulder. "Have you given up your mission or should I expect to see you at Sig Chi Saturday night?"

I open my mouth to give a snarky reply, but Coop's words echo in my head.

Turnabout is fair play.

The cocky cockblocker—try saying that three times fast—has blocked me twice now. *Twice.* Surely, he doesn't expect me to just take it lying down?

No freaking way.

If the arrogant jockhole wants to play dirty, it's game on.

I smile sweetly at Coop, meeting those gorgeous blue eyes head-on. "I guess you'll find out Saturday night."

18

COOPER

My roommates and I roll into Sig Chi like the kings of campus amid shouts of "Five and O, baby!" and "Wildcat Nation!"

Fucking right, we do. We stomped Michigan State today, making Waverly the only undefeated team in the Big Ten.

Shit's getting real.

The hopeful chatter of the talking heads is getting louder. Their predictions of a championship run harder to ignore.

And the pressure?

It's no joke. Not only because it's my last shot at a national championship—at a chance to break Waverly's fifteen-year drought—but because of everything that comes after.

The draft. Graduation. The future.

But mostly the draft. I need to be a first-round pick. The second and third rounds make bank, but the money isn't guaranteed.

There are no guarantees in life.

Isn't that the truth?

Our conference is always underrated, and despite a tough schedule and a winning record, the only way to secure a spot in the championship game is to go undefeated. Otherwise, you're at the mercy of the selection committee.

That's a problem for another day.

Tonight, we're celebrating. The music is loud, and the party is in full swing, but with Wildcat pride roaring through town, I doubt campus police will make an appearance.

Unless it's to congratulate us on kicking ass today.

I bump fists and slap open palms as we weave through the crush of sweaty bodies, making our way to the kitchen at the back of the house.

That's where Sig Chi keeps the good shit.

Reid, Parker, and Vaughn follow my lead. On the field, Reid is our captain, but on Greek Row, where it's all about the swagger, I'm in my element. Tonight, my element is all about a good time.

Hell, we deserve to celebrate and enjoy our last season as Wildcats.

Not to mention all the perks that come with it.

"Hey, Cooper." A curvy blonde squeezes past me in the tight hall, her breasts skimming my chest. "It's been a while. Find me later?"

I flash Zoe a grin. "I'll be around."

"Damn." Parker thumps me on the back. "That's got to be a record, even for you." He turns to Reid. "What's it been? Like two minutes since we walked through the door?"

Reid smirks and shakes his head. "Not even."

I turn, glancing over my shoulder at Parker. "Just so you know, the record is actually twenty-eight seconds."

Parker howls with laughter as we shoulder our way into the kitchen and head straight for the fridge.

"What'll it be, boys?" I open the door, revealing a case of lager, a nearly empty case of German wheat beer, and some bougie shit with a wave on the can.

Reid and Parker opt for the lager and Vaughn, true to form, takes one of the white cans.

I grab a wheat beer for myself and use the bottle opener on the side of the fridge to pop the top. The beer is cold, and it goes down easy as I tip my head back and chug half the bottle.

"You keep that up, and we'll have to carry you home," Reid says, giving me a pointed look.

"That was one time." I cringe at the memory. It was our first big loss of the season freshman year, and I drank myself stupid, passing out on the lawn in front of our dorm. Reid and the others had to drag me up to my room and sneak me past the RA. "I've matured since then."

I've also put on fifteen pounds of solid muscle and increased my alcohol tolerance.

Vaughn snorts. "This from the asshole who wrapped all of our keys in duct tape last week."

"I told you it wasn't me." I tip my bottle at him. "You better believe I'd own that shit if it was."

And I for damn sure wouldn't have wrapped my own stuff. Talk about a pain in the ass. My keys are still sticky.

"Better watch your back." Reid leans against the counter and crosses his ankles. "Looks like the reigning king of pranks is about to be dethroned."

"No way." I smirk. Locker room pranks are my jam. "Nobody can touch me."

Facts.

Reid might be on to something, though. Coach went on a rampage after Spellman, our kicker, busted his leg during a preseason dare, so I've been keeping a low profile. But I haven't forgotten the itching powder in my jock strap the first week of practice.

Not cool.

"Jesus." Vaughn takes a pull on his beer. "I didn't think it was possible, but your head might actually be bigger than your biceps."

"And yet it's still smaller than your beard," I shoot back, eying the giant bush on his face as Reid and Parker convulse with laughter. "Soon it's going to need its own zip code."

Vaughn flushes and gives me the finger, which is basically our love language.

The guy is like a brother to me, but he really needs to lighten up.

Life's too short to be taken so seriously. Once you figure out what really matters, you fight like hell to protect it, and let all the rest go.

"Is that jealousy I detect?" I flex, showcasing the biceps I've worked so hard to strengthen. "If you want to touch them, all you have to do is ask."

"Hard pass."

"Your loss." I wink at him and drain my beer in one long chug. Then I toss the empty into the recycling bin and grab another from the fridge.

My phone vibrates in my pocket. I pull it out to check my messages and grin when I see a familiar name on the screen.

Padawan: Leather pants. Yay or nay?

Padawan: NM. Leather pants=trying too hard, right?

Leather pants? Who is this girl?

Just ask.

No way. I'm not trying to ruin a good thing.

Yeah, because a DeLaurentis giving dating advice is a great fucking idea.

I bitch slap the voice in my head and tap out a reply.

Me: Leather pants are always a good idea.

Damn right they are. I stare at the screen, ignoring the guys, and wait for the three little dots to appear. She doesn't let me down.

Padawan: I don't know... I don't want to look desperate.

Pretty sure desperate people don't worry about looking desperate, but I'm not exactly an expert on the subject.

Me: If you're not feeling it, skip them.

Me: Trust me, the sexiest thing you can wear is confidence.

Padawan: You're right. I'm probably being extra.

Padawan: Thanks.

I slip the phone in my pocket and turn my attention back to my roommates. "Well, gentlemen, if you'll excuse me, I'm going to go find someone who appreciates my finer assets."

The guys snicker and as I'm walking away, someone makes a crack about my finer assets.

I don't bother replying.

Nope. I just strut into the hall, my assets on full display.

When I enter the living room, I'm greeted by another round of Wildcat cheers.

Waverly fans are nothing if not loyal. They're as pumped about the winning season as the guys on the team.

I make small talk as I weave through the crowd, but it doesn't take long to spot Zoe.

Our eyes meet through the crush of bodies and she waves me over to where she's dancing with a couple of Tri Delts.

What the hell.

She's a cool chick, and we always have a good time.

"Cooper!" She flashes a bright smile, revealing perfect white teeth. "You found me."

"You're kind of hard to miss." I flick my eyes to the bright red dress she's wearing. Scratch that. It's definitely a shirt. It might be belted at the waist, but it's too short to be anything else. Not that I'm complaining. Zoe's got great legs.

Quinn's are better.

They're also off limits.

Which is what I tell myself every time I think about touching her again.

"Where have you been hiding out?" Zoe asks, a sultry smile on her full lips. "I haven't seen you around all semester."

I take a pull on my beer and rake a hand through my hair. "Coach is keeping us busy. You know how it is."

"Whatever he's doing, it's working," the brunette to Zoe's right chimes in. She has a tiny Wildcat painted on each cheek. "You guys killed it today."

"Thanks. Our new kicker is a godsend."

When Reid proposed poaching talent from the women's soccer team, I thought he'd lost his damn mind, but Carter's holding her own. On the field and on the team.

"Don't be so modest." Zoe squeezes my arm, and it takes all my self-control not to laugh. No one has ever accused me of modesty. "You looked good today."

So good, I'm staring down the Waverly record for receiving yards. As long as Reid and I both stay healthy, I'm practically a lock.

"Oh, I love this song!" Zoe's eyes brighten as the opening notes of *Hot Girl Summer* fill the living room. "Dance with me?"

She grabs my hand and drags me toward the center of the room where the sea of bodies is thickest.

Zoe's a good dancer and I follow her lead as she molds her body to mine. We dance for five songs straight, and I'm parched when the DJ finally mixes it up, dropping a Def Leppard throwback.

Disappointment flashes across her face, but it's quickly replaced by a smile as she punches a fist in the air and sings along, belting out the lyrics along with everyone else.

I'm not much of a singer, so I take the opportunity to drain my beer as Zoe rocks out next to me, her body moving in time with the swaying crowd.

When she notices I'm not joining in, she bumps her hip against mine. "What's wrong? Surely you didn't use up *all* of your stamina on the field today."

A husky laugh sounds from my right. "Only one way to find out."

Quinn.

Before I can say a word, she steps forward, slips an arm around my neck and pulls me in close, lowering my mouth to hers. Our eyes meet, and with a boldness I didn't know she possessed, Quinn crushes her lips to mine.

The kiss is rough and demanding, all the things Quinn isn't.

It's fucking hot.

Her tongue glides along the seam of my mouth, coaxing my lips apart, and my resolve wavers.

Rules are meant to be broken.

Not my rules.

I should—

Quinn's tongue plunges into my mouth, incinerating what's left of my self-control with quick, sure strokes, her tongue caressing mine in a way that sends a bolt of white-hot lightning straight to my cock.

She tastes good.

Sweet, like strawberries.

Smells good too. Like flowers and sunshine and happy shit. I can't get enough of it. Can't get enough of her.

Noah's going to kick your ass.

He can try.

Not the point, asshole.

The hell? Two seconds ago, my inner voice was all about breaking the rules.

What is even happening right now?

Good fucking question.

Quinn tangles her fingers in my hair, nails scraping seductively against my scalp as she pulls me closer. Her tongue makes another aggressive sweep of my mouth, and just like that, she releases me.

The taste of summer lingers on my lips, the only proof Quinn's kiss wasn't a drunken hallucination.

A smug grin tugs at the corners of her mouth as she turns to Zoe. "Hello, there."

Shiiit.

"Wow." Zoe's cherry red lips pucker in distaste. "Just... Wow."

I should probably say something—do something—but my brain is on a thirty-second delay. If I'm being honest, I'm holding out for the instant replay. The one where Quinn's soft lips are pressed to mine, her hot, wet mouth taking without hesitation. Without restraint.

"What can I say?" Quinn cocks a hip, and— *Fuck.* Is that satisfaction lighting her eyes? "I'm a bold one."

"You're something alright." Zoe gives me a tight smile and turns on her heel, stalking back to the Tri Delts.

The blood flow slowly returns to the big head, and warning bells clang in my thick skull.

Quinn's up to something. It's not the first time my lips have been ambushed by a beautiful woman, but Quinn's not exactly a card-carrying member of the Cooper DeLaurentis fan club. And she knows I won't help with this messed up sex quest.

So why did she just jam her tongue down my throat?

Only one way to find out.

I level my gaze at Quinn, taking in the chunky heels, high-waist jeans, and black crop top. She looks damn good, but I'm not about to be distracted by the slice of creamy skin revealed by her midriff. Not this time.

"What the hell do you think you're doing?"

19

QUINN

"Turnabout is fair play." I smirk up at Coop and give myself a mental high-five. "Or have you forgotten?"

A muscle in his jaw twitches, the only outward sign I've gotten under his skin. "Are you fucking with me right now?"

"That depends." I make a show of tapping my chin and drink in the look of shock on his face. *Priceless.* "Are you enjoying it?"

God knows I am. I couldn't have timed this better if I'd tried. The fact that he was getting cozy with a gorgeous blonde when I arrived? If that's not karma, I don't know what is.

"I don't know," he says, cool amusement replacing confusion. "I'm still deciding."

He glances around the crowded living room, giving me an unobstructed view of his profile. So I do what any self-respecting woman would do. I look my fill.

Cooper might be an arrogant jockhole, but he's got a killer jawline.

My gaze drifts south, admiring his broad chest and rock-hard biceps, which are on full display, muscles straining against the soft fabric of his t-shirt. He's wearing low-slung jeans that highlight the deep V of his abs, and it's all I can do not to drool.

The guy is all muscle.

Is it any wonder half the women on campus are in lust with him?

I have a flash of momentary guilt. Not for blocking Cooper—he had it coming—but for the blonde he'd been dancing with.

My little revenge plot screwed her too.

Coop turns back to me, blue eyes dancing with laughter, as if he knows exactly what I've been thinking.

"You're lucky Noah isn't around. He'd kick my ass if he saw us kissing."

"Relax." I pat his chest—for reasons—and mentally catalogue the fact that his pecs are like concrete. "Noah's all talk."

He hasn't seen the inside of a gym since high school. The odds of him throwing down with a DI football player are about as good as my odds of getting laid tonight.

So, basically, zero.

"You know, I was really hoping you'd given up on this insane quest of yours."

Did he just—

"Did you just call me crazy?" I plant a hand on my hip and glare up at him. Even with three-inch heels, Coop towers over me.

"Did I?" He grins, looking down his nose to meet my heated stare. "Or did I say the mission was insane?"

"Semantics."

He shrugs. "We can stand here all night arguing or we could get in on the beer pong tourney."

So not happening. The last time I played, I spilled an entire pitcher of beer on one of the Sigs. "Wouldn't we have to wait, like, forever?"

Coop chuckles. "Do you really think they'd make me wait in line?"

I roll my eyes. He's right, but that doesn't make it any less obnoxious. "You're an ass."

"Says the girl who showed up tonight just to cockblock me."

"That's not the only reason I came." I flash him a saccharine smile.

"Don't remind me." He plants his giant palms on my shoulders and spins me around so my back is to him. "Come on, Mowery. You owe me."

"Don't call me Mowery," I protest, allowing him to steer me through the sea of bodies.

"Whatever you say, sweetheart."

I stifle a groan and bite back a snarky reply. Cooper's annoying pet names are the least of my worries because there's a raucous group surrounding the beer pong table, whooping and hollering.

The better to laugh when you make a fool of yourself.

Maybe I can just make a run for it.

Cooper wouldn't actually chase me down, right?

The crowd parts for us, giving me a front row view as one of the frat bros sinks a shot, forcing the other team to drink.

This is a bad freaking idea.

I'm mentally tallying all the ways this could go wrong, preparing my argument, when Coop drapes an arm over my shoulders and bellows, "We've got next game!"

Warmth spreads through my body at his touch, and I want to lose myself in the moment. To bask in the feel of his arm wrapped protectively around me. But I don't have that luxury because the table's nearly clear.

"Are you sure you don't want to find another partner?" I have to shout to be heard over the music. There's a speaker on the other side of the table, making normal conversation damn near impossible. "I'm shit at beer pong."

Understatement.

Coop smirks and squeezes my shoulder. "How bad can you

be? All you have to do is throw the ball into the cup. Piece of cake."

So much for remembering everything.

Panic takes root in my stomach and my palms begin to sweat. The memory of the last game I played runs through my brain like a highlight reel.

"I'm a walking disaster, Cooper. I don't have an athletic bone in my body!"

The music fades as I impart that last gem—because of course it does—and several heads turn my way. The girl to my left snickers, but I ignore her, shifting to face Coop.

His arm slips from my shoulders, but I don't let myself dwell on the loss of contact.

"You should find another partner. One of the guys from the team. Or the frat."

Or literally anyone who isn't me.

Coop studies me, full lips pressed flat as if he's considering.

He's about to cave—I'm sure of it—when Noah appears at his side, cheeks flushed and eyes bright.

"You should listen to her." He slaps Coop on the back and adds, "Partnering with Quinntastrophe can only end one way."

An emotion I can't identify flashes across Cooper's face, but it's gone in an instant, replaced by his usual cocky grin. "And what way is that?"

"Disaster."

Noah's right, but the knowledge does little to take the sting off his words.

Just once, it would be nice if he had a little faith in me.

"I'll take my chances," Coop says smoothly. "I've got a good feeling about Quinn. Who knows? She just might be my good luck charm."

"More like bad luck charm." Noah grins and claps Coop on

the back. "When you end up drunk and covered in beer, don't say I didn't warn you."

When it's our turn, I step up to the table with Cooper, smiling despite the growing knot in my stomach.

Coop fills our cups and lines them up, forming a neat triangle. Then he takes his place next to me, standing so close our shoulders brush. There's nothing intimate about it, but tell that to my body. Awareness prickles over my skin, every nerve ending on high alert, every hair standing at attention.

"Relax, Quinn." The way he says my name—with casual familiarity—has some of the tension leaking from my body as he turns and winks at me. "We've got this."

If only I shared his confidence, but nope. I've got nothing. Unless Coop's prepared to carry the team, this is a disaster in the making.

Gavin and Brandon, the Sigs who won the last game, eye us from the other end of the table.

"We'll do you a solid and let you go first, DeLaurentis." Gavin gives me a slow once-over, a shit-eating grin on his face. "You're going to need it."

Asshole.

"I tried to tell him," Noah says, shaking his head. "I've got next."

He's so sure we're going to lose, he directs the statement to the other end of the table.

A red haze tinges my vision, because what the fuck?

"Ignore them," Coop orders, offering me a ball. I take it, careful to avoid touching him. I'm already up in my feelings. I don't need to be swooning over Cooper when there are ten half-full cups of beer in arm's reach. "Better yet, make them eat their words."

Before I can respond, he flicks his wrist and his ball goes sailing across the table.

It lands in the center cup with a splash.

A loud cheer goes up from the onlookers and Coop throws his hands up in the air, arms spread wide, like he's the freaking king of campus.

Which he basically is.

"Sink yours and we get 'em back."

So, no pressure then.

I line up my shot, aiming for the back row, and let it fly.

The ball arcs through the air, clearly on a collision course with Gavin's face. He swats it away at the last second and drunken laughter goes up from the crowd.

Technically, he's not supposed to block the ball unless it bounces on the table, but who can blame him? Even I wouldn't expect him to take a shot to the face.

"Huh." Coop chuckles, the low rumble humming across my skin. "You really are shit at beer pong."

Brandon lines up his shot, sinking the ball in the back left corner.

Looks like I'm drinking this round.

Gavin's next, but thankfully his ball bounces off the rim of the center cup. Coop snatches it out of the air with a triumphant grin.

I fish Brandon's ball out of the corner cup, resigned to chugging a warm beer.

Coop shakes his head and wiggles his fingers in a *hand it over* gesture.

"I'm the one who missed," I remind him. "I should be the one to drink it."

"Not happening."

He reaches for the cup and I hand it over. If Coop wants to do the drinking, who am I to argue? The less I drink, the less chance I'll make a monumental ass of myself.

That's the spirit.

He drains the cup in one long gulp and sits it on the edge of the table before taking his shot. This time, he hits the cup at the apex of the triangle. The ball circles the lip, and I hold my breath, silently willing it to drop into the cup. It does.

Hallelujah.

At least one of us doesn't suck.

"Nice shot." I roll my own ball between my fingers. "We'd be unstoppable if I had your skills."

If only.

Coop arches a brow. "You can."

Yeah, in my dreams.

"I appreciate your opt—"

I don't get to finish the thought. Coop's behind me in a flash, repositioning my body, his hand covering mine as he lifts my arm and lines up a shot.

"You can do this," he says, breath hot against my cheek. It's distracting as hell. Does he really think I can concentrate with his mouth just inches from mine? "It's all in the wrist. Just relax and when you breathe out, release."

"Oh, is that all?" I squeak as he mimics the shot with our joined hands.

"Trust me." I can practically hear the smile in his voice when he adds, "What do you have to lose?"

That would be nothing.

Coop releases his grip on me and steps to the side.

I draw a steadying breath, pull my arm back and exhale, letting the ball fly.

It sails across the table, arcing toward the misshapen triangle, and I swear to God time slows as it bounces off the rim of the first cup and plops into a cup in the back row.

Holy crap.

I did it.

"I did it!" Adrenaline courses through my veins as I clap my hands together. "I actually freaking did it!"

"Yeah, you did." Coop gives me a lopsided grin and, for a second, it looks like he's going to pull me in for a hug. But one glance at Noah has him raising his hand for an awkward high five instead. I slap his palm, grinning like a fool. "I knew you had it in you."

"I'm glad one of us did." Because I sure as hell didn't.

I never imagined it would be Cooper DeLaurentis who saw something in me I couldn't see in myself, let alone help bring it to the surface. The more I get to know Cooper, the more I wonder if I've misjudged him. If there's more to the cocky player than meets the eye.

"Give yourself some credit." He rakes a hand through his hair, pushing the blond locks off his forehead. "Hasn't anyone ever told you confidence is sexy?"

I freeze, his words echoing in my head. It's not the first time a guy has shared the sentiment.

Hell, it's not even the first time tonight.

What are the odds?

The odds of two guys imparting the same sage wisdom seem slim, but the odds of Cooper being Frat Boy Yoda have to be slimmer. No way. There's no way he's the rando I've been texting. He probably has a harem of women sliding into his DMs, so why would he bother chatting with a woman he doesn't even know?

It's ridiculous.

Imposs—

"You still with me?"

I blink, bringing the party back into focus. Coop's staring at me, eyes narrowed in suspicion. "Huh?"

"We're up." He lifts my hand and drops a ping-pong ball into my open palm. "Ready to kick some Sig ass?"

"As ready as I'll ever be." I smile, attempting to match his easy grin.

"We make a good team. When we're not fighting."

I arch a brow. "You mean when you're not interfering in my sex life."

"I wouldn't need to interfere," he says, a dangerous edge to his voice, "if you'd just drop this ridiculous mission."

Anticipation hums through my body, a visceral response to that soft growl, but I hold my ground, all his prior good deeds forgotten. "Not. A. Chance."

20

QUINN

It's Sunday afternoon, and like most of Wildcat Nation, I'm nursing a hangover. The only difference is that mine stems from an unprecedented run at the beer pong table, not a celebratory drinking binge.

I groan and reach for my water bottle, which is on the nightstand next to my bed.

Homework and hangovers are not a thing, and don't ever let anyone tell you different.

I've been staring at my laptop for an hour and I've only produced about fifty new words on my term paper. At this rate, it'll take me all semester to finish it.

Serves you right bragging about being hangover-proof.

I really should've known better.

Still, I shut down the snarky little voice in my head. I don't need that kind of negativity in my life.

No, what I need is a decent topic for my term paper. Not to mention a solution for my virginity problem. Five weeks into the semester and I'm no closer to ditching my v-card than I was day one.

If that's not the definition of an epic fail, I don't know what is.

I sigh and press the backspace key, deleting the last sentence I wrote.

It's trash and I know it.

There's a knock at my bedroom door, and when I look up, I find Haley peeking in.

"Got a minute?" She pushes the door open with her foot. She's hiding something behind her back and there's a mischievous glint in her dark eyes as she grins, revealing a row of brilliant white teeth. "I have a surprise for you!"

My stomach drops. Haley's last surprise was a creepy doll painting that gave me nightmares for a month.

Please don't let it be another creepy AF painting.

I rack my brain, trying to remember what she's working on in her art classes. There's new media—whatever the hell that is—and glassblowing, which seems harmless enough. Last week, she brought home an adorable little pumpkin with a curly stem.

"Ta da!" Quick as a flash, Hales reveals her creation, holding it out like an offering on her upturned palms.

It's clear glass, so it's hard to make out the detail, but it's about eight inches long with a rounded head and—*OMFG*. Is that a dildo?

"Please tell me you didn't make a cock in your glass blowing class."

She snorts with laughter and sashays across the room, flopping down on the end of the bed. "I so did. You should've seen Ronan's face when she had to critique it." She thrusts the toy toward me and I have no choice but to take it. "Got an A on it too, because my bullshit explanation was fire."

No surprise there. Haley's mastered the art of delivering off-the-cuff creation stories with unflinching sincerity.

"Do I even want to know?" I tilt my head to admire the life-like veins along the shaft. I may be a virgin, but I've seen enough sex toys to know what a proper cock looks like.

Hales shrugs. "Probably not, but that doesn't mean you get to tuck it away in a drawer. That baby needs to be on display."

So not happening. "My mom would have heart failure if she saw this sitting on my dresser."

Haley waves off my protest and flops back on the bed. "I'll bet the old broad has a major kink and you just don't know it."

"Eww!" I screech, dropping the dildo and covering my ears. "Can we not talk about my mom's hopefully non-existent sex life?"

"Fine, but for the record, I think your mom would fully support owning your sexual health." She shifts onto her side and props her head up on her hand. "What are you working on? Please tell me it's a new article for The Collegian."

I shake my head. "Nope. No article this week."

"Why not?"

"Nothing to tell. It's been a quiet week." I scrape my hair back into a ponytail and secure it with a hair tie from my wrist. "I spilled tacos on myself in the Quad, but that's like a two on the scale of one to Quinntastic."

Haley's face falls. "Really? That's all you've got?"

"Try not to look so disappointed." I toss a pillow at her. She catches it and props it under her head. "What can I say? I had a good week. Not even one disaster."

Which is pretty much a miracle.

"Not even at the Sig party?" Haley grins. "That is impressive. Noah must be so proud."

I pull a face at the mention of my brother. He's still on my shit list after last night. "Nope. No sexcapades last night. I actually spent the night playing beer pong."

That gets her attention.

"You? Played beer pong? And no one got hurt?"

"Is that really so hard to believe?"

Haley lifts a brow, letting her eyebrows do the talking.

Smart woman.

"Cooper and I had quite the run, if you must know." I shoot her a smug grin, remembering the way his hand felt cupping mine. "We won six games in a row."

Not a house record by any stretch, but damn good, given my lack of actual skill.

"You were hanging out with Cooper DeLaurentis again?" Haley sighs, a wistful look on her face. "Do you have any idea how lucky you are? There's no shortage of women who'd trade their soul for a night in his bed."

Irritation sparks in my chest—Cooper's more than a freaking sex object—but I tamp it down. It's not my place to defend him. Besides, she's not saying anything I haven't thought a hundred times.

How's that for hypocrisy?

"Maybe that's why he enjoys harassing me." I pause, considering. "Because there's zero chance of us hooking up."

Not with his virgin rule and Sig Chi's hands-off sibling policy.

If I hadn't ambushed him last night, he never would've touched me.

Warmth floods my chest at the memory of our kiss.

It was rough. Commanding. Incendiary.

Everything I'd expected, and not at all what I'd expected because I'd been the one driving it, not Cooper.

It meant nothing.

I know it on a cerebral level, but the knowledge didn't stop my body from reacting with deep-seated desire, need radiating from my core the instant our lips touched. The press of Cooper's soft lips on mine? The way his tongue caressed mine with sure, sensual strokes?

It was even better than my wildest fantasies.

"Maybe," Haley says, pulling me back to the conversation. "But the guy isn't exactly hurting for friends."

She's right, but what other explanation could there be?

"Whatever. It doesn't matter anyway. Despite Cooper's cock-blocking, my goals haven't changed. Operation Spontaneous Hookup is still a go."

Haley bites her lip, eyes softening. "It's been five weeks, Quinn. Maybe it's time to take a break. Some things can't be rushed. It'll happen when the time is right."

Her words hit me like a sucker punch to the gut.

She means well. I know she does—know she only wants the best for me and doesn't want to see me hurt—but I'm not ready to throw in the towel yet.

I'm a lot of things, but a quitter?

Not in this lifetime.

"I'm not taking a break." There's been an idea percolating in the back of my mind for weeks, and sure, it's a little out there, but it's like Coop said. What do I have to lose? *Nothing*. "I've got a new plan."

I grab my phone off the nightstand and unlock the screen.

It's now or never.

I open my texts and scroll to the last message from Frat Boy Yoda.

"What are you doing?" Haley demands, pushing herself into a sitting position.

"Propositioning the rando." I tap out a message. "The one with the eastern PA number."

"You can't be serious." She crawls over and positions herself so she can read the message over my shoulder. "Shit. You're really doing this."

I can't decide if it's shock or awe in her voice. Maybe both.

I'm not exactly known for making big moves, but I'm tired of riding the hot mess express.

It's time to take control of my life and stop letting fate decide my path.

This new plan isn't exactly spontaneous. It'll take some planning. Maybe even some travel, but I'll make it work.

Desperation or inspiration?

Only time will tell.

Heart slamming against my ribcage, I reread my text and press send.

21

COOPER

THE ONLY THING better than watching football on a Sunday afternoon is kicking Parker's ass at Madden. We're chilling in the living room, sitting side-by-side on the couch while Reid lounges in an armchair, nose buried in a textbook. How he can study with the endless stream of trash talk is anyone's guess.

"Fourteen-zero."

Parker shrugs. "Still early, princess."

"Exactly." I flash him a smug grin. "Still plenty of time for me to run the score up on your ass."

"Don't get cocky," Reid warns, not bothering to look up as my kicker sends the ball sailing downfield on-screen. Parker's receiver runs it back for a twenty-yard gain before my gunner tackles him. "Remember what happened last time."

How could I forget? Parker spanked me like a newborn and spent the next week rehashing his victory. "He got lucky."

"Keep telling yourself that." Parker snickers and taps furiously at his controller as his offensive line takes the field.

My phone buzzes, vibrating on the coffee table before me. I glance down long enough to see that it's a text from Padawan before turning my attention back to the screen.

Parker's QB throws a bullet downfield, but I'm ready for him. My defensive back picks it off with ease and runs it back, diving into the end zone and executing a perfect somersault.

"What was that you were saying?" I press the taunting command and my DB spikes the ball.

"Your sportsmanship is unparalleled," Parker deadpans.

"You know it." I wink and blow him a kiss. "Don't be a sore loser."

"Game's not over yet, asshole."

Might as well be. Football is as much a mental game as it is physical, and I'm in his head now. It's just a matter of time until I roll out my victory dance.

I grab my phone off the coffee table and read the message from Padawan.

The hell?

I must've read it wrong. There's no way—

I reread the message.

Padawan: This is probably crazy, but would you be interested in meeting up? To hook up? One night. No strings. Just sex.

Dread slithers up my spine.

It's not the first time I've been propositioned via text, but something about this feels wrong.

Probably because there's only one girl you know who would text a random stranger for sex.

No fucking way.

Tension coils low in my gut as I tap out a reply. I'm probably overreacting, but I need to know.

Me: I'm flattered, but why me? I seem to recall you saying all douchey frat guys are the same.

I press send and stare at the screen, waiting for the reply bubbles to appear.

Nothing happens.

Shit. Was that too aggressive? What if I scared her off?

"Are we doing this or what?" Parker gives my phone a pointed stare.

I drop the phone on the table and pick up my controller. Staring at the unread message won't make her reply any faster. I need to chill. Play it cool. Distract myself by kicking Parker's ass at Madden. "Ready when you are."

It's a bald-faced lie, but swagger's gotten me this far.

We resume the game and Parker's got possession. I miss a block, but drive him back on the next down. He's third and long when my phone buzzes.

I try to ignore it, but it's impossible.

Just as I reach for my phone, Parker snaps the ball. I fumble the controller and he picks up the first down.

"Getting sloppy, princess."

"It's one play." I jerk my chin at the screen. "Let's see what else you've got."

Relax. The message will be there when the game is over.

We go through another set of downs, and I swear to Christ it's the longest drive of my life, which is ironic since it's only a video game.

"Oh, how the mighty have fallen." Parker turns to look at my bouncing knee. It's going a mile a minute, but I can't seem to relax. I just want this game to be over so I can check my phone. "Never thought I'd see the day when Cooper DeLaurentis cracked under pressure."

"Big words for a guy who has yet to see the end zone."

"Don't you worry." He slaps me on the back. "I'm coming for you, baby."

My phone buzzes again, reminding me I have an unread message.

Like I could possibly forget.

Just a few more minutes.

Parker snaps the ball. I'm slow to respond, and my defense is a mess. I watch in disbelief as his QB runs it into the end zone. He doesn't bother with in-game taunts. The asshole jumps off the couch and starts dancing right next to me.

My phone buzzes.

Fuck it.

"Can you take over for me?" I toss my controller to Reid and grab my phone off the table. "I need to take this."

"Aw, come on. Don't do me like that!" Parker whines. "Shit was just getting good."

I ignore him and jog up the steps to my room. Inside, I kick the door shut and sink down on the edge of my bed before opening the message.

Padawan: It's possible I was hasty in my assessment. The fact is, I have terrible luck. Especially when it comes to guys. But you seem decent, and you like Star Wars, and I thought maybe you could help me deal with the problem of my virginity, since according to your area code, we both live in PA.

Fucking hell.

I can almost hear the words pouring out of Quinn's heart shaped mouth. No filter. No pretense. Just frank honesty.

My pulse throbs at my temple.

Any doubt I had that Quinn and Padawan are one and the same has been erased, but I have to be sure.

I bring up my contacts and scroll to Noah's name. When he added his number back a few weeks ago so he could harass me about frat business, I was less than enthused. Now I'm grateful. I draw a steadying breath and tap to reveal his number.

It's one digit off from Padawan's. Because they probably share a cell plan.

The reveal is entirely anticlimactic.

Maybe I knew deep down this was coming, but is Quinn really so desperate to be rid of her virginity that she's going to meet some random guy for sex?

That's messed up. And unsafe. For all she knows, I could be a serial killer.

It puts the lotion on its skin.

Has she even seen that movie? Maybe I should offer to watch it with her.

The thing is, I support her agency—and God knows I love sex—but how am I supposed to stand by while she makes a huge fucking mistake?

Because it's her mistake to make.

And what? I'm supposed to spend the rest of my life feeling like an asshole if something bad happens to her?

Me: How do you know I'm not like, a serial killer or something?

Padawan: The odds of meeting a serial killer are less than 1 in 20k. I looked it up.

Of course she did.

I scrub a hand over my face, racking my brain for a way out of this. A way to convince her this is a bad idea.

My phone vibrates in my hand.

Padawan: And yes, I already tried the hookup apps with no luck.

Before I can think it through, I'm typing a response.

Me: Yeah? What happened?

Padawan: Chad turned out to be a thirty-something IT guy who lived in his mom's basement and was obsessed with Cheetos.

I snort-laugh, because damn. This girl.

Me: How do I know you won't take one look at me and change your mind?

Padawan: Trust me. I won't.

Padawan: I don't have a car, but if you come to College Park, I'll spring for the hotel room.

Jesus. The way she talks about losing her virginity is almost transactional.

I've had my share of random hookups, but there's always attraction. Passion. *Orgasms.*

Quinn deserves at least that much.

Hell, she deserves more.

Quinn deserves a man who will worship her all night long. A man who won't relent until he's wrung every last drop of pleasure from her curvy little body and who leaves her writhing in ecstasy.

There's only one way to ensure Quinn gets the pleasure she deserves.

I have to be the one who gives it to her.

The realization hits me like a linebacker, and the air punches out of my lungs.

What about rule number two? Thou shall not fuck a brother's sister.

Extenuating circumstances.

There's no stopping Quinn, and surely it's better for bro code if her first time is with someone who wants her to enjoy the experience and not a one-sided hookup with some selfish asshole who doesn't even get her off.

She's a virgin.

A virgin who isn't tangled up in her feelings. She's not looking for an attachment or a boyfriend or a guy who can sweep her off her feet.

Quinn's only looking for one night.

Even I can do one night without screwing it up.

Without losing my focus.

Nothing has to change. We do this and we go our separate ways.

Quinn, back to whatever it is she does in her free time and me back to football.

Back to an undefeated season with an eye on the championship game. On the draft. On the future.

I can't believe I'm even considering this.

It goes against every rule I have for hookups. But that doesn't stop my fingers from flying over the screen as I type my reply.

Me: Would next Saturday work?

It's nearly two weeks away. Plenty of time for one of us to come to our senses.

Padawan: It's Homecoming. Might be hard to get a room.

Not for me. I've already reserved a suite at The Wildcat Inn, the nicest hotel in town. I book one every year just in case my parents decide to come watch me play. At least this year the reservation won't go to waste.

Me: Don't worry. I'll take care of everything.

22

QUINN

"THANK you for supporting the fight against childhood cancer." I hand over three softballs in exchange for a crumpled five-dollar bill. Then I stuff the cash in my apron pocket and step back to watch as the newcomer approaches the dunk tank.

May the force be with you.

I've been at this for nearly an hour, and I have yet to see anyone dunk the Sig inside.

Still, we're raising money for a good cause, and that's what matters.

It's Wednesday night and the HoCo carnival is in full swing. The carnival is one of my favorite Waverly traditions. The HUB lawn is filled with booths offering snacks, games, and even a smattering of rides. Each booth is run by a student organization and all the money raised is donated to charity.

It's noisy and nostalgic and always a good time.

A catchy song blasts from the K-Pop Music and Dance booth next door and the scent of caramel corn permeates the air, making my mouth water.

I'd kill to be wandering the lawn with Haley, stuffing my face with deep fried goodness, but Noah roped me into covering his shift at the dunk tank so he could get in line for the Tri Delt kissing booth.

I should have known better than to believe him when he promised he'd only be gone for a few minutes.

The line for the kissing booth stretches so far down the crowded aisle I can't see the end.

My line is abysmal by comparison.

Which is shocking because aren't there a ton of women on campus who'd enjoy dunking obnoxious frat bros?

Says the girl who's planning to lose her virginity to one.

Nervous energy coils low in my belly.

Only three more days until my meetup with—

I really should've asked Frat Boy Yoda for his real name.

It's not too late.

Nope. The plans are set. The last week and a half has been relatively disaster free, and I will not test the universe by asking for his name.

Besides, what difference would it make?

None.

I'm doing this. Finally. At The Wildcat Inn.

I have no clue how he managed to swing a room at The Inn on one of the busiest weekends of the year, but I'm not about to look a gift horse in the mouth. A posh hotel room is certainly more appealing than a dirty Greek Row bedroom.

At least the sheets will be clean.

Because this is what my life has come to.

Maybe I should write up that little gem for Call-Me-David.

I snicker and I'm still laughing at my own joke when Noah returns with Cooper at his side.

At the sight of them, Jeremy, the Sig in the dunk tank, lets out a whoop of joy and shouts, "Get your ass up here, DeLaurentis! Your throne awaits."

Without waiting for a reply, Jeremy climbs to his feet and scrambles down the ladder for the shift change, bone dry.

Cooper gives him a slow once-over and turns back to Noah. "Are you sure this is the best utilization of my skills? I think the kissing booth would better showcase my talents."

Noah rolls his eyes. "Nice try. You get to skip meetings and pretty much every other Sig obligation because of football. The least you can do is support us and help raise money for the children's hospital."

"Childhood cancer," I amend. Because apparently, I can't help myself.

Both guys turn, noticing me for the first time.

Coop grins and lifts his chin in greeting, while Noah heaves a beleaguered sigh. Like I'm not doing him a favor by being here.

Siblings are *so* fun.

Coop jogs over to the dunk tank and drags a hand through the water. "Jesus, that's cold." He flashes Noah a wicked grin and shakes the water off his hand. "Maybe I could just make a donation instead?"

Why am I not surprised? I swear, the guy doesn't take anything seriously.

"Worried about shrinkage?" I challenge. "Afraid it'll ruin your image on campus?"

He smirks and plants his hands on his hips. "I've never had any complaints."

"There's a first time for everything."

He swaggers toward me, stopping when we're toe to toe. We're so close I can feel the heat rolling off his body and when he speaks, the fresh scent of peppermint lingers on his breath. There's fire in his eyes and as his gaze bores into me, the memory of our one and only kiss comes rushing back.

"Sweetheart, you could dip me in an ice bath and I'd still deliver."

My breath hitches, and I open my mouth to respond, but no words come out.

I should not be attracted to Cooper DeLaurentis. He's everything I despise in a guy. Cocky, controlling, thoughtful.

What? No.

Okay. Fine. He's not exactly the arrogant jockhole his reputation suggests, but that's hardly the point.

Cooper doesn't do virgins. Or girlfriends.

Well, that escalated quickly.

It really did.

I mentally backpedal. It's not like I actually want to date Cooper. It was a hypothetical thought. Who could blame me? The guy *can* kiss.

#Facts.

"Dude. We all get it. You've got a big dick," Noah barks. "Now get in the tank and away from my sister."

Cooper winks at me and turns on his heel.

I watch in fascination as he strips off his shirt, revealing the most droolworthy abs I've ever had the privilege of seeing, and climbs into the tank.

If you ask nicely, he'll probably let you touch them.

So not happening.

"How's it going?" Noah asks, yanking my attention from Cooper, who's perched on the dunk bench like a preening peacock, a giant grin plastered on his face.

"Traffic could be better."

"It'll pick up." Noah chuckles and shakes his head. "I spread the word that DeLaurentis would be in the tank at six."

Like magic, a group of cheerleaders arrive, their faces painted and their smiles bright. I watch as they go through the line one by one, doing their best to drop Coop in the cold water. A few of them hit the target, but despite their impressive power, he doesn't go down.

For his part, Coop doesn't hesitate to heckle them, his deep voice carrying beyond the booth. It helps draw interest from the passing crowds and our line starts to grow.

Noah takes over collecting cash and I hand out balls, pulling double duty since I also have to collect them from the ground around the dunk tank every few minutes.

We have a steady stream of players for the next twenty minutes and I'm feeling much better about our fundraising efforts—despite the fact that Coop has yet to come off the bench—when a bunch of football players roll up to the booth.

I recognize a few of them, mostly seniors. Austin Reid, Waverly's star quarterback. Smith and Parker, both tight ends. Vaughn, a left tackle. There's a brunette woman with them and surprise washes over me when I realize it's Kennedy Carter, the Wildcats' new kicker.

She's been killing it, despite the team's loss to Nebraska last week.

Talk about a dark day in College Park.

Hopes and dreams crushed by the tens of thousands.

Alcohol flowing like a river.

No shortage of tears.

Fortunately, Wildcat Nation is resilient, and most of us have faith Waverly can still bring home a national championship.

To be honest, I'm surprised the team is here tonight. I figured they'd be busting their asses on the practice fields. They've got Ohio on the schedule this weekend and there's no love lost between the teams. It's always a brutal game and tensions will run high, both on the field and off.

The football players sling catcalls at Cooper as Noah collects their money.

He eats it up, flexing his arms and blowing them kisses like he's been waiting all night for their arrival.

I roll my eyes and dole out the balls. The guys jostle for position, all wanting to go first, but after Parker fails to hit the target and Coop shreds him for having shit aim, they push Reid to the front.

Not a bad play. After all, he's got the best arm on the team.

I smile brightly and hand the team captain three balls. "I'll personally refund your money if you dunk him."

Reid grins. "Are you kidding? I'd pay double."

Carter laughs and shakes her head as the guys tell Coop to kiss his ass goodbye.

Reid rolls his shoulders, winds up, and lets it rip.

The ball streaks toward the target like a bolt of lightning and anticipation flutters in my chest.

It misses.

It actually freaking misses.

Coop howls with laughter as the ball hits the backdrop and falls to the ground, landing in the grass.

"Is that the best you can do? I've seen toddlers with better aim."

Reid laughs good-naturedly and tosses a ball in the air, catching it easily. "I'm just getting warmed up."

He adjusts his stance, and this time, when he hurls the ball, I know it's going to hit the target. I can feel it.

One big fat helping of cosmic justice coming right up.

The ball slams into the bullseye with a loud *crack*.

Nothing happens.

No release. No splash. No sputtering jock.

Even Coop looks shocked.

The surprise doesn't last long. He immediately returns to heckling Reid. "Damn, I wish I had this on film. Coach will never believe it."

The corners of Reid's mouth tighten, and I can't blame him. The guy got robbed.

Stupid, defective rental tank.

Reid looks like he's debating his next throw when a guy wearing a backward ball cap jumps the line. "Need me to show you how it's done?"

The newcomer is tall and trim. Well-built, for sure, but compared to the football players, he's downright skinny. He's got a few guys with him and one of them is wearing a Waverly baseball hoodie.

Oh, shit.

It's no secret the two teams have a longstanding rivalry. Noah once told me that's the reason the Sigs don't allow baseball players to rush the frat. Too much potential for trouble until Coop graduates.

"I don't want any trouble," Noah barks from the front of the booth. "If you want to support childhood cancer, cool. If not, move along."

"It's all good." Reid doesn't take his eyes off the baseball players. He rolls his neck and holds out his last ball. "If you think you can do better, McCoy, by all means, give it a shot."

McCoy takes the ball, flashing a victorious grin at his buddies.

One of the football players mutters, "asshole," but we all pretend not to hear it.

I can't speak for the rest of them, but I don't care who dunks Coop. I just want to see him take a bath.

Yes, it's shitty, but what can I say? That *is* the point of a dunk tank.

And the guy's been talking smack like it's his job.

McCoy moves to the throwing line, positioning himself like he's on the pitcher's mound. His back is straight and when he winds up, lifting his front leg, I have to admit his form is better than Reid's.

Yeah, because he's probably an actual pitcher.

He releases the ball and his follow through is on point. The ball hurtles toward the target and I give silent thanks I'm not on the receiving end of that throw. It slams into the bullseye with a resounding *crack* and a cheer goes up from the baseball players.

Their cheers are short-lived.

Coop is still on the bench, a shit-eating grin on his face.

How is that even possible?

I shoot a glance at Noah. Did he rig the tank so Coop wouldn't mess up his perfect hair? I wouldn't put it past him.

But, no. He looks as perplexed as the rest of us.

"The fuck?" McCoy shouts, glaring at Coop. "This thing is clearly broken. That ball was easily going eighty-five miles per hour."

Now it's the football players' turn to laugh.

"Don't be salty," Coop calls. "You didn't stand a chance, McCoy. Not when I've got my lucky lady at my side."

He points to the top of the tank where he's wedged a sparkly pink stuffed animal—a freaking unicorn—into the chain-link fence that protects him from getting hit with a stray ball.

Carter snorts and rolls her eyes. "I told you they deserved each other."

"Excuse me?" I ask. Because how can I not?

She turns to me, a wide grin transforming her pretty face. "I won the unicorn at one of the game booths, but I gave it to Coop because only a guy who preens as much as he does could appreciate such a glorious creature, right?"

I snicker. "I think I love you."

"Her name," Coop shouts indignantly, "is Starlight Twinkle."

That sends everyone into a fit of laughter, and when I recover, I move to collect the balls from around the tank. I toss one after another into my bucket as the others wait their turns. I'm moving fast, doing my best not to flash them my ass every time I bend over to grab a ball, but I'm already flustered when Coop whispers, "What? No kiss hello today?"

I glance up, heat flooding my cheeks, and my foot tangles in one of the extension cords used to light the booth. I stumble forward, hands out to brace my fall, and crash into the bullseye, the full weight of my body pressing into the lever.

Oops.

There's a metallic screech, and Coop's eyes go wide as the bench drops out from under him. He hovers in midair for an impossibly long second, gaze locked on mine, before dropping into the icy water with a splash.

23

COOPER

THE WATER IS cold as hell. Did the Sigs fill this thing with ice cubes or what? I wouldn't put it past the pricks. My muscles lock up in protest and I sputter to the surface, spitting a stream of frigid water from God knows where.

I never should've let Noah talk me into this. I'll bet Coach would've written me an excuse note. Something about protecting his star receiver from injury.

A cool breeze blows through the booth, raising a fresh wave of goosebumps on my arms.

I haul myself back up on the tiny ass bench, doing my best to ignore the hysterical laughter coming from the watching crowd.

It could've been worse. McCoy could've dunked your ass.

I never would've lived that shit down.

Back in position, I glare up at Starlight Twinkle and comb my fingers through my hair, pushing the damp strands back from my forehead.

So much for being good luck.

Then again, I was doing just fine until Quinn interfered.

I shouldn't have made that joke about us kissing. I could tell by her face she was shook. It was stupid, but I couldn't help myself. Besides, with all the smack talk, there's no way Noah could've overheard.

"That's a good look for you, DeLaurentis!" McCoy shouts, pointing and cackling like a hyena.

"I make everything look good," I shoot back, resisting the urge to give him the finger. This is a family affair, and Coach would have my ass for representing the team that way. "Too bad the same can't be said for you and your boys."

McCoy smirks and as the baseball players turn to go, he raises a hand to high-five Quinn. I can't hear what he says, but when she slaps his palm, a bright smile on her face, something ugly twists my gut.

Fucking baseball players.

"I don't want to alarm you," Reid says, approaching the tank the way one might approach the lion exhibit at the zoo. "But I think your unicorn is broken."

"My unicorn is just fine, fuck you very much." It's the best I can manage with my attention fixed on Quinn.

Reid laughs and shakes his head. "Either way, that was the funniest thing I've seen all day. Remind me to thank Coach for cutting practice short."

"Yeah, yeah."

We make plans to meet up after the carnival to grab something to eat, and he takes off with Carter and the rest of the guys, no doubt rehashing my tumble into the ice bath.

Christ. I hope they didn't catch it on film. I have no interest in becoming a meme. Especially with my father's re-election campaign reaching a fever pitch. The old man wasn't kidding when he said Mullaney was turning the screws. The polls show them neck and neck, and if anything goes wrong—if I embarrass him in any way—there'll be hell to pay.

It's just a fundraiser.

Yeah, fuckin' right. The media can twist even the most innocent footage when there are clicks to be earned. Growing up a politician's kid, I've seen it time and again.

It wouldn't be so bad if it only affected my asshole father, but shit rolls downhill and when the senator isn't happy, no one's happy.

Just a few more months.

The words have basically become my mantra, driving every decision I make, both on the field and off. Once that NFL contract is signed, I'll be free.

Until then, I've got to walk the line.

A new player approaches the tank and I push all thoughts of my father—and the election—from my mind.

The next half hour flies by. There's a steady stream of traffic, but no one manages to hit the target.

Thank Starlight Twinkle for small favors.

Mid-October in Central Pennsylvania isn't exactly freezing, but it's not what you'd call a tropical paradise either.

When Noah gives the signal to close up shop, I grab my unicorn and get my ass out of the tank. No need to give Quinn another opportunity to dunk me. Not when she'd likely take the universe up on the offer.

I'm rifling through my bag, looking for something to use as a towel, when a throat clears to my left.

I glance up to find Quinn watching me.

"Here to gloat?"

My swim trunks are still damp and cling to me in all the wrong places, but it is what it is. I might be a jackass, but I'm not about to scratch my balls in front of Quinn.

"I have no idea what you're talking about." She flutters her lashes, doing her best to look innocent. I'm not buying. "I tripped. It was an accident."

"Right," I drawl. "I'll bet you didn't have any accidents when Jeremy was in the tank."

"He didn't bring in much of a crowd." She shrugs, the corner of her mouth twitching. "You were like, the star of the show."

I knew it. The little vixen dunked me on purpose.

Should've seen it coming after the stunt she pulled at Sig Chi a few weeks ago.

Not that I'm complaining. That kiss was scorching hot, and I'm looking forward to a repeat performance.

"Anyway." She clears her throat and is it my imagination or are her cheeks flushed? *Probably just the cold.* "I thought you might need a towel. Noah brought a few over from the house."

She holds out a lump of gray terrycloth.

I climb to my feet and take the towel. Her fingers brush against mine and a jolt of electricity slides up my arm, warming my chest. "Should I consider this a peace offering?"

"I didn't know we were at war." Quinn lifts her chin defiantly. "Anyway, you should put some clothes on before you catch a cold."

"It's scientifically impossible to catch a cold from just being outside," I say, making no move to follow her advice. "But if I'm making you uncomfortable—"

"You're not."

Bullshit. I shake out the towel and use it to dry my chest, rubbing in quick circular motions Miyagi-Do style. Quinn watches, eyes going dark. She bites her lip, plumping the tender flesh between her teeth, and my cock twitches in response.

It's all I can do not reach for her.

Keep your dick in your pants, DeLaurentis.

Homecoming. Saturday. The Wildcat Inn.

Just a few more days.

Quinn's attention is fixed on my chest—which, not gonna lie, is flattering—so she doesn't notice me watching her.

Should I tell her the truth? That I'm the guy she's been texting? I've been wrestling with this question for the last week and a half and I still don't know the right answer.

It's fucking distracting.

Time is running out, and I want to do the right thing, but I don't know what that is. I'm totally out of my depth. I only know that I don't want to screw this up for Quinn.

What if she's disappointed when she finds out it's me?

Or worse, pissed?

Fact: There are a lot of women on campus who want to sleep with me, but Quinn Mowery isn't one of them.

Shit. Maybe I should tell her.

No. That's stupid, right? She'll call the whole thing off and who knows what she'll try next. At least with me, she's safe. Even if she's disappointed, I'll make sure it's good for her. I'll make sure it's special.

A night she'll never forget.

"Yo, DeLaurentis." Parker's voice slices through my thoughts, announcing the return of my roommates who, it turns out, have the world's worst timing. "Hurry the hell up. I'm starving."

Quinn's cheeks flush a deeper shade of crimson, like she's just realized she's been caught staring. "So, um, thanks again for being a good sport about the dunk tank."

"It was for a good cause." But that doesn't mean I can't get her back just a little. I shake my dripping hair like a wet dog, flinging the ice-cold water droplets in her direction.

She squeals and jumps back, covering her face with her hands.

When she peeks out from between her fingers, I flash her my trademark grin.

"Oops."

I pull on my sweatshirt and grab Starlight Twinkle, tucking

her protectively under my arm as I sling my bag over my other shoulder.

Quinn sputters, at a loss for words.

"See you around, sweetheart."

24

QUINN

I CROSS the elegant lobby and head straight for the elevator, head down, purse clutched in my hands. I can't say with certainty, but I'm pretty sure it's a close approximation of the walk of shame. Realistically, I know there's not a soul in the hotel who knows why I'm here, but the knowledge does little to quell my raging nerves.

There might as well be a flashing light over my head that says '*I'm here for sex.*'

My palms sweat as I press the up button on the elevator bank. An older couple wearing white Wildcat jerseys joins me, offering polite smiles.

"That was some game," the man says, shaking his head. "Best Homecoming game I've seen in ages."

I nod, silently willing the elevator to hurry. It was a goddamn nail biter, but the Wildcats managed to punch one in as the clock ran out, pulling off the win against Ohio. Normally such a close game would've had me losing my mind, but football is the least of my concerns today.

The elevator finally arrives and there's a quiet *ding* as the doors glide open.

When the passengers exit, I hurry inside and push the button for the third floor. Frat Boy Yoda texted the room number earlier, which was a relief since I'd rather not suffer through an uncomfortable meeting in the lobby, surrounded by strangers.

And yet you're meeting a stranger for sex?

Whatever. I never said my logic was foolproof.

I turn to the older couple, desperate to focus on anything but my impending hookup, and they confirm they're also going to three.

Perfect.

It's a short, awkward ride, but it feels interminable. When the doors finally slide open, my feet are cemented to the floor.

Oh, God. What if he's gross and I can't go through with it? Or worse, what if he's not attracted to me and he bails? I'm not sure my ego can take another rejection.

Why the hell did I ever think this was a good idea?

It's not too late to back out.

I could ride the elevator right back down to the lobby and walk out, with my dignity and my virginity intact.

"Are you okay, dear?" The couple has exited the elevator and the man has a hand braced on the door, holding it open. The woman is staring at me, concern etched in the deep lines of her face. "Do you need help?"

"No. No, I'm fine." I force a smile and step out of the elevator. "Just daydreaming."

More like freaking the eff out, but she doesn't need to know that.

I watch as they make their way down the hall, whispering quietly. Then I rally my courage and check the directory on the wall.

Room 335 is to the left. The opposite direction from the retreating couple.

I heave a sigh of relief and check my reflection in the mirror across from the elevator. It hangs above a table so I can only see the top half of my body, but it's perfect for checking hair and lipstick.

Or, you know, stalling.

Put on your big girl pants and get moving.

The voice is Haley's, but I know deep in my gut that it's right. The longer I delay, the better the odds of something going wrong.

I draw a deep breath, square my shoulders, and put one foot in front of the other, willing my nerves to settle.

When I find the room, I raise my fist and knock before I can change my mind.

There's still time to bolt if he looks like a creep.

There's a quiet *snick* as the doorknob turns and the electronic lock disengages.

Holy shit. I'm really doing this. My stomach rolls, twisting itself in a knot.

Just breathe.

I suck in a shallow breath, heart slamming against my ribcage.

The door opens slowly and— *No freaking way.*

It's a trick of the light. It has to be. The soft glow casting shadows or something.

I blink.

Once.

Twice.

Third time's the charm.

But nope. The man before me remains unchanged.

Cooper.

"I— I'm sorry." Heat scorches my cheeks and I pray the floor will swallow me whole. I have no doubt he knows exactly what I'm doing at the Wildcat Inn, and he's never going to let me live it down. "I must have the wrong room."

I step back, prepared to make a hasty retreat and never think of this moment again.

"Quinn."

I turn, unable to meet his eyes as humiliation crawls up my spine.

"Padawan."

The name freezes me in my tracks, and like a puppet on a string, my head jerks up.

"You don't have the wrong room." He tucks his hands into the pockets of his jeans. "I'm the douchey frat guy you've been messaging." He smiles, but it's not his usual cocky grin. There's a softness to it, an uncertainty I've never seen before. "Your words, not mine. I actually think I'm a pretty decent dude."

My throat closes and it becomes hard to breathe. To think.

I can't— This cannot be happening.

It's too cruel. Too—

"Is this some kind of joke?" I demand, voice unsteady. "Do you think this is funny? Have you been sitting around with your football buddies laughing at the naïve little virgin? God, I am so stupid." I push a stray lock of hair out of my face. "I should've known."

I've suffered some serious indignities, but never in my life have I felt this deep, cutting level of mortification. I don't even wait for a reply. Nothing he says can make this better. I speed walk down the hall, moving as fast as my heels will allow.

I don't make it ten steps before Cooper is blocking my path, his wide shoulders making it impossible to pass.

"Don't go," he says, voice quiet. "It's not what you think, Quinn. This isn't some fucked up joke. Not to me."

"Oh, really?" I wrap my arms around myself. "What is it then? Why are you here?"

Maybe I really am a fool because I actually want to hear what he has to say.

He rakes a hand through his hair, looking unsure for maybe the first time in his life. "I want to help. It's clear you're determined to lose your virginity, and I hate the idea of you having sex with some random guy you've never met, which, by the way, is completely unsafe for about a million different reasons."

Oh, good. We're back to this again.

"So, what?" I hiss, lifting my chin. "You thought you'd play knight in shining armor and I'd be so honored to experience your magical penis that I'd just fall at your feet in gratitude?"

His eyes go wide and the hint of a smile tugs at his lips.

Which, fair, because yes, I just said magical penis, but he's not getting off that easily.

No pun intended.

"You lied to me."

For weeks.

The worst part? I actually thought we were becoming friends.

Or, if not friends, frenemies at least.

"I never lied to you," he growls, stepping into my personal space. We're so close I can feel the heat rolling off his body, smell the intoxicating scent of his cologne. See the way his pupils have gone wide, nearly swallowing the cerulean irises. "You never asked my name."

He has a point, but I'm too pissed to care.

"It didn't occur to you that maybe you should volunteer the information when you realized it was me you were talking to?"

How long has he known, anyway? Did he know the night we met up at The Den?

I can't believe I've been talking to Cooper DeLaurentis all this time, asking him for advice.

It's unreal.

This is like B grade romcom fodder.

"I wanted to tell you, but I wasn't sure how." He closes his eyes and takes a deep breath, exhaling slowly before he meets my stare again. "Can we go back to the room and discuss this in private?"

I open my mouth to argue, but he's right. The last thing we need is an audience.

"Fine, but don't think for a second that you can sweet talk your way out of this."

25

COOPER

QUINN TRAILS me into the room, and I'm nervous as fuck. Probably because one wrong word—one wrong move—will have her bolting. Anger rolls off her in waves, but there's hesitation written all over her face, and that means there's still a chance I can salvage the night.

Give her space.

It goes against every instinct I possess, but I move to the far side of the room and lean against the ornately carved desk, crossing my ankles.

The relaxed posture is fake as hell, and completely at odds with the shit show in my head, but I'll do whatever it takes to put Quinn at ease.

She already thinks you're an asshole.

Which is why I need to let the angry tirade from the hall roll off my back, even if her assumptions burn like acid in my gut.

Does she really think I'm such a prick that I'd do all this just to humiliate her? To hurt her?

The urge to ask is nearly overwhelming, but I swallow the question down, afraid of the answer.

"Would you like a glass of wine?" I gesture to the bottle chilling in an ice bucket on the desk.

Wine isn't really my thing, but the guy at the store assured me it was good quality, and I figured it would help set the mood.

She opens her mouth—probably to decline—but hesitates.

The moment stretches between us, each second ticking by painfully slow, but I force myself to wait her out.

Just like running down the play clock.

Quinn scans the room, her attention landing on the king-size bed with its blue and gold brocade comforter and mountain of pillows. She swallows, and when she finally answers, there's a touch of relief in her words. "That would be great, actually."

Thank Christ.

I could use a glass myself. If nothing else, it'll give me something to do with my hands. I pour two glasses and offer one to Quinn.

"I meant what I said before." I hold her gaze, willing her to hear the truth in my words. "I want to help. We can do this and then you can go back to hating me tomorrow."

My chest tightens at the prospect.

She freezes, the wineglass halfway to her lips. "I don't hate you, Coop."

I quirk a brow, and to my surprise, Quinn smiles.

"To be fair, you are a pain in the ass."

"Yeah, but I'm a charming pain in the ass."

At least, that's what I've been told.

Quinn takes a hasty sip of her wine, and it's clear she's trying to hide another smile.

You've still got it, DeLaurentis.

"Now that we've established you don't hate me." I place my untouched wine on the desk. "I'd like to present my qualifications."

Quinn snorts and lifts her wineglass in a mocking salute. "By all means."

"First, as we've already agreed, I'm charming."

"If you do say so yourself," she cuts in, eyes dancing with amusement.

"Don't interrupt. I'll lose my place and have to start all over." Quinn laughs, the sound light and sweet and so damn endearing. *Focus, asshole.* I clear my throat and gather my thoughts. "As I was saying, I'm charming. Sexy. I know my way around a woman's body. All of which makes me the perfect partner for a one-night stand."

"That's it?"

My palms begin to sweat. "Uh, yeah."

What else is there? What am I missing?

Orgasms. I should've mentioned orgasms.

Quinn shakes her head and crosses her free hand over her stomach. "I can't believe I'm actually considering this."

Anticipation fills my chest, and for all my experience, I can't remember the last time I was so desperate to touch a woman. Quinn is gorgeous and the slinky green slip dress she's wearing is sexy as fuck, but it's not the dress that has desire humming along my skin like an electrical current.

It's Quinn herself.

The snarky, quick-witted, strong-willed woman who doesn't back down. Who gives as good as she gets and always brings a smile to my face. Who, despite all odds, has become a friend.

I definitely didn't see that coming.

"You can have any woman you want," Quinn says slowly, as if voicing her thoughts. "But you're here with me. You booked this room. Brought a bottle of wine. Blew off a hard-won homecoming celebration." She pauses, biting her lower lip. The naked vulnerability nearly does me in. "You're actually taking this seriously."

"Yes." For her.

To help her.

"If we do this, we're in agreement that it's a onetime thing, no strings attached?"

I nod, not daring to speak.

She narrows her eyes. "And we never speak of it again?"

The corner of my mouth twitches, but I nod again. She doesn't have to worry about me talking. After all, I'm the one breaking all the rules here.

Shit. I can't believe I'm going to have sex with Noah's little sister.

Noah's little sister, who also happens to be a virgin.

This literally breaks every rule I've set for myself since arriving at Waverly. Since determining I need to keep my head down, my nose clean, and my eye on the prize.

It's just one night.

One night with Quinn isn't going to screw up my dreams of becoming a first-round draft pick. I can handle this. I'm Cooper-fucking-DeLaurentis.

Quinn takes a long drink of her wine before continuing. "You realize there's like a ninety percent chance something will go wrong, right?"

I grin and wink at her. "Never tell me the odds."

"Okay." She gives a firm nod—ignoring my killer Star Wars reference—and for a second, I'm not sure which of us she's trying to convince. "Let's do this."

Quinn sits her wine on the dresser and reaches around to unzip her dress.

"Whoa." I'm across the room in a few long strides, hands gripping her wrists and locking them in place. "What's the hurry? We have all night."

"All night?" she echoes, voice unsteady.

"I'm going to do this right, Quinn." I trail a finger down her bare arm as I look her over, taking in the thin satin dress and sky-high heels. "You deserve a man who will worship your body and make you writhe with ecstasy. A man who will wring every last drop of pleasure from that sweet little virgin pussy."

She gasps and a slow flush spreads over her cheeks and down her neck.

"Would you like that?"

She nods, her clear green eyes locked on mine.

It's not enough. Consent matters, especially when you're a high-profile athlete.

"I need to hear you say it, sweetheart."

Her breath hitches and before she can respond, I brush my lips against hers. The kiss is light and tender, completely at odds with the filthy words that just came out of my mouth.

It's erotic as hell.

"Tell me you want this as badly as I do," I murmur, voice husky as I release her wrists and slip an arm around her waist, pulling her closer. She's soft and warm and her body melts against mine as I trail open-mouthed kisses across her chin and down the column of her neck, twisting my free hand in her hair.

Damn, she smells good.

Like pumpkin and vanilla. Is that even a thing? If not, it should be.

Anticipation sizzles down my spine, and my cock thickens.

I want this. I want her.

Just for tonight.

"Cooper." She plants her hands on my chest and pulls back, just enough to meet my eyes. "I want it all. I want you."

I crush my lips to hers and this time there's nothing tender about the way I claim her mouth. This kiss is demanding, fueled by desire and pure unbridled lust. My tongue glides along the seam of her mouth and when she opens for me, deepening the connection, a groan of pleasure is my only response.

It's hands down the hottest kiss of my life, and still, it's not enough.

Her fingers skim feather light over the hard muscles of my abdomen, stopping only when the hem of my shirt is firmly in her grasp. She tugs on the soft material and pulls it over my head before tossing the shirt on the floor. The instant it's gone, her lips are pressed to mine, hungry for more.

It's a silent request, and I'm happy to oblige.

I allow myself to explore the luscious curves of her body, cupping her small breasts and brushing the hardened nipples with my thumbs.

Quinn arches into my touch, a needy whimper escaping her parted lips.

"No bra," I purr, lifting a brow. "Did you leave your panties at home, too?"

"Only one way to find out." She rolls her hips in a slow, torturous motion that has my cock straining against the zipper on my jeans.

Does this woman have any idea how sexy she is?

I'd like nothing more than to bury myself inside of her, but tonight isn't about what I want.

It's about Quinn and what she needs.

I lower my hands to her thighs, my calloused palms gliding north as I push the hem of her dress up, confirming she's bare underneath.

A slow smile spreads over my face and I drop to my knees, something dark and ravenous taking hold at the sight of this gorgeous woman standing before me, her most intimate parts on display.

I lean forward and press a kiss to her stomach, the smooth creamy skin soft against my lips. Then I make my way south, leaving a trail of kisses in my wake.

Quinn shivers and her thighs clamp together.

"I— You don't have to—" she stutters, unable to finish the thought as I blow a hot breath against her pussy.

She bites her lip, but it's too late to stop the quiet whimper that escapes.

"I want to." I nudge her thighs apart. "Relax, Quinn. I've got you."

I palm her ass and pull her closer. Before she can utter another protest, my tongue is on her. I lick her with one long, lazy stroke right up the center.

The sound that erupts from her lips is music to my goddamn ears.

I did that.

I'm the one wrenching those needy little noises from Quinn and it feels so damn good.

I give another slow lick before circling her clit with my tongue and sucking hard.

Judging by her gasp of pleasure, she likes it.

Her legs quiver and she threads her fingers in my hair. To hold on or pull me closer, I don't know. Don't care. I only know that I never want this moment to end.

Desire courses through my veins, arousal coiling deep in my balls as I lick and suck, devouring Quinn like a ripe peach on a hot summer afternoon. The little mewling sounds she makes are testing my control, but I've already promised myself we won't have sex until she's come at least once.

Maybe twice.

I slip a finger inside of her and she moans, the sound deep and guttural.

"Do you like it when I fuck your pussy like this?"

I slowly withdraw the finger and slide it back in.

"Yes." The admission is half sigh, half plea as her body clenches around my finger. "I need more, Cooper."

The way she says my name all breathy and pleading has my

chest swelling with pride. I slide another finger into her and Quinn gasps when I curl them, stroking her G-spot. She rolls her hips and her grip on my hair tightens as she pulls me closer, bringing my mouth back to her pussy.

Fuck yeah.

I suck her clit hard and she tips her head back, losing herself in the moment.

She looks so damn good, so relaxed, like for once she's forgotten all of her troubles, her bad luck, and whatever else has her caught up in that pretty head of hers. Her guard is down, and I'm the one she's chosen to let in. To share this moment.

Just for tonight.

Quinn's orgasm comes hard and fast and she cries out as her body clamps down on my fingers with renewed intensity.

I hold her, supporting her weight until the last wave of pleasure has passed, and then I pull her down on the bed, so she's sitting in front of me.

"I— That was amazing," she says slowly, like she's having trouble forming complete thoughts with all the post-orgasm dopamine clouding her brain.

"Like I said, we have all night." I grin, entirely self-satisfied. "No need to rush."

I climb to my feet, eyes locked on Quinn. Not gonna lie, I'm aching to be inside this woman. Not only for the release, but to show her how good it can be and to prove that she's not fucking cursed.

She just hasn't been with the right guy.

I pull a condom from my back pocket and toss it on the nightstand.

The foil packet slides over the edge, and I swoop down to catch it. I'm mentally praising my tight reflexes when my head slams into the corner of the small table.

"Sonofabitch!"

The pain is sharp and intense, like getting crushed by a three-hundred-pound linebacker. It hurts like a motherfucker.

I jerk upright, barely managing to keep my balance as the room spins around me.

Something hot and sticky drips down my face. I press a hand to my forehead, and when I pull it away, the sight of my own crimson blood tells me everything I need to know.

Fuck. Me.

26

QUINN

CHRIST ON A CRACKER. This cannot be happening. Coop reaches out to steady himself, grabbing the closest piece of furniture, which isn't furniture at all, but a lamp. The delicate lampshade crumples under his weight and he nearly topples over.

I leap to my feet, heart pounding, and wedge myself under his left arm.

My knees buckle under his bulk and he nearly sends both of us crashing to the floor, but I manage to steer him to the bed. I make a mental note to step up my gym routine and give him a quick once-over. There's a gash on his forehead and his eyes are unfocused.

"Are you okay?"

That'll be stupid questions for one hundred, Quinn.

Right. The guy just face-planted into the nightstand. Of course he's not okay.

"I'll be fine." Coop presses a hand to his forehead in an attempt to staunch the bleeding. "I've taken worse hits in football."

Doubtful, but this isn't the time to argue.

"We need to get some ice on that." I haul ass to the bathroom and grab a crisp white towel, ignoring the guilt that niggles at my conscience. Then I move to the desk and fill the towel with ice from the wine bucket before returning to Coop's side. "This should help slow the bleeding."

He stares at me blankly, but makes no move to resist as I press the makeshift icepack to his forehead.

He hisses at the initial contact, but doesn't complain.

After a few seconds, he lifts a hand to the ice pack and takes over.

"I'm so sorry." I wring my hands as I sit down next to him. "This is all my fault."

"This isn't your fault. I'm the dumbass who smashed his face into the nightstand." He shifts, turning to face me. "I can only imagine what the talking heads would say about my footwork if they could see me now."

"I'd worry less about the media and more about your head." I lean forward, gently lifting the edge of the towel. "It's really bleeding. A lot."

"Head wounds always bleed more." He shrugs. "And I had a few zrinks tonight."

I straighten. "A few what?"

"Drinks."

"That's not what you said the first time." I narrow my eyes and search his face for evidence of a concussion. What are the signs, anyway? I should check WebMD.

"Are you trying to peer into my soul? Because I usually save that for the second date," he says with a hint of his usual humor.

That has to be a good sign, right?

Maybe, but no way is Cooper DeLaurentis getting brain damage on my watch. I'm just about to get my phone and Google the shit out of concussions when he flashes a disarming smile.

"Just give me a few minutes, and then we can try again."

"Try again?" I echo.

"Yeah." He gestures to the expansive bed behind us, and my cheeks heat as I recall every desperate noise I made while he was going down on me. *Aka, giving me the best orgasm of my life.* "You don't really think a bump on the head is going to stop me, do you?"

"You don't really think I expect you to go through with this," I say, crossing my arms, "when you're bleeding from *your head.*"

I put extra emphasis on the last two words, because WTF.

"Quinn." He speaks slowly, carefully enunciating his words. "I'm a DI athlete. I don't quit."

I roll my eyes. "That's not the flex you think it is, Cooper."

"Beg to differ. No way am I going to throw in the towel because of one minor setback. Not like those other assholes," he mutters, looking totally affronted. "This is your night, and I'm going to make sure it's perfect."

I appreciate the sentiment. I do. But he can't really think I'm just going to slap a Band-Aid on his head and get back to business.

"Trust m—" The words die on his lips and he squeezes his eyes shut. "Is this what getting stabbed in the brain with an ice pick feels like?"

My pulse flutters, and not in a good way.

"You should see a doctor. You might have a concussion." I stand. "I'm calling the front desk."

"No way." He stumbles to his feet and positions himself between me and the phone on the desk. "I'm fine. Really. No harm, no foul."

"Coop—"

"The hotel is packed with Wildcat fans. The last thing I need is for word of this to get out." He points to the icepack with his free hand. "Coach will freak. The news will make a big deal out of nothing. There will be all kinds of speculation and press and shit I don't need." He pauses and when he speaks again, there's a defeated edge to his voice. One I've never heard before. "My father is up for reelection in a few weeks. If I make the wrong kind of headlines, he'll blow a gasket."

I chew my bottom lip, torn. I get what he's saying. My parents weren't exactly thrilled when I got caught hooking up on the golf course. Or when I had to do community service for destruction of property, but his injury could be serious.

"I'm fine, Quinn."

Water from the icepack drips down his face and from what I can tell, he's anything but fine.

"I don't believe you."

"I find your lack of faith disturbing," he shoots back, sinking down on the edge of the bed.

"Did you just go dark side on me?" I throw up my hands. "That's it. Put your shirt on. We're going to the ER."

Ignoring his protests, I slip into the bathroom and grab another towel, which I use to make a fresh compress. We switch icepacks and I throw the old one—now soaked with blood—in the trashcan.

"I really don't think this is necess—"

"I swear to God, Cooper. If you don't come with me right now," I say, jabbing a finger toward him, "I'll stuff you in a laundry cart and wheel you out right through the lobby for all the world to see."

Twenty minutes later, we roll into the Emergency Room with its too bright lights and antiseptic stench. One look at the crowded waiting area, where a dozen people sit in uncomfortable looking chairs watching HGTV reruns, and Coop groans.

Dammit. Frustration wells up from the pit of my stomach. He's only just stopped insisting he's fine, and I have no interest in rebuffing a fresh round of protests.

I hook my arm through his and drag him straight to the check-in desk.

We wait.

And wait.

And wait.

Coop pulls out his phone as I watch the minutes tick by on the overhead clock.

I make it a whole five minutes before cracking.

"Excuse me." I tap gently on the plexiglass that separates the triage nurse from the waiting area. In the time we've been waiting, the woman hasn't looked up once. Not that Coop seems to care. He's watching highlights from today's game, phone in one hand, icepack in the other. "My friend hit his head and needs immediate medical attention."

The nurse, a harried looking Black woman with tired eyes and a sour expression, finally looks up. It's clear she's had a long shift. And judging by the monster sized coffee on the desk, she's planning for a long night.

I'm not unsympathetic—dealing with the public sucks and I'm sure she's seen some shit—but Cooper's head is gushing like Old Faithful.

The nurse pushes a clipboard across the counter, sliding it through the tiny window at the bottom of the plexiglass divider. "I'll need you to fill out these forms as completely as possible."

I grab a pen from the cup on the counter and snatch up the clipboard, skimming the paperwork.

I fill in what information I can while the nurse asks Coop a series of questions about his injury and pain level. He turns on the charm, flashing her a winning smile, and it's all I can do not to roll my eyes. I swear, the guy could be rocking a full-on concussion and he'd still be the world's biggest flirt.

When the nurse finally runs out of questions, she tells us to take a seat in the waiting area.

Un-freaking-believable.

"He's bleeding." I point to his head. "And you want us to take a number?"

She gives Coop an aggrieved look, and he grins like they're sharing an inside joke, which only pisses me off more.

"This is exactly what's wrong with healthcare in America." I huff out a breath and gesture to the overflowing waiting area.

The nurse sighs. "I'll let you know when a doctor can see you."

"Thank you," Cooper says, pulling me toward the waiting area.

"Fine," I call over my shoulder. "But if Waverly's star wide receiver dies in your waiting room, it's not my fault!"

Coop snorts and shakes his head. "It's just a scratch, Quinn. I don't have a concussion."

"Well, if you do, it'll probably be healed by the time you see a doctor."

He gestures to two empty chairs by the door and I follow his lead.

"I've had concussions before," he whispers conspiratorially. "I'd definitely know if I had one."

"Yeah, and I'm sure you'd be *so* forthcoming about it too." I flop down in the left chair and cross my arms. Coop might be able to charm the nurse, but I'm not falling for it. God knows one of us needs to act like a responsible adult here. "Should I call your parents and let them know what's going on?" I straighten, dread curling low in my stomach as I turn to him. "Are they in town?"

I can't believe I didn't think of it sooner. It's homecoming. College Park is overflowing with alumni. Coop is on the freaking football team.

"They aren't here," he says, voice flat. "I reserved a room at The Inn, but..."

They bailed. He doesn't have to say the words to get his point across.

His earlier comment comes back to me, and I remember the look on his face as he talked about his father's re-election campaign. Maybe the senator isn't a family man or maybe he's a workaholic, giving everything to his constituents and leaving nothing for his son, but whatever the case, it's obvious from Coop's shuttered gaze he doesn't want to talk about it.

I'm curious as hell, but the least I can do is respect his wishes.

After all, he wouldn't be in the ER if it weren't for me.

"Probably for the best." I nod slowly. "Can you imagine explaining this to them?" I sure as hell can't. "The prospect facing Wildcat Nation is terrifying enough. If the doc benches you, I'll be flayed online."

A smile tugs at the corner of his mouth. "Now you're just being dramatic."

I'm really not.

"Clearly you haven't been following the news on Spellman." I lift my chin even as panic takes root. Spellman is the Wildcats' starting kicker. Or he was until he got hurt and Carter replaced him. "The media hasn't exactly been kind to the woman they say is responsible for his injury."

The commentary has been brutal.

I'd never hold up under that kind of pressure.

"Then I guess it's a good thing you aren't responsible for my current condition," he says smoothly.

I snort because we both know that's a big fat lie.

"This is on me." He gestures to his bloody forehead. "I'm the one who forgot to bring Starlight Twinkle for good luck."

Before I can even unpack that statement, Coop's name is called, and he's ushered through a pair of greige automatic doors, leaving me open-mouthed in the waiting area.

27

COOPER

THE NURSE LEADS me to a sterile gray exam room that smells like disinfectant and despair. The lights are too bright and the exam table too small. My legs dangle uncomfortably over the end as she takes my vitals and grills me on my unremarkable medical history. Once she's done, I'm left alone to wait for the doc, which is just as boring as it sounds.

Talk about anticlimactic.

This definitely isn't how I imagined the night ending.

I pull out my phone and check my messages. There are a bunch of texts congratulating me on today's win and a few asking where I'm partying tonight. I delete them all, stopping only when I see a message from my mom.

Mom: You played well today. I'm so proud of you.

Just not proud enough to show up.

Anger sparks deep in my chest, a smoldering flame that's never truly extinguished.

It's not her fault. I know it on a cerebral level, but it doesn't take the sting off the fact that in four years, she hasn't attended a single game.

Don't be a dick. She'd be here if she could.

I drag in a steadying breath and slowly exhale. The paper liner on the exam table crinkles when I shift, loud and abrasive in the quiet room.

Me: Thanks.

It's short and to the point, but it's been a long day and I'm tapped. My head is throbbing like a motherfucker, and I don't have the energy to pretend everything is fine or that it doesn't hurt that my own parents can't be bothered to come watch me play ball.

Mom: Your father's town hall went well today.

She knows I don't give a shit about his dog and pony show. It's her way of letting me know why she couldn't attend the game. Why he wouldn't let her.

Not that it matters.

If it wasn't the town hall, it would've been something else.

Mom: Just a few more weeks and we can put this election behind us.

Until next time.

She doesn't say it, but she doesn't have to. If re-elected, this will be his last term in the Senate. We both know he's got bigger aspirations. Which is why it's so important to keep his image as a family man intact.

Mom hates campaign season as much as I do. All the smiling and faking it for the cameras. Meeting strangers and pretending to be the perfect wife to the perfect husband.

What a joke.

Me: Did you talk to him about Senior Day?

I don't know why I even asked.

Because you're a glutton for punishment.

They aren't going to come. They didn't come to my first game. Why would they come to my last?

Mom: Have you spoken with your professors about election day?

My pulse quickens, and I grip the phone more tightly as I reread the message.

Mom: Your father promised that if you join us at the hotel on election day, we'll be able to take a day off to come see your game.

His word isn't worth shit.

He doesn't keep campaign promises, so why would he keep a promise to his family?

The prospect of having my mom by my side on Senior Day is a powerful lure, and the bastard knows it. He always knows where to apply pressure. What lies to tell.

What words to twist.

It's what makes him such an excellent politician.

Just a few more months.

We just have to hold on for a few more months and then we can start over—*without him.*

The door to the exam room opens with a quiet click and a middle-aged doc with dark hair and tired eyes enters, a stethoscope hanging limp around his neck. His white jacket is pristine, but his scrubs are wrinkled and he looks like he's had a long night.

I know the feeling.

"Mr. DeLaurentis?"

"Yes, sir."

The words sound oddly formal in the cramped, uncomfortable room, but I'm not only representing the Wildcats here, I'm representing my father, and any misstep will be held against me in the future.

"I'm Dr. Mackey." He taps the screen of his tablet, not quite meeting my eye. "You played a good game today."

Fucking right, I did.

Two TDs *and* I broke one hundred-yards against our conference rival.

On Homecoming.

The only thing better will be winning the national championship.

"Thank you." There's a time and place for the cocky player routine and this isn't it. "Ohio is a tough competitor."

The doc smirks. "The Wildcats are better."

I shrug, a smile tugging at the corners of my mouth.

"What happened? Too much celebrating?" He jerks his chin toward the gash on my head as he steps to the sink and washes his hands. "There seems to be a lot of it going around tonight."

That explains why he looks so tired. Not that I'm surprised.

"No, sir. I dropped something and when I bent to pick it up, I clipped my head on the nightstand. No big deal, but my—" *Shit.* How to describe Quinn? The doc turns back to me, drying his hands on a paper towel. There's an amused curiosity in his dark eyes I'm not about to indulge. "My friend thought I should get it checked out."

He nods and pulls on a pair of latex gloves. Then he moves in to inspect the damage.

"Have you been drinking?"

"No." I had a few beers with the guys, but that was hours ago.

Thank Christ. Alcohol and ER visits are the kiss of death for an NFL draft hopeful.

Not to mention the child of a prominent politician.

Dr. Mackey gently prods my forehead, and searing pain radiates from the point of contact.

I grit my teeth.

"All right, Mr. DeLaurentis. I'm going to give you three words I need you to repeat and remember for later. Understand?"

I nod.

This isn't my first concussion check, and I doubt it will be my last.

Between Quinn and football, it'll be a miracle if I make it to the end of the season without another one.

Fuck.

Quinn must be freaking out. She warned me something like this might happen, but I didn't listen. I just plowed ahead like always, confident in my decision.

You really think you could have predicted this?

Nope. It's too goddamn ridiculous.

What kind of asshole concusses himself trying to do the deed?

It's not a concussion.

At least, it better not be.

Fear grips my chest, squeezing like a vise. I can't afford to ride the bench. Not now. Not when I'm so close to making my dreams a reality.

"Field. Grass. Blue."

I repeat after Dr. Mackey, committing the words to memory.

This is what I get for trying to play the hero. For trying to be the good guy. For breaking fucking bro code and my own damn rules.

The doc examines my eyes and asks a series of inane questions.

"What day is it?"

"Saturday."

Aka, the Homecoming that will live in infamy.

"How many receiving yards did you have today?"

"One hundred twenty-six."

Like I could forget.

"Have you ever had memory problems?"

"No."

But I've got plenty of memories I'd rather forget.

When the onslaught of questions finally ends, Dr. Mackey grins and pats me on the shoulder. "It's a nasty cut, but I don't see any sign of a concussion."

My shoulders relax, relief welling up from the pit of my stomach.

"We'll just get you stitched up and you can be on your way."

He leaves briefly and returns with a tray bearing the tools of his trade.

The doc numbs the area with a local anesthetic and sets to work while I do my best not to think about the fact that he's sewing my face back together. Easier said than done when he's explaining the care and cleaning of the absorbable sutures.

At least you won't have to come back to get them removed.

Truth. My schedule is already insane. I don't have time for extra appointments.

"That takes care of the stitches." Dr. Mackey peels off his gloves and tosses them in a waste receptacle. "Do you remember the three words I asked you to memorize earlier?"

"Field. Grass. Blue."

I've been running them through my mind for the last ten minutes, waiting for this moment.

"Good." He gives a curt nod. "You're all set, Mr. DeLaurentis. Be sure to let Coach Collins know you took a knock on the head." The doc levels me with a firm stare that suggests this isn't his first time dealing with a D1 athlete. "You need to take it easy for a couple of days."

Like hell.

"Yes, sir."

"No contact at practice. If you have any difficulty with memory loss, nausea, or headaches that don't cease with a couple of aspirin, see the team doctor." He hands me a business card. "I'm just a phone call away if you or Coach Collins have any follow-up questions."

"Thanks, doc."

I pocket the card, doing my best to ignore the skepticism rolling off Dr. Mackey in waves.

"I'm serious. Your entire future isn't worth one game."

Easy for him to say.

He's not one injury away from losing it all. From failing his mother and himself.

"I understand." I slide off the table and offer my hand. The doc shakes it, his grip firm and reassuring. "We've got a bye week, so it shouldn't be too hard."

The lie comes easily, proving I just might have the makings of a career politician after all.

Like father, like son.

28

QUINN

"*GIRL*." Haley grins at me over the top of The Collegian. "Today's article is fire. And also, like, the most relatable content ever."

"Right." I sigh and slump back in my chair, unable to match her enthusiasm. "Because what virgin hasn't sent their would-be partner to the freaking ER?"

Haley rolls her eyes, but she can't suppress the grin that splits her face.

"I was talking about the part where you both tried to make it perfect—luxury hotel, wine, the whole bit—and it still sucked. That's literally the definition of first times. They're always clumsy and awkward." She snort-laughs. "And they sometimes end in stitches."

I shoot her a look that's darker than my French roast. It's Tuesday morning and we're holed up in a corner booth at Daily Grind. I'm procaffeinating with my second cup of coffee, but it's doing little to improve my mood.

Haley drops the newspaper on the table. "Quit sulking."

If only it were that easy. "I reserve the right to sulk indefinitely."

After all, I deserve it. The hottest guy on campus gave me a toe-curling orgasm and then *boom!* We're in the ER getting his face stitched back together.

Worst. Luck. Ever.

"I still can't believe Coop is the guy you've been texting." She sips her tea, holding the mug with both hands. "That's some freaky shit."

"Tell me about it." I'm still shook.

Because even when I wondered if it could be true, I never seriously considered it. The very idea was just too far-fetched and convenient. Like a feel-good movie that overlooks the glaring plot holes.

And the plot hole?

Only the fact that my phone number is one digit off from Noah's.

I should've figured it out when Fray Boy Yoda told me he was trying to text his buddy.

Yeah, because your brain is always in top form in the middle of the damn night.

Plus, there were the Witcher dreams.

Whatever. It doesn't matter anymore.

I can't go back. I can't unknow the feel of Coop's lips on mine. Can't forget the way his mouth licked and sucked and—

"You're thinking about him, aren't you?" Haley wiggles her brows suggestively. "The sexy bits."

My cheeks flush and I shove my coffee away. "No."

"Liar." She smirks and crosses her arms. "Look, I love B, but if your brand of hot mess means you get to hook up with hard bodied athletes, I don't think you get to complain about being a virgin anymore." I open my mouth to protest, but she throws up her hands in a defensive gesture. "I don't make the rules."

I lean forward, resting my chin on my hand. "The rules are stupid."

"Preach."

"It probably sounds naïve, but I really thought it was going to happen this time. We were so freaking close." And, yes, I was mad at first, but once I had time to think it over, I realized Coop was the right guy for the job. I wanted it to be him. "Everything was perfect. He was being so sweet and I was so comfortable. So relaxed."

"Oral sex tends to have that effect when it's done right." She pauses, a devious glint in her eyes. "Which just proves the rumors about Cooper DeLaurentis and his wicked tongue are true."

"Haley!" I practically hiss her name as I glance around. "Someone will hear you."

She shrugs. "What do I care? I'm a sexually empowered woman."

"Yeah, and I fully support that, but I don't need rumors about Coop and I getting around campus," I whisper. "There's a reason I don't use real names in my articles."

"Maybe you should. You'd get twice as many comments online."

"Or I'd be the butt of twice as many jokes. Hard pass."

My life is already a dumpster fire. I don't need to add jokes about my inability to get laid into the mix.

"Suit yourself. What are you going to do about He-Who-Must-Not-Be-Named?"

It's the million-dollar question. One I've been asking myself for the last two days.

"There's nothing to do." Well, aside from sulking and wallowing in shame. "I doubt he'll ever speak to me again after Saturday night."

The realization hurts more than it should.

I reach for my lukewarm coffee and take a sip, letting the dark roast soak into my tastebuds.

"Or he'll pursue you relentlessly because he wants another taste of your sweet virgin nectar."

I choke, coffee halfway down my throat, and spray French roast all over the table.

"You cannot say shit like that when I'm drinking!" I grab a napkin and mop up the mess as Haley shakes with laughter. "Seriously. What were you thinking?"

"I was thinking Cooper is on his way over here right now."

I look up from my mess, glaring at her. "Not funny."

"Then I guess it's a good thing I'm not joking."

My stomach drops and my palms go clammy. I don't have it in me to turn around because I know exactly what I'll see, and I'm not prepared to face Coop yet.

I didn't even brush my hair this morning.

Too late to do anything about it now.

I wipe up the last of the coffee and toss the dripping napkin into my nearly empty mug as Coop appears at our table, looking like God's gift in tight, low-slung jeans and a black compression shirt that hugs every dip and curve of his sculpted body.

My cheeks flush and my skin tingles at the memory of those powerful arms wrapped around me. Of having those calloused hands on my thighs. Of having those talented fingers rip sobs of pleasure from my lips as I climaxed.

"I had a feeling I might find you here," he says, a crooked smile playing across his full lips.

I lift my gaze, forcing myself to meet his eyes, which makes it impossible not to look at the neatly stitched gash on his forehead. The bruise is fading and just a hint of purple remains, but it does little to assuage my guilt.

"So, what?" I demand, falling back on our old routine. The one where we bicker instead of peeling our clothes off. "Now you're stalking me?"

"Hardly." He shoves his hands into the pockets of his jeans. "Don't you ever go to class?"

"Like you have room to talk." I lift my chin and offer him a sweet smile. "Exactly how many times have you crashed one of my coffee dates?"

Haley clears her throat. "Speaking of class. I should get going or I'll miss my studio time."

She grabs her bag and slides out of the booth, avoiding my eyes.

Haley doesn't have class, and we both know it. She probably thinks she's doing me a favor by giving me some one-on-one time with Cooper, but that's the last thing I want right now.

"Are you sure you can't stay?" My voice is too high, too desperate. "I thought your class was canceled."

"Nope." She shoots me a quizzical look and slings her bag over her shoulder.

"Then ditch." I pause, scrambling for something—anything—to change her mind. "We'll get cupcakes. My treat!"

If I'm a pumpkin whore, Haley's a cupcake slut. She has never said no to a cupcake. Not even once.

"I'll buy you a dozen," Coop says, fishing a twenty-dollar bill out of his pocket and offering it to her. "*If* you give us a few minutes alone."

Haley's eyes light up and she snatches the bill from his hand. "Deal."

I gape at her. There's no other word for it. She just sold me out. "Traitor."

She blows me a kiss and promises to save me a cupcake before she turns on her heel and saunters up to the counter, leaving me alone with Cooper.

He slides into the booth, sitting opposite me.

The playful guy who just bribed my BFF is gone. His eyes, which are normally so clear, are like storm clouds, and there's not a hint of amusement in his words when he speaks. "We need to talk."

My stomach clenches and for a second, I think my coffee might make another spectacular reappearance.

He's pissed. I get it. The other night was a disaster and once he's said his piece, we'll go our separate ways.

No more Sig Chi parties.

No more late-night texts.

No more...Coop.

The worst part? I can't even blame him. The guy can have any woman he wants, and he doesn't need a walking disaster screwing things up or ruining his shot at the NFL.

"I really am sorry about the stitches." I fold my hands in my lap where they can't do any damage. "I totally understand if you never want to see me again."

I said all of this on Saturday night, but maybe he's forgotten. Or, more likely, blocked it out. Either way, there's no such thing as too many apologies when you put someone in the ER.

"Wait." Coop straightens and his brows knit together. "You think I'm mad about what happened at The Inn?"

Obviously.

I bite my bottom lip, stalling. Because knowing it and hearing it are two very different things.

"I'm not upset about Saturday night." He shakes his head, blond locks falling over his forehead. "That was an accident, Quinn. It could've happened to anyone."

I shoot him a pointed look.

"Well, maybe not just anyone," he amends, lips twitching.

His words should be a relief, but I can't let go of the tension coiled deep in my belly.

"If you're not mad about what happened at the hotel," I ask, wringing my hands. "What exactly do we need to talk about?"

29

COOPER

A BETTER QUESTION WOULD BE, what don't we need to talk about?

First things first.

There's a copy of The Collegian on the table and it's open to the article that inspired this little chat.

My pulse accelerates at the sight of that damn headline.

Another One Bites the Dust.

"What the hell is this?" I slide the paper across the table and stab the article with my pointer finger.

Never in a million years did I think my sex life would be headline news.

No, that's not quite true. I've always known it was a possibility, which is why I'm careful. It just never occurred to me that I needed to be on my guard with Quinn.

She frowns. "It's a newspaper. Surely, you've seen one before."

Ignoring the sarcasm, I lean forward and rest my forearms on the table. "My father is up for reelection. If word gets out that I'm the guy in this story—" I pause, choosing my words carefully. "Let's just say it won't be good for his campaign."

Or his family.

"Did you actually read the article?" She arches a slender brow in silent challenge. "If so, then you know it's anonymous. You have nothing to worry about."

Yeah-fucking-right.

The media are relentless. One whiff of this and all hell will break loose.

"Because there are so many guys strutting around campus with three stitches in their forehead?"

She shrugs, her delicate shoulders rising and falling easily. "I'm sure you're not the only one. It was Homecoming."

"What does that have to do with anything?"

"Maybe you don't remember this because of all the painkillers, but the ER was packed. Besides, most people will just assume you got banged up during the game."

She's not wrong. Cuts and bruises are part of the sport, but not everyone will be fooled so easily.

"My roommates are not most people." I rub the back of my neck. "And before you say it, they're athletes, not idiots."

Annoyance flashes in her eyes. "Would they really sell you out to the press?"

"No." I'd stake my life on it. "They're good guys."

I should just tell them what happened and get it over with. The best defense is a good offense, and the longer I keep it a secret, the longer they'll bust my balls trying to get to the bottom of it.

She relaxes. "Trust me, I don't want my identity getting out any more than you do."

"Good. Then you understand why I prefer not to be included in any future articles."

She makes a noncommittal sound—which is probably the best I can hope for since it's all anonymous—as I pick up the paper, looking at the article more closely.

A. Ginger.

"Nice byline. But if you're so worried about people learning your identity, why write the articles in the first place?"

I can't imagine documenting the private details of my sex life —or lack thereof—for forty thousand strangers.

"I'm a writer." Quinn fiddles with her empty coffee mug, not meeting my eyes. "It's what I do."

Maybe. But there's got to be more to it. Otherwise, why not write about— *Fuck*. I don't know, *anything* else.

"But why these stories? They're pretty damn personal."

I shouldn't press—I hate it when people get into my business —but I can't help myself. Everything I know about Quinn is surface level.

I didn't even know she was a writer before today.

Now? Now I want to know everything there is to know about her.

"I share my story," she says, tucking a strand of hair behind her ear, "because maybe there are other girls like me who need to see it to know they aren't alone."

Her words land like a helmet to the groin.

"Girls like you?" I shake my head. "What does that even mean?"

She shifts, still toying with her hair. "You know, girls of the hot mess variety."

Is that all she sees when she looks in the mirror? Just the thought of it chafes.

"Quinn, I've met a lot of women, and trust me, none of them are quite like you."

Her head jerks up and from her wide-eyed expression, it's clear I've said the wrong thing.

No surprise there. I'm not exactly great with words and I don't have a lot of experience in this area. When it comes to women, my strengths are flirting and meaningless sex, not sincere confessions of the heart.

Not that this is a confession of the heart.

Fuck. What am I even saying?

"That was supposed to be a compliment." The tips of my ears grow hot, but I forge ahead. "I just meant that you're incredible. Smart. Funny. Sexy."

The corner of her mouth lifts. "You think I'm sexy?"

Relief floods my veins.

This, at least, is familiar territory.

"You know I do." How could she not after Saturday night? "Which brings us around to the other reason I wanted to talk to you."

She lifts a brow, but says nothing.

"I think we should try again." I glance around, making sure we don't have an audience. "You know, sex."

"Are you out of your mind?" She leans forward, the corners of her mouth dipping low. "Are you sure you don't have a concussion? I knew I should've talked to the doctor myself."

"I don't have a concussion. I'm simply committed to finishing what I start."

It's one of the few good qualities my father instilled in me.

"No way." She shakes her head vehemently. "I'll find someone else."

Like hell.

"This has already gone too far." She points to my stitches. "I will not be responsible for you getting hurt again. Or worse."

I chuckle. "Or worse?"

"Who knows? Next time you could break a bone or your—" She blushes, her gaze dropping to my lap. "You know."

"I can assure you my cock is just fine."

Aside from being sexually frustrated.

I've spent the last two days fantasizing about Quinn's lush little body, and I'm not too proud to admit I've jerked off more in the last forty-eight hours than I have in my entire college career.

"Good." Quinn sniffs. "I suggest you keep your distance if you'd like to keep it in working order."

I honestly can't tell if she's kidding or if she really thinks she might somehow break my dick.

Either way, I'm not so easily discouraged.

"Like I said. I always finish what I start." I pause, pitching my voice low. "As long as you're committed to this Virgin Quest, I'm not going anywhere."

"Then I guess it's a good thing it's not up to you," she retorts, matching my energy.

A slow grin spreads over my face and my cock twitches in anticipation. This is the sassy little spitfire I can't get enough of, and if I have to fight dirty—just this once—so be it.

The music is loud and no one's paying attention to us.

We're in a corner booth, completely out of the way.

Practically invisible.

"Come on, Quinn. Just give me one more chance. The team has a bye this week and I can't think of a more satisfying way to spend my Saturday night than licking that gorgeous little pussy of yours." I lick my upper lip and she wriggles in her seat, no doubt remembering the feel of my tongue on her clit. "I can still taste you on my tongue. So sweet."

I'm getting hard just thinking about it.

She nods slowly. "It was...nice."

Nice? If she's trying to insult me, it won't work.

"Liar. We both know there was nothing *nice* about the way you came on my tongue."

Her cheeks flush and I'd lay odds I'm not the only one reliving Saturday night in my head.

"I don't know." She bites her lip, the tender flesh plumping around her teeth. "What if things go wrong again?"

"They won't." I won't allow it. I'll be better prepared this time. "I'll take care of everything."

Her features soften and the sight of all that vulnerability nearly does me in.

"I want to, but—"

"No buts. I have a plan." One that doesn't involve hotels and wine and too much damn pressure. "You can trust me, Quinn. Just say the word."

She nods, green eyes glittering with conviction. "Yes."

30

QUINN

I CAN'T BELIEVE I'm doing this—*again.*

For the love of God, please let me lose my virginity in spectacular fashion tonight.

Well, not too spectacular. I want orgasms, not ER visits, which have ruled my thoughts for the last five days. But now it's Saturday night and I'm standing at Cooper DeLaurentis's front door, prepared to lose my virginity once and for all.

There's no going back.

Not that I'd want to.

Last Saturday may have ended in disaster, but everything leading up to it was **chef's kiss*.*

Coop may not do strings, but what he lacks in commitment he more than makes up for with his mouth. And his fingers. And those rock-hard abs.

And, okay, yes, if I'm being honest, he's actually a nice guy when he's not being a cockblocking jackass.

Which, I'm learning, is more often than not.

Nerves grip my stomach, twisting it in knots as I stare up at the nondescript townhouse.

College Park Apartments is a popular complex among

student athletes, but it's my first time here. The community is a winding maze of apartment buildings and townhouses, but I'm pretty sure I'm in the right place because Coop's Audi is parked out front.

I raise my hand and knock before I can second guess myself.

Several seconds tick by and doubt creeps up my spine.

The townhouse is dark. There are no light in the windows, not even the soft blue glow of a tv screen.

Maybe Coop changed his mind. Or maybe I got the time wrong.

Shit. What if I'm at the wrong apartment?

Yeah, because they always give two units the same number.

I glance at the sign above the door.

Eleven fifty-seven.

There's a quiet shuffling inside and a loud *thwack* as the lock is thrown back.

A bead of sweat rises between my breasts and I silently curse my stupid nerves as the door opens, revealing Coop's smiling face.

His hair is damp, and he's dressed casually in gray sweatpants and a navy Wildcats t-shirt, which is a relief since I also dressed for comfort in leggings and a Waverly U hoodie.

"Sorry." He shoves a hand through his hair, pushing the wet strands back from his forehead. "I was in the shower."

"No worries."

He turns, swinging the door wide.

I slip past him, inhaling the comforting scent of Ivory soap and laundry detergent as I step into the living room. To my left there's an open staircase, and to my right are several oversized chairs and couches arranged around an enormous flat screen tv.

Typical.

Coop closes the door and heads for the back of the townhouse, where light spills through a wide entryway, casting shadows on the hardwood floor.

"Hungry?" He turns to glance over his shoulder. "I ordered pizza."

"Sure." I clear my throat. "I could probably eat a slice."

Yeah, right. My stomach is so tangled up, I couldn't force down pizza if I wanted to.

I trail him into the kitchen, which is surprisingly clean. There's no clutter. No dirty dishes in the sink. The only thing on the granite counter is a bunch of bananas and a pizza box with paper plates and napkins stacked on top.

"What can I get you to drink?" He opens the fridge, giving me a glimpse of what has to be the most organized fridge on campus. *Marie Kondo would be proud.* "We've got beer, water, Powerade, orange juice, some weird green smoothie shit, and Coke."

"Water is fine."

He grabs two bottles of water and pushes the door shut.

"I didn't take you for such a neat freak," I say, leaning a hip against the counter.

"I'm not. That's all Vaughn." He flashes me a wicked grin. "Sometimes I move stuff around just to mess with him."

Why am I not surprised?

Speaking of roommates. I glance around, straining my ears as Coop offers me the water.

I accept and twist off the top. "Where is everyone tonight?"

The townhouse is eerily quiet.

Or you're being hypersensitive because you expect the worst.

Ugh. You know what's the worst? My inner monologue.

"They're out partying." He shrugs. "Probably making the most of the bye week."

Of course. Coop would be out living his best life if it weren't for me.

He scoops up the pizza box and nods to the hall. "You wanna head up to my room? We can watch a movie or something while we eat."

It's on the tip of my tongue to suggest we eat in the kitchen, but that's probably my nerves talking, so I nod and we make our way upstairs.

Coop's room is at the back of the house and despite his claims that Vaughn is the neat freak, his room is spotless. There's a computer desk by the window with a laptop and a stack of textbooks on top, but a queen-size bed with a gray and navy comforter takes up most of the room. The bed is flanked by a small, functional nightstand on one side—with Starlight Twinkle resting on top—and an ensuite bathroom on the other. A flatscreen tv hangs opposite the bed and there's a bulletin board above the desk with articles and game schedules pinned to it, but there's not much else to see aside from a Wildcat flag and a few ball caps hanging on hooks.

Definitely not what I expected from Cooper and his larger-than-life personality.

There's nothing personal about it.

That's when it hits me. There's not a single picture to be found. Not of his family, his friends, or even the team.

It doesn't matter. You aren't here to get to know him.

At least, not in that way.

Anxiety fills my chest and I sink down on the edge of the bed, water bottle clutched in my hands.

This is a bad idea. We should've eaten in the kitchen. He'll probably scald his mouth on hot cheese and then he'll drop his pizza and the grease will burn his cock and—

"Relax, Quinn."

I glance over to find Cooper staring at me, laughter dancing in his cerulean eyes. "I'm relaxed."

He chuckles. "If you relax any further, you're going to burst a blood vessel."

Okay, fine. So I'm a little tense.

How could I not be after last week's trainwreck?

"Why don't you bring up Netflix and find something for us to watch?" he suggests, opening the pizza box and filling our plates. "The remote's on the nightstand."

I grab the remote and queue up Netflix. I don't have the patience to search for a movie, so I find *The Witcher* and press play, picking up where Coop evidently left off.

"A woman after my own heart." He nods approvingly and hands me a plate. Then he climbs onto the bed, leaning against a pile of pillows as he stretches out, crossing his ankles. "Come sit by me."

It's more order than request, but I don't argue as he pats the spot next to him.

Perching on the edge of the bed isn't exactly comfortable and if I don't chill the eff out, this night really will end in disaster.

I scoot back so we're hip to hip and curl my legs under me.

The opening credits play on-screen and Coop dives into his pizza, but I can't bring myself to eat.

We watch in silence for a few minutes and when Coop finishes, I give up any pretense of hunger and offer him my plate.

"Want mine? Turns out I'm not actually hungry."

He eyes it, but eventually shakes his head. "I'd better not. Technically, I'm not supposed to be eating pizza. I'll put it on the nightstand in case you change your mind later."

Fat chance of that happening, but I give him the plate anyway.

"If you aren't supposed to be eating pizza, then why do it?"

He shrugs. "Why do I do anything?"

Fair point.

I'm pretty sure he's not supposed to be deflowering virgins, yet here we are.

Again.

"Relax, Quinn. I promise not to bite." He flashes me a wolfish grin. "Unless you're into that sort of thing."

"I'm a virgin." I try to infuse my words with false bravado, but they come out breathy and unsure. "I don't actually know what I'm into."

Coop's eyes are a blue flame as he studies me, trailing a finger up my thigh. "I can help you with that, too."

"Of that, I have no doubt." A nervous laugh forces its way from my throat. "I'll bet you've helped tons of girls right here in this very bed."

More than I care to think about.

He freezes, his finger coming to a stop on my upper thigh. "I'm not in the habit of inviting women over."

"Oh, really?" I arch a brow and make a show of looking around the room.

"Smartass." He hooks an arm around my waist and pulls me down on top of him so we're face-to-face, my breasts pressed to the hard planes of his chest, his hand resting on the swell of my hip. "This is different. We're friends."

Desire stirs low in my belly, yawning awake like a cat that's been napping in the sun.

If this is what it feels like to be his friend, I'm all in.

Coop and I have chemistry—last weekend proved it—and I'm not going to waste our night together obsessing over what he has or hasn't done with other women. I don't want to be that girl. Besides, what does it matter?

We're just friends.

Friends who exchange sexual favors.

God, it sounds so dirty when you put it like that.

"Hey. Stay with me, Quinn." He cups my cheek, his calloused

fingers scraping over my skin. "Don't disappear into that pretty head of yours."

Despite my nerves, I smile. "I wouldn't dream of it."

Truth. I want to savor every second of our time together.

I lean down, but before I can even brush my lips against his, he's reaching up, claiming my mouth with his own. The kiss is hot and hungry and when he slides his hands under my sweatshirt, skimming his fingers along my bare flesh, a ripple of desire radiates from my core, electrifying every nerve ending in my body.

He deepens the kiss, lips soft, yet commanding as his tongue sweeps into my mouth, massaging and stroking and reminding me of all the wicked ways he can use it to give pleasure.

A quiet whimper cuts the air and when he finally pulls away, I'm gasping for breath.

Sweet baby Jesus.

I can't remember the last time I was so thoroughly kissed.

Probably never.

Coop stares up at me, and though I can't explain it, there's desire in his eyes.

He wants me.

Maybe even as much as I want him.

It's a heady realization and my confidence swells.

"Lose the shirt," he rasps. "I want to see every gorgeous inch of you."

I sit up and straddle him, pinning his hard body between my thighs. His erection is long and thick and I ache to feel him inside me as I pull the sweatshirt off over my head.

"So damn perfect." His big hands settle on my hips, his thumbs tracing slow circles over my leggings, moving closer to my core with each pass. "I've been looking forward to this all week."

"Me too."

I unhook my bra, slip it off, and toss it on the floor.

Coop exhales through gritted teeth and then his hands are skating up my sides, cupping my breasts, kneading and exploring, thumbs sweeping across the rosy peaks. His hands are warm and his movements sure as he sits up and takes my right breast into his mouth, nipping and sucking and teasing.

My eyes drift shut and the world fades away.

It's just me and Cooper and pleasure.

I arch into his touch and he devours me like a starving man. His teeth clamp down on my nipple and I moan as a delicious wave of pleasure/pain radiates through my limbs.

Being with Coop feels so natural. So right. *Safe.*

Gone are my inhibitions. My fears. My bad-freaking-luck.

I'd give anything to hold on to this feeling of liberation.

But I've only got one night. One night to throw all my inhibitions out the window.

I grab the hem of Coop's t-shirt and pull it over his head, forcing him to release my breast as I reveal the six-pack abs that have starred in my fantasies every night this week.

Though it's mid-October, his skin still has the golden-brown hue of a summer tan, something I haven't experienced a day in my life. I can't leave the house without SPF 50 or I burn to a crisp.

He looks up at me with hooded eyes and then we're kissing again, his fingers tangled in my hair as I scrape my nails over his pecs, exploring every ridge and plane of his muscular torso.

The ache between my legs reaches a fever pitch and I roll my hips, grinding shamelessly against his cock. Coop groans and I repeat the motion, savoring every sinful inch.

It feels incredible, but it's not enough.

I need more.

"We should take off our pants."

Coop grins. "I like the way you think."

He flips me over with mind-blowing speed and before I can catch my breath, he's stripping off my leggings, that hungry look in his eyes as he peels them down over my calves, leaving me naked before him.

I'm splayed out like an offering—*one sacrificial virgin coming right up*—but I don't feel self-conscious.

I just feel...ready.

It's taken seven weeks to get here, but I wouldn't change a thing. Maybe the universe did me a solid when Cooper carried me out of Sig Chi that first night, because instead of losing my virginity to a guy who couldn't even remember my name, I'm going to give it to a man who will put my comfort—my pleasure—first.

Who needs love when you've got a friend like Cooper?

I smile up at him, a new kind of warmth filling my chest. "I'm glad it was you in that hotel room. There's no one else I'd trust with my body."

Coop freezes, fingers gripping the waistband of his sweatpants. His cock strains against the soft gray fabric, proof he's as ready as I am.

Finally.

His ears turn a violent shade of red and he mumbles something that sounds like, "I'll be right back."

Then he turns and disappears into the bathroom without a backward glance. I sit up and watch in disbelief as he closes the door, leaving me naked and alone in his bed, virginity intact.

What the ever-loving fuck just happened?

31

COOPER

Fuck. Fuck. Fuck.

I brace my palms on the bathroom counter, replaying the last thirty seconds in my head.

Quinn's admission; it was too much.

My muscles locked up, and I couldn't move. I just stared down at her, stretched out before me like a gift I didn't deserve, that fiery hair splayed across my pillow, miles of soft, creamy skin on display. The moment she met my gaze, her emerald eyes churning with desire, my chest had tightened.

And like a complete jackass, you bolted.

I stare at my reflection in the mirror, cursing my stupidity.

Is this what it feels like to crack under pressure?

Impossible. I'm a DI athlete. I *thrive* on pressure.

Maybe it's performance anxiety.

No fucking way. Cooper DeLaurentis doesn't get performance anxiety.

Still, I glance down. Just in case.

My dick is still hard, tenting the front of my sweatpants.

I exhale, the breath rushing out of me in a screwed-up combination of relief and frustration.

This can't be happening. It's like some Freaky Friday shit. Quinn's ready to go and I'm hiding in the bathroom having a goddamn crisis of conscience.

And what do you think Quinn is doing right now?

Probably freaking out. Thinking I'm another asshole who's going to bail on her.

Condoms. I'll tell her I forgot the condoms. I put some in the nightstand earlier, but she doesn't know that.

I open the lower cabinet and grab a strip of foil squares before turning my attention back to the asshole in the mirror.

"Chill the fuck out." I glare at my reflection. "You can do this. It's one night. Not even you can destroy a person in one night."

Don't be so sure about that.

Fuck. The last thing I want to do is hurt Quinn.

Which is why I'm going to go slow and make sure her first time is perfect.

Then we can go back to being friends. Or strangers. Or whatever.

I scrub a hand over my face. The last time I felt this insecure, I was fifteen and lost my virginity to a cheerleader two years my senior. I'd been wasted, and it certainly hadn't been special for either of us.

Quinn deserves better.

Hell, I'm going to make it so good the next asshole who touches her will have to work twice as hard to make her come.

The thought leaves a sour taste in my mouth, but I shrug it off.

What she does after tonight is none of my business.

I roll my shoulders and turn from the mirror, yanking the door open.

Quinn's sitting on the edge of the bed, arms wrapped around herself as *The Witcher* plays quietly in the background.

"Sorry about that." I flash a smile and hold up the condoms. "Figured we'd need these before we go any further."

Her eyes widen, and fuck me, I feel like the world's biggest prick for bolting.

"I thought maybe you changed your mind."

"Not a chance." I approach the bed like a lion stalking its prey and toss the condoms on the nightstand. I gesture between us. "This is happening, and no cosmic interference is going to stop us tonight."

Quinn slips off the bed, standing naked and gorgeous before me. She reaches for the waistband on my pants, but I capture her wrists, pinning them between us as I claim her mouth, pouring all my pent-up frustration and desire into the kiss.

She moans softly and then she's biting my lower lip, pulling it gently between her teeth.

White-hot need explodes at the base of my spine and my balls draw up so tight the slightest breeze would probably set me off.

"So fucking sexy." I push her back onto the bed. A slow flush fills her cheeks as I drop to my knees before her. "Sweet too, if I remember correctly."

There's nothing I'd like more than to bury myself between her thighs, but I haven't forgotten my promise.

Hell, I've been looking forward to this all week.

Just the thought of Quinn coming on my tongue has my mouth watering.

Without prompting, she spreads her legs.

I spread them wider.

"Good girl."

She's already wet, the soft pink folds of her pussy glistening like a goddamn peach.

I don't waste another second. I lower my mouth and feast.

Quinn writhes as I work her with my tongue, licking every

luscious inch of her. I grip her thighs, holding her in place as she threads her fingers through my hair, pulling me closer.

"I could do this all night," I murmur, circling her clit with my tongue and sucking hard.

She cries out, arching her back and pulling my hair, her inhibitions forgotten.

Pride swells in my chest and I lap at her tender flesh with renewed vigor, sliding a finger into her tight channel.

"So fucking tight."

She whimpers as I slip another digit inside, and it doesn't take long for those needy sounds to morph into eager pleas.

"Cooper. I need you inside me." She bites her lip, the now familiar vulnerability lighting her eyes as she looks down at me. "Please. Before something goes wrong."

"Nothing's going to go wrong." I won't let it. This is her night. "But if that's what you want—"

"It is."

I nod and climb to my feet, stripping off my sweatpants.

I couldn't deny her, even if I wanted to. Not when she's looking at me like I'm the answer to her prayers.

It's a dangerous thought, but I cast it off. I'm not about to get tangled up in my head again.

I made a promise to Quinn, and I intend to keep it.

Her eyes go wide at the sight of my cock and she licks her lips, incinerating all rational thought.

I want this girl so bad it fucking hurts.

My balls ache as I grab a condom from the nightstand and tear it open.

Quinn watches as I roll it over my length, but says nothing.

Then she scoots back on the bed and I nudge her thighs apart as I stretch out above her, her hardened nipples grazing my chest in a promise of things to come. I prop myself up on one arm and position myself at her entrance as she looks up at me from under her lashes.

Say something.

I search for the right words, but come up empty. I've never been great with words. Actions on the other hand... I cup her cheek and lower my mouth to hers. The kiss is slow and languid. A silent reminder that we have all night. That we don't have to rush.

That I'll be ready when she is, whether it's right now or six hours from now.

"I'm ready." Her voice is steady and firm, and I won't insult her by asking if she's sure.

Quinn's made up her mind, and she knows exactly what she wants.

I brush my lips against hers, nipping at the tender flesh as I slowly sink into her, inch by painstaking inch.

She tenses beneath me, fingers digging into my lower back, and I freeze, tension coiling between my shoulder blades.

"Don't stop."

Her eyes lock on mine and something passes between us. An unspoken request.

With one quick thrust, I bury myself to the hilt.

Our hips slam together and electricity sizzles up my spine.

Quinn gasps and I pepper kisses along her neck and jaw as her body adjusts to my size. When I make my way back to her mouth, she crushes her lips to mine, the kiss hot and hungry and full of longing as her tongue mates with my own, caressing and probing and begging for more.

She whimpers and I begin to move. Slowly. So slowly. I pull out and sink back into her wet heat, knowing this is as close to heaven as I'll ever get.

It's fucking torture—*the best possible kind.*

The need to bury myself hard and fast is nearly impossible

to resist, but as Quinn relaxes, her limbs become fluid. Her hands skate down my back, a slow, steady exploration that feels better than it should.

At first, her touch is feather-light, but then she's gripping my ass, begging me with her eyes and actions, encouraging me to move faster.

Harder.

Deeper.

Our bodies crash together in perfect harmony, the sound of our heated flesh slapping together, driving my arousal to new, maddening heights.

She moans and then she's grinding against me, nails digging into my shoulders as she rolls her hips, chasing her own pleasure.

"That's right, sweetheart. Use me. Use me however you want. I can take it."

That last bit might be a lie. Sweat beads along my hairline and I'm so close to coming it's taking all my self-control to hold my orgasm at bay, but no way am I going to come first.

I roll my pelvis, angling for the spot that will give her the most intense orgasm.

She whimpers and I do it again, repeating the motion over and over until she's panting for breath, begging for release.

"I'm going to—" She cries out, my name on her lips as her muscles contract with pleasure.

Quinn's face is fucking radiant when she climaxes, eyes bright, lips parted, and the way she says my name, chanting it like a prayer, has me pumping harder, faster, desperate to deliver every last drop of pleasure her sweet little body can handle.

Her pussy grips me tight and in just a few more strokes, I'm chasing her over the edge.

My orgasm explodes like a sonic blast, the shock waves pulsing through my limbs with no end and no beginning as I give one last thrust, burying myself so deep I can't tell where I end and Quinn begins.

I hold her tight, riding out the aftershocks of my orgasm as a shy, sated smile curves her heart-shaped lips.

"That was..." She pauses, as if searching for the right words, and my pulse spikes. "Well worth the wait."

"Damn, right." I pinch her ass and she squeals, wriggling beneath me. "The best things in life are always worth the wait."

Truth. I'm one lucky bastard to be sharing this moment with her.

After, we lay entangled, a mess of arms and legs and blazing red hair and—

Holy shit. I can't feel my toes.

Maybe virgin vaginas really are magical because that was the best damn orgasm of my life.

Or maybe it was just that good with Quinn.

We have chemistry. There's no denying it. But could sex be like that every time?

There's only one way to find out.

I reach for her just as she climbs out of bed. Oblivious, she picks up her discarded sweatshirt, fumbling to turn it right side out.

I push myself up on my elbow. "What are you doing?"

"Getting dressed."

I glance at the clock on the nightstand. It's barely ten.

"I came over to have sex and we did it, so..." She gestures awkwardly at the door.

"You're not going anywhere, sweetheart." I crook my finger and gesture for her to return to bed. "We're not finished here."

32

QUINN

CONSCIOUSNESS TUGS at me and I pull the blanket over my head, blocking out the bright rays of sunshine determined to pry my eyelids open.

Just five more minutes.

The alarm hasn't even gone off yet.

Shit. Did I forget to set it?

I blink awake slowly, a thick fog muddling my thoughts. It's dark under the covers. Warm. Cozy. And there's a comforting weight across my midsection.

I glance down to find a muscular forearm curled around my waist.

Cooper.

The memories of our night together come rushing back, the warmth in my chest expanding until it's possible I'm glowing from the inside out.

I had sex last night.

Three times.

And it was...intense.

I didn't even know it could be like that.

I've had plenty of orgasms courtesy of my vibrator, but they were like foreplay compared to sex with Coop.

Now, here I am, curled up in his arms, my back pressed to the hard planes of his chest, soaking up his body heat and savoring the warm afterglow of great sex.

Oh, no.

I'm wrapped in Coop's arms.

That's a direct violation of our no strings agreement.

Dammit. I never should've slept over. But I'd been so tired after the second time that I just crashed, and then we had sex again around four and—

I need to go. *Now.*

Coop already has an irrational fear of virgins. Waking to find one curled up against him like a lovesick fool probably qualifies as his own ninth circle of hell. I need to get out of this bed before he wakes up and decides I'm planning our freaking wedding.

So not happening.

We agreed this was a onetime deal and I have no plans to get attached.

I lie still, hardly daring to breathe as I listen to the steady rise and fall of his chest. When I'm certain he's out cold, I gently lift his arm and slip out of bed. He's stretched out on his side, hair adorably sleep mussed and sticking up at odd angles. Blond stubble lines his jaw and heat floods my body at the memory of it scraping against my thighs last night.

Coop really is a man of many talents.

But I doubt awkward morning after conversation is one of them.

I scoop up my sweatshirt and leggings, noting the pleasant soreness between my legs.

Marathon sex will do that to a girl.

Does three times count as marathon sex?

I'll have to ask Haley.

Later.

Right. Clothes. I scan the room, but my bra and panties are nowhere in sight.

I tiptoe around the bed and find my bra peeking out from under Coop's side, but no amount of searching reveals my very expensive, very lacy panties.

A small price to pay for amazing sex.

I tug on my leggings and dress quickly before slipping into the hall and closing the door silently behind me.

The house is quiet as I make my way downstairs and I'm just about to let myself out the front door when I realize I don't have my keys.

Shit.

My chest tightens and I rack my brain, trying to remember the last time I had them.

Did I put them on the kitchen counter when I came in?

I head for the kitchen and as I near the entry, I see my Wildcat keyring laying on the counter.

Thank God.

The prospect of sneaking back into Coop's room to search is unthinkable. I hurry in and grab the keys. Just as I'm turning back to the door, there's a blur of movement to my right.

A startled cry bursts from my lips and my soul exits my body as Austin Reid, Waverly's star quarterback, closes the fridge.

"Sorry." He sets the bottle of orange juice he's holding on the counter and I can't help but notice his clothes have the same wrinkled look as my own. "I didn't mean to scare you."

"No worries," I squeak, voice high and pitchy.

Holy-freaking-shit.

I'm talking to Austin Reid and I'm not wearing any underpants.

Will he know?

Of course he will.

I probably smell like sex and have a wicked case of bedhead. Plus, there's the whole sneaking out of the townhouse at the ass crack of dawn, doing the walk of shame.

Well, maybe not shame, because there's not an ounce of that in my body right now.

What Coop and I shared was amazing.

Reid cocks his head and peers around me. "Are you a friend of Parker's?"

"No."

His brows shoot up, transforming his face into a mask of surprise. "Vaughn?"

"Um, no."

Reid's surprise turns to suspicion, and his jaw hardens. "Did you sneak in? Do I need to call campus security?"

"What? No." This is getting really awkward. Maybe I can just—

"Bruh."

I spin to see DJ Parker—sans shirt—scratching the back of his head as he looks me over. Vaughn is right behind him, his giant body filling the doorway to the living room and blocking my only escape route.

Damn. They're stealthy for big guys. I didn't even hear them approach.

"Is this another one of Coop's stalkers?" Parker steps around me and grabs the bottle of juice off the counter. "It's too damn early for that shit." He turns to me. "No offense."

"None taken." Heat floods my cheeks. Is this some kind of joke? "I'm not a stalker."

Parker smirks. "Yeah, that's what they all say."

"All?" I can't even hide my disbelief. This is too freaking weird. I knew Coop lived with other players, but meeting guys I've only ever seen on tv or online with no goddamn panties is not how I pictured this morning going. "You mean this has happened before?"

"So you admit you're a stalker?" Parker glances at Vaughn. "You're getting all this, right?"

Vaughn just shakes his head, a gesture that's twice as intimidating given his massive beard.

"No. I just meant..." I turn to Reid, but his face is impassive. *No help there.* "You can't be serious. Do I look like a stalker?"

"That's the thing, isn't it?" Parker opens a cabinet and pulls out a glass. "No one looks like a stalker." He pauses, like he's actually considering it. "Except that weird dude with the knit cap who hangs out on the corner of College Ave and Pullman. That dude definitely has a stalker vibe."

"Marty?" Vaughn moves to lean against the counter.

Parker rolls his eyes like we're all sharing some inside joke. "Of course Vaughn knows his name."

"What?" Vaughn frowns. "He's a good dude. Just down on his luck. I bring him sandwiches sometimes."

Parker's right. It's too early for this crap.

"Um, can we just?" I gesture toward the door. "You know what? I'm going to go."

I make it all of two steps.

"Not so fast." Reid plants his hands on his hips. "You still haven't told us how you got in."

Un-freaking-believable.

Clearly the universe is trying to make up for lost time since last night was disaster free. It's the only explanation for the fact that every single of one of Coop's roommates is in this kitchen grilling me instead of sleeping off a hangover.

"Oh, my God." I throw up my hands. "I told you. I'm not a stalker."

"There's no rule that says stalkers can't be hot." Parker twists the top off the juice bottle, and I watch, dumbstruck, as he fills his glass. “Besides, it wouldn’t be the first time.”

Wait. Does that mean Cooper had an honest to God stalker?

I have to know. “Are you serious?”

Parker huffs out a breath, a sly smile curving his full mouth. “It’s happened like three times.”

I guess that explains the virgin rule.

“I believe they call that a trifecta,” Vaughn deadpans.

I scan their faces. “Is it really so hard to believe Cooper invited me over?”

“YES,” they respond in unison.

Well, then.

“He’s never invited a girl over.” Reid arches a brow. “And he definitely doesn’t do sleepovers.”

Oh, for fuck’s sake. This is what I get for sleeping with a guy who has a harem of women trailing after him. I have no one to blame but myself for this trainwreck.

“I have an idea.” I jangle my keys. “How about I leave and we all pretend this never happened? Cool?”

I turn on my heel, not waiting for a reply, and trip over my untied shoelaces.

Vaughn darts forward, catching me before I faceplant on the hardwood floor.

Despite his imposing size, his hands are gentle as he rights me.

“You okay?” he asks, voice gruff.

“Other than my pride?”

That gets a smile out of him. “Pride is overrated.”

“Thanks.”

“Oh, shit.” Parker slaps his palm on the counter. “I knew you looked familiar. You’re the girl from the dunk tank, right?”

I tip my head to the ceiling and sigh. “If I say yes, can we forget this entire conversation ever happened?”

Reid chuckles, but it's Vaughn who responds.

"If you say yes, I'm going to make you breakfast." He grins and bumps my shoulder. "Forget trouncing Ohio. Seeing Coop take an ice bath was the highlight of my HoCo reel."

"Glad I could be of service." I gesture toward the door. "This has been fun and all, but I've got to go. You know how it is." I smile sweetly. "A stalker's work is never done."

They howl with laughter as I haul ass for the front door, silently praying Coop is still sound asleep upstairs.

33

COOPER

THE SCENT of frying bacon greets me as I enter the kitchen and my stomach rumbles in a Pavlovian response.

No surprise there.

I'm starving and I didn't get much sleep.

Worth it.

Last night was incredible. Best sex of my life, in fact. Not to brag or whatever, but that's saying something because I've had my share of hookups.

It was different with Quinn, though. She was so damn responsive, her appetite ravenous. Best of all, not one thing went wrong.

At least, not until I woke up and found her side of the bed empty.

Talk about a kick in the nuts. I didn't even hear her slip out.

Did she wake up with regrets?

Not possible.

Quinn enjoyed her time in my bed. Her actions—her words—are proof enough.

So why did she sneak out like a thief in the night?

Probably because some asshole made it clear he didn't do strings, including morning afters.

"What'd I tell you?" Parker smirks at me from the kitchen table where he's nursing a glass of OJ. "Our boy can't resist the smell of frying meat."

I ignore him and pour myself a glass of juice from the bottle on the counter.

Vaughn's busy at the stove, scrambling eggs, and Reid is playing sous chef, chopping fruit right next to him. They both turn, giving me curious stares.

"What?" It's not unusual for us to have breakfast together, but they're all giving off weird vibes and I'm too tired to play guessing games this morning.

"Now the real fun begins." Parker rubs his hands together like an old school villain. "Where should we start?"

I empty my glass in three long gulps. "As usual, I have no idea what you're talking about."

Though I'd be lying if I said I didn't have my suspicions. That they're all up so early after a night out isn't what you'd call typical. Especially on a bye week. We don't get a lot of opportunities to sleep in during the season, and they're never wasted.

"Come on, man. Don't keep us in suspense." Parker rocks his chair backward, balancing on two legs. "We know you had a sleepover with the dunk tank girl."

So much for hooking up on the DL.

It's only a big deal if you make it a big deal.

I grab some plates from the cabinet and set the table. "So?"

Reid and Vaughn exchange a look, but say nothing as they carry food to the table.

"So," Parker says, dragging the word out. "Cooper DeLaurentis doesn't do sleepovers."

I shrug. He's right, but it's not like I can explain the situation. I'm not even sure I understand it.

"Just tell me one thing," he presses. "What exactly does a Cooper DeLaurentis sleepover include? Was there cuddling? Did you whisper sweet nothings in her ear?"

I shoot him a dark look and raise my middle finger. "I don't kiss and tell, asshole."

True, but I'm also kind of freaked out. I've never had a girl sleep over before. I hadn't planned for Quinn to stay the night. One thing led to another and it just sort of happened.

Not that I'm complaining.

Hell, I was hoping for morning sex.

"They probably stayed up late braiding each other's hair," Vaughn says, laughing at his own joke.

"Come on, man. Give us something." Parker makes a pouty face. It's pathetic as fuck and has zero chance of changing my mind. "At least tell us if she's the same girl who gave you the stitches on Homecoming?"

"She didn't give me the stitches."

That was just bad luck. The worst kind.

Parker doesn't miss a beat. "But it was the same girl?"

I ignore him and shovel food onto my plate, piling it high with fruit and protein. Bacon isn't strictly on my diet, but I'm feeling too damn good to care, despite the fact that my roommates are busting my balls.

Vaughn drops into the seat next to me. "At least he didn't end up in the ER this time."

"Maybe that knock on the head rebooted his system." Parker leans forward, the front legs of his chair crashing to the floor. "Are you going to quit playing the field and wife up?"

Vaughn snorts and scoops fruit onto his plate. "I'll believe it when I see it. Coop doesn't know how to keep his dick in his pants."

I spear a piece of melon with my fork. "You make it sound like I just walk around whipping it out all over campus."

I haven't done that since freshman year. I'm older and wiser now.

Reid shoots me a meaningful look. "She's a regular at Sig Chi, right?"

Jesus. Not him, too.

"Relax. She's not dating one of the brothers." I'm all about no strings sex, but I'm not a complete prick. "She's Noah's sister."

Reid freezes with his fork halfway to his mouth. "Dude. That's ten times worse."

No kidding.

"What the hell were you thinking?" he asks, dropping the fork to his plate.

"From the sounds of it," Vaughn deadpans, "there wasn't a lot of thinking involved."

Parker snickers. "So much for rule number two."

I scrub a hand over my face.

"Quinn is an adult with her own free will and agency." Which is all well and good until Noah finds out I slept with her. "That said, it's probably best if Noah doesn't find out."

Reid curses. "This has disaster written all over it. Noah will lose his shit if this ends up on social media."

No chance of that happening.

"It was a onetime thing. Quinn won't tell anyone. She's not the bag 'n' tag type."

It's one of the things I like best about her. She doesn't treat me like some untouchable football god. She sees me for exactly who I am now—not for my NFL potential—and she doesn't hesitate to call me out when I deserve it.

Which is why I can't believe she left this morning without even saying goodbye.

If we weren't friends, I might feel used.

What's the protocol here, anyway? Should I call and check up on her?

No, that's stupid.

You could ask Vaughn.

He's the only guy I know who's legitimately in touch with his feelings.

My gaze slides to the Bearded Wonder. He's slicing his fruit like Miss Manners is going to pop in and evaluate his technique at any minute.

Vaughn must sense me staring at him, because he looks up. "What?"

I smirk. "Nothing. Just admiring your delicate table manners."

"Watch carefully," he shoots back. "I'm sure you could learn a thing or twenty."

Yeah, there's no way am I asking him for advice. I'd never hear the end of it.

Which reminds me...

I turn to Reid. "Where did you spend the night? I noticed your bed wasn't slept in."

He scrapes the last of the eggs from his plate and pops them in his mouth, taking his sweet ass time. "The high school recruits kept me busy."

It sounds like a bullshit excuse to me, but what do I know? Coach would never ask me to babysit a bunch of eager minors. Just another perk of my well-deserved reputation.

Parker narrows his eyes. "They kept you busy *all* night?"

"I asked Johnson to watch them for a couple of hours while I was at study group, so naturally he got them wasted." Reid stands and collects the empty dishes. "I came back to find them puking their guts out and then campus police showed up."

Parker grimaces. "Coach is gonna be pissed."

"They didn't take names." Reid shrugs, not meeting my stare. "With any luck, Coach won't find out."

Yeah-fucking-right.

There's more to the story. Something Reid isn't saying. I've known him long enough to know when he's holding back, but I've got my own problems to deal with right now. If he wants to talk, he knows where to find me.

I slide my phone out of my pocket and pull up my messages.

Nothing.

Disappointment nips at my consciousness, but I shut that shit down.

Getting up in your feelings never solves anything. Better to take action.

Like texting Quinn.

To make sure she got home safely.

I tap out a quick message, my thumb hovering over the send button.

What am I doing? I'm not the kind of guy who texts the morning after. It sends the wrong message. One that implies strings.

I tap the backspace key, deleting the message one letter at a time.

If Quinn needs something, she'll let me know.

Just like she said goodbye this morning?

She's never been shy before.

There's a first time for everything.

Screw it. I'm overcomplicating things. It's a text message. Not a marriage proposal.

I retype the message, but I still can't bring myself to press send.

"Forget about the recruits," Reid says, voice slicing through my thoughts. "We need to buckle down and focus on this week's game. Wisconsin's looking good. They're going to make us work for it."

He's right. I need to get my head on straight. National titles don't win themselves. We're 6-1. This isn't the time to get distracted. We lose another game and we can kiss our championship run goodbye.

Plus, Coach let slip that there will be NFL scouts in the stands this week.

No pressure.

I stand and lock my phone, dropping it in my pocket. "Who's up for a run?"

Surely six miles around campus will be enough to pound all thoughts of Quinn from my head.

34

QUINN

SEX HAS ADDLED MY BRAIN.

It's Monday evening and I haven't been able to think of anything but orgasms for the last thirty-six hours. It's becoming a real problem, especially since Call-Me-David caught me daydreaming in Creative Nonfiction this morning. Priya bailed me out, but I didn't miss the disapproving way he stared at me for the rest of the class.

I'm sure it won't affect my grade on the latest assignment.

Yeah, right.

I sigh and return my attention to the laptop balanced on my knees. The article I've just written for The Collegian is ready to submit, but I can't bring myself to press send. I'd hoped—naïvely—that writing about my night with Coop would curb my rampant desire, but it seems to have had the opposite effect.

My gaze slides to the nightstand.

There's no rule that says you can't masturbate at 8pm on a Monday.

True, but I'm not sure my rabbit vibrator can live up to the reality of sex with Cooper.

Or the fantasies that have since taken up residence in my head.

So. Many. Fantasies.

All of which will go unfulfilled, since our hookup was a onetime deal.

Stupid-freaking-rules.

Heat pools between my legs and I squirm, my backside burrowing into the soft mattress.

So much for satisfying my craving by writing about my night of toe-curling, mind-blowing, life-altering sex.

If anything, it's amplified my need.

Who knew losing your virginity could leave you in a permanent state of lust?

Only every sexually active person ever.

It would certainly explain Haley and Bryan's on-again, off-again relationship.

After all, they say makeup sex is the best kind of sex.

Yeah, this train of thought so isn't helping.

I force my attention back to the article on-screen, my mouse hovering over the submit button.

Why am I even hesitating?

Because sharing the intimate details of your life with forty-thousand strangers is no joke.

It's never stopped me before.

I've written about embarrassing moments. Failed hookups. Awkward *I-wouldn't-believe-it-if-it-hadn't-happened-to-me* encounters of the humiliating variety.

This feels different. For the first time, I'm not sure I want to share my story. I want to keep my night with Cooper for myself.

Because it was your first time or because you're catching feelings?

I stiffen. The former, obviously.

Even I'm not foolish enough to fall for a guy who thinks commitment is a four-letter word.

Coop doesn't do relationships. Until two nights ago, he'd never even invited a woman over.

When he confessed as much, I'd thought it was a line. That he was telling me what he thought I wanted to hear.

Sunday morning's inquisition proved me wrong.

The way his roommates grilled me would've been comical if it had happened to someone else.

Which is pretty much my entire brand.

Still, I can't deny I'm flattered he made an exception for me.

Despite Coop's reputation, he's not the obnoxious player he pretends to be. Under all the swagger and sarcasm, he's got a big heart. One he clearly feels the need to hide behind that infuriating smirk.

The realization fills my chest with warmth.

Because we're friends. Not because I'm falling for him.

That's a one-way road to heartbreak.

Which is why my time is better spent focusing on my term paper for Call-Me-David. Now that I've dealt with the pesky problem of my virginity, I can turn my full attention to not failing Creative Nonfiction.

Wishful thinking, sis.

Unfortunately, that doesn't change the fact that I have five weeks to write a twenty-page essay on a lesson or experience that shaped me in some way.

I scrape my hair into a ponytail and secure it with a scrunchie from the nightstand.

There has to be something I can write about.

Like having sex for the first time?

I bite my lip. It's been done before, and it'll be done again, but could I actually do it? I'm not sure I could look Call-Me-David in the eye afterward. Not when my name will be printed at the top of the paper.

Then again, it's not like I've got a lot of other options.

Ugh. Why did I ever think it was a good idea to sign up for this class?

Because you enjoy writing and virtually every degree you've considered requires it.

I huff out a breath. I hate it when my subconscious is the voice of reason.

My phone buzzes with an incoming text, and, grateful for the distraction, I grab it off the nightstand.

Cooper: How's my favorite ginger?

I grin and flop back on my tower of pillows.

Me: I thought Emma Stone was your favorite ginger?

There's a long pause before the floating dots appear, but I wait him out because the alternative is working on the essay from hell.

*Cooper: You're moving up in the world. *winking emoji**

Eat your heart out, Emma Stone.

Cooper: You good?

I stare at the screen, unsure how to answer. On the surface, it's a straightforward question, but there are a million ways to interpret it. He could be asking about my day, my health, or the fact that we screwed our brains out on Saturday night. His meaning is anyone's guess.

So, like the coward I am, I take the easy way out.

Me: Yeah. You?

Cooper: Rough practice. No one told Coach that corporal punishment was canceled. Swear to God, the man is a sadist. I couldn't do another burpee if I wanted to.

Me: Oof. What did you do?

Cooper: Why do you assume I did something?

I laugh as I type my reply.

Me: Because I've met you.

*Cooper: Fair enough, but this time I'm entirely innocent. *angel emoji**

I snort. We both know he doesn't have an innocent bone in his body. Frankly, it's one of his more endearing qualities.

Cooper: A couple of guys on the team got into a scuffle with the baseball team. They were talking trash about Carter.

Because she's a woman. He doesn't say it, but he doesn't have to. She's killing it on the field, so what else could it be?

Me: Misogynistic pricks.

Cooper: Right? Maybe you can put that in your next article.

Me: Not likely. My editor has this whole thing about avoiding defamation lawsuits.

There's a lull in the conversation and I turn my attention back to my laptop. Maybe I can pull a few lines out of this article as a jumping off point for my paper, though I'm still not sure what the overarching theme would be.

How *did* sex change my life?

Aside from the obvious, it's too early to tell.

My phone buzzes and another message pops up.

Cooper: Let me get this straight. You can write about your sexploits, but you can't write a hit piece on the baseball team? So much for freedom of the press.

I snort-laugh and mentally add sexploits to my vocabulary.

Me: Thanks again for Saturday night. I owe you one.

Cooper: You don't owe me anything. Trust me, I had a great time.

My pulse quickens and that molten heat returns to my core.

Fan-freaking-tastic. Now all it takes is a text for me to get aroused.

Me: I wish there was something I could do to return the favor.

The instant I press send, I reread the message and groan. Nothing says thirsty like sending suggestive texts to your commitment phobic one-night stand.

Cooper: It's all good. Anyway, I just wanted to make sure you were okay.

I stare at the message, brow furrowed, before typing a reply.

Me: Why wouldn't I be okay?

Cooper: I've heard some women are sore after their first time and since we did it three times...

I can almost see his ears turning red as he types. It's sweet that he cares enough to check in, and it proves my theory that he's not the arrogant player he pretends to be—not entirely anyway—but that doesn't mean I can't give him a hard time.

Me: And you figured that since you're SO big, I must be one of those women?

The floating dots appear, and I laugh out loud when a Big Dick Energy meme pops up on the screen. My fingers fly over the keyboard as I type my reply.

Me: I don't think that phrase means what you think it does. Go look it up. I'll wait.

35

COOPER

"I KNOW what Big Dick Energy is," I mutter, opening the browser on my phone.

I've got BDE in spades.

"What are you mumbling about?" Parker leans over to peer at my screen.

The entire football team is holed up in the academic center for study hall. Like practice, it's a requirement for student athletes to ensure we maintain passing grades.

My roommates and I share a table in the back corner of the room, but despite the open laptop and stack of textbooks before me, I haven't gotten much done.

I'm too damn tired to think, thanks to Coach Collins and the practice from hell.

Just the thought of physical activity is enough to make me hurl right now.

So, yeah, I should be working on this week's case study for my International Relations class, but I'm not feeling it.

Talking to Quinn is far more interesting.

"You can Google BDE all you want," Parker says, smirking.

"But the only way you're going to get it is if Reid's energy rubs off on you."

"We should be so lucky." Vaughn looks up from his laptop, gaze sliding from me to Parker. "If it hasn't happened by now, it's never going to happen."

Ignoring them, I read the definition filling my screen.

Big Dick Energy (noun): Understated but unshakeable self-confidence. Confidence without cockiness.

Well, shit. Quinn was right. Talk about a misnomer.

I close the browser and type my reply.

Me: Quiet confidence is overrated.

Quiet confidence doesn't get one hundred thousand screaming Wildcat fans on their feet. It doesn't get the talking heads excited. Doesn't attract scouts from all over the country.

Unless you're Reid. Somehow, he makes it look easy.

If he wasn't my best friend, I'd envy him.

"Forget BDE." Parker pretends to study me. "What you've got is more like fuckboy vibes."

"Fuckboy implies manipulation." I smirk. "I don't have to manipulate women to get laid. My partners know where I stand on relationships."

Which is probably why Quinn snuck out without saying goodbye.

Whatever. The rules exist for a reason and no matter how cool she is, I can't go breaking them. Not now.

Not when I'm so close to getting out from under my father's thumb.

The knowledge doesn't change the fact that I enjoy talking to Quinn.

She's funny. Real. The kind of girl my mom would like.

The kind of girl you'd break, given the opportunity.

Not happening. We're just friends.

That we can text without resorting to dick pics and sexts is refreshing. Not that I'd ever send a dick pic because the internet is forever and my mom doesn't need to see that shit, but I've gotten my fair share of tit shots.

None of them can compare to Quinn.

Just the thought of her perfect tits has my cock stirring.

I'll have to work on that. I've never been friends with a woman before, but I'm pretty sure there's a rule that prohibits hard-ons.

My phone vibrates and I pick it up, expecting a response from Quinn. No such luck. It's my second favorite Mowery.

Noah: Halloween party. Saturday night. Bring your boys. We'll celebrate your win over the Badgers.

Fuck yeah, we will.

Wisconsin's defense is solid, but Reid and I have been studying their game tape. Our O-line will be ready. This time next week, we'll be 7-1.

One step closer to the championship game.

Me: We'll be there.

I've got the perfect costume.

"Halloween party at the Sig house Saturday night," I announce.

"I'm down." Parker taps his pen on the table. "Think I can go as a Big Ten football player again?"

"That's lame as hell." Vaughn gives him the side-eye. "Why bother dressing up if you aren't even going to try?"

I chuckle. "Relax, Chewbacca. Not all of us have an organic costume."

Across from me, Reid chokes on a laugh.

"Or were you planning to go as Hagrid this year?"

Vaughn strokes his beard. "My shit is way neater than Hagrid's."

"Keep telling yourself that, O' Bearded One."

"For fuck's sake. If I feed you, will you guys shut up already?"

Reid pushes his textbook aside and upends his bag. Protein bars, trail mix, and apples tumble out, forming a munchie mound in the center of the table. "Some of us actually need to study."

We descend on the food like a pack of ravenous wolves.

I grab a protein bar and tear it open. "You always did know the way to my heart."

"Yeah, well, the way to mine is silence," he shoots back, repositioning his textbook. "I have an exam in career management and I've got to pull at least a B."

At that, we all pipe down. It's no secret Reid works hard to make grades and none of us wants to be the reason he misses the Dean's List. It shouldn't matter. He's the captain of the team and one of the best damn quarterbacks in the country. His future is with the NFL, but he's clearly taken Coach's lectures about the Waverly tradition of academic excellence to heart.

I delete Noah's text and open the conversation with Quinn. She still hasn't responded, but it's all good.

I'm confident enough to text twice in a row.

Me: Will I see you at the Sig Halloween party this weekend, or are you done with Greek Row now that you've completed your mission?

I devour the protein bar while I wait for a reply. It's bland and gritty, but beggars can't be choosers. I'm shining an apple on my shirt when she finally responds.

*Quinn: *shrugging emoji* I may swing by for a bit. See what trouble I can get into. What about you?*

Me: I'll be there. I've already got my costume.

It's a classic.

Quinn: Oh? Do tell.

Quinn: No, wait. Let me guess. Han Solo?

A slow grin spreads across my face as I type a reply.

Me: The only way I'm going as Han is if you go as Leia.

Quinn: Hard pass. Can you imagine me in a white dress?

Yes. Yes, I can. It would be fucking glorious. All that sexy red hair coiled in tight buns, just waiting to be unleashed.

Blood rushes to my cock and I have to adjust myself before replying.

Me: If you're worried about stains, you could always wear Leia's iconic gold bikini.

*Quinn: *eyeroll emoji* Yeah, then I'd just have to worry about freezing my ass off.*

And what a sweet little ass it is.

Quinn: If you're not going as Han, what are you going as?

I could tell her, but what would be the fun in that?

Me: If you really want to know, you'll have to swing by Saturday night and see for yourself.

36

QUINN

HALEY and I roll up to the Sig house just before eleven with Bryan and his roommates. We pre-gamed at their apartment, and after two beers, I can see why Haley didn't want to set me up with any of them. Cam and Isaiah are nice enough, but J is severely lacking in the maturity department.

Exhibit A? He's dressed as a banana and has an *Eat Me* sign pinned to his crotch.

The Halloween party is in full swing as we make our way up the front steps, passing a sexy angel/devil duo making out against the railing. The guys hand over a few bills at the door, but Haley and I get in for free because we're awesome like that.

"Think Coop will be here tonight?" Haley asks, adjusting her headdress as the Sig collecting cash doles out red plastic cups.

I don't have time to answer.

"How would Quinn know?" Bryan slings an arm across her bare shoulders. They're dressed as Cleopatra and Mark Antony and Haley's costume is fire, making my black bodysuit look tame by comparison. "Please tell me y'all aren't joining his fan club? He might be a great wide receiver, but the guy is a womanizing douche."

Irritation burns in my gut. No way am I going to stand by while he throws shade. Not when his roommate is wearing an *Eat Me* sign. "Where do you get off calling him a douche? You don't even know him."

"Neither do you," he shoots back.

An impish smile spreads across Haley's lips. "Actually..."

I shake my head. "Drop it, Hales. Let's just have fun, okay?"

I'm not about to let her dish on my night with Cooper just to prove a point. Bryan's entitled to his opinion, even if it's wrong.

Because he is wrong, isn't he?

Haley hooks her arm through mine and pulls me forward, shrugging off Bryan's possessive hold.

The house is vibrating as we enter the crowded foyer, and Nicki Minaj is blaring from the speakers, the loud bass rocking the floorboards beneath our feet. The place is wall-to-wall bodies, as if all of Wildcat Nation came out to celebrate the win over Wisconsin. It's the same all up and down Greek Row, costumed undergrads stumbling from one house to another, plastic cups in hand.

"This is sick!" Haley's eyes go wide at the sight of a girl who, although it's fifty degrees out, appears to be wearing nothing but a few handfuls of strategically placed cotton candy. "Mark my words, this will turn into an orgy before the night is over."

"Did someone say orgy?" J asks, appearing at her side with a lascivious grin. "Count me in."

Haley rolls her eyes and makes a beeline for the keg, pulling me along behind her. "I need another drink before I can deal with that fool."

That makes two of us.

We fill our cups in the living room and it's not long before Bryan and Haley disappear onto the dancefloor, leaving me alone with the three stooges.

"I fucking love Halloween," J says, grin widening as a girl

wearing a sexy gumball machine costume walks past. "I'd stick my coin in her slot any time."

Gross.

I can't believe Bryan even suggested setting me up with this guy.

"Don't be a dick," Cam says, elbowing him in the stomach. "Quinn doesn't want to hear that shit."

"Ignore him," Isaiah adds. "He's NSFV."

"NSFV?" I echo.

"Not safe for virgins."

Heat floods my cheeks and I take a long sip of my beer, hiding my face behind the stupid red cup.

I'm going to kill Bryan. *Painfully*.

"Bruh." Cam shoots Isaiah a WTF look. "Poor form."

"What?" Isaiah looks from Cam to me. "I didn't mean anything by it. Virgins are cool." He gives me a nod. "I used to be one, when I was like fifteen."

Oh. My. God.

This has to be a joke. It can't possibly be my real life.

I tip my beer back and drain the cup.

"I'm going to get another drink." I don't bother adding that I'll be right back, because that would be a lie.

I weave through the crush of sweaty bodies only to discover the keg is kicked.

It'll take a few minutes for the Sigs to bring in a replacement, but I've been to enough of these parties to know there'll be another one in the kitchen. I duck out of line and make my way down the back hall, passing a Squid Game contestant, a guy in a Top Gun flight suit, and a girl wrapped in yellow caution tape.

I do a double take.

Why didn't I think of that?

Because it's my everyday state of being, which probably invalidates it as a costume choice.

It's quieter in the kitchen and there's no line for the keg, so I step right up and grab the faucet. It sputters when I press down, but eventually the amber liquid trickles out. It's slow going and my cup is only half full when I hear a familiar rumble of laughter behind me.

"I've been looking for you all night," Coop says, breath hot against my cheek. "I was starting to think you wouldn't show."

His fingers skim my hip, just the barest contact, as he reaches around to pump the keg. My heart slams against my ribcage and I watch, breath held, as the beer flows freely, filling my cup to the top.

Be cool.

I drop the faucet and turn to face him. He's standing so close my breasts brush his chest, but I doubt he can feel it through his armor. He's dressed as Thor, blond hair scraped back from his face, muscular arms on full display.

It's a good look for him.

Especially the leather pants, which hug his trim hips like they've been painted on.

"Thanks for the assist." I sip my beer, careful not to spill any on my costume. "If you hadn't come along, I'd have been here all night."

He quirks a brow. "Something tells me you would have managed just fine."

"Don't be so sure about that." I grin up at him. "I'm forbidden from ever pumping a keg. House rules."

He leans against the counter and crosses his ankles. "Now this I've got to hear."

Not a chance. He's already heard more than enough embarrassing Quinntastrophe stories.

"Let's just say the last time I tried to pump a keg, things went horribly wrong." I glance around, realizing for the first time that we have the kitchen to ourselves. There's no one else around and despite the loud music pouring in from the hall, it's strangely quiet. "What about you? Why are you hiding out in the kitchen? Shouldn't you be surrounded by your adoring fans?"

He played a great game today. There must be plenty of women eager to help him celebrate.

My stomach twists at the realization.

Coop shrugs. "I'm just here for the candy."

Of course. "You mean the eye candy?"

He smirks and holds up a bowl of Reese's peanut butter cups I hadn't noticed.

Because you were too busy checking out his biceps.

"Shh." He leans in close, whispering conspiratorially. "Don't tell. I'm not supposed to be eating sugar. Or carbs. But these things are my kryptonite."

"Wrong universe, pretty boy." I flash him a teasing smile. "I don't think Thor has a kryptonite."

"Whatever." He preens, lifting his chin and flexing his biceps. "I'd dress up like Superman—I totally have the legs for blue tights—but with this face, Thor is sort of inevitable."

No lies detected.

Until this moment, I've never had a thing for the Asgardian God of Thunder, but I'm currently rethinking my position because Cooper makes those leather pants look damn good.

Better than Geralt?

Abso-freaking-lutely.

"It's like you and this hair." He tugs on one of my curls, igniting a fire in my belly. "Black Widow?"

I nod and sip my beer, not quite trusting myself to speak. What are the odds we'd both show up dressed as Marvel superheroes?

Pretty good, apparently.

"It was this or Jean Grey and—"

"She's got a lot of baggage," he says, finishing my thought.

"Exactly." How is it possible this guy, who takes nothing seriously, gets me when my own family doesn't? I sigh, mentally cursing the universe for being a cruel-ass bitch. "What can I say? I'm a simple woman."

Coop huffs a laugh. "There's nothing simple about you."

Just like there's nothing simple about the fact that I want this man to bend me over the counter and fuck me right here and right now.

Two-night stands really should be a thing.

My core clenches as he gives me a slow once-over, his clear blue eyes raking over every curve of my body before settling on my mouth.

When he finally speaks, his voice is a seductive rasp that speaks directly to my ovaries. "That's a great costume."

I glance down at the black jumpsuit, getting a bird's-eye view of my meager cleavage. The costume doesn't leave much to the imagination, but in this case, it doesn't matter because Coop's already seen every freaking inch of me..

Just like I've seen every sinful inch of him.

A deal is a deal.

Which is why I need to stop lusting over the cocky wide receiver and get on with my life.

I force a smile, tamping down my errant emotions. I will not be a clingy virgin. Or is it former-virgin? *So not the point.* "I should probably let you get back to the party."

"I have a better idea." He wraps his free arm around my shoulders and steers me toward the door. "How about you hang with me tonight and keep the jersey chasers at bay?"

I open my mouth, to say what, I have no idea, but he stops mid-stride and presses a finger to my lips.

"Look at these pants." He pauses, giving me ample time to admire the way the leather hugs his muscular thighs and accentuates the bulge of his sizable cock. *Like I needed a reminder*. "They'll descend like vultures the second you abandon me."

"And that's a problem why?" The instant the words leave my mouth, I want to suck them back in.

Coop's personal life is none of my business. We're just friends.

Friends who have scorching hot chemistry.

"It's a problem," he says, tucking me back under his arm. "Because I've already found my kryptonite."

The Reese's.

I sigh and steal a peanut butter cup from his bowl. He watches silently as I open the foil wrapper and pop it in my mouth, letting the chocolate melt on my tongue.

Might as well enjoy it.

From the looks of things, a foodgasm is the only pleasure I'll be getting tonight.

37

COOPER

This is a terrible idea.

It doesn't matter. No way am I letting Quinn out of my sight. That jumpsuit is tight as hell, highlighting every luscious curve of her body.

Douchey frat guys would be all over her.

Not happening. Just the thought of some asshole pawing at Quinn has my pulse thrumming.

"Easy there, big guy." Quinn looks up at me, the corner of her mouth lifted in a half-smile. Her lips are painted a sinful shade of cherry red, and the urge to rub my thumb across her lower lip is almost too strong to resist. "You squeeze any tighter and my head is going to pop off."

I loosen my grip on her shoulders as we enter the living room.

"Sorry." I flash her a wicked grin. "We can't have that. You go down and the ladies are likely to rush me."

She rolls her eyes and steals another peanut butter cup from my bowl. "It's good to know you have your priorities in order."

"Prioritization is critical if you want to make it as a student athlete."

Facts. My days start at five-thirty and rarely end before midnight during the season.

"I'll keep that in mind. You know, in case I develop a case of late-onset athleticism."

"Smartass." I give her a squeeze, pulling her in close again. Even with her boots, which have a chunky heel, she's tiny next to me. I could practically put her in my pocket. *Now there's an intriguing idea.* "Want to play beer pong?"

She shrugs. "I'm game."

That she agrees without a single disclaimer or disparaging comment about her bad luck or lack of skill feels like a big fucking win.

We make our way to the beer pong table and I call next game.

A couple of the guys gathered around the table steal glances at Quinn, but a few well-placed glares take care of the problem.

Quinn is totally oblivious to the attention as she fishes another Reese's out of my bowl.

She starts to open it and pauses. "I should probably lay off the candy, huh? Just in case."

Without waiting for an answer, she tosses it back in the bowl.

"Just in case what?"

"Just in case it makes a reappearance later. I doubt they taste as good the second time around."

I chuckle. "Let me get this straight. You aren't worried about hangovers, but you're worried about the possibility of puking up your guts?"

"Priorities," she says, each syllable layered with sickly sweet sarcasm.

I shake my head and turn back to the game just in time to see a ping-pong ball fly over the side of the table. It bounces against the hardwood floor and rolls between Quinn's feet.

She turns, and when she bends over to pick it up, every head in the vicinity swivels to look at her perfect ass.

Assholes.

"Show a little respect," I bark as Quinn rights herself, holding the runaway ball aloft.

She hands it to one of the players just as Noah appears, a nearly empty bottle of lager in hand. His eyes are red-rimmed, and it's clear he's been drinking for a while. Probably started during today's game and never stopped.

"What the hell are you wearing?" he demands, positioning himself between Quinn and the guys at the beer pong table.

She frowns, a tiny wrinkle forming between her brows. "Isn't it obvious? I'm Black Widow."

A damn fine one. Her ass looks like a dream in that skinsuit.

I want to sink my teeth into it and never let go.

But I know better than to say that aloud.

Noah scoffs. "You couldn't think of something a little more..." He waves a hand, gesturing to encompass the entirety of her.

She cocks a hip and crosses her arms, which only emphasizes the hint of cleavage revealed by the low-cut jumpsuit.

What I wouldn't give to tug that zipper down.

Focus, DeLaurentis. This isn't the time for R-rated fantasies.

"Dude." I knock him on the shoulder. "If you're going to shame anyone, it should be the pricks gawking at her ass like a bunch of pervs."

Noah blinks. Then he turns to the guys gathered around the beer pong table. "The next person who looks at my sister's ass is banned from the house for the rest of the semester!"

Now there's a rule I can get behind.

Unfortunately, Quinn doesn't agree. She huffs out a breath and rolls her eyes. "Cool it with the mantrum, Noah. I'm an adult, in case you haven't noticed."

Pretty sure he's noticed, hence, the mantrum.

Not that I blame him. If Quinn was my sister—which, thank Christ, she's not—I wouldn't want this bunch of drunk assholes staring at any part of her.

I'm all for personal agency and I don't want this night to end in ruin, so I clap Noah on the back and grin. "Relax man. I'll keep the handsy douchebags at bay if you want to grab another beer."

Works like a charm.

"Thanks." He nods and turns to his sister. "Do me a favor and stay out of trouble, Quinntastrophe."

Her cheeks flush as he disappears into the crowd.

"Forget about him." I nudge her with my shoulder. "It's the beer talking."

"We both know that isn't true."

Yeah, we do, but Noah's a dumbass and Quinn doesn't need—or want—me fighting her battles, so I swat her on the ass instead. "Looks like we're up."

Her eyes go round, but her body language relaxes, Noah's dig forgotten.

We approach the table and the winning team announces they're going to take a break, making noise about needing to take a piss.

Quinn frowns at their retreating backs. "Do they really think Noah would ban them for the rest of the semester?"

"Evidently." I smirk and drop my candy dish on the edge of the table. "Though I doubt Noah's going to remember much of anything in the morning. I don't think he got your hangover-resistant genes."

Quinn laughs. It's a full-throated belly laugh that's sexy as hell and my cock stirs with interest.

"Can we get next game?" Parker shouts, rolling up the table with Vaughn at his side.

No one protests—which could be a result of Noah's threat or

a show of respect for today's win over the Badgers—and we begin setting up the cups.

Quinn hands Parker a pitcher of beer and his eyes light up. "Dunk tank girl!"

She rolls her eyes. "My name is Quinn."

He passes the pitcher to Vaughn and gives her an approving thumbs up. "Looking good, Quinn. I'm digging that costume." His grin widens, and he gestures to the batons strapped to her back. "If Coop steps out of line, do you get to spank him?"

She arches a brow, returning his smile. "I haven't tried that yet, but who knows? The night is young. Maybe if you're nice, I'll let you borrow one and you can give it a go yourself."

Parker guffaws and turns to Vaughn, who's filling the cups. "I knew I liked this girl."

"Simmer down." I toss Parker a ball. "If anyone's getting spanked tonight, it's you." I squint and cock my head, pretending to think. "What's it been, like, six months since you and Vaughn won a game of beer pong?"

"Seven," Vaughn corrects, continuing to pour.

"The man makes a good point." Parker rubs his jaw. "We should mix it up. Can't have the Avengers teaming up on us. I'll take Black Widow. You can have Thor and his mighty hammer."

I give him the finger, but I don't have time to argue because Quinn shakes her head and steps between us.

"No way. If we're splitting teams, I get Vaughn." She gestures between Parker and I. "You two egomaniacs can take all your drama to the other end of the table."

"Works for me." Vaughn snickers, setting the pitcher aside as Quinn saunters toward him, her backside swaying with every step. "Birds of a feather and all that."

The fuck?

In the three years I've known Vaughn, not once has it occurred to me he might be capable of stealing my date.

No, not my date. My teammate.

Whatever. It's basically the same thing.

Which isn't even the point.

Look at the guy. He's about as smooth as oatmeal.

I shudder. I fucking hate oatmeal. It's boring—*just like Vaughn.*

And yet, Quinn chose him over me.

It's a fucking travesty.

One I'm never going to live down if Parker has anything to say about it.

My humiliation is compounded when Quinn and Vaughn both sink their first shots, forcing us to drink and getting the balls back.

They've knocked out three cups before Parker and I even get a chance to shoot.

"Damn." Parker fishes a plastic ball out of a cup in the back row. "Quinn's got skills."

The irony isn't lost on me since I'm the one who helped her improve her form.

Was that only a few weeks ago? It feels like a lifetime.

Fall semester is always rough, but with my father's election looming and the pressure to put up big numbers heading into the draft, this semester has been especially brutal.

The only positive is that a busy schedule makes it easy to dodge my father's calls. He left me a message this morning, but I haven't listened to it yet. The last thing I need is him yapping in my ear on game day.

"Bottom's up," Parker says, handing me a cup.

I drain it in a single gulp, and when it's my turn, I sink my shot, forcing Vaughn to drink.

Parker misses on his turn. So does Quinn.

They both have to drink, but on the next round, Quinn

redeems herself. She and Vaughn sink their shots one after the other, getting the balls back again.

The onlookers cheer and I shoot Parker a dark look. "Since I'm carrying you anyway, do you want to just climb on my back?"

He gives me the finger, but puts one in on his next turn.

Quinn's up next and she must be feeling confident because the little smartass starts talking smack.

"You know, Parker. You just might be onto something." A mischievous grin curves those ruby red lips. "I'm starting to think Cooper might be into spanking after all."

If she only knew how right she was.

My cock stiffens and I shift my weight, subtly adjusting myself as she leans forward to line up her shot. I've got the perfect view of her tits, that sexy little hollow between her breasts drawing my gaze.

What I wouldn't give to run my tongue over every inch of her exposed flesh right now.

Was her zipper that low twenty minutes ago?

Nah. She must've pulled it down when I wasn't looking

Christ almighty.

If she keeps this up, I'll have a full-blown erection by the time the game is over.

The woman's got me by the balls, and judging by the smug look on her face, she knows it.

It's a good thing Reid isn't around to see this. He'd never believe it. Cooper DeLaurentis brought to heel by a tiny slip of a redhead?

No way.

I shake off the thought.

What the hell am I thinking? Quinn's not looking for romance, and it's safe to say I'm the last guy on campus who'd be considered boyfriend material.

So what if we hook up more than once?

It doesn't have to mean anything. We can keep it casual.

Hell, casual is my middle name.

Quinn and Vaughn hand us our asses over the next few rounds, and when Vaughn sinks a ball into our last cup, I'm almost glad the humiliation is at an end.

"No pressure." Parker hands me a ball for the mandatory redemption shot.

This thing is over. He hasn't hit a cup in the last three rounds. The odds of him sinking one now are slim.

We take our shots and both of us miss.

"Drink up." Vaughn slides the remaining cups across the table.

We make quick work of the beer, which has grown warm and tastes like ass. I grab my candy dish—because no way am I leaving my Reese's behind—and step away to make room for new players.

Quinn and Vaughn follow, apparently deciding to quit while they're ahead.

"You're not going to stick around and clobber some other unsuspecting fools?"

"Nah." Quinn pretends to buff her nails on her jumpsuit. "I prefer to spend the night basking in your complete and total annihilation." She grins. "But first, I need to use the bathroom. If I drink another thing, my suit's liable to split."

She gives a little finger wave and heads for the stairs.

I follow.

I promised Noah I'd look out for his sister, and I always keep my word.

Quinn maneuvers through the crowd easily, while I'm stopped by well-wishers and jersey chasers looking for a hookup. Any other time, I'd be down, but there's only one woman I want riding my cock tonight.

Quinn.

By the time I catch up to her, she's halfway down the upstairs hall.

I close the distance between us in a few quick strides. She must hear me approaching because she turns just as I reach for her, eyes going wide as I pin her against the wall, cupping her face and crushing my lips to hers. I coax her mouth open with my tongue, savoring the taste of chocolate and beer that linger on her lips. Her body melts against mine and she moans, but I swallow that down too.

I'm a greedy bastard and I'm not about to share. Not one look, one taste, one sound.

When it comes to Quinn, I want it all.

She draws back, smiling against my mouth. "What are you doing?"

"Inviting you back to my place."

She bites her lower lip, the tender flesh as ripe as a strawberry. "Are you sure?"

White-hot need coils deep in my balls and I roll my hips, cock gliding over her belly. I need to be inside this woman right fucking now.

"I've never been so sure of anything in my life."

38

QUINN

THE INSTANT COOP closes his bedroom door, I launch myself at him, hooking my fingers in the collar of his armor and using it to lower his mouth to mine. The kiss is hot and needy, fueled by seven days of unsated sexual desire and too many fantasies to count. Our lips crash together, a messy mating of tongues and bodies as he palms my ass, digging his fingers into the soft flesh and pulling me closer.

His erection is thick and hard against my belly and my panties grow damp at the prospect of pleasure.

God of Thunder, indeed.

He spins us around, slamming my back against the door. The impact radiates down my spine, culminating in a fiery ball of desire that pools between my thighs like molten lava. Then his mouth is on my body, lips cutting a path across my jaw and down my throat as he licks and sucks and—

Sweet baby Jesus.

His teeth clamp down on my throat—a teasing nip—and my pussy clenches, my hips grinding of their own accord as he shoves his thigh between my legs, delivering the delicious friction I so desperately crave.

I shamelessly grind against him, chasing my pleasure as his hands explore my body.

"This jumpsuit should be illegal," he murmurs, toying with the zipper that hangs just above my breasts. "I haven't been able to think of anything but peeling it off since I saw you standing in that kitchen, your sweet little ass on display."

There's nothing little about my ass, but my heart flutters nonetheless.

"In fact, I think you wore it just to tease me." A wolfish grin transforms his face, and his eyes grow dark as they meet mine. "Were you trying to get my attention, Quinn?"

No. *Yes.* My breath hitches. "Did it work?"

I don't mean to say the words, but they spill out of my mouth anyway.

He presses my hand to his cock, using it to stroke himself. "You have my undivided attention."

"G-good." It's all I can manage with desire short-circuiting my brain.

He cups my chin, and when he speaks, his voice is low and gravelly, the words vibrating in my chest. "When you crave release, you come to me. No one else. I'll give you what you need."

Once again, the words are less request and more order.

Anticipation sizzles across my skin like an electrical storm, but I can't make a habit of bending to his whims. Even if they align with my own.

"You think you know what I need?"

"Damn, right." He lowers the zipper on my jumpsuit and cool air kisses my bare breasts. I shiver as he trails long fingers down my abdomen, dipping them inside my panties. He circles my clit and I arch into his touch, the breath hissing from my body as one of those fingers slides inside me. He repeats the motion, stroking me gently, just the way I like it, and my eyes roll back in my head.

"Cooper." His name is a breathy moan on my lips. One that begs for more. More heat. More pressure. More everything.

He pulls away and I gasp at the loss of contact.

"That's right, sweetheart. I'm the only one who knows what you need. The only one who knows how you like it." He cups me, his thumb pressing down on my clit through the thin fabric of my costume. "This pussy belongs to me."

Oh, God.

This is better than porn.

As long as he keeps touching me, he can have my pussy and every drop of pleasure that comes from it.

Work out the details later.

Right. Be in the moment. Hell, I want to live in this moment forever.

"Say it, Quinn. Tell me it's mine," he growls, breath hot against my cheek, "and I'll make you come so hard you forget your own name."

Yes, please. "I'm yours."

Any pretense of restraint slips away with those words.

I want this man and I want him now.

"Good girl." He raises those glistening fingers to his mouth, the ones that were just inside of me, and licks them, long and slow. When he reaches the tips of his fingers, he sucks them into his mouth. His cheeks go hollow, like he doesn't want to leave a drop behind, and there's a loud *pop* when he finally releases them. "So sweet."

Curiosity takes root and I release the button on his leather pants.

"I've never—" Heat floods my cheeks as I lower his zipper and I silently chide myself. There is absolutely no reason to be embarrassed. Cooper knows I'm inexperienced. Just like I know there's so much more he can teach me. "I want to taste you."

He groans and his eyelids fall to half-mast as I drop to my knees before him, releasing his cock and shoving his pants down.

His erection stands proudly before him and from this angle, it looks even bigger than I'd remembered.

There's no way it's going to fit in my mouth.

It's impossible.

"I can't tell you how many times I've dreamed of this." He tangles his fingers in my hair. "Of having those ruby red lips wrapped around my cock."

It's all the encouragement I need.

I grip the base of his cock and lick the bead of moisture pooling on the head. It's sweet and salty at the same time. Not quite what I'd imagined, but in the best possible way.

He watches, transfixed, as I lick him again, swirling my tongue around the tip like I'm tasting an ice cream cone.

I repeat the motion and his grip on my hair tightens, but he makes no move to rush me as I trail the flat of my tongue down the underside of his shaft.

He's frozen in place, posture rigid. His chest barely moves as I look up at him from under my lashes, but there's the hint of a smile on his face.

Emboldened, I wrap my lips around his shaft, easing him into my mouth. He hisses, the air whistling between his teeth.

Shit. Am I doing it wrong?

"Don't stop," he pleads, a desperate edge to his words.

Pride fills my chest. *I* did that. *I* put that needy tone in his voice.

Cooper may be big and bad on the football field, but right now, I hold all the power.

I suck gently, rubbing the head of his cock with my tongue,

and he moans, a deep rumble that has every nerve in my body quivering with desire.

"Show me how you like it."

I want to know how to please him. To make him feel as good as he makes me feel.

Hunger flashes in his eyes and he guides my mouth to his erection.

I open without hesitation.

Coop has always handled me with care. This will be no different. He won't push too hard or too fast, but even if he loses control, I'll welcome it. Welcome the opportunity to watch him revel in the same toe-curling pleasure he's given me.

He's long and thick and when the head of his cock grazes the back of my throat, I stiffen, nearly gagging on the fullness.

"Easy." He massages the base of my skull, his fingers moving with expert precision. "Relax for me, sweetheart."

I exhale and close my eyes, willing the tension from my body.

He moves slowly, rocking his hips as he slides in and out, the musky taste of him coating my mouth.

I lick and suck, relishing the pressure at the back of my throat as he shows me how to work him simultaneously with my hand. It takes me a minute to get the hang of it, but judging by the animalistic sounds he's making, Coop's enjoying this lesson as much as I am.

When his thrusts become less controlled, his grunts more erratic, I increase my pace, sucking harder and pressing my thighs together as my arousal spirals higher.

"Quinn. I'm going to come."

Yeah. Me too.

Which is something I never would have thought possible without physical contact.

Coop grips my shoulders, holding me in place. A quiet sob

escapes as he withdraws, leaving me frustrated and on the verge of climax.

He pulls me to my feet. "I want to come inside of you."

I was fully prepared to let him, but I know what he means, so instead of arguing, I strip off my clothes as he does the same.

Cooper finishes first and by the time I step out of my jumpsuit, he's rolling a condom over his length.

There's a look of pure desire on his face when he turns to me, hooking his hands under my thighs and lifting me into the air even as he presses my back to the wall.

He brushes his lips across mine. "This is going to be hard and fast."

I nod. "Don't hold back."

He seats himself to the hilt with one quick thrust. Blistering heat explodes in my core and I cry out, digging my nails into his shoulders as he withdraws and thrusts back into me with one frenetic movement.

As promised, the sex is hard and fast, his body pinning me to the wall as he angles his hips, pelvis rubbing my clit with each delicious thrust. Our sweat slick bodies slap together, making the filthiest, most erotic sounds as my pleasure spirals higher and higher. When I finally fly over the edge into that dark oblivion, pulling Cooper along with me, the power of our shared release nearly splits me in two.

Cooper lets out a roar worthy of any Wildcat and I give silent thanks we've got the place to ourselves. He leans into me and we stay like that for a while, bodies an exhausted tangle of damp, relaxed limbs.

Eventually, he pulls out, lowering me gently to the floor.

My legs are shaky as hell, but I'm definitely not complaining. Judging by the big ass grin on Cooper's face, he feels the same way.

He glances around the room and when his gaze settles back

on mine, he rubs the back of his head, looking unsure. "Stay the night?"

"I don't know..." The last thing I want to do is crowd him. I know how he feels about sleepovers and everything they imply.

"If you stay," he says, wiggling his brows, "I can guarantee at least two more orgasms."

My chest tightens, but the feeling is so fleeting I can't tell if it was relief or disappointment. "When you put it like that, how could I possibly refuse?"

39

COOPER

SUNLIGHT STREAMS THROUGH THE WINDOW, an unpleasant reminder that I forgot to close the blinds last night. No surprise there. My mind—and body—were otherwise occupied.

Quinn's curled up next to me, her head resting on my chest. She fits perfectly against me with her hand pressed to my abdomen and one leg draped over mine.

It's like the spot was carved out just for her.

I watch her as she sleeps, which isn't as creepy as it sounds. Or maybe it is. It's not like I have a lot of experience in this area. I've never woken up with a woman before, and I'm curious.

Her breathing is slow and even and every time she exhales, a wisp of that scarlet hair flies up in the air, tickling my chest on the way down.

My fingers itch to brush it back from her face, but I don't want to wake her.

We didn't get much sleep last night. Not that I'm complaining. I'll take great sex over sleep every day of the week.

Even on a Sunday, the one day I don't actually have to be up at the ass crack of dawn.

Quinn stirs, making this sexy little purring sound, and my cock springs to life, tenting the sheet.

I tilt my head, checking to see if she's up, but nope, her eyes are still closed.

Morning sex will have to wait.

I stare up at the ceiling, tracing idle circles on Quinn's back as I mentally run through my schedule for the upcoming week.

We've got Indy on the schedule Saturday, so Reid and I will need to book time with the O-line to watch film. It's an away game, which means less prep time, but at least we're flying. Busing it to Indiana would be torture. Just like the upcoming exam in Applied Regression Analysis—aka stats—my least favorite part of the PoliSci curriculum. Then again, maybe it won't be too brutal since we're just a few weeks from finals.

Finals. Something else I'm not ready to think about yet.

I can't afford to let my grades slip any more than I can declare my intention to enter the draft.

Best-case scenario, my old man would lose his shit. Worst? I don't even want to think about it.

Just a few more months.

One day—*one step*—at a time.

I can keep my professional aspirations quiet for a few more months, even if it means no NIL agreements, no agents, and no informal meetings with NFL scouts, something Reid's father is pushing hard.

Lucky bastard.

If only my father were half as supportive.

My cell vibrates on the nightstand and the Imperial Death March fills the room with its ominous vibes.

Fuck. Fuck. Fuck.

The literal last thing I want to do is talk to my father right now, especially with Quinn in my bed. But I've been dodging his calls for days and he knows this is my day off.

If I don't answer, there'll be hell to pay.

I slide out from under Quinn, gently lowering her head to the pillow as I sit up. Then I grab my phone and swipe accept, turning my back to her as I bring the phone to my ear.

"Cooper."

Well, good morning to you too.

"Hey, dad."

"It took you long enough." His words are clipped, his tone irritated. "I thought you were going to send me to voicemail again."

It's too early for this shit, but I scrub a hand over my face and swallow my annoyance.

"No, sir. Sorry I missed your calls." The apology is insincere as hell and we both know it. "It's been a busy week."

That at least is true.

He makes a dismissive sound and there's a rustling of papers on his end. "I'm calling to confirm you'll be at the hotel on election day. Elliot sent you the details. I trust you've received them."

Unfortunately. The election is next week and despite the quid pro quo offer he made my mom regarding Senior Day, I haven't spoken to my profs about missing classes yet.

Nothing like putting it off until the last minute.

Whatever. It's no secret I don't want to go, just like it's no secret he only needs mom and me there for the sake of appearances. After all, how would it look for him to be photographed without his loving family on such a big night?

"I need to clear it with my professors. Things have been busy with football and I haven't talked to them yet."

"Which is why Elliot took the liberty of speaking with them on your behalf. They've all agreed to excuse your absence so you can spend the day at the command center." There's more shuffling of papers. "One of them even offered to give you extra credit if you write a five-page essay on the implications of the election. Professor White-something." There's a long pause, but I don't bother providing the correct name. Not when his asshole assistant just added a five-page paper to my To Do list. Like I have time to write another fucking paper. "Anyway, I'm sure you'll figure it out."

I always do.

"Yes, sir."

"Good. Your mother and I look forward to seeing you bright and early next Tuesday." Rage burns deep in my gut at the emphasis he puts on the word mother. "And Cooper? Wear a suit."

We disconnect and I throw the phone across the room. It bounces off the drywall and drops to the floor, landing unceremoniously on the carpet.

"Is everything okay?"

Dammit. How could I forget Quinn was here?

Her hand settles on my back, the tentative touch like a brand on my heated skin.

"Sorry about that." I exhale, forcing the tension from my body before I turn to face her. "I didn't mean to wake you."

A shy smile curves her lips as she pulls the sheet up to cover her breasts. "It's your place. You can be as loud as you want." She gestures to the phone. "Want to talk about it?"

Do I? Yes.

Can I? No.

I shove my fingers into my hair, pushing it back from my face. "It's nothing. Just family stuff."

She nods and for a second, I think she's going to say something, but she presses her lips flat, like she's holding whatever she wants to say in.

Because you're acting like an asshole.

Like father, like son.

"I won't push," she finally says. "But I'm here if you want to talk."

She sounds like my high school counselor, and I'm kind of digging it. When was the last time I had an honest conversation with anyone but Reid?

That would be never.

And even he doesn't know what a prick my father is.

"Actually, there is something I'd like to ask you." I wipe my palms on the sheet. It's probably crazy, but what the hell. "This is sort of a weird request, and you can totally say no, but would you want to hang with me on election day? I have to make an appearance at the hotel where my father and his donors are gathering to watch the polls. It'll be lame as hell, but the food's good and I'm excellent company."

Quinn frowns and presses the back of her hand to my forehead.

"What are you doing?"

"Checking to see if have you have a temperature." She smirks. "So I can decide if it's you asking or if it's your cock."

I roll my eyes, but it's actually a great idea. Bathroom sex would make election day infinitely more tolerable. First I have to get her to agree to go. "If I promise sex, will you come?"

Quinn tilts her head, but there's a familiar twinkle in her eye. "This sounds a lot like prostitution."

"Nah. Just think of it as one friend doing something nice for another friend." I grab a strand of her wild hair, twisting it around my fingers. She's got a serious case of sex hair and I'm digging it. "You wanted to return the favor. Here's your chance."

She doesn't owe me anything for helping with the Virgin Quest, but it would be nice to have moral support on election day.

I drop a kiss on her shoulder. I'm not above playing dirty,

and orgasms are the best incentive I have at my disposal. "I promise to make it worth your while."

"This is a formal event, right?"

I shrug.

"Are you sure you want me to go?" She forces a self-deprecating laugh. "This idea has disaster written all over it."

Anger stirs in my gut and I want to throat punch every asshole—including her brother—who's ever made her feel like she's less than because of her shitty luck.

"Any woman on campus would be happy to accompany you," she adds quietly.

Problem is, I don't want just any woman at my side. I want Quinn. "True, but inviting another woman to an event with *my parents* would send the wrong message, whereas you and I are on the same page."

Just sex.

No strings. No drama. No damage.

Quinn snorts and scrunches up her nose. "I'm pretty sure every woman on campus knows where you stand on relationships."

"Trust me. I'm doing everyone a favor by being upfront. I'm not boyfriend material."

I never will be.

"Next Tuesday?" she asks.

"Yup."

"I can do it. I've only got one class and I can ditch."

I should probably ask if she's sure, but I'm not about to give her an out. Not when the thought of her company is the only thing that makes the prospect of spending an entire day with my father bearable.

Another thought occurs to me. "This will be off the record, right?"

She nods. “Relax. Politics isn’t my thing. I only write human interest pieces.”

I feel like a dick for asking, but you can never be too sure. In my experience, media types have a flexible moral code.

Sort of like politicians.

I press a chaste kiss to her lips. “Thanks.”

“What are friends for?” She cups a hand to the back of my neck and pulls me down on top of her so we’re skin to skin. “You know, besides orgasms.”

“You’re incorrigible.” I fucking love it.

Quinn rolls her hips, bringing my cock to attention. “I learned from the best.”

40

QUINN

COOPER TAKES the turnpike exit ramp at an alarming speed, his white-knuckled grip on the steering wheel doing little to put my nerves at ease.

To say it's been a tense drive from College Park to Philadelphia would be an understatement. Cooper's shoulders have the rigid look of a man about to face the firing squad and he's barely said a word during the three-hour drive.

So, yeah, my anxiety is at an all-time high as we near the hotel where we're supposed to spend the day with the senator and his strongest political supporters.

Cockwaffles. Why did I ever agree to this?

Because Coop looked like he needed a friend after that awful call with his father.

Hell, he looked like he needed a drink.

And since drinking your feelings is frowned upon, I'd opted for the next best thing: sex. Which had the added bonus of multiple orgasms for me.

Unfortunately, sex isn't an option at the moment.

Too bad. Cooper in a suit is **chef's kiss**. The soft black fabric hugs his body like it was tailor made for him and his shirt is open at the collar, revealing just enough smooth tan skin to set my pulse thrumming, which definitely isn't helping with the anxiety sitch.

I don't want to pry, but I'm starting to question the wisdom of agreeing to this little outing.

Not only because there's a high probability I'll embarrass Cooper, but because I'm walking into the situation completely blind.

I know nothing about his family, other than what I gleaned from the internet, and I don't have the first clue what I'm supposed to say to his parents.

Start small and work up to the big stuff.

"What are your plans after college and the NFL?"

So much for starting small.

Cooper's head swivels toward me, but his expression is unreadable. "I never said I was going into the NFL."

"I figured it was a given." I shift in my seat, angling my back toward the door so I can look at him. "You're not planning to play pro ball?"

He shrugs. "It's complicated."

"How complicated can it be?" I mirror his shrug. "Either you want to play pro ball or you don't."

Talent isn't even a question. Not for Cooper.

"I'd like to play in the NFL, but my father doesn't approve." He rolls his shoulders and adjusts his grip on the steering wheel. "It's a major point of contention. Please don't bring it up today."

I have a million and one questions—namely, *What kind of asshole doesn't support their kid's dreams?*—but I don't want to press.

Cooper is already wound tight.

I nod slowly, thinking it through. "If you don't play football, you'll...what? Go into politics like your father?"

Coop's a PoliSci major. It's the obvious answer.

"Maybe." He huffs out a breath. "I enjoy the work, and I take pride in giving back to the community, but my father and I don't see eye to eye on several key issues. Most notably, women's rights."

I add women's rights to my mental list of topics to avoid.

At this rate, we'll be limited to the weather and not much else.

"Working in politics doesn't mean you have to follow in your father's footsteps. You can always carve your own path."

A better path. Which wouldn't be hard, since his father sounds like a pompous ass.

Like every career politician ever.

"What about you?" Coop asks, turning the tables on me. "What are you going to do after school?"

"No clue." I sigh and slouch down in my seat before remembering that wrinkles aren't a good look. I straighten and smooth the fabric of my little black dress. "I haven't declared a major yet."

I have to declare by the end of spring semester, which isn't terrifying at all.

It's just my entire life.

Coop hums noncommittally.

"What's that supposed to mean?"

It's a rhetorical question. Of course I know what that sound means. I've heard it from my brother often enough to know it's the crushing sounds of judgment.

Calamity Quinn, at your service.

"I just figured you'd be doing something with your writing." He flicks the turn signal and darts a quick glance over his shoulder before changing lanes. "I've been following your column. It gets a lot of hits online."

"It does." More than most columns in The Collegian. "I love

to write, but I can't see myself writing human interest stories for the rest of my life."

"Why not?"

There's genuine curiosity behind the question, like he actually cares about the answer.

"Tales of my disastrous escapades are funny now, but at twenty-six? At thirty?"

"Not so much," he says, finishing my thought.

"I don't know. I can't see myself applying to the journalism department, anyway."

Hard pass. Modern journalism is a mess I want no part of.

"Have you ever done any creative writing?"

"Ouch." I snort-laugh. My column is nothing if not creative. "You sound like my Creative Nonfiction prof."

Coop reaches over and squeezes my knee, his thumb brushing my outer thigh. "You know what I mean. Like shorts stories and stuff."

"A little." His hand remains on my knee, a warm, reassuring distraction. "I tried to write a book once."

I clap my hands over my mouth. I've never told anyone about the half-written romance novel on my laptop.

"What happened?"

"Nothing happened." That was the problem. "I got busy, and it seemed silly to waste time on something that would never see the light of day."

"Let me get this straight," he says, a devious smile curving his lips. "You wouldn't give up on the Virgin Quest come hell or high water, but you quit writing because you didn't know if your work would ever be published?"

It sounds stupid when he puts it like that.

"No, I just thought—" What had I been thinking? "It just seemed unrealistic. Telling people you want to write novels is like saying you want to make it as a musician or a dancer. No one would ever take me seriously. Least of all my parents."

So, basically, nothing would change?

Stupid voice of reason.

"Anyway, I can't afford to pin my college career on making a living as a novelist." The student loans won't pay themselves and I have no interest in moving back home. "My parents dealt with all this"—I gesture to myself—"for eighteen years. They don't need me bringing my mess home to crash on the couch after graduation."

Coop scoffs. "You make it sound like you're a burden."

"Did you forget the story about the golf cart? Because—" I pause. "Actually, forget all about the golf cart."

No need to remind him he's bringing a delinquent to his father's election day festivities.

"Quinn." He rubs my knee, his calloused fingers sending a shiver of desire right up my spine. "You need to own that shit so no one can use it against you. The mess, as you call it, is part of your charm. It's part of what makes you so adorable and it's the reason people love your column. You're relatable."

I scrunch up my face and turn to him. "You think?"

"I know." He strokes lazy circles with his fingers, working his way up my thigh. "We've all had those moments."

"Yeah, well, if you keep that up,"—I stare pointedly at his hand—"we're going to have an entirely different kind of moment."

Cooper smirks and for the first time all day, the smile reaches his eyes. "You say that like it's a bad thing."

"It is when I'm about to meet your parents."

The light in his eyes dims and I mentally curse myself.

"It's not too late to bail. We could get a hotel room and—"

"Nice try, DeLaurentis." I swat his arm playfully. "You're not getting off that easily."

Not yet, anyway.

41

COOPER

I CLIMB out of the car and hand the keys over to the hotel valet who calls me sir like I'm a slick forty-something businessman instead of a cocky twenty-something student.

Nothing like setting the tone for the day right out of the gate.

My nostrils flare as I exhale, and I remind myself it's not his fault this day is going to suck balls.

Should have brought Starlight Twinkle.

No way. The last thing I need is my dad's bad juju tainting my lucky unicorn.

"Wow." Quinn steps out of the Audi and joins me on the sidewalk. It's just past noon and Broad Street is teaming with bodies. "I didn't think it would be so..." She gestures to the elegant limestone façade and gilded doors leading into the bright lobby. "It's a lot."

The Belle Tower is one of the swankiest hotels in Philadelphia. Nevertheless, it's a concession. If my father had his way, we'd be at the Four Seasons, but his donors enjoy the feel of old money, something my family has never known.

"Don't sweat it." I loop a red silk tie around my neck and

button my top button. "Remember, they're just people like you and me."

Quinn arches a brow that clearly calls *bullshit,* and a smile breaks across my face.

"Let me help you with that," she says, stepping closer and taking the ends of my tie.

I can do it myself, but I'm not about to turn down an opportunity to feel her hands on my body.

Besides, I know better than to go inside without ensuring it's perfectly straight.

My father would have a shit fit.

Quinn ties the knot with deft fingers, a skill I choose to believe she learned from Noah. She tightens it at my neck before smoothing the fabric over my abs.

"I suddenly feel underdressed." She gives me a slow once-over and tucks a strand of hair behind her ear, something she only seems to do when she's nervous. "Haley was right. I should've worn heels."

"Hey." I cup her chin and tilt her face to mine. "You are gorgeous, with or without heels."

If I weren't so damn stressed, I'd have pulled over for a quickie on the way here. The little black dress she's wearing is a classic, but it leans just this side of sexy with a wide neckline that reveals the gentle slope of her clavicle.

Who knew bones could be so sexy?

I rest a hand on her lower back, cursing the lack of privacy. I'd like nothing more than to claim her mouth and show her just how much I like the dress, but we have an audience.

One that isn't accustomed to Greek Row PDA.

"We might as well get this over with."

The sooner the better.

Just like ripping off a band-aid.

We enter the lobby and Quinn's eyes go wide. "Holy crap. This place is like something out of Bridgerton."

I have no idea what Bridgerton is, but I had the same reaction my first time here. The combination of polished marble, gilded woodwork, and crystal chandeliers isn't what you'd call subtle opulence.

We take the elliptical staircase and make our way up to the ballroom, which is humming with energy. A guy near the door is quoting the polls, which are currently predicting a second term for my father, who's done a masterful job of painting himself as a man of the people.

It's total bullshit.

Our ancestors may have been blue-collar dock workers, but my father hasn't done a day of hard labor in his life. Not that you'd know it by hearing him talk.

I scan the crowded room, marking the bar, and spot my parents near the stage. Because of course there's a dais for my father to impart words of wisdom and give some farcical speech about democracy when the race is called later tonight.

Like me, he's tall and broad shouldered, but that's where the resemblance ends. My fair coloring and good looks are all my mom, who's practically invisible in the crowd of reporters and sycophants gathered around them, angling for face time.

My father spots us as we approach and I paste on a smile that's fake as hell—just like his—as he disentangles himself from the crowd of well-wishers.

Quinn and I wait in silence as the last of the hangers-on disband.

Finally, my father turns to us, a practiced smile on his face. At his side, my mother's smile is one hundred percent authentic.

Relief floods my veins.

It's been nearly three months since I left for training camp and though we talk on the phone regularly, it would be easy for her to conceal trouble at home.

I lean down to hug her and the comforting scent of Chanel No. 5 fills my nostrils as she rubs my back, just like she did when I was little.

We separate and I turn to Quinn, who looks like she's doing her best not to fidget.

"Quinn, this is my father, Steven DeLaurentis." A muscle in his jaw twitches at the informal introduction, which just goes to show what a narcissistic bastard he is, expecting me to use his title when introducing him to my friends. "And this is my mom, Lauren."

My mother positively beams at Quinn, clearly getting the wrong idea.

She's going to be sorely disappointed when she realizes we're just friends.

"Mom. Dad. This is my *friend* Quinn."

They shake hands and exchange greetings, but when my father turns back to me, his cool demeanor is back in place.

"I didn't know you were bringing a guest."

I make a point of glancing around the crowded ballroom. "What's one more?"

"That seems to be your philosophy in life."

I let the dig roll off my back. It's just the first of many I'll receive today.

"It's so nice to meet you," my mother gushes, falling into the role of peacemaker. For as long as I can remember, it's been her way to smooth things over between my father and I. "It's been ages since Cooper brought anyone home to meet us."

With good reason.

Quinn smiles, her posture relaxing almost imperceptibly. "It's nice to meet you, too."

"How exactly do you two know each other?" my father asks, just the tiniest bit of disapproval tainting his words.

He's good at that. Keeping the slights so mild, you wonder if you imagined them.

"Her brother is a Sig." *No need to get into the messy details.*

At that, he nods approvingly. Like her family affiliation somehow makes her more worthy in his eyes.

Hell, it probably does. He was a Sig himself, which was the only reason I bothered to rush when he suggested it. It wasn't worth the fight to refuse.

We make small talk for a few minutes, and when Elliot, my father's assistant, appears, it's clear our time is up.

Fine by me.

The less I have to deal with the old man, the better.

I promise my mom we'll find her later, and when they leave, I turn to Quinn.

"Good news. It's an open bar."

She grins and shakes her head. "Only you would suggest using my fake at a political rally, or whatever you call this thing."

"It's fine. They won't even card you." I hook my arm through hers and steer her toward the bar. "It's literally the only upside to these events."

At the bar, I order a beer. Quinn, taking my advice, opts for a glass of white wine.

Drinks in hand, we make a tour of the ballroom. After all, that's the whole reason I'm here. To be seen and play my role as the perfect son in the perfect all-American family.

It's mind-numbingly boring and after only an hour of making small talk with my father's guests, I'm ready to scratch my eyes out.

We complete our circuit and commandeer a small, high-topped table in the back of the room.

"I'm sorry I dragged you along today." I lean down, resting

my forearms on the table. "I'm actually interested in politics and I'm bored out of my mind. I can only imagine how you feel."

She waves me off. "It's fine. It's not like I had big plans for the day. Besides, I owed you one."

"You don't owe me anything, Quinn."

"Exactly." She grins, that mischievous light in her eyes. "Now we're even."

"We're far from even. By my count—"

"Cooper!" I turn to find Tom, my old boss, smiling at me, drink in hand. "I thought that was you."

"In the flesh." Tom is one of the few people on my father's team I genuinely like, and this time, I don't mind making introductions. "Tom, this is my friend Quinn. Quinn, this is Tom Anderson, the Field Director for my father's campaign. I interned with him over the summer."

"He did great work." Tom claps me on the back. "We were sorry to lose him."

"According to the polls, you managed just fine without me."

"Yeah, but we'd have done even better with you." He turns to Quinn and stage whispers, "Cooper was our secret weapon with the AARP crowd. The men enjoyed talking sports and the women— Well, I don't have to tell you how charming he can be."

She laughs good-naturedly. "No, you really don't."

"That reminds me." Tom's attention swings back to me. He's all business now. "Your father said you're interested in working on The Hill when you graduate in the spring. I've got a lead on a Staff Assistant position I think would be a good fit. I can send you the details."

I nod, feigning interest. "That would be great."

I hate lying to Tom, but I don't have a choice. Not when my father is using me like a cog in his political machine.

Irritation skitters up my spine, but I breathe through it, forcing myself to focus on the conversation.

"What exactly does a Field Director do?" Quinn asks, all wide-eyed innocence. "I've always been curious about the composition of a political campaign."

Her face gives nothing away, but I know the truth. She doesn't give a shit about campaign roles or Tom's duties. She's redirecting the conversation.

To spare me.

The realization nearly blows me away.

That this woman could ever think she does more harm than good is a fucking travesty.

She's an angel.

And just for tonight, she's mine.

42

QUINN

MY WINE GLASS IS EMPTY, and my mouth is parched when Tom finally excuses himself. Cooper's been quiet, leaving Tom and me to carry the conversation. The only thing that seemed to penetrate his thoughts was talk of Wildcat football.

Even that was short-lived.

The moment Tom suggested Cooper could end his football career on a high note by winning the national championship, he'd completely shut down.

I reach across the small table, touching Coop's forearm. "Are you okay?"

"I could use another drink." He raises his beer and drains the bottle. "How about you?"

"I'd kill for a glass of water."

"Smart." He nods, flashing me a conspiratorial grin. "This thing is like a marathon. Pacing is key." He checks the time on his phone. "Two hours down, eight to go."

"Eight hours?"

Sweet baby Jesus.

"Don't worry. If they don't call the race by ten, I'll make our excuses so we can duck out. My father can hardly complain given the long drive back to College Park. I'll tell him you have an early class."

"Oh, I see how it is." I cross my arms, feigning indignation. "I'm the scapegoat."

"Nah. You're the eye candy." His brows shoot up. "Wait. Am I allowed to say that?"

I grin. "If you have to ask..."

"That came out wrong." He moves around the table, his large body all but pressing me to the wall. "What I meant to say is, you're beautiful and we should find a bathroom where I can worship you like the goddess you are."

Heat rushes to my core.

He thinks I'm a goddess?

No one's ever called me a goddess before.

So not the point.

Even if I wanted a quickie in the bathroom—which, let's be honest, I do—we absolutely cannot go through with it.

It would be wrong.

And *oh-so-right*.

"What do you say?" Coop drags a finger down my arm, leaving a trail of goosebumps in his wake.

"I need to go to the bathroom."

He straightens. "Yeah?"

"Alone."

His face falls, but there's a hint of laughter in his eyes. "Spoilsport."

"That's me. Quinn Mowery, spoiler of sports."

May as well add it to my growing list of nicknames.

Coop grins. "I'll get another round of drinks and meet you back here."

We split up and I head off in search of a ladies' room.

When I finally locate it, I'm about to burst and I'm hauling ass because I don't want to pee myself, so of course I run into Cooper's mom.

Literally.

As in, I hit her with the heavy wooden door as she's exiting the restroom.

She makes a sort of surprised sound and I shriek like a banshee as my bladder tries to execute an unplanned evacuation.

Thank God I've been doing my Kegels.

"I'm so sorry." I clap a hand to my chest, where my heart is trying to leap out of my ribcage. "Are you okay?"

Mrs. DeLaurentis smiles. "I'm fine. No harm done."

"Are you sure? I'm so sorry. I'm such a klutz." I'm rambling, but I can't seem to stop. "Because if you're okay, then I'm going to…" I glance at the row of stalls, unable to utter the word *pee* in front of this woman.

"By all means, don't let me stop you," she says, totally unfazed.

Talk about cool, calm, and collected.

It's probably a necessity when you're married to a US senator.

Or, you know, when you're responsible for raising a hellion like Cooper.

I walk stiffly to the first stall, clenching my pelvic muscles for all I'm worth, and lock myself inside.

It takes all of two seconds to pull down my tights and underwear, but when I relax my body, nothing happens.

I've never had a shy bladder, but apparently today is going to be a day of firsts.

First time in Philadelphia.

First time meeting a senator.

First time I couldn't freaking pee because Cooper's super sweet mom is still out there and I can't bear the thought of her listening, even though I know it's the most natural thing in the world.

FML.

My bladder is going to burst. Is that even a thing?

It's about to be.

The sound of running water echoes through the marble bathroom, and I practically sob with relief.

I quickly take care of business and when I exit the stall, Mrs. DeLaurentis shuts off the faucet.

She dries her hands on a thick towel and drops it in a basket under the sink as I wash my hands. My gaze slides to the left and I study her reflection in the mirror.

It's easy to see where Cooper gets his good looks. His mother has the same honey-blond hair, though hers is pulled back in a smooth chignon, and her eyes are such a startling shade of blue, it's hard to believe she's not wearing contacts. Even her suit is impressive, wrinkle free and tailored to her slender frame in a way that's both feminine and professional.

The woman is everything I'm not. Polished. Patient. *Perfect.*

I have no idea why she's still here, and I'm not about to ask.

Not after I just nailed her in the face with a door.

Just be cool.

"It really is so nice to meet a friend of Cooper's," she says, turning to me as I dry my hands. "He hasn't had a girlfriend since he was in the sixth grade, if you can believe it. Too busy with football."

Crap. Did she just say girlfriend?

Talk about missing the mark.

"Cooper and I are just friends." Friends who screw like rabbits and make lame Star Wars jokes. We're definitely not a couple. "I know everyone thinks men and women can't be just friends, but Cooper and I make it work."

For the love of all that is holy, stop talking.

"We're like peanut butter and jelly. Milk and cookies. Tacos and cheese."

Condoms and lube.

I bite down on the inside of my lip before any more nonsense can slip out.

Mrs. DeLaurentis smiles and there's a kind of knowing in her eyes. It's a look that tells me she isn't buying what I'm selling.

And you're surprised by this why?

I am laying it on pretty thick.

"You're good for him," she says. "We talk regularly and he's been happier this semester than he's been in a long time."

"Oh, I don't think I can take credit for that, Mrs. DeLaurentis."

She waves off my comment. "Please, call me Lauren."

I nod, but I can't seem to push her name past my lips. It's too weird. She's an adult.

So are you.

Debatable. Especially compared to this woman, who's an adultier adult than I'll ever be.

"I'm glad Cooper has finally met a nice girl. Someone who sees him for who he is and not just his skill on the field."

"I—" How am I even supposed to respond to that? *Very. Carefully.* "He's a great guy. And a really good friend."

Oh, God. Please let this end before I make a bigger fool of myself.

"Cooper deserves to be happy." She smiles warmly, her eyes crinkling at the corners just like Coop's do. "He puts on a front, but deep down, he's actually quite sensitive. Not like those other boys who just—" She shakes off the thought. "Well, I'm sure you know what some of those boys are like."

It's all I can do not to laugh because only a mother could believe Coop isn't sewing his wild oats and banging his way across campus.

"Once he joins the NFL," she continues, "having stability will be even more important for him."

I stiffen. This feels like a trap. Coop said his parents didn't know about his plans.

No, he said his father didn't know about his plans.

Still, I'm not sure what to say, so I just stand there like an idiot, saying nothing.

"A girl like you could help keep him grounded."

Anxiety tightens my chest. She's right about Cooper. He has a good heart. He's not at all what I expected based on his reputation. Even now, it's hard to reconcile the guy I met that first night with the man I've come to know. He's sweet. Smart. Loyal.

But I'm not the one who will keep him grounded.

What we have isn't real, even if I wish it was.

I can't exactly say that to his mother, though. Not when she's looking at me like I'm the greatest thing that's ever happened to her son. "I'll do my best."

She touches my arm. "That's all a mother can ask."

I follow her lead as we exit the bathroom. When she reaches for the door handle, the sleeve of her jacket rides up and I glimpse a nasty bruise on her wrist.

"Ouch." The observation pops out before I have time to think it through. "That looks like it hurt."

I'd know. I've had my share of ill-timed bruises over the years.

Lasting reminders of my status as a literal walking disaster.

"Oh, it's nothing." She holds the door for me and after I slip through, she adjusts the sleeve of her jacket, once again the picture of perfection. *#lifegoals.* "I have a bit of a clumsy side. Cooper may have gotten his looks from me, but he definitely got his father's grace."

It's hard to believe this beautiful, confident woman has a clumsy bone in her body, but it explains *so* much.

43

COOPER

THE LAST FEW hours have stretched on interminably, even with Quinn's company. I'm going to owe her another favor after this, because I had way more fun helping her with the Virgin Quest than she's having right now.

She's too polite to say it, but I'm pretty sure she'd rather be doing homework.

Or waxing her legs.

Or pretty much anything else.

I can't blame her. I'd rather be at study hall screwing around with my roommates. Watching my father socialize with his cronies is nauseating.

How can they not see that he's a lying, manipulative bastard?

Because they choose not to.

The polls closed an hour ago, and the ballroom has grown increasingly crowded as fundraisers and supporters pour in to watch the final projections. My father is leading Mullaney by a full point, and even though the news stations aren't likely to call the race until all the ballots are counted, his team is making noise about claiming victory.

Democracy at its finest.

I turn to Quinn, who's working her way through a plate of hors d'oeuvres. "It shouldn't be too much longer now."

"As long as you keep the food coming, I'm good." She wipes the corner of her mouth with a napkin. "You need to try this crab and avocado toast. It's to die for."

She offers me the appetizer in question, which is a thin piece of toast with avocado spread and spongy chunks of crab sprinkled on top.

I shake my head. "Die being the operative word."

"Oh, my gosh." She snatches it back and drops it on her plate. "Are you allergic to seafood?"

"If by allergic, you mean totally repulsed by the texture of it in my mouth, yes."

She rolls her eyes. "There's something very wrong with you."

"Took you long enough to figure it out."

"Seriously." She shakes her head in disbelief. "Who doesn't like crab?"

I shrug and take a pull on my beer. People always react this way when they find out I don't like seafood. Most of the time, I just lie and say I'm allergic to avoid the questions, but I don't want to lie to Quinn, even over something so trivial.

"So, wait." She frowns, that adorable wrinkle forming between her brows. "Is this weird texture aversion exclusive to crab or do you like, hate all seafood?"

"That would be option two."

Her eyes go wide and she plants her hands on her hips. "I don't think we can be friends anymore."

"Or you could look at the bright side." I nod to her plate. "You never have to worry about me stealing your shrimp cocktail. In fact, I'll give you mine."

She cocks her head, pretending to think it over. "You make a good point, but that also means no sushi bars or crab boils or—" She flushes. "Not that we'd be doing those things, anyway."

I open my mouth to respond when Elliot appears at our table. "We're going to need you onstage, Cooper. Senator DeLaurentis is going to give an address and we need the whole family present."

His eyes bore into me, which is his passive aggressive way of letting me know he's not leaving without me in tow.

I grab Quinn's hand, which earns me a disapproving look from the chief minion.

"Relax, Elliot. I'm not planning to bring her onstage, but I'm not going to just leave her here alone, either." I wink at him. "I'm a gentleman."

Quinn smothers a laugh and follows me to the front of the room, where there's a door leading backstage. It's dark and we climb the handful of stairs carefully before finding a place to wait in the wings.

A gold curtain blocks us from view, and, not gonna lie, I wish I'd thought of this sooner because it's the perfect place to pass a few hours making out with a gorgeous woman.

But I can't say that because there are too many of my father's lackeys around.

The door at the bottom of the stairs opens and my parents slip through.

"That reminds me," Quinn whispers in my ear. "I finally figured out why you're completely unfazed by Calamity Quinn."

My gut clenches at that fucking nickname, but this isn't the time to get into it.

"Your mom told me she has a klutzy side too, so I guess that means you're used to it."

Ice freezes my veins. "What are you talking about?"

"Your mom had a bruise on her wrist. When I commented

on it, she told me you get your grace from you father and that she has a clumsy streak, like me."

Sonofabitch.

A red veil drops over my vision just as my mother walks past, smile fixed in place.

"What is it?" Quinn asks, voice tinged with worry. "Did I say something wrong?"

My father crests the stairs just then, fully in politician mode, looking like the king of the world. He claps me on the shoulder and says something about DeLaurentis men being winners, but I don't hear him.

I only hear the blood rushing through my ears, whispering the truth I've always known.

Abusive, cheating bastard.

Just like his father before him.

Like all DeLaurentis men.

Red-hot fury pulses through my limbs as I grab the front of his jacket and swing him around, slamming his back against the wall.

Quinn gasps and steps aside, but I only have eyes for my father.

"What the fuck did you do to her?" I growl, breathing hard. "Why is there a bruise on her wrist?"

His eyes go wide and he glances around for help, but short of calling security, no one's getting between the two of us. Certainly not Elliot with his pinstriped suit and outdated pocket square.

"This isn't the time," he hisses. "You're making a scene."

"You're goddamn right I'm making a scene."

"Your father's been under a lot of stress," my mother says, her words a quiet whisper, as if even she knows they're bullshit. "It's not a big deal."

Not a big deal?

No decent man puts his hands on a woman and the fact that he's got her defending him pushes my fury to a whole new level.

"From where I'm standing," I grit out, "it's a pretty big fucking deal."

"You need to calm down, son." Sweat beads along his hairline and I can see the wheels turning as he tries to weasel his way out of taking responsibility. "The ballroom is full of reporters. This isn't a good look for either of us. If I recall correctly, Waverly has a strict no tolerance policy for violence."

Fuck. Fuck. Fuck.

He's right. If word gets out I hit my father, my ass will be benched for the rest of the season. No championship game. No NFL combine. No draft.

His back may be to the wall, but he still has all the power.

Just a few more months.

I bite back a curse.

"If I find out you laid one finger on her after today, there's no amount of bad press that will stop me from beating the shit out of you." He struggles, but I hold tight to the lapels of his jacket. "You will piss blood for a week, old man. Not. One. Finger."

He doesn't say a word, but for the first time in my life, I see genuine fear in his eyes.

Good. He should be afraid. He should know how it feels to cower and wonder if the next blow will be the one that puts him in the hospital. *Or worse.*

"Cooper." My mother's quiet plea breaks through the red haze clouding my vision. She touches my forearm, her slender fingers gentle despite the violence roaring through my veins. "That's enough. You've made your point."

Doubtful. The bastard's as thick as a cinderblock wall.

"Let's go, Quinn." My jaw is clenched so hard it's a struggle to get the words out. "We're leaving."

I'm not about to stick around and celebrate this bastard.

I release him with a rough shove, slamming his back against the wall one more time. Anger flashes in his eyes, but when he straightens, his face is a blank mask.

If only his constituents could see him now.

On stage, the emcee wraps up his introduction and thunderous applause fills the ballroom. I don't spare my father a second glance as I kiss my mother's cheek and promise to call her in the morning.

I turn on my heel and push through the fire door, exiting into the hall. Quinn is right behind me, hurrying to keep up with my brisk pace. I exhale and force myself to slow down.

She doesn't speak as we descend the stairs and exit the hotel. It's just as well. I have nothing to say about the scene upstairs.

Just the memory of the bruise on my mom's wrist has my blood pressure skyrocketing again.

I rip off my tie and stuff it in my pocket as we wait for the valet to bring the Audi around.

It's going to be a long ride back to College Park.

Beside me, Quinn looks shellshocked.

Can't blame her. I doubt this is how she pictured the day ending. Or, maybe, like the rest of the world, she bought into my father's bullshit family man persona.

Christ. I hope she didn't vote for him.

The car arrives, and I tip the valet before sliding in behind the wheel. We buckle up and I stomp on the gas pedal, more than ready to put this day in the rearview mirror.

I turn up the music, but the thumping bass does little to drown out my thoughts.

Just a few more months.

Once I sign with the NFL, I'll have the resources to get my mom out of there. To protect her.

I'm so damn close, and yet there's nothing I can do for her

now. I don't have the money or the connections to take on my father.

It's frustrating as hell.

I just want to take care of her and make sure she's safe, something she's always done for me.

And part of that is keeping our story out of the press.

I dart a glance at Quinn. She's been quiet for most of the ride, but it's clear the silence is for my benefit. "This better not end up in one of your stories."

Hurt flashes across her face at the accusation, but it's quickly replaced by hard-earned stoicism. "I'd never do something like that, Cooper."

Guilt squeezes my chest.

It was a dick comment. Quinn would never betray me like that, but I can't afford to take chances. Especially since my judgment is obviously shit.

"Do you want to talk about it?"

"No." I'd rather get blindsided by a two-hundred-and-fifty-pound linebacker.

Quinn covers my hand, which rests on the gearshift, with her own. "I'm here if you change your mind."

Not gonna happen.

Not in this lifetime, anyway.

By the time we pull up to Quinn's place, it's after midnight and I'm ready to crawl out of my skin. It's been a long, stressful day and I'm exhausted.

"Thanks again for coming with me." I drum my fingers on the steering wheel. "Sorry it was such a shit show."

"Hey." She hooks a finger under my chin and turns my head, forcing me to meet her eyes. "You have nothing to apologize for, Cooper. You didn't do anything wrong." She grins. "For what it's worth, I voted for the other guy."

I laugh in spite of myself and just like that, the tension between us fades.

She looks up at me from under her lashes, eyes sparkling in the streetlight, and suddenly, the only thing that matters is feeling her sweet lips on mine.

I kiss her, slow and deep, feeding the part of myself that is never sated, that always craves more when it comes to Quinn.

When she finally pulls away, there's a mischievous grin on her face. "Do you want to come in?"

44

QUINN

I LEAD Cooper to my room and close the door behind us as I flip the light switch. Haley's staying at B's tonight, and we have the place to ourselves, but I'd feel weird leaving the door open. I may be inexperienced, but I'm pretty sure exhibitionism isn't my thing.

Don't knock it 'til you've tried it.

Fair enough. There's not much I wouldn't try at least once where Cooper is involved.

"I'm glad you decided to come in for a bit."

"Like I could ever refuse you."

I stretch up on my toes and kiss him as he threads his fingers through my hair. My scalp tingles and it feels so freaking good, I never want him to stop. But tonight isn't about me.

It's about Cooper.

He's had a rough day, and even if he doesn't want to talk about it, I know the physical connection will bring some comfort. At least, I hope it will.

I strip off his jacket and toss it over the desk chair. Then I unbutton his shirt, my fingers moving down the line of tiny buttons until I reach his belt.

"Someone's in a hurry," he murmurs, brushing my hair back from my face.

Accurate. "Do you have any idea how good you look in a suit?"

He smirks. "I do."

"There's a fine line between confidence and cockiness." I unfasten his pants and shove them down as he steps out of them. "It should be illegal to look this good."

"Tell me about it." He drops a kiss to my collarbone. "This patch of skin right here has been driving me crazy all day. You don't know how many times I've thought about running my tongue over it just to get a little taste."

Warmth blossoms in my chest and then I'm kicking off my shoes, reaching for the zipper on the back of my dress.

Cooper spins me around and my hands fall to my sides as he unzips me, peppering kisses down my spine as he goes. His mouth is wet and hungry and my nipples ache at the mere prospect of contact. When the black wool falls to the floor, pooling around my feet, he goes to work on my tights, peeling them down ever so slowly and stripping my panties too.

Goosebumps rise on my thighs, but I forget all about them the instant Cooper's teeth clamp down on my right ass cheek.

"Oh!" I barely have time to process the sting before his tongue descends, licking and massaging the pain away. "*Ohhh.*"

Desire ignites between my legs like wildfire and I turn to him, cupping his chin and pulling him to his feet.

Tonight is about Cooper, but it's also about firsts.

"Lie down on the bed."

His brows shoot up at the command, but he does as instructed, stretching out on top of the comforter, his cock jutting proudly toward the ceiling.

Nerves take hold as I pull a condom from the nightstand, but I push them aside and tear the foil packet open.

Coop watches as I climb onto the bed, straddling his legs. He's rigid beneath me as I roll the condom down his length, but the intensity of his stare suggests he likes what he sees.

That makes two of us.

I will never tire of admiring the contours of his chest or the deep v that leads to his pelvis.

How many crunches does it take to get that kind of definition, anyway?

Too many.

Which is why I look my fill. That kind of dedication should be rewarded, after all.

Coop's eyelids dip low as I hover above him, positioning his cock at my entrance.

He caresses my thighs with his big, calloused hands and when he speaks, his voice is a sexy rasp that has my core clenching with need. "Ride me, sweetheart."

I'm already wet, my body desperate and aching for the fullness only Cooper can deliver.

I lower myself slowly, savoring every glorious inch as he fills me up and *oh*—

Sweet Jesus.

Tension coils deep within me, every nerve in my body tingling with pleasure.

Cooper's eyelids slam closed, and the breath hisses out of him. "You feel so damn good."

Maybe it's the angle. Maybe it's the way he bit my ass earlier. Or maybe I'm just getting better at sex, but I'm halfway there already and his words give me the confidence to take control.

Own that shit.

"Relax." I rock my hips gently. "Tonight, I get to take care of you."

His eyes snap open, locking on mine with a new kind of intimacy. The weight of it presses down on me, heightening every sensation as I move against him, chasing our mutual pleasure.

"So damn beautiful."

Coop grips my hips, but he doesn't rush me or try to take control. He seems perfectly content with my languid love making as his fingers skim up my sides to cup my breasts, which are heavy with arousal. When he sweeps his thumbs over my nipples, I moan and order him to do it again.

A lazy smile stretches across his full lips, but he does as he's told and I arch into his touch, grinding against his pelvic bone.

Another wanton moan bursts from my lips, but I'm past the point of modesty. This man has licked and sucked and explored every inch of my body. There are no secrets left between us.

Not physically, anyway.

"I had no idea you could be so bossy," he says, trailing a finger down my abdomen. "Not that I mind. I'm actually kind of digging it."

I open my mouth to issue another command, but the words die on my lips when he licks his thumb and presses it to my clit. The little bundle of nerves sends a wave of indescribable pleasure straight to my brain and I quicken my pace, rubbing against his slick finger as I ride him, pushing us closer to the explosive finale.

"That's my girl." He rolls his hips, and the angle introduces a new sensation that has my toes curling so hard they freaking cramp. "I wish you could see how sexy you look right now."

My cheeks heat at the compliment and I revel in the knowledge that I've given him a reprieve—however temporary—from the day's events.

"Come for me, sweetheart." He all but pants the words, and for the first time, I notice the sheen of sweat lining his brow. He's almost there. "I want to watch you come all over my cock."

"I want it too." God, do I want it. "I'm close."

So close.

He increases the pressure on my clit and stars explode behind my eyelids. I throw my head back, arching into his touch as I take and take and take. And then I'm flying over a cliff, Cooper's name on my lips as I break over and over, his pleasure rushing in like the tide as his hips crash against mine. He buries himself deep, cock pulsing inside me as he rides out the powerful orgasm.

After, as we lay tangled in bed, his fingers toying with my hair, mine tracing circles on his chest, he clears his throat. "I really am sorry about today."

"Don't be." I force myself not to look up, to keep my voice even so I don't spook him. "I'm glad you didn't have to face it alone."

And pissed he had to face it at all.

"I knew the day would be shitty, but I didn't expect—"

He doesn't have to finish the sentence. The meaning is clear. He hadn't expected me to shine a spotlight on his father's domestic abuse.

I hate that I caused Cooper pain—hate that his father is absolute trash—but I can't bring myself to regret telling him what I saw, no matter how tactless the delivery.

If only I'd realized sooner.

God, I'm such an idiot. His mother's words about being a klutz replay on a loop in my head and I'm reminded of every movie ever where the abused spouse covers for their abuser with thinly veiled lies.

"My father's always been a bastard." Cooper's voice is thick with emotion. His chest vibrates beneath my head and I want to wrap my arms around him, but I don't dare move. Not when he's talking freely. "Over the years, he's gotten very good at hiding that part of himself from the public. After all, who'd vote for a politician who beats his wife and kid?"

My stomach roils, anger and disgust filling the space that just moments ago was aglow with softer, warmer sentiments.

"For a long time, I thought his Jekyll/Hyde personality was normal. That if mom and I just tried harder, if we could be a little better, he wouldn't have to punish us. That's what he always said, anyway."

My heart aches at the thought of a smaller, defenseless Cooper suffering at the hands of that monster.

"Eventually, I realized that no matter how hard we tried, he'd always find a reason." His body stiffens beneath me and the fingers that just moments ago were tangled in my hair, stop moving. "My mom protected me the best way she knew how—by using herself as a shield and taking the brunt of his rage—but it was never enough. No matter how many bruises he left, how many ribs he cracked, how many lips he split."

I mold my body to his, pressing my breasts and belly flush to his side, providing comfort the only way I know how, through touch. Cooper's never been this vulnerable with me before and something tells me I'm the exception, not the rule. Do his friends even know he's carrying this dark secret?

Probably not.

He wouldn't want to worry them with his troubles.

After all, he's made an entire college career out of being the good-time guy. The laid-back jock who can always be counted on to deliver a laugh.

"The summer I turned sixteen, I had a growth spurt." There's a wryness to his voice and I can almost imagine a bittersweet smile twisting his lips. "I came home from practice one day to find him hurting my mom and I lost it. I pinned him to the wall and promised that the next time he laid a hand on her, I'd repay every bruise tenfold. Things were better for a while after that. It was a relief to know I could finally protect her the way she'd protected me for so long. But then I left for college like a selfish asshole, and without me there to keep him in check..."

He trails off, and it's clear the guilt of not being home to shield his mother from abuse weighs on him.

No one should have to bear that burden. Especially a child. Being forced to choose between building a future and protecting those they hold dear?

That's no choice at all.

"I would've stayed," he says stiffly. "But playing ball is the only hope I have of getting her out. My father is too wealthy, too well-known. Too fucking connected. He'll never let her go, and I don't have the resources to fight him. Not in the press and certainly not in a courtroom. He's got friends in high places and a cutthroat legal team that would shred whatever baby lawyer I could afford. That's why I've spent the last four years busting my ass to ensure I'll be a first-round draft pick. The money I'll earn from an NFL contract is the only chance I have of getting my mom away from him. The only chance we have of starting over without him in our lives."

The admission rips the air from my lungs.

No wonder Cooper is so focused on football. He views it as the only solution to a problem—a situation—he's never been able to fix. The pressure to perform must be crushing.

I always knew being a top tier athlete would carry a lot of pressure, but this... It's beyond anything I could have imagined.

Yet he shoulders the burden silently and without complaint.

My heart squeezes at the unfairness of it all.

"Anyway." He clears his throat. "I just thought you should know."

Because this is the reason he doesn't do relationships. He doesn't trust himself. Or maybe he simply doesn't know what a healthy relationship looks like.

You could show him.

Even if that were true, he'd never agree. Would he?

That he hasn't sworn me to secrecy again speaks volumes. Maybe it's a sign he's finally ready to let someone in.

"Thank you for sharing this with me." I wrap my arms around him, holding him tight. His skin is hot, and he smells like sex, but I wouldn't have it any other way. "You're nothing like your father, Cooper. You can't keep punishing yourself for his mistakes."

In one swift movement, he rolls us over so that I'm pinned to the mattress beneath him. One look into those clear blue eyes and it's obvious he's ready to put this conversation—this night—behind us.

"You just might be onto something," he drawls, cock nudging at my belly. "Why punish myself when I've got you to do the job for me?"

45

COOPER

I WAKE with Quinn curled in my arms and the knowledge that if I don't get my ass out of bed soon, I'm going to be late for strength training. Quinn mumbles something unintelligible and snuggles up closer, pulling the comforter tight around us. The blanket is hot AF and I'm burning up, but it's a small price to pay for a night of great sex.

Liar.

Fine. Last night was about more than sex.

I still can't believe I told her about my father. I've never told anyone before, because who would believe me?

Quinn.

She listened without interrupting. Without making excuses for his behavior. Without questioning a single word of my story.

It was almost enough to give me hope others might believe it, too.

But I can't take the risk. Not when I'm entirely without resources.

Just a few more months.

With herculean effort, I slip out of bed and begin collecting my discarded clothes. The room is chilly and though it's a welcome relief against my heated skin, it's not worth the tradeoff of leaving Quinn's soft curves behind.

My cock stirs and I steal a glance at the bed.

Focus, asshole.

My pants are wrinkled as hell and hardly appropriate for the gym, but I slip them on anyway. I keep a change of clothes in my locker, so at least I won't lose time stopping by the apartment. I throw on my shirt and pull out my phone to check the time.

Five-thirty.

I'll be cutting it close. Training starts at six.

I button my shirt and slip on my shoes before darting one last look at the bed.

Quinn looks like an angel curled up under that ridiculous pink comforter, hair spread around her head like a halo.

Sneaking out is a dick move, but I hate to wake her so early. We didn't get much sleep last night and even if she's got an 8am class, she can still grab another hour of rest.

I find a pen and sheet of paper on her desk and I'm scrawling a note by the light of my phone when a quiet laugh breaks the silence.

"Were you actually going to leave me a note?" Quinn asks, voice groggy from sleep.

She flips on the bedside lamp and I turn to find her sitting up, hair tangled and still wearing my undershirt. It looks good on her. She should sleep in one of my shirts every night.

I toss the pen on the desk, abandoning the note. "You say that like it's a bad thing."

"Not at all." She grins. "I just didn't know it was part of the Cooper DeLaurentis sleepover experience."

"There's a lot you still don't know about the Cooper DeLaurentis sleepover experience."

There's still a lot *I* don't know, since this is only my third one.

I cross the room in a few quick strides and drop a tender kiss on her lips. "Sorry to cut and run, but I've got strength training at six and Coach will kill me if I'm late. We've got Michigan this week, and he wasn't happy I missed practice yesterday."

"No worries. I don't want you to be late on my account." She bites her lower lip, and I can practically see the wheels spinning in her head. Impressive considering my brain is currently running on autopilot. "I know you have training, and I respect that, but there's something I want to say before you go."

Awesome. That doesn't sound terrifying at all.

"What's up?" I ask, trying to sound casual.

"So, the thing is, I want more."

"More what? Sex?" I flash her a wicked grin. "I'm down."

Quinn laughs and shakes her head. "That's part of it, but not all of it."

My smile falters. "What else is there?"

"Don't freak out."

Yeah, because good news always comes after those words.

"I can't keep sleeping with you." She fists the comforter in her hands, but she might as well punch me in the balls. "Not without some kind of commitment. I'm just not built that way. And after last night..."

Last night was intense. I won't deny it. Hell, I won't even deny it changed things between us, but dating? Like an actual relationship? That's like— I don't—

Fuck.

I rake a hand through my hair.

"I'm not sure what to say here."

That's the understatement of the century.

"I didn't mean to spring this on you, and I don't expect an answer right away." She tucks a wild strand of hair behind her ear. "In fact, I'd prefer you take some time to think it over, because what we're doing? It's a relationship, even if you're afraid to call it one."

"I'm not afraid of a label."

She arches a brow, clearly skeptical. I can't blame her. The words sound defensive to my own ears, so I can only imagine how they sound to hers.

"I get it," she says quietly. "After yesterday, I understand better than ever why you have trouble with commitment, but you aren't your father, Cooper. You'd never hurt me."

Not intentionally, but intentions don't matter when it comes to hurting the people you care about.

I care about Quinn.

The realization pulls me up short. I don't know how it happened or even when it happened, but sometime over the last two months, she's become important to me.

My hands tremble and I shove them into my hair, willing them to steady.

If I don't do this, if I don't at least try, I'll lose her.

No more hookups. No more cuddling. No more impromptu coffee dates at Daily Grind.

Eventually, she'll meet someone else. Someone safe. Someone who isn't fucked in the head and doesn't have daddy issues. Someone who can give her everything she needs, maybe even love.

Just the thought of another guy touching Quinn has my gut clenching.

I can't lose her.

What about the rules?

The virgin rule is already out the window. So that just leaves rule number two.

Which also went out the window the second I touched her. Noah just doesn't know it yet.

If I had my way, he never would.

Dammit. Why is this so complicated?

The rules exist for a reason. But we've already broken them

and my life hasn't gone into a death spiral. Quinn and I are getting along great and I'm playing the best ball of my life. Could it really hurt to try?

If things go sideways, we can always call it quits.

Way to be an optimist, asshole.

Okay. That's probably not the best outlook on dating, but I'm new to all this.

Quinn stares up at me, hope and uncertainty warring in those Coke bottle eyes and something in my chest cracks.

I put that look there. That uncertainty. It's the same look she gets when she talks about being a trainwreck or when Noah calls her those stupid nicknames.

A hot ball of fury throbs in my gut.

I will not be one of the people who make her doubt herself. Who makes her feel like she doesn't deserve the things she wants most out of life.

"I don't need more time."

Her brows knit together in confusion. "You don't?"

"I've never dated." I close my eyes and inhale a steadying breath. *Please don't let me screw this up.* "I don't know if I can give you what you want, but I'm willing to try."

The smile that breaks over her face is radiant and I can't believe I ever hesitated. There's nothing I wouldn't do to see her look at me that way just one more time.

"We can start slow." She pushes up on her knees and crawls to the edge of the bed, looking up at me from under her lashes. "We could start with dating exclusively." She pokes me in the chest. "Which, in case you're not familiar with the term, means you won't be hooking up with anyone else."

"Done." Why would I want to hook up with anyone else when I've got Quinn? "But you have to stand in front of me when we tell Noah."

Quinn snort-laughs. "You can't seriously expect me to

believe you're afraid of Noah. You're like four inches taller than he is. What's he going to do? Ban you from the house?"

"How about we don't find out?" I snake an arm around her waist and pull her in for a kiss. It's chaste as hell, but I have no interest in showing up at the gym with a boner.

The guys would never let me hear the end of it.

When she pulls away, there's a mischievous glint in her eyes. "How about we do?"

She dives for the phone on the nightstand, giving me a prime view of her bare ass, and taps out a quick message. I don't get a look at the screen until after she's pressed send.

*Quinn: I'm sleeping with Cooper. Deal with it. *happy devil emoji**

Fuuuck. "That's definitely not how I would have delivered the news. Surely there was a more tactful way to communicate our status."

I can't quite bring myself to say the word *relationship* yet.

She smirks. "Yeah, but what would be the fun of that?"

I pinch the bridge of my nose. It's too early for this sibling shit.

On the bright side, Noah's probably still asleep. Maybe he won't see it and—

Her phone vibrates with an incoming message.

Noah: I swear to God if you're messing with me...

Noah: Are you with DeLaurentis right now? He better have fucking pants on.

Noah: This isn't funny, Quinn!

She tosses the phone on the bed without replying.

"Aren't you going to answer him?"

"Nope." She flashes me a smug grin. "I'm going to let him sweat it out. Seems like it'll be a lot more fun that way."

"Fun for who?" I grumble, rubbing the back of my neck as I imagine all the ways Noah's going to make my life miserable within the frat.

"Me, obviously." She scoots to the edge of the bed again and gives me a quick peck on the lips. "Now get moving. I will not be the reason you're distracted."

It's a little too late for that.

When I roll into the team weight room fashionably late, my roommates descend like vultures, cornering me before I even have a chance to warm up.

"Where were you this morning?" Reid asks, wiping the back of his hand across his forehead. He was probably one of the first to arrive. He always is. "Your bed was empty when I looked in."

A raucous cheer breaks out down the aisle, buying me some time, as a bunch of guys cheer on a defensive tackle who's doing squats with an obscene amount of weight on the bar.

"I stayed at Quinn's place." No point lying. They've probably already guessed the truth.

"We figured y'all stayed out late celebrating the senator's big win," Vaughn says. "But another sleepover? Sounds serious."

The mention of my father sours my mood instantly.

"Dude." Parker smirks and slings an arm around my shoulders. "I don't know what's going on with you lately, but you're freaking me out. It's like invasion of the body snatchers or some shit." He grabs my chin with his free hand and turns my head to face him. "Have you been body snatched? Blink once for yes and two for no."

I blink.

Because what the hell?

Vaughn smacks Parker on the back of the head. "If he was body snatched, do you really think the aliens would let him tell you?"

Parker shrugs.

"I saw the movie," Vaughn continues, far too serious given the topic. "The aliens take complete control of your brain and your nervous system and everything." He shudders. "Talk about freaky."

"It's too early for this crap." I shake my head and pull out of Parker's reach as he and Vaughn discuss the merits of getting body snatched. "I'm going to do squats. Some of us are actually here to work out."

Reid snorts, but follows me to an empty power rack and helps me load weights on the bar. The defensive line is still going strong with their chant, making conversation impossible.

It's just as well.

I'm not exactly itching to tell him Quinn and I are exclusive. Not only because I want to keep the news to myself for a while, but because he'd probably join the body snatching conspiracy theory. Then again, he might be the only one to understand since he spent half the season sneaking around with Carter, our new kicker. Either way, I've got enough drama in my life without fanning the flames.

What I need right now is focus. With only three games remaining in the regular season, I can't afford to get distracted. Not when my mom is counting on me.

46

QUINN

"Girl, you are so lucky." Haley flops down on my bed as I stand before the mirror, swiping mascara on my lashes.

It's Sunday night and I'm getting ready for my first official date with Cooper. I'm nervous as hell and the butterflies in my stomach have been swarming all day. Which is ridiculous. The guy has feasted on every inch of my body. It doesn't get much more intimate than that.

"Where are you guys going?" Haley asks, her reflection wiggling its brows at me in the mirror. "You know, in case B and I want to join you."

"Don't you dare." I'm open to a double date in the future—assuming Bryan agrees not to be an ass—but no one is crashing our first date. "I've been looking forward to this all week."

Haley snickers. "You don't say?"

I stick my tongue out at her and gesture to the laptop on the bed. "My paper is open on the desktop, if you're still up for a proofread."

"Like you even need to ask." She pulls the laptop closer and taps the touchpad before losing herself in my words.

I finally finished my term paper for Call-Me-David. Coming

up with a topic was like slogging through quicksand, but after I spent some time thinking about Coop's advice—to own my vibe and not let others use it against me—I found clarity. Once I decided to write about my Virgin Quest and learning to accept myself for who I am and embracing my chaos as fuel for the creative well, the words had flowed from my fingertips. I'm still a work in progress, but I finally understand what Call-Me-David meant when he said my pieces lacked depth.

After all, poking fun at myself and devaluing my thoughts and experiences invited everyone else to do the same.

I carefully apply lip gloss to my bottom lip and press my lips together.

The last few weeks have been incredible—aside from Noah's continual digs about me going behind his back—but With Cooper's hectic schedule, it's been hard to plan anything. We mostly see each other at Daily Grind or at bedtime, though sleeping is hardly a priority.

A crimson flush stains my cheeks.

It's possible I've been greedy in that respect. I have no clue how Coop powers through his days on so little sleep, but I've been mainlining coffee like it's my job.

Which is why I'm going to make sure he gets to bed early tonight.

No late-night sex marathons for us. Just good old-fashioned, restorative sleep.

Cooper's been stressed about football and now that I know the root of his ambition, I can hardly blame him. Though he's been playing well, the team barely pulled out a win against Michigan last weekend. Thankfully, yesterday's away game against Rutgers was a blowout.

Just one more regular season game to go.

But even that's a temporary relief because then it's on to bowl games.

So, yeah. Cooper's got a lot on his mind, which is why I'm not pushing him for labels. Although we spend almost every night together, I'm not even sure he's told his friends we're dating. But he's not seeing anyone else and for now, it's enough.

Even if I am falling for him.

Hard.

"This is good," Haley says, cutting off my train of thought. "Like, really good. If Call-Me-David doesn't give you an A, he's an idiot."

"Thanks." Priya had said the same thing more or less, but it never hurts to have multiple sources of feedback. "Let's just hope he's not an idiot because I can't afford anything less than an A on that paper."

Haley sits up, giving me an appraising stare. "Your ass looks great in those jeans, by the way."

"Maybe I should attach a picture to my term paper."

"Couldn't hurt." Haley flips the laptop around. "Just submit the paper already and be done with it. The longer you hold on to it, the more you're going to second-guess yourself."

God, she knows me so well.

I have a tendency to over-edit. And overthink. And basically drag projects out until the last possible second while turning myself into a basket case.

Haley arches a brow and stares pointedly at the laptop.

I sigh and tap a few keys, pulling up my email. Under her watchful gaze, I type a brief email to Call-Me-David and attach the file. My finger hovers over the send button, but then Haley clears her throat and I tap it, anxiety curling deep in my chest as the email blasts off into cyberspace.

"There." Haley wipes her palms together as if she's just completed hard labor. "Now you can enjoy your night out without worrying about Call-Me-David."

As if such a thing is possible.

"How's your final project for Professor Ronan coming along?" I dab on a light, floral perfume and give myself one last look in the mirror. I have no idea where we're going—despite asking Cooper at least a dozen times—so hopefully jeans and an emerald green sweater fit the dress code.

Haley grins. "I have all the pieces for my sculpture complete, but I haven't assembled them yet. I enjoy keeping Ronan in suspense."

"Suspense?" I snort-laugh. "I think you mean terror."

Based on the stories I've heard, the professor doesn't appreciate Haley's flair for the dramatic. Or her innate ability to push boundaries.

Her loss.

"Whatever." Haley shrugs. "It's going to be epic."

The doorbell rings and Haley trails me into the hall, because, as she's told me on several occasions, she's never not going to ogle the man candy.

Fortunately, Coop considers it a compliment.

I open the front door and Cooper steps in, looking sexy as sin in dark jeans and a navy Henley that brings out the color of his eyes. Something like a growl rolls off his lips, and he hooks an arm around my waist and grabs my ass, pulling me in until I'm flush against him. Then his lips descend on mine, ravenous, despite the fact that it's only been forty-eight hours since we last saw each other.

His tongue glides along my upper lip and I melt into him, biting back a moan as he makes a seductive sweep of my mouth.

God, I've missed this.

Has it really only been two days?

Coop groans and the hard ridge swells against my belly.

"That's it," Haley announces from somewhere behind us. "I'm going to watch porn."

I laugh and Coop releases his grip on me with a wolfish grin.

"What can I say? You look good enough to eat." He pauses. "You know, we could just order in."

"Nice try." I poke him in the chest playfully. "You're taking me out. Otherwise, this is just a booty call."

Coop heaves a theatrical sigh. "Dating has so many rules."

"I could write them down." I quirk a brow. "Would that make it easier for you to remember them?"

"Very funny." He swats me on the ass. "For future reference, I am one hundred percent open to booty calls. I will never be offended if you stop by unannounced for sex."

A few minutes later, we're settled in the Audi, cruising down Wildcat Ave. Cooper has the heat on full blast and I know it's entirely for my benefit, since he's like a walking radiator. A cold front has settled over College Park and while I'm bundled up in a puffy North Face parka, he doesn't even have a jacket.

"Where are we going?" I ask as local shops and restaurants slide by in a blur.

"It's a surprise." He turns, giving me a devilish wink. "I've held out this long. I'm not about to crack now."

I roll my eyes. "Have I mentioned that I hate surprises?"

"Only like once or fifty times." He reaches over the center console and squeezes my knee. "Trust me. This is a good surprise." He pauses and glances over his shoulder before changing lanes. "Did you finish your paper?"

"I did. Haley also convinced me to submit it, which I am now seriously regretting."

"No sense stressing about it now. Besides, I'm sure it's great."

"Let's hope Call-Me-David agrees."

"Don't let one pretentious asshole's opinion derail you." He gives my knee another gentle squeeze. "You've got genuine talent, Quinn. There are plenty of people who are interested in reading your work and hearing what you have to say."

He's right. I know he's right, but it's not that easy to just forget about it.

I'm not wired that way.

Cooper pulls into Tadashi, a popular Japanese restaurant, and my stomach rumbles in approval. "We're getting sushi?"

"Yeah." He pulls into a spot near the entrance and kills the engine. "I know you like it, so I thought I'd give it another try."

Warm fuzzies fill my chest, and I lean across the center console to kiss him.

"Thank you. This is really sweet." Especially since he looks like he's about to toss his cookies at any moment. "Are you sure you don't want to go somewhere else?"

"No." He cocks his head to the side. "Why would you think that?"

I grin. "Because you look a little green around the gills."

He groans and rolls his eyes. "Spare me the fish jokes."

"Only if you agree to let me do the ordering." Something tells me it's in my best interest to make the selections for both of us. I don't need him trying to eat an octopus just to impress me.

Cooper grins. "Deal. As long as I get to choose dessert."

47

COOPER

THIS WAS A TERRIBLE FUCKING IDEA. Why did I ever think I could stomach raw fish? I know it's a delicacy and that loads of people enjoy it, but I'm not one of them.

Quinn stares at me expectantly as I pick up my chopsticks.

She ordered a wide variety of what she called basic rolls in hopes I'll find something I like, but it's not looking good. For starters, it's fish. One roll looks like a dragon. Like, it literally has eyeballs and a tail and whatever that thing that expands around a lizard's neck is called.

I'm trying to be open-minded, but it's kind of hard when your dinner is staring you in the eye.

It's creepy AF.

"Start with the tuna roll." Quinn points to a seaweed wrap containing pink fish and rice. She sounds so hopeful. I want to enjoy it, if only to make her happy. "It's like entry-level sushi. You can dip it in a bit of soy sauce for added flavor."

I pick it up with my chopsticks and shove it in my mouth before I can overthink it.

The seaweed wrap is surprisingly crunchy, and the rice has a hint of vinegar that isn't so bad, but then the tuna hits my tongue and *nope*.

I chew quickly and chase it down with a long drink of water.

Quinn chuckles. "I'll take that as a no."

"Maybe we could start with something a little less fishy," I suggest, popping a bit of ginger in my mouth to cleanse my palate.

"How about a California roll?" She picks up a roll that's coated with rice and seeds and offers it to me with her chopsticks. "This one has—"

"Don't tell me." It's probably better if I don't know what's inside.

I take the bite and I'm pleasantly surprised to discover it contains avocado, but then I hit a spongy texture that can only be crab and I'm out. Not even the prospect of Quinn feeding me every roll on the plate is enough to continue.

I choke it down—because I'm not a complete heathen—and drain my water glass.

Quinn chuckles. "I take it that's a no, too?"

Dammit. This night is turning into a complete disaster.

"I don't know what I was thinking." I scrub a hand over my face. "All I wanted was to take you on a proper date and I'm screwing it up." I gesture to the California roll, feeling like a complete asshole. "I can't even handle the most basic item on the menu."

"You haven't screwed anything up. It's the thought that counts, and it was really sweet of you to give sushi another try." She laughs and nudges me under the table with her foot. "Besides, if you're not eating, that just means more for me."

"Eat up." I'll gladly watch, as long as she's happy.

"So." She picks up a piece of the dragon roll. "Only one more regular season game to go."

"Maryland should be an easy enough game." I drag a finger

through the condensation on my water glass. "Most of the seniors are already looking forward to bowl games and the guys who want to go pro are looking for agents, if they don't already have them."

Quinn chews slowly, a thoughtful look on her face. "Do you have an agent?"

"No. I need to keep my plans to go pro quiet as long as possible. My father will take it as a personal insult that I'm not following in his footsteps, and my mom doesn't need to deal with the fallout."

"Won't that hurt you when it's time for the draft?" she asks, picking up a tuna roll.

"Sweetheart, I'm one of the best wide receivers in the country." Number three, to be exact. "I won't have any trouble finding an agent when the time comes."

Quinn takes a delicate bite and I fill the silence.

"Coach Collins has been great about letting scouts in to watch practice and, thanks to Reid, I've gotten looks from guys all over the country. As long as things don't go sideways, I've got a damn good shot at a first-round draft pick."

"You just said you're one of the best receivers in the country." She frowns. "You don't think any of the scouts come to see you?"

I shrug. Probably, but it's not like I can chat them up and find out. I've been very careful not to express interest in going pro, both on camera and off. "It doesn't matter either way. There are always teams looking for receivers. I'll find a spot."

"Who's your dream team?"

"My dream team?"

She rolls her eyes. "You know, the team you'd play for if you could pick any team in the league."

I honestly don't know. I don't have the luxury of worrying about coaching staff, or winning records, or any of the normal stuff. Even if I did, it wouldn't matter. The draft will determine my new home.

"Given the choice, I'd pick a west coast team."

Understanding flashes in her eyes, and she reaches for my hand again. "You deserve so much more than you were given."

Maybe. Maybe not. But at least I've got a way out.

We chat about classes and football and the upcoming Thanksgiving break. Quinn's planning to go home for the holiday, but I'm going to stick around campus and prep for the Maryland game. Plenty of the guys on the team will do the same and the coaching staff will ensure we get our turkey dinner. It won't compare to my mom's cooking, but at least it'll be a tension free meal.

When we leave the restaurant an hour later, Quinn's got an entire bag of leftover sushi dangling from her wrist.

"If there was any remaining doubt that I'd make a shitty boyfriend, this date has probably cleared it up," I say, tucking her into the passenger seat.

Quinn laughs and shakes her head. "I'm a simple girl, Cooper. I don't need all the frills. I just need you."

"I'll keep that in mind." I lean down and kiss her, slow and deep, showing her with my mouth what words could never say. Then I close the door and jog around to the driver's side, where I slide in behind the wheel.

"Why don't we drive through somewhere and get you something to eat?" she suggests as the engine roars to life. "You've got to be starving."

"I really am." I chuckle and throw the car in gear. "For our next date, I'm taking you to a burger joint. Or a pizza place. Or literally anywhere that doesn't serve fish."

"Tacos," she says, lightly. "You can never go wrong with tacos."

"I like the way you think."

We drive through a local taco place and I park at an overlook with a great view of Wildcat Stadium. It's dark tonight, but under the light of the full moon, I can still make out the sloped walls and Wildcat logo on the back of the scoreboard.

It's hard to believe my time at Waverly is ending.

Just one more game.

Senior Day.

I unwrap the taco Quinn hands me, but my appetite has evaporated.

"You look like you're a million miles away." She turns to face me, curling her feet beneath her. "What's on your mind?"

"This week's game against Maryland is Senior Day." I keep my gaze fixed on the stadium below, unable to meet her eyes. "I got a text from my mom today. She and my father are planning to attend."

Quinn doesn't respond right away, and I'm grateful because it means she won't spit meaningless platitudes.

"How do you feel about that?"

Fuck if I know. I wanted them to come. Hell, I bargained for it, but now the price feels too high.

"I'm not sure." I rub the back of my neck. "In the four years I've been at Waverly, they haven't attended a single game. How screwed up is that? Their first game will be my last."

"Oh, Cooper." She rests a hand on my thigh. "That says nothing about you and everything about them."

"It's my father's doing. My mother hasn't exactly had a choice in the matter." She doesn't get a choice in most things. That's the way it's always been, but that's all going to change after the draft. "To be honest, I'm surprised they're coming after the blowup on election night."

Though I'm sure my father will be on his best behavior with so many cameras around.

"I'm glad your mom is going to be there to see you play and escort you onto the field. I know how much she means to you."

"I'd like you to be there too. On the field with me."

I hadn't planned to ask this of her. Hadn't planned to just blurt out an invitation, but the words feel right.

"Are you sure?" She hesitates. "Taking the field with your family feels like a girlfriend's role."

"Isn't that what you are?" We haven't put labels on our relationship—yes, I can now say relationship—but it doesn't change how I feel about Quinn.

Her cheeks flush and she leans across the console to kiss me. Her lips are soft and warm and featherlight as they brush mine. "I'd be happy to escort you on Senior Day."

Relief floods my veins.

"Thanks. If you can stomach a meal with my father, maybe we can all go out to dinner after the game."

Quinn nods, though her features are tight with concern.

I can't blame her. My father is an asshole of the highest order. But if I have to put up with his presence to spend time with my mom, so be it. He'll be out of our lives soon enough.

"My mom adores you." I chuckle. During our last call, she spent twenty minutes gushing about what a sweet girl Quinn is. *If she only knew*. "She'd like to get to know you better, if you can make it."

Quinn beams. "There's nowhere else I'd rather be."

48

QUINN

It's the Saturday after Thanksgiving and while I'd normally be lounging around in joggers, nibbling on leftover pie and binging holiday movies, today I'm dressed to impress. Or, at least, I hope I am. I never really paid attention to what the girlfriends and families wore for Senior Day in the past, so I opted for black dress pants and an emerald green sweater that highlights my best feature: my hair.

The Wildcats play their last game of the regular season today and since I promised Cooper I'd escort him onto the field for Senior Day, Noah grudgingly drove me back to College Park last night. He moaned and groaned the entire way about cutting his break short, but it was a small price to pay.

I wouldn't miss this for the world.

God knows Cooper needs all the support he can get with his father in town.

We're supposed to have dinner after the game and I'm nervous AF. Coop assured me I have nothing to worry about, because his parents will just pretend the election night drama never happened. Apparently, it's their MO.

The knowledge hasn't exactly calmed the tangle of knots in my belly.

Not that I expected it to. There's too much riding on this game.

I've never been so anxious about a freaking football game in my life. I'm not sure if it's the stress of spending time with Cooper's parents or the fact that it's the Wildcats' last game of the season before bowl games are announced.

Probably both.

Which has only hammered home the amount of stress Cooper carries on a daily basis.

That he hasn't cracked under the pressure is a testament to his will and strength of character.

Traffic on campus is a nightmare and by the time my bus arrives at the stadium, I can barely sit still. Nervous energy courses through my veins as I step out onto the sidewalk with throngs of Wildcat fans, most of whom are decked out in blue and white Waverly apparel.

The parking lot is a sea of jerseys and the air hums with Wildcat pride. Everywhere I look there are students and alumni drinking and celebrating and playing cornhole alongside pop-up canopies as they tailgate and prepare for kickoff. The smell of grilled meat lingers in the air and somewhere to my left, a group of guys are doing a loud, raucous Waverly cheer.

A smile breaks over my lips.

Wildcat Nation is famous for its team pride. So famous, in fact, we've got one of the loudest stadiums in the country, giving our guys an extra edge for home games.

I make my way through the crowd and circle around to the players' entrance. There's a pleasant looking security guard at the door and when I provide my name, he gives me directions to the media room, where the families are supposed to wait.

Since I suck at directions and don't want to get lost, I pull out my phone and text Coop.

Relief washes over me when he appears a moment later, already dressed for the game.

It's the first time I've seen him up close in uniform and he looks so damn big and intimidating with his pads on. It's sexy AF. He smiles, flashing that crooked half-grin I adore, and pulls me into a hug, shaggy hair falling over his forehead.

"It's about time." Despite his smile, there's an undercurrent of anxiety in his voice. One I've never heard before. "I was starting to think you were ditching me."

"Not a chance." I poke him in the ribs, but I'm pretty sure it hurts me more than it hurts him, because *pads*. "It's a madhouse out there. It probably would've been faster to walk."

"No worries." He hooks a thumb over his shoulder. "The seniors and their guests are hanging out down the hall. You want to go join?"

"Sounds good."

He takes my hand, interlacing our fingers, and leads me down the hall.

Twenty feet from the door, we hit a wall of sound.

"I probably should have warned you." He ducks his head sheepishly. "It's a little loud. Emotions are running high today."

No doubt. "I can handle it."

It certainly can't be any worse than the parking lot.

We enter the stadium's media room, which must be nearing capacity. I've seen the coaches and players give interviews in this space a thousand times, but I never imagined I'd step foot inside. There's a large atrium above and sunlight streams through the overhead windows, illuminating the lengthy blue and white desk at the front of the room. Rows of chairs have been lined up facing the desk, but despite the abundance of seating, most people are gathered around the periphery, talking in small, animated groups.

Unease creeps up my spine as I scan the room, imaging all the things that could go wrong.

Do not embarrass Cooper.

I squash the thought under my mental boot heel. I'm a strong, confident woman. I've got this.

Besides, judging by Cooper's damp palm, he's nervous enough for both of us.

"Dunk tank girl!" Parker hollers, drawing *all* the attention as he approaches. He starts to sling an arm across my shoulders but seems to think better of it. He pivots and holds out his fist.

I grin and bump it. There's just something about this guy that's irresistible, despite the fact that he insists on using that stupid nickname.

At least it's not Quinntastrophe.

Vaughn and Reid take up positions on either side of Parker as he rambles on.

"Your boy was starting to get worried." He smirks at Cooper. "He thought maybe you wised up and moved on."

So they do know we're dating.

The realization makes me ridiculously happy, and I'm light as air as I exchange greetings with Vaughn and Reid.

Cooper unlocks his phone and checks his messages.

I'm surprised his parents haven't arrived, but I'm not about to draw attention to it.

His friends, however, lack my restraint.

"What time are your parents due in?" Reid asks.

If they aren't here yet, they'll be cutting it close.

The Senior Day presentation is being held just before kick-off, which is in forty-five minutes.

Coop locks the screen and tucks the phone in the waistband

of his pants, but his voice is carefully neutral when he answers. "They'll be here soon."

I squeeze his hand and he returns the gesture, the corner of his mouth lifting in a smile.

"Speaking of parents." Parker rubs his hands together. "We hear you're meeting DeLaurentis's parents today." He turns to Vaughn. "Remind me again what that means."

The left tackle grins, eyes alight. "Where I'm from, meeting the parents means things are getting serious."

"Where you're from, people still marry their cousins," Coop shoots back.

Vaughn's cheeks flush. "That's bullshit and you know it."

"The man makes a good point," Parker says, nodding. "Our boy went from permanent bachelor, to wifed-up and meeting the parents in a hot minute." He turns to me. "No offense, Quinn."

"None taken." I've already met Cooper's parents, but since it was a disaster, I'm perfectly content to let them think this is our first meeting.

Reid huffs out a breath. "There's nothing wrong with having a girlfriend."

It's the wrong thing to say because Parker and Vaughn howl with laughter.

When Vaughn finally catches his breath, he looks from Cooper to Reid and says, "Oh, how the mighty have fallen."

"Don't you assholes have your own people to bother?" Coop grumbles.

"Chill, princess. We just wanted to say hi to Quinn and meet the parents." Parker smirks. "We figured if she gets to meet them, we do too. You know, since we've been putting up with your sorry ass for the last three and a half years."

At the reminder of his parents' absence, a muscle in Cooper's jaw flutters.

They haven't attended a single game in four seasons and they can't even bother to show up on time? My heart aches for this man. He's been trying to downplay it, but he's been looking forward to having his mom visit. To having her escort him onto the field and watch him play. What kind of monster would stand in the way of that?

The kind who terrorizes his family and lies to his constituents.

Red-hot fury floods my veins.

All Cooper wants is what every child should have; unconditional love.

It's such a precious gift, and yet so easy to take for granted. After all, how many times have I complained about my annoying, overbearing family? More times than I can count. But I know deep down that it comes from a place of love.

Seemingly unaware of the tension that's descended over our group, Parker glances around slyly and pats his stomach. "Where's your mama, Vaughn? I need to get another one of those homemade cookies."

Vaughn sighs disapprovingly. "You can have one after the game. All that sugar will have you crashing in the fourth quarter."

Parker's jaw drops. "Are you seriously gatekeeping the cookies right now? That's stone cold, man."

"Think of it as an incentive to play well."

"I always play well," Parker says, puffing out his chest.

I laugh, because how can I not? Cooper's friends are hilarious, and it's clear they have a deep bond, just like me and Hales.

Coop's phone rings and his face sags in relief as he pulls it from the waistband of his pants and swipes accept. We all go silent and when he disconnects, there's a genuine smile on his face, the first one I've seen all day.

"They're here."

49

COOPER

LEAVE it to my father to show up at the last possible second. Nerves taut, I retrace my steps down the hall to the player's entrance, Quinn at my side.

When mom texted this morning to say they were running late and that they'd meet me at the stadium instead of the apartment as planned, I'd worried they were canceling. When Quinn arrived and I still hadn't heard from them, I'd worried something had gone wrong. That maybe my father changed his mind, and I'd be taking the field alone today.

No, not alone.

Quinn will be at my side, no matter what.

I draw a steadying breath as we turn the corner and I spot my parents waiting near the door, just as Quinn had been earlier.

My mother beams at us, her gaze drifting to our intertwined hands before returning to my face.

This time I'm not worried about her getting it wrong or reading too much into the situation. Quinn *is* my girlfriend and I'm fucking crazy about her.

Quinn drops my hand as we approach my parents, and I

open my arms wide to embrace my mom. She lifts her arms and her black cape—which is way too fancy for a football game—falls away, revealing a splint on her wrist.

I freeze, my blood running cold.

This is why they're late. Why my father wanted to meet at the stadium instead of the apartment. He thought if they arrived right before kickoff, when there was a crowd around, I'd keep my mouth shut.

Thought I wouldn't follow through on my promise.

Mom's eyes dart to the splint and she folds her arms back in the voluminous fabric of the cape, hiding them from view. "It's so good to see you both."

"I wish I could say the same," I bite out, rage building deep in my gut. "What happened to your wrist?"

"Oh, it's nothing," she says, a self-deprecating laugh spilling from her lips. "You know how clumsy I am."

How many times have I heard that lie over the years?

Too many to count.

She cups my cheek with her good hand. "Don't worry about me, sweetie. This is your day."

My gaze slides to my father, who stands idly by, as if the entire conversation is beneath him.

It's the final straw.

My pulse throbs at my temple and I explode like a goddamn supernova, unleashing years of pent-up rage and frustration.

"What the hell happened this time?" I shout, getting right in his face. The bastard flinches at the ferocity of my words, but he doesn't back down. He never does. "Did she forget to iron your favorite shirt? Burn your toast? Tell me, Dad. What exactly did she do to deserve a broken wrist?"

"It's just a sprain, Cooper. I'm fine. Really."

Is she fucking serious right now?

Like a sprain is so much better than a broken bone.

"Keep your voice down," my father orders through clenched teeth. "Don't make a scene."

"Don't make a scene?" I echo, breath coming hard and fast. *Un-fucking-believable.* "I wouldn't have to make a fucking scene if you'd keep your hands to yourself, you piece of shit!"

His eyes harden and he steps forward, fists clenched. "How dare you speak to me that way."

"How dare I?" My heart pounds against my ribs, beating double-time as I grab the front of his jacket and slam him up against the plate-glass window. His head rebounds off the spotless surface and his feet scramble for traction as he struggles to right himself. "How. Dare. You. What kind of sick fuck needs to hit a woman to feel powerful?"

"Cooper." Quinn's quiet voice cuts through my rage and I relax my grip.

"It's not his fault," my mom says, pleading on his behalf. "It's mine. Your father is under a lot of pressure and—"

A red haze blurs my vision as I draw my fist back and drive it straight into his face. Searing heat slices across my knuckles, and I welcome the pain as I raise my fist again.

I'm about to throw another punch when a small hand clasps my biceps and a familiar voice begs me to stop.

It's too late for words.

The only thing this man understands is violence.

I jerk my arm, shaking off the restrictive grip, and from the corner of my eye, I see Quinn stumble back. She trips over her feet and nearly lands on her ass, but Reid appears out of nowhere and swoops down to catch her just as powerful hands clamp down on my biceps, pulling me off my father before I can land another blow.

He slumps against the wall, cradling his busted jaw, as I struggle to break free of Parker and Vaughn.

"What the hell is going on?" Reid demands, lifting Quinn to her feet.

"Trust me," I hiss. "The bastard had it coming."

The hall falls silent and all eyes turn to my father.

Ever the politician, he straightens, pulling himself up to his full height as he smooths the front of his jacket. "Let's go, Lauren. We're leaving." He issues the cool command like he's ordering one of his minions to fetch him a coffee. "It seems we aren't wanted here."

My mother darts an apologetic glance my way and then hurries to his side, head down.

No. *Nononononono.*

If she doesn't leave him now, she'll never leave. I know it the way I know I can run a forty-yard dash in 4.29 seconds. This is the moment. The one when she has to choose.

The one that will decide the rest of our lives.

"Mom, no. You don't have to go with him. Please." My voice is high and tight, but I'm not too proud to beg. There's nothing I wouldn't do for my mom. "I can keep you safe. We'll figure this out."

"There's nothing to figure out," my father says icily. "Your mother and I are leaving."

He turns on his heel and pushes through the exit, my mother trailing behind him.

The worst part? She doesn't even look back.

I watch in stunned silence as the door slams shut behind them, the metallic clang echoing through the quiet hall.

"FUUUCK!" Hurt and anger squeeze my chest like a vise as I shrug off Parker and Vaughn.

I close my eyes and tip my face to the ceiling.

This cannot be happening. I did everything right. I've worked so damn hard.

"It's going to be okay," Quinn whispers, tentatively resting a hand on my arm.

Her touch is like a brand. A painful reminder of the moment my life crumbled right before my eyes. The moment I became just like him. "Don't touch me."

There's a sharp intake of breath, and she withdraws her hand. "Cooper."

I force myself to meet her stare. To look into her eyes and see the hurt and confusion swirling in their emerald depths as my roommates look on.

"I mean it, Quinn. Don't touch me." I step back, desperate to put distance between us. To cleanse my nostrils of her sweet floral scent. "We're through."

The words are bile on my lips, a fetid poison that took root long ago, and I know deep down in that dark part of my soul that this is the only way to protect her—*from me.*

"What?" She shakes her head, as if clearing her thoughts. "What are you talking about?

"I'm talking about the fact that I nearly put you on your ass. If it weren't for Reid, you could've been hurt."

"That wasn't your fault." Her voice climbs an octave. "I slipped on the tile. These boots have zero tread. I should have thrown them out ages ago."

"Do you even hear yourself right now?" I shake my head in disgust. At her. At myself. At my parents. "You sound just like her. Today, you slipped. What about next time? Will you tell people you ran into a door? Or that you fell down the stairs? No fucking way, Quinn. I will not be the one who breaks you."

"You can't break me, Cooper. I'm not a doll." She throws her hands up in the air. "I'm a grown ass woman and only I get to decide what breaks me."

It's a nice sentiment, but it's total bullshit. "I think you mean who."

Quinn's nostrils flare and she takes a step forward. I take another step back.

"You would never hurt me. That's not who you are." She pauses, lowering her voice. "I wouldn't be dating you if I thought you were a threat to me."

If only it were that simple.

"I'm pretty sure my mom didn't think my dad was a threat to her when she married him. Look how that turned out."

"You're not thinking rationally right now." She holds up a hand. "When you calm down—"

"I don't need to calm down. I know exactly what I'm saying." I shove my fingers into my hair to keep from reaching for her. If I let myself touch her, even once, my resolve will splinter. "I knew dating was a bad idea, but I did it anyway because I'm a selfish asshole, just like my father. I thought maybe I could be different, but fuck. It hasn't even been a month and I've already hurt you."

My gut clenches at the realization.

Like father, like son.

"You didn't hurt me, Cooper. Look at me." She sweeps an arm down the length of her body. "I'm fine. No scrapes, no bruises. Nothing."

I drag in a breath, willing my heart rate to slow.

"You got lucky this time. There won't be a next time." I won't allow it. "I mean it, Quinn. We're through."

Tears well in her eyes, but I don't look away. I deserve this. Deserve to have that painful image burned into my retinas so that every time I close my eyes, I'm reminded of Quinn.

Reminded that, no matter how much I care about her, she deserves better.

"Can someone please explain why half of my seniors are not in the media room where they belong?" Coach Collins barks, storming down the hall with his clipboard in hand. "Y'all are worse than the damn freshmen." He glowers at us, and for the first time, I don't have a snarky reply. "Go line up in the tunnel. We take the field in five minutes."

Coach retreats down the hall, grumbling about the fact that he shouldn't have to babysit seniors and my roommates hustle after him, leaving Quinn and me alone.

I wait a beat, searching for the right words to say goodbye, but come up empty.

It's just as well. There's nothing I can say that will fix this, fix us. My actions today spoke volumes.

I turn and follow my teammates, each echo of my cleats on the tile floor a blow to my chest, chipping away at my heart until it finally splits right down the middle.

When I reach the tunnel, I line up with the other seniors. I'm the only one who doesn't have an escort.

It doesn't matter.

I did the right thing. I just have to get through the Senior Day presentation and then I can get back to focusing on what matters: football.

The Defensive Coordinator gives us the green light, and the guys ahead of me march out one-by-one with their families. When it's my turn to take the field, Quinn falls in step with me, her hand brushing mine.

I don't look at her. I can't. It hurts too damn much.

"You don't have to talk to me," she says quietly. "Or look at me. But you shouldn't be alone on the field tonight."

Her words land like a punch to the gut. Because despite everything that happened in the hall, despite the fact that I walked away without so much as saying goodbye, she still showed up.

Shame burns the back of my throat, but I swallow it down. "Just so you know, this changes nothing."

50

QUINN

I SWIPE a tear from my cheek as the countdown clock on the corner of the tv screen races toward zero. Though I'm curled up on the couch in my apartment, the excitement in the stadium is almost palpable when the final score is announced. As predicted, the Wildcats defeat Maryland, finishing the season 11 and 1.

Given the day's events, it's somewhat anticlimactic.

Nothing like getting your heart smashed to bits to put things into perspective.

I grab a tissue from the box on the coffee table and blow my nose—*again*. Then I add the tissue to the discard pile with the others. Soon, I'll have an entire Kleenex village filled with salty tears and snot, a painful reminder of everything I've lost.

At least you still have your pride.

I managed to stave off the tears until after kickoff when I'd bolted from the stadium. The thought of sitting in the stands with one hundred thousand screaming Wildcat fans was unthinkable. There was no way I could paste on a smile and cheer for Cooper.

Not after he'd shattered me into a million tiny pieces.

I barely made it through the Senior Day presentation, his words playing on a loop in my brain.

Don't touch me.

Each word had been sharper than the last, piercing my chest like a blade.

Even worse was the way he'd compared himself to his father.

Just the memory has my stomach churning with nausea.

The front door swings open and Haley stalks in, brushing snow from her coat and hair. I'd been so focused on the game, I hadn't noticed the tiny flakes swirling outside the living room window. I glance back at the tv and sure enough, snow is falling on Wildcat Stadium. The sports anchor is talking through the final results of the game as she waits for the MVPs to join her on the sideline.

No doubt Cooper will be tagged for an interview.

He played in incredible game.

Never let it be said that Cooper DeLaurentis doesn't perform under pressure.

"Spill." Haley kicks off her sneakers and tosses her coat on a chair. Her gaze lowers to the coffee table in front of me, and she lifts a finger. "Hold that thought. This calls for wine. Lots and lots of wine."

I sigh. "We're out."

The first thing I'd done when I got home was change into sweats. The second was search the pantry for wine.

Haley grins. "I keep an emergency bottle of red in my closet for moments such as this."

Thank God.

Maybe it'll help take the edge off.

She returns a few minutes later with a bottle of wine, two glasses, and a bar of dark chocolate that she tosses into my lap.

"What happened?" she asks, plopping down next to me on the couch.

She pours the wine generously and hands me the first glass. I take a long sip, letting the bold flavor coat my mouth as I savor the notes of black cherry and vanilla.

Then I unload the whole awful story.

By the time I'm done rehashing the scene at the stadium, there's a fresh wave of tears ready to stake their claim in the Kleenex village and my glass is empty. I reach for the wine bottle, but Haley beats me to it.

"Let me get this straight," she says, filling my glass nearly to the rim. "He broke up with you, in front of all of his friends, and you still took the field with him and smiled while thousands of rabid fans cheered for his dumb ass?"

A laugh-sob bursts from my lips and wine sloshes over the rim of my glass, soaking my fingers. "I couldn't let him go out there alone."

Not after I'd promised to be at his side, and certainly not after his parents left.

Haley shoots me a dubious look. One that says I shouldn't give a damn about his feelings since he pulverized mine.

"He was hurt and angry." I blink back tears and use a napkin to sop up the wine on my fingers. "His own mother abandoned him. Can you even imagine what that feels like?"

I sure as hell can't.

"Well, when you put it like that."

"It was awful, Hales." I take a gulp of my wine to avoid another spill. "Cooper's been working his ass off to give her a way out, and she just left without saying a word. He was crushed. You could see it in his eyes." Haley opens her mouth, probably to say something disparaging about Mrs. DeLaurentis's parenting skills, but I cut her off. "She's a victim, too."

Haley flops back against the couch cushions and breaks off a generous piece of the chocolate bar. "This whole situation is fucked."

"Tell me about it."

My phone vibrates in the pocket of my hoodie and when I pull it out, there's a message from Noah. Besides Haley, he's the only other person I messaged about my breakup with Cooper. I'm probably going to get a shit ton of '*I told you so*' messages, but since I'm going to get them anyway, I figured it was best if he heard it from me first.

Call it a lesson learned the hard way.

Noah: Do you want me to kick his ass? Because I will.

"Please tell me that isn't Cooper groveling via text?" Haley frowns and pops the chocolate in her mouth. "I swear to God, that boy better grovel in person if he knows what's good for him."

"It's Noah." I type a snarky reply and delete it. He didn't make a single crack about how this was inevitable. He didn't gloat. Heck, he didn't even use one of those stupid nicknames I hate.

He's serious.

Because while Cooper's his friend, I'm his sister.

Me: That won't be necessary, but I appreciate the offer.

I'd prefer he doesn't get his teeth knocked out on my behalf. Our parents spent a small fortune on his orthodontics and they'd never forgive me.

Noah: If you change your mind, you know where to find me.

Not happening. There's been enough fighting for one day.

I'm about to put my phone away when another message pops up.

Noah: Look, I can't believe I'm saying this, but if that dumb fuck let you go, then he doesn't deserve you.

Fresh tears spill over my cheeks and I swipe them away. Maybe Noah's more evolved than I give him credit for.

Me: Thanks.

I reach for another tissue, and Haley pulls me in for a hug.

"It's going to be okay," she says, giving me a squeeze. "Karma will get him, eventually." She pulls back, a sly smile spreading over her lips. "With the clap, if she has a sense of humor."

"Haley!" I may be wallowing in despair, but I haven't quite reached the level of wishing STIs on him.

And I definitely don't want to think about Cooper hooking up with another woman. Not now. Maybe not ever.

"What?" She shrugs. "It's curable."

"So is a broken heart." That's what I've been told, anyway. "I just can't believe it's over. I really thought we had something."

"Maybe after he cools off, he'll change his mind." She snorts. "I can't tell you how many times I've said something to B in the heat of the moment that I wanted to take back later."

I bite my thumb nail, considering.

"I don't think there's anything I can say that will change his mind. Not if he sees himself in the same light as his father."

Which is equal parts ridiculous and infuriating.

Haley's brows pull low and there's a dark fury in her eyes when she says, "You're sure he didn't—"

"Yes, I'm sure." She doesn't even need to finish the question. I know exactly what she's asking. "It was an accident. I was wearing those stupid booties I bought online—the ones that don't have any traction on the sole—and I slipped on the tile. You know how maintenance polishes the shit out of the floors on campus."

It's not the first time I've slipped on a freshly waxed floor and it probably won't be the last.

"Fast fashion trash." Haley sighs. "I told you to throw those away last year."

"Yeah, well, I didn't listen." Now I'm paying the price for cute, dysfunctional shoes.

Go me.

A dull ache throbs in my chest and I rub it absently.

"What's done is done. Cooper needs to come to terms with his issues because no one else can do it for him." No matter how much I wish I could. "I may be a work in progress, but I will not chase after a guy who doesn't think I'm worth the effort."

"Preach." Haley raises her glass and then takes a hearty drink.

"If I've learned anything from this entire experience, it's that I have to know my value and not settle for less than what I deserve." Ironically, Cooper taught me that. "I deserve a guy who loves me as much as I lo—"

Oh, no.

Haley's eyes go wide. "You love him."

I sit with her words—*my words*—for a minute, letting them sink in.

I'm in love. With Cooper DeLaurentis.

Before today, I hadn't recognized the warm, glowy feeling.

Attraction? Sure.

Lust? Absolutely.

But love? *Undeniably.*

I love the way he makes me laugh. The way he believes in me, even when I don't believe in myself. The way he gives everything he has to the people he cares about, while keeping nothing for himself. I've never known a sweeter, more loyal person and though he tries to hide it, Cooper's big heart and protective nature shine through in everything he does.

"What's that quote?" I whisper. "'*Tis better to have loved and lost than never to have loved at all.*'"

"Screw Cooper and his future clap diagnosis," Haley declares. "If he doesn't know love when he has it, he doesn't deserve it. For the record, you are totally worth the effort. When you're ready to date again, I'm going to help you find Mr. Perfect."

Pretty sure I've already found him and he doesn't want me.

"Thanks, Hales. You're a good friend, but I think I'm going to stick with my battery-operated boyfriend for the foreseeable future."

We both burst out laughing and I laugh so hard, my emotions get tangled up and a fresh wave of tears stream down my face.

"Are we crying because we miss Cooper or because BOB can't hold a candle to him?"

"Both." I shrug and use the palms of my hands to wipe the tears from my cheeks. "The guy has moves."

"I freaking new it." Haley's eyes narrow. "I take back everything I said about him. I hope he gets his head out of his ass and comes crawling back so you can have incredible makeup sex and tell me all about it."

I huff out a laugh, because as ridiculous as it sounds, I hope so, too.

51

COOPER

*W*HAT THE HELL *happened last night?* There's a gremlin in my head banging steel drums like he's auditioning for an eighties hair band and my mouth is so dry it's like the fucking Sahara. I roll over and try to open my eyes, but they're glued shut.

Not cool.

My stomach lurches and bile rises in the back of my throat, but since I can't peel myself off the bed, I swallow it back down.

I'll just lie here until it passes.

Or until I die.

Whichever comes first.

My temple throbs like a motherfucker and suddenly that joke isn't so funny.

How much did I drink last night? I haven't been this hungover since freshmen year.

With good reason.

I'm too old for this shit. I feel around on the nightstand, hoping for a bottle of water, but all I find is Starlight Twinkle.

An irrational sense of annoyance takes hold and I fling the stuffed animal across the room. There's a quiet *thunk* as she hits the wall and slides to the floor.

If she was really good luck, I wouldn't be hungover.

"Oh, good. You're awake."

I lift an arm and raise my middle finger in the general direction of Reid's voice. It sounds like he's near the door, but since I can't open my eyes, it's hard to be sure.

"I brought water." His heavy steps cross the room and then he's pressing a cold plastic bottle into my hand. "Drink up, asshole."

"That would require sitting up."

"Jesus. You smell like you just came off a two-week bender."

He's not wrong. My hair is damp and I'm pretty sure the sour stench of sweat and alcohol is all me.

I manage to open one eyelid. "Thanks for the water. You can go now."

"Not a chance." He moves to the desk and plants himself in the chair, leaning back and locking his hands behind his head like he's settling in for a nice long chat. "We need to talk."

I'm dying and he wants to hold social hour?

Fuck. That.

"I believe our bromance has a hangover clause that precludes the discussion of serious topics while said hangover is *murdering your best friend.*"

Reid snorts. "If you can use words like *preclude*, you're fine." He pauses, and when he continues, there's concern in his voice. "Last night was pretty intense."

"No shit."

I hardly remember yesterday's game. Only that I couldn't wait for it to be over so I could get blitzed and forget Senior Day altogether.

Mission accomplished.

"Cooper."

I groan and drag myself to a sitting position. Reid using my full name is the team captain equivalent of a mom using your middle name.

Mom.

My chest tightens at the memory of the splint on her wrist and I send up a silent prayer that her evening was less eventful than mine. The old man was pissed when he left and the thought of him hurting her because of my actions cuts deeper than any blade ever could.

That shit goes straight to the soul.

I breathe through the pain. There's nothing I can do about it right now.

Because I'm hungover and because she chose him.

I scrub a hand over my face and blink against the piercing afternoon sun. It's too damn bright, and every ray of light is another blow to my throbbing head.

According to the clock on the nightstand, it's almost three.

Not that it matters. I have nowhere to be.

No class. No practice. No Quinn.

When I'd imagined sleeping late today, this wasn't how I'd pictured things going. My fantasy had included celebratory sex and lots of it.

That fantasy had fizzled out right along with any chance Quinn and I had.

My throat tightens as the full impact of my actions hit home, and it's suddenly hard to draw a proper breath. Quinn and I are over. I'll never hear her sweet laugh again. Never kiss her soft lips. Never fall asleep with her wrapped in my arms where she belongs.

No. Quinn doesn't belong anywhere near me. My actions yesterday proved as much. I was completely out of control.

If anything had happened to her, I couldn't live with myself.

I twist the top off the water bottle and drain half of it in three long gulps.

"I'm sorry about the shit show yesterday." I take another hit off the water bottle. "I never meant for you or the other guys to get involved."

"You don't need to apologize. Not to me anyway." Reid leans forward and rests his elbows on his knees. "If anyone should apologize, it's me. I'm sorry you never felt like you could talk to me about the stuff with your parents."

Is he serious right now?

"You have enough to worry about with school and football and all the scouts trying to get on your balls." I roll my eyes, which is a dumb move because it hurts like hell. *Just one of the many reasons you shouldn't get blackout drunk.* "I wasn't about to unload my problems on you."

"Cooper, I'm your best friend. You can tell me anything."

"You mean like how you told me about you and Carter?" It's a low blow, but what can I say? I'm a salty little bitch when I'm hungover.

Reid frowns. "You and I are going to have to work on our communication skills."

I smirk. "You think?"

"Want to talk about what happened yesterday?"

Nope. "What is there to say? My father is a violent bastard and my mom won't leave him. You saw her." I shake my head, unable to keep the disgust from my voice. "Even now, when I'm so close to getting the money I need to support her and help her break away, she chose him. She chose that bastard, knowing he'll hurt her again. Knowing it's just a matter of time."

Reid's quiet. Contemplative.

I'm not surprised. It's always been his way.

It's just as well, because now that I've started, I can't seem to stop. Just like yesterday when I slugged my father. I've never hit anyone in my life, but if Vaughn and Parker hadn't held me back, I don't know how far it would've gone.

Too far.

"The funny thing is, I used to think she was protecting me. Staying because she knew that if we took off, life would be hard, and we'd struggle to make ends meet. But now? Now I'm so close to being able to save her and it's still not enough."

I'm not enough.

The knowledge doesn't sting as much as it should, thanks to the alcohol numbing my system.

"It's not your job to save her." Reid frowns. "She's the parent. It was her job to protect you."

I shoot him a dark look. "She did the best she could."

And I won't sit here and listen to anyone talk shit about my mom.

"I didn't mean to imply otherwise." He throws up his hands in self-defense. "But she's an adult. She has to make her own choices. Just like you and Quinn."

My temple throbs at the mention of her name.

"Leave Quinn out of this. She has nothing to do with my family situation."

"Bullshit." Reid scoffs. "Based on what I saw yesterday, she has everything to do with it."

No. I won't allow her to get tangled up in my father's web. In *my* web.

Like father, like son.

The only thing yesterday proved is that DeLaurentis men are only good for one thing: destruction.

I got lucky yesterday. If anyone else had witnessed the fight with my father, I'd have been benched and it would've been a matter of time until the media picked up the story.

Hitting my father was reckless. That loss of control could've cost me everything.

Then again, maybe it did.

It sure as hell feels that way right now.

Reid leans back in the chair, studying me like he's trying to break down a defensive play. "If Quinn has nothing to do with your family situation, then why did you break up with her?"

Shame scorches a blistering trail up my spine at the memory of our heated exchange.

"You were there. You saw what happened."

"What I saw was you breaking up with a woman who clearly cares about you. And even though you cut her off at the knees, she still showed up when you needed her."

That's not how it was. I wasn't trying to cut her down. I was trying to protect her.

"She could've been hurt," I bite out. "I don't need that shit on my conscience."

If I hurt Quinn... Just the prospect has my throat closing up again.

You think words don't hurt? She was wrecked yesterday.

Better my words than my fists.

"I grew up with a man who hit first and asked questions later." I rub the back of my neck, which is hot and clammy. "When I was a kid, I never knew when the next beating would come or how severe it would be, only that it was inevitable. Just like I knew my mom would use her body as a shield, taking the brunt of my father's rage."

I pause, taking a sip of water to soothe my parched throat.

"It was fucking terrifying. I used to lie in bed at night wondering why no one else could see the monster behind the politician's smile. Why only my mom and I had to face it. When I was finally big enough to put a stop to it, when I could feel the rage boiling under my skin, I swore I'd never give in to the anger. I'd rather be alone than terrorize the people closest to me."

It was a solid plan, too. I was perfectly content with one-night stands until I met Quinn.

She changed everything.

Made me think that just maybe I could be a better man than my father. Made me think I was capable of feelings other than misplaced anger.

Yesterday had shown me just how wrong I was.

"You're not your father, Coop. In the four years I've known you, you've never hurt anyone."

A bitter smile curves my lips. "I believe my father would disagree."

The bastard had it coming.

It's no excuse. I know better than anyone that actions have consequences. My actions yesterday were inexcusable. Full stop.

"There were extenuating circumstances," Reid says, like the fact that I attacked my father is no big deal. "But since you're determined to think the worst of yourself, let's talk numbers. Did you resort to violence when that freaky stalker chick snuck into our dorm freshman year and got naked in your bed?"

Hell no. I'd let the RA deal with it.

"Did you retaliate against Professor Langdon when she called you a dumb jock sophomore year?"

Now way. I'd aced her class and made her eat her words when I got the top score.

"Exactly how many women have you hurt since coming to Waverly?" Reid presses.

"None!" I wipe my palms on my thighs and study my hands. "I've never laid a finger on a woman."

"Well, there you go, dumbass."

"I nearly put Quinn on her ass yesterday."

"That wasn't your fault. She slipped. We all saw it."

God, I wish that was true. But I know better. I've seen first-hand where that kind of thinking can lead.

"Don't make excuses for my behavior," I growl. "That's how it starts."

"I'm not excusing shit. You shrugged off her touch. So what?

That isn't what caused her to fall." He lets out a frustrated sigh and rakes his fingers through his hair. "Those floors were over polished. Hell, Parker's mom slipped on the way in."

I stiffen. "She did?"

Reid grins. "Yeah. Gave the security guard hell for it, too."

Were the floors really that slippery?

Dammit. I don't remember. I'd been wearing my cleats, and I'd been so caught up in my anger, the only thing I'd processed was the splint on mom's wrist.

"Look, you can spend your life punishing yourself for your father's mistakes or you can take your shot and make your own damn mistakes."

If only it were that easy.

"I won't take that chance. Not with Quinn."

"You're one stubborn bastard, I'll give you that." He pauses, changing track. "Do you love her?"

"Of course I fucking love her." The words explode from my mouth, surprising us both. But now that they're out, there's no turning back. "She's incredible. Smart, sarcastic, quirky as hell. And the sex—"

"TMI." Reid flinches like he's dodging a mental image of Quinn and I. "The point is, you'd never hurt Quinn. But taking that chance, it's her choice, not yours. You get to decide if you want to be with her, but that's got to be about you and your feelings. You don't get to decide if she wants to be with you. That's a choice only she can make."

Fuck.

He's right. The realization hits me like a three-hundred-pound linebacker.

The night I met Quinn, I hadn't trusted her to know the right path for herself. I'd taken away her agency instead of giving her the space to choose what was best for her. I'd been so sure I knew what she needed, but I'd been wrong.

I was wrong then, and I'm wrong now.

My stomach rolls, and this time it's not from alcohol. "I think I made a mistake."

"Oh, you definitely made a mistake." Reid chuckles. "The question is, what are you going to do about it?"

"I have no idea." But I'd better figure it out quick because there are only two weeks left in the semester.

52

QUINN

It's Monday morning and I'm curled up in a booth at Daily Grind, cramming for finals and trying not to think of Cooper, which is easier said than done since Wildcat football is all anyone on campus wants to talk about.

Case in point, the guys at the next table are discussing the best way to score tickets for the upcoming bowl game.

I put on my headphones, blocking out their annoying chatter, and return my attention to the study guide before me. I don't have time to sit around obsessing over football. And I definitely don't have time to feel sorry for myself or wonder what Cooper's doing and if he's dating anyone new.

Riiight.

Okay, fine. Yes, I've obsessed. But only between classes. And at night. So, basically only when I'm awake and not studying.

Whatever. At least I've steered clear of Greek Row. Not that it's been a challenge. I'm hardly in the mood to drink and party, especially with exams starting next week.

I've got a Calculus final that, judging by my current performance on this study guide, is going to kick my ass, and Call-Me-

David is supposed to post the grades for our final papers today, which has me refreshing my email every five minutes.

It's a step up from constantly checking my phone, hoping there'll be a text or call from Cooper. I spent all day last Sunday hoping he'd come to his senses and ask to meet up.

Spoiler alert: he did not come to his senses and ask to meet up.

So, yeah. My new post-Cooper plan is to keep my head down, get through finals, and go home for the holidays to lick my wounds in private while eating *all* the sugar cookies.

Maybe by the time spring semester starts in January, I'll be able to handle the prospect of facing him. Of seeing him on campus and watching him hook up at parties.

Doubtful.

They say you never forget your first love, but even if it's not true, Cooper will always hold a special place in my heart. Not only because he was my first, but because he was the first person to believe in me and to encourage me to follow my dreams, no matter the odds.

My phone buzzes on the table and I snatch it up, more than ready to take a break from the study guide from hell. I open my email to find a canned message from Call-Me-David. Grades have been posted for the Creative Non-Fiction term papers.

I log into my student account, mentally cursing the slow Wi-Fi as the page loads.

When the grading matrix finally pops up, I scroll straight to the bottom.

A+.

Holy crap. I got an A+. From Call-Me-David.

There's a note in the comments section and I zoom in to read it.

Excellent work, Ms. Mowery. This was one of the best papers I've read all semester. It really highlights your tremendous growth as a writer.

Pride washes over me and I tap my feet on the floor, biting back a squeal. I did it. I actually freaking did it.

"This calls for a celebration." Preferably one of the carb variety.

Before I can get up, my phone vibrates again. It's a message from Priya.

Priya: How'd you do?

Me: A+. I think maybe I had too much coffee and I'm hallucinating. You?

Priya: Girl, you earned that A+. Your paper was gold. I got an A.

*Me: *high five emojis**

Unlike me, Priya's been pulling A's all semester, so her final grade is a lock.

I scoot out of the booth and grab my mug, carrying it up to the counter for a refill.

I'm scanning the daily specials as I make my way toward the line, deciding between a slice of pumpkin bread and a death by chocolate muffin, when I hit a wall.

"Oof."

Strong hands grip my shoulders and awareness crackles over my skin like static electricity. When I look up, I'm staring into the most stunning crystal blue eyes I've ever seen.

Cooper.

My chest tightens, forcing the air from my lungs. He looks good. Lighter somehow. Unburdened. His eyes are bright and though he's in desperate need of a haircut and shave, the shaggy look suits him.

"Quinn."

I yank my headphones off, looping them around my neck.

"Hey, Cooper. I didn't see you there." *Fucknuts.* He probably thinks I plowed into him on purpose. Which I so didn't. "Just getting a refill."

I hold up my mug, in case he needs proof I'm not stalking him.

A slow smile spreads across his face and my stupid heart melts just a little.

Traitor.

"Excuse me." I move to step around him, pretending I'm totally fine bumping into the man who broke my heart.

That's right, no clingy exes here. Just a cool, confident woman.

"Actually, I was hoping to run into you." He sweeps an unruly lock of hair off his forehead. "How have you been?"

Miserable, thanks.

"Busy. Studying for finals." I shrug and gesture half-heartedly. "You know how it is."

God, this sucks.

Never in a million years did I think things between Cooper and I could get this awkward.

"Yeah, it's been a crazy week."

I don't know what to say to that, so I change the subject. "Congratulations on making the Peach Bowl."

If the Wildcats win, they'll advance to the championship game. Coop and I may not be a couple anymore, but I know winning a national championship means the world to him. Waverly hasn't won a title in fifteen years. They're due.

"Thanks." He shifts his weight and stuffs his hands into the pockets of his jeans. "It's a hell of a way to ring in the new year."

Images of a raucous post-bowl game celebration flood my brain and tears sting the back of my eyes.

Don't think about it.

I blink, banishing the tears before they can fall. I will not cry in front of Cooper. "Think you guys are ready for Clemson?"

He frowns. "I didn't come here to talk football."

That makes two of us, but the way he says it, part disappointment, part chastising, is too much.

The hurt and anger that have been stewing on the back burner for the last week finally bubble over.

"What did you come here to talk about?" I ask with a simpering smile. "How you broke up with me in front of all your friends? How you completely shattered my heart without the courtesy of an adult conversation? Or maybe you wanted to talk about how you thought it was your place to swoop in and save me from myself?"

For such a smart guy, Cooper can be really dense. How many times is he going to make the same mistake before he gets a freaking clue?

"If we could just—"

I don't let him finish. He's already said his piece. This time, he can damn well listen.

"Honestly, who do you think you are?" I poke him in his big stupid chest. "I might be a mess, but at least I learn from my mistakes, unlike some people."

"Everything okay here?"

We both turn to find Noah staring at us, eyes narrowed, hands planted on his hips in what I can only assume is meant to be an intimidating gesture. He's wearing a plaid blazer and bowtie, which pretty much ruins the effect.

Still, I appreciate the brotherly concern.

"We're good." I exhale slowly, releasing the last of my anger. "I was just heading back to my seat."

I have nothing more to say, and I'm not interested in hearing what Cooper has to say to me. He had his chance, and he blew it.

Without another word, I return to my table, forcing myself to take slow, measured steps.

Do. Not. Look. Back.

I hold out until I slide into the booth.

Cooper and Noah are having a heated conversation, probably about me, but I'm out of steam, so I grab my pencil and turn my attention back to the Calc study guide.

Not my circus.

Not anymore.

I stare at the worksheet for what feels like an eternity, but the numbers swim on the page. I'm not even sure what problem I was working on anymore.

This is pointless.

Thanks to Cooper, my concentration is shot. I should probably just pack it in and head back to the apartment where I can avoid all talk of Wildcat football and sexy exes.

I'm shoving my notes inside my bag when Cooper places Starlight Twinkle on the table, along with a copy of The Collegian.

"I'm sorry, Quinn. I fucked up."

My heart squeezes at his words, but it's too little, too late.

"I believe we already established that fact." I zip my bag and slide toward the end of the bench. "Now if you'll excuse me."

I gesture for him to get out of the way, but the stubborn ass doesn't move.

"Just give me five minutes." He nods to the paper, worry creasing his brow. "Have you read it yet?"

"No." The word is sharp and clipped and I don't want to be a shrew, so I add, "I've been a little busy studying for finals."

His face relaxes and something like relief flashes in his eyes. "Read it. Please."

"I really don't have time—"

"Please," he repeats, sliding the newspaper across the table.

I glance down at the paper, which is open to an article titled *Jockhole Seeks Miracle.*

My gaze flicks to the byline. Cooper DeLaurentis.

"What is this?" I ask, hating the waver in my voice.

"An apology. A damn good one, if I say so myself." The ghost of a smile graces his lips. "But it's probably best if you judge for yourself."

Cockwaffles.

Cooper wrote me an apology letter and published it in The Collegian?

My pulse skitters and I clasp my hands together to keep them from shaking.

For a guy who's built his reputation as a playboy one hookup at a time, and who values his privacy above all else, that's a pretty big freaking deal.

Any NFL scout who Googles his name will see it.

Future employers.

Voters, if he ever runs for office.

That's about as vulnerable—and transparent—as it gets.

So read it already.

My fingers tremble as I reach for the paper.

Quinn,

The day I met you, my life changed for the better. Whether you realize it or not, you showed me what it means to take risks, to be unyielding in the pursuit of my goals, and most important of all, what it means to love.

Until you came along, I thought love meant protecting those you care about, and while that's certainly part of it, you showed me that love has many facets, that it's bigger than any one person or principle.

Through your words and actions, you taught me that love requires respect, partnership, and trust. And when I had the opportunity to reciprocate, I fumbled the ball. I let my insecurities get the best of me, and I took away your agency, justifying my actions with the misguided notion I was protecting you. I was wrong, and for that, I'm sorry.

I've made a lot of mistakes in my life, but the one I regret most is breaking your trust. You call yourself a disaster, but to me, you'll always be a miracle. My smart, beautiful, chaotic miracle. You showed me what it is to love unconditionally, and despite all my faults, you chose me.

I can't change the past, no matter how much I wish I could, but if you give me another chance, I won't let you down again.

— COOPER

TEARS SPRING TO MY EYES, and I don't bother trying to fight them as I turn my gaze back to Cooper. He *loves* me. A warm flush heats my skin, covering every inch of my body.

If someone had told me three months ago that Cooper-the-cockblocking-jockhole-DeLaurentis would fall in love with me, I'd have called them a damn liar.

But here we are. Two broken souls, trying desperately to find our way back to one another.

I want to forgive him. How could I not?

It's the most beautiful apology I've ever read. It proves he's finally come to his senses, that he understands it's not his place to decide what's best for me.

But he's right, it doesn't change the past.

Cooper is a protector by nature. It's not something he can just turn off at the flip of a switch. No matter how heartfelt and touching these words are, there's no guarantee he'll live up to them in the future, that he'll be able to stop himself from over-stepping if he doesn't agree with my choices.

That's something I can't—*won't*—accept, even if it means walking away from the man I love.

53

COOPER

QUINN LOOKS up at me and—*fuck*—there are tears in her eyes. I made her cry again. I'm absolute shit at relationships. And breakups. And, apparently, at apologies too.

It's like the dating failure trifecta.

I clear my throat and gesture to the empty seat across from her. "Can I sit down?"

She blinks, but says nothing as a tear slips free, cutting a path down her cheek before falling onto her sweatshirt.

She's going to say no. I can see it in her eyes, in the way she's hesitating.

A bead of sweat slides between my shoulder blades.

Why is it so damn hot in here?

Focus, asshole.

"Please. Just give me a few minutes, and then, when I'm done, if you never want to see me again, I'll leave you alone."

It won't be easy to keep that promise, but I'll respect her wishes, whatever she decides.

Third time's the charm.

Finally, Quinn nods and I slide onto the bench.

Thank you, Starlight Twinkle.

The cafe noise fades away, and for a long minute, we just stare at each other.

When I finally open my mouth to speak, no words come out. My brain is a total blank slate. I don't know what to say, and I don't want to say the wrong thing, because I only have one shot here.

I can't afford to blow it.

This is what I get for seeking inspiration from teen romcoms.

I'm going to be the laughingstock of campus and I still won't have the girl.

Unacceptable.

"I don't know how to say this, so I'm just going to say it," I blurt out. "I was foolish and pigheaded to think I could choose for you. You were right. It wasn't my place."

"And you came to this conclusion how?" she asks, toying with the edge of the newspaper.

"I had some help." I rub the back of my neck, remembering Reid's tough love. "Reid helped me see that what I was doing wasn't so much protection as steamrolling."

"Smart man."

I shrug. "He has his moments."

Quinn studies me for a long time before asking, "Do you still think I need to be protected from you?"

"No." I exhale and roll my shoulders. This is the hardest part. The part that still scares the hell out of me. "If you say you slipped on the floor, then I believe you. I'm not proud of the way I lost my temper with my father. Or the way I shrugged off your touch. But I've had time to process and put the day into perspective. Before last Saturday, I'd never hit anyone in my life. It's not an experience I plan to repeat."

Ever.

"Good." She nods slowly. "I'm glad you've come to realize what the rest of us already know. You're not your father, Cooper.

You're not a bully or an abuser." She reaches across the table and takes my hand, wrapping her small fingers around mine. *That has to be a good sign, right?* "You have never given me cause to fear you, and you never will. It's not who you are at the core."

I silently vow to live up to her faith in me.

I'll do whatever it takes to avoid letting her down again.

"What about your parents?" she asks. "And football?"

"I spoke with my mother earlier this week." It had been a tough, but long overdue call. "I let her know I wouldn't be coming home again, and I offered to help her get out if she decides to leave. She wasn't exactly receptive to the idea."

With some coaxing, she agreed to talk to a domestic violence counselor, and I emailed her some resources I found online. My expectations are low, but who knows? Maybe a professional will get through to her in a way I can't.

"Oh, Cooper. I'm so sorry." Quinn squeezes my hand and I swear to God, it's like coming home. "That couldn't have been an easy conversation."

"It wasn't, but it was a step in the right direction. For both of us." I finally realized that if my mom doesn't want to leave, I can't make her. I can only be ready to support her if, and when, she makes that choice for herself. "I also told Coach Collins that I'm planning to declare for the draft." I chuckle. "He said it was about damn time. For all his bluster and sideline antics, Coach is a good guy. He offered to help me with agents and scouts, but we've agreed to put all of that on hold until next semester. I've got until January seventeenth to officially declare, so I just want to focus on the championship game for now."

"That's great news. You shouldn't have to hide your dreams from anyone." She picks up the newspaper and shakes her head. "I can't believe you did this."

"A big screw up requires a big apology. I'm hoping it will

earn me a second chance." I flash her a playful smile, hope surging in my chest. "Is it working?"

"I'm still deciding." She drops the paper on the table and there's a mischievous glint in her eye. "The internet is probably going to turn you into a meme."

"My roommates already did." Using my free hand, I pull out my phone and show her the text message.

She laughs and claps a hand over her mouth. "Why am I not surprised?"

"It's all good." I slide the phone back into my pocket. "It'll be worth it if I get you back."

Quinn shakes her head, those fiery curls bouncing with every move. "You realize the internet is forever, right?"

I shrug. "So are the best relationships. Seems like a fair trade to me." Her cheeks flush, but she doesn't respond, so I nod to our joined hands and press my advantage. "Does this mean I'm forgiven?"

My heart leaps into my throat and I wait with bated breath as she bites her lower lip, considering. It's so goddamn sexy, it's all I can do not to lean across the table and kiss the hell out of her.

"Did you mean what you wrote in the paper?"

"Every word." It took me days to write that letter. To get every word just right. Call it a side effect of acting like a carefree prick for the last four years. "Give me another chance and I'll prove it."

She pulls away and crosses her arms, fixing me with a hard stare. "So you're saying that if I want to streak across campus after my last final, you're going to stand by and watch?"

"Why the hell would you—"

Quinn clears her throat and her right brow arches in consternation.

I clamp my mouth shut so hard a muscle in my jaw twitches. "Yes. In fact, I'll make a sign to cheer you on."

"With glitter?"

"Whatever you want, sweetheart." I'll cover myself in glitter and parade around campus if it'll make her happy.

She grins and her entire face lights up. *Christ, I've missed that smile.* "I'm going to hold you to that."

"I'd expect nothing less." I lean forward, resting my forearms on the table. "I love you, Quinn, and I know I'm far from the perfect boyfriend, but I promise to give it my all every day for as long as you'll have me."

I just need one more chance. This time, I won't blow it.

"I love you, too." She leans forward and brushes her lips against mine.

The kiss is soft and gentle and not nearly enough after six days apart.

"You call that a kiss?" I cup the back of her head and draw her in closer, claiming her mouth with mine as my lips move over hers, relearning the shape and taste of her, committing every exquisite detail to memory.

When I release her, her lips are swollen and her pupils are blown wide. "I think we have an audience."

"Let them look." I've always avoided PDA, mostly because of my father's rules and the fear of his wrath, but I'm done playing it safe. I'm ready to live my life to the fullest.

No more holding back.

No more worrying about what the media might say or how my actions might impact my father's career.

"Let me rephrase," Quinn says, voice husky. "I think we should go somewhere more private to finish this conversation."

My cock twitches in agreement. "Your place or mine?"

"Mine's closer." She slides out of the booth and slings her bag over her shoulder, making a beeline for the door.

I grab Starlight Twinkle and follow Quinn out into the blustery morning. It's freezing and the smell of snow hangs heavy in the air as I tuck her under my arm, fitting her body to mine. "I've missed this."

"Me too," she says, breath forming a small white cloud before her lips. "My bed is so much warmer when you're in it."

I lean down and kiss the top of her head. "Happy to be of service."

I could live a thousand lifetimes and I'd never get enough of this woman. I'll never tire of her kisses or her sweet laughter or the way she challenges me at every turn. I could live a thousand lifetimes and I'd want to spend every single one of them catching Quinn.

EPILOGUE

12 MONTHS LATER…

QUINN

It's Sunday night and I'm curled up in bed with my laptop, working on my romance novel. It's been slow going, trying to squeeze in writing time around classes and real life, but I'm almost finished with my first draft.

With any luck, I'll write *The End* before the holidays, which would be amazing since I'm spending winter break at Cooper's place in Nashville. The Titans drafted him in the first round and though he always said he wanted to play ball on the west coast, Tennessee suits him.

It suits me too, since it's only a ninety-minute flight.

We see each other as often as we can, but the last few months have been tough. The team works six days a week during the season and maintains a rigid schedule for practices, training, and game prep.

Cooper's thriving though, and that's what matters.

My phone vibrates and I grab it off the bed, heart sinking when I see it's a voice call.

We were supposed to Facetime tonight, but something

must've come up.

I swipe accept and lift the phone to my ear. "Hey, babe."

"Hey, gorgeous. What are you up to?"

"Working on my manuscript. I think I'm going to have a first draft by the end of the year."

"Outstanding."

I laugh. "No, outstanding is how well you played today. You looked great out there."

Cooper's having a breakout year. He's been killing it on the field and the Nashville fans love him. When I visit, we can't eat in a restaurant without getting swarmed for autographs, which inevitably leads to Cooper's ears turning red as they heap on the praise. It's so freaking adorable.

"Thanks," he says, voice echoing through the line. "Coach told me I better stay healthy, so I told him he should give me more time off."

If only.

As much as I love watching Cooper play, I can't wait until the season is over so we can spend more time together.

"Are you still at the stadium?"

"No. Why?"

"Just wondering. There's a weird echo on the line."

"Strange. I don't hear it on my end." Of course not. Stupid freaking technology. "My signal isn't great, which is why I didn't bother with Facetime."

"It's okay," I say, trying to keep the disappointment from my voice. "Just think, in a few more weeks, we'll be together."

"True," he drawls. "But I don't know if I can wait that long. What are you wearing?"

I glance down at my faded blue and white Wildcat sweats. "I'm wearing those silky green pajamas you bought me. The ones with the lacy top and the little bow above the ass."

"Yeah?"

"Yeah." *Real talk*: long-distance relationships are hard. Sometimes little white lies are necessary to spice things up. "I love the way the fabric feels against my skin, almost like you're right here with me, touching me."

"Sexy little liar."

My gaze shifts to the bedroom door where Cooper stands in dark jeans and a black leather jacket with a bag slung over his shoulder.

"How did you—"

I don't finish the thought. He drops his bag and I vault off the bed, leaping into his arms.

He catches me easily and I wrap my legs around his waist as I crush my lips to his. The kiss is hard and deep and our teeth grind together, but I don't care. I want to be as close to him as possible. He tastes like peppermint and chocolate, and when his tongue makes an expert sweep of my mouth, a quiet moan spills from my lips.

"How are you here right now?" I ask when we finally come up for air.

"I missed you, so I hopped a flight after today's game."

I laugh and shake my head. A year ago, such a thing would've sounded ridiculous, but his contract affords him the luxury of last-minute travel, even when his schedule doesn't.

"How long can you stay?"

"Just the night. I have to head back tomorrow for practice."

"You flew all the way up here to surprise me for just one night?"

"Yes?" he says, sounding unsure.

"Best. Boyfriend. Ever." I drop another kiss on his lips, this one slow and sensual.

"Tell me about it." He carries me to the bed. "Since we only have one night, we should probably make the most of it."

I release my grip on him, lowering my feet to the floor even as I slide the jacket off over his broad shoulders and get to work on the button of his jeans.

Cooper chuckles and tugs on the waistband of my sweatshirt, pulling it over my head, before removing his own shirt and kicking off his shoes. "My sexy little liar."

I shrug, refusing to feel guilty about my fib. "What did you expect? There's nothing sexy about this getup."

"Trust me," he purrs, lowering my sweatpants and sinking to his knees before me. "I can make anything sexy."

Truth. The man once gave me an orgasm while eating a hot dog.

He looks up at me from under long, fair lashes and I know we won't be getting much sleep tonight.

My body clenches with desire, and heat pools between my legs.

"I've missed you," he rasps, and for a second, I'm not sure if he's talking to me or my pussy.

Does it matter?

No, no it does not.

His breath is hot against my core and when he presses his lips to my slick folds, his tongue cutting a path right down my center, I nearly come on the spot.

"I've missed you, too." I tangle my fingers in his hair, gripping the thick strands and guiding him to the cluster of nerves that will intensify my pleasure.

He doesn't disappoint. His tongue darts out, swirling and licking, delivering divine pressure just where I need it most. There's nothing in the world like this feeling and the tension in my belly coils tighter as I spiral toward release.

It feels so damn good, but it's not enough. It's never enough with Cooper.

"I need you inside me," I pant, pulling him to his feet.

A wolfish grin curves his sensuous mouth and he shoves his

pants down, releasing his cock. I watch, every nerve in my body humming with desire as he fists himself, giving his length one long, hard stroke.

Then we're tumbling into bed, a tangle of arms and legs as our bodies come together, Cooper burying himself between my thighs with one confident thrust.

Six months ago, I went on the pill as a precaution, but honestly? Having the freedom to be skin-to-skin with Cooper has made the sex so much hotter. The slide of his skin against mine as he sinks into me, driving us both toward climax is delicious, but the level of trust, of intimacy, has made us that much closer.

He captures my mouth with a slow, languorous kiss, and when he rolls his hips, rubbing his pelvis against my clit, I moan into his mouth, a desperate plea for more.

Cooper quickens his pace and rational thought drifts out of reach. He knows just how to work my body, how to deliver the most intense pleasure followed by toe-curling orgasms. It's not long before I'm coming, my body clenching tight around his as his name spills from my lips, and then he's coming too, his cock pulsing within me as he rides out the aftershocks of his release.

Afterward, as we're lying tangled in the sheets, he whispers, "I have a surprise for you."

~

COOPER

We get dressed and I lead Quinn to the living room, Starlight Twinkle stuffed in the back pocket of my jeans. I left her gift by the tiny little shrub she and Haley call a Christmas tree. The thing can't be over two feet tall. It's so small it has to be displayed on the coffee table just to be seen.

I make a mental note to buy the biggest tree I can fit in my apartment so Quinn and I can decorate it together when she comes to visit in a few weeks.

"What is this?" she asks, planting her hands on her hips as she studies the package sitting on the floor next to the coffee table.

"Your Christmas gift." I smirk and swat her on the backside. "I thought that would be obvious from the wrapping paper."

"Smartass." She pretends to glare at me, but she can't pull it off. Not with the big ass grin on her face. "Christmas isn't for another three weeks."

"I couldn't wait any longer." I snake an arm around her waist, inhaling the pumpkin and vanilla scent I've missed so much, and plant a kiss on her forehead. "Open it."

Her eyes go wide. "Now?"

"Yes, now." I give an exaggerated eye roll because I can't resist fucking with her. "You don't really think I came all this way just for sex?"

She laughs, and the sound is music to my ears.

I love Nashville. The people are great and the city has a vibrant nightlife, but I can't wait until Quinn graduates so she can join me there while she writes her heart out.

Quinn settles on the floor next to the box, which is bigger than the Christmas tree, and shoots me a dubious look. "How did you ever get this on the plane?"

"I bought an extra seat." Her jaw falls open, and she looks from me to the bright red box with its pristine white bow and back again. "What? I wasn't going to send it through baggage check."

It would've been hell on my wrap job.

"OMG. You're ridiculous."

She doesn't know the half of it. "Thank you."

I gesture for her to open the gift and she obliges, carefully pulling the end of the white ribbon. The bow disappears, and the ribbon slides to the floor as she tears the paper away.

My heart flutters and I shove my hands in my pockets so Quinn won't see them shaking.

I've never been great at giving gifts—haven't had much need—and it took me months of research to plan this out.

Hopefully she likes it.

It'll be a real kick in the balls if she doesn't.

Quinn opens the top flap of the brown cardboard box and her eyes go wide.

"Oh, wow." A giddy smile breaks over her lips as she reaches inside. "I can't believe you got me a MacBook Pro. Cooper, this is amazing." She slides the laptop box onto her lap, handling it like it's a precious treasure, before turning her gaze back to me. "Thank you."

"According to the online chat boards, this is the best machine for an aspiring writer. Lots of memory and all the bells and whistles you'll ever need for creating graphics and editing videos."

She scrunches up her nose. "When did you find time to research laptops?"

"I made time." No matter how busy life gets, I'll always make time for Quinn. With all the changes in the last year, she's been the one constant. The one to keep me grounded. The one I turn to when things get rough. The one who never loses faith in me. "Keep going."

She looks around for a second, like she's searching for another gift, and then she peeks inside the box.

"What's this?" She pulls out another package wrapped in bright red paper.

My palms begin to sweat. "Open it and find out."

She tears off the paper and laughs when she finds an external hard drive and another box wrapped in red paper.

"I'm sensing a theme."

"Every writer needs a backup hard drive to save their work." That's what it says online, anyway.

Quinn opens the next box, and she squeals with delight as a stack of colorful notebooks spill out. "They're so pretty," she says, hugging them to her chest. "I'm never going to write in them."

I chuckle. "I believe that means you're well on your way to being an author."

Evidently that's a thing writers do. Hoarding pretty notebooks they'll never write in. Seems like a waste to me, but who am I to judge?

Quinn pulls out another red box. "Exactly how many boxes are nested in here?"

Too many. Watching her unwrap them one by one is torture.

I really didn't think this through.

"My precious," she whispers, opening a pack of limited-edition gel pens.

If I weren't so damn nervous, I'd make a Gollum joke, but every second that ticks by is another thread frayed from my already taut nerves.

I exhale slowly as Quinn pulls out the next package, which is only 5x5, and tears into it.

"Oh, my God." She pulls a stack of rainbow Post-it Notes from the box and sets them on the coffee table. "You know me too well."

She removes the last gift-wrapped package, holding it in her palm as she studies it, completely oblivious to the tension that's oozing from my pores like stale beer.

This is it.

Sweat beads along my hairline and my pulse quickens as she unties the white satin ribbon tied around the box.

Christ. I'm going to pass out before she even opens it.

"Let me guess. Paperclips?"

I open my mouth to reply, but my throat is closed up tight. I couldn't squeeze a word out if I wanted to, so I just shrug. Then I reach around to my back pocket and rub my fuzzy pink unicorn for good luck.

She shakes the package, holding it close to her ear. "Too quiet to be paperclips. Unless it's just one." She smirks. "Which I wouldn't put past you."

What's in that box is way more valuable than any paper clip. Not just because of the price tag, but because of what it represents.

Quinn tears off the paper, revealing a black velvet box.

Her gaze darts to me, and I finally find my voice. "Open it, sweetheart."

She swallows, throat bobbing delicately, and lifts the lid.

At the sight of the diamond ring inside, her hands tremble.

It's a three-carat emerald cut stone set in a platinum band. Simple yet elegant, just like Quinn.

I fall to my knees in front of her, nerves fading away. "Marry me, Quinn. I know it's only been a year, but this has been the best damn year of my life." A quiet sob slips from her lips and she claps a hand over her mouth. "I love you, and I can't imagine my life without you in it. We can wait until after graduation. We can wait five years if that's what you want, but I need you to know there's no one else I want to share my life with. You're it for me, Quinn. You're my person."

I just hope I'm hers.

I've never wanted anything—including a future in the NFL —as much as I want Quinn to be my wife.

Please say yes.

Hell, I'll beg if that's what it takes.

I'm just about to start when she finally speaks.

"Yes." She nods, tears glistening in her eyes. "Yes. I will absolutely marry you, Cooper." *Thank you, Starlight Twinkle.* Relief and joy flood my veins and I lean in to kiss her, but she cuts me off, holding up a finger. "On one condition."

I freeze, my emotions doing a complete one-eighty. "There are conditions?"

"Just the one." She cups my cheek, a mischievous smile curving her sweet lips. "You have to tell Noah."

"Done."

I should've seen that coming. He hasn't quite forgiven me for breaking up with her last year, but I'll win him over. He's important to Quinn and her happiness means the world to me.

"I love you." Quinn leans in and wonder—*fucking wonder*—fills my chest as I kiss my fiancé, secure in the knowledge that I get to spend the rest of my life loving this incredible woman.

Thank you for reading Catching Quinn! For more of Cooper and Quinn's story, visit www.jenniferbonds.com to download the Bonus Epilogue for a must-read glimpse of their future!

Need more Wildcat shenanigans in your life? Grab Parker's story, Scoring Sutton.

www.jenniferbonds.com

ALSO BY JENNIFER BONDS

Waverly Wildcats

Holding Harper

Claiming Carter

Catching Quinn

Scoring Sutton

Protecting Piper

The Harts

Miles and Miles of You

Not Today, Cupid

Royally Engaged

A Royal Disaster

Royal Trouble

A Royal Mistake

The Risky Business Series

Once Upon a Dare

Once Upon a Power Play

Seducing the Fireman

ABOUT THE AUTHOR

Jennifer Bonds writes sizzling contemporary romance with sassy heroines, sexy heroes, and a whole lot of mischief. She's a sucker for enemies-to-lovers stories, laugh-out-loud banter, over-the-top grand gestures, and counts herself lucky to spend her days writing swoonworthy romance thanks to the support of amazing readers like you!

Jen lives in Pennsylvania, where her overactive imagination and weakness for reality TV keep life interesting. She's lucky enough to live with her own real-life hero, two adorable (and sometimes crazy) children, and one rambunctious K9. Loves Buffy, Mexican food, a solid Netflix binge, the Winchester brothers, cupcakes, and all things zombie. Sings off-key.

To connect with Jen, visit www.jenniferbonds.com to sign up for her newsletter and be the first to know about new releases, giveaways, and exclusive content! You can also find her on Facebook, Instagram, and TikTok @jbondswrites.